WHO W

The Assassin

PHOENIX

Was he the elegant middle-aged Frenchman who flew to Libya to accept an assignment to commit an "impossible" assassination?

Was he the crude German peasant who withdrew a half-million dollars deposited by prospective employers in his Swiss bank account?

Was he the young American jazz piano player who became the passionate lover of a sex-hungry black model in Paris?

Was he the handsome young Irish revolutionary plotting a bloody massacre for the IRA?

Was he the genial old Jewish gentleman who made the most influential Zionist lawyer in New York a proposition impossible to turn down?

He was all of them and none of them—and yet he had to be found and stopped before the last perverse piece of his icily calculated perfect plan fell into place to complete the most diabolical design for death in our time. . . .

PHOENIX

is the newest name for terror!

PHOENIX

AMOS ARICHA
& ELI LANDAU

A SIGNET BOOK
NEW AMERICAN LIBRARY
TIMES MIRROR

NAL BOOKS ARE ALSO AVAILABLE AT DISCOUNTS IN BULK QUANTITY FOR INDUSTRIAL OR SALES-PROMOTIONAL USE. FOR DETAILS, WRITE TO PREMIUM MARKETING DIVISION, NEW AMERICAN LIBRARY, INC., 1301 AVENUE OF THE AMERICAS, NEW YORK, NEW YORK 10019.

SIGNET TRADEMARK REG. U.S. PAT. OFF. AND FOREIGN COUNTRIES
REGISTERED TRADEMARK—MARCA REGISTRADA
HECHO EN CHICAGO, U.S.A.

SIGNET, SIGNET CLASSICS, MENTOR, PLUME AND MERIDIAN BOOKS are published by The New American Library, Inc., 1301 Avenue of the Americas, New York, New York 10019.

First Signet Printing, June, 1979

1 2 3 4 5 6 7 8 9

PRINTED IN THE UNITED STATES OF AMERICA

This story of a Libyan plot to assassinate an Israeli political leader is entirely fictitious. However the names of some real world leaders and some actual international political events have been incorporated into the story for purposes of creating an authentic fictional background.

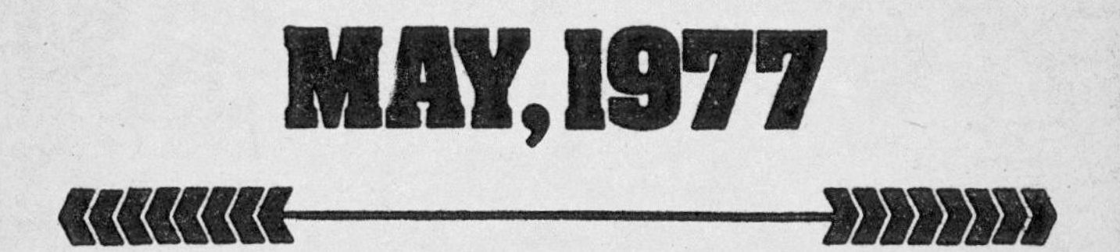
MAY, 1977

John Palmer, the U.S. intelligence chief at the American Embassy in Paris, was a tall man with a youthful face that belied his fifty years. His look of innocence had misled many people in the past. He was, in point of fact, a well-seasoned veteran of the CIA, with a keen sense of discernment. From the start of his conversation with Hans Kirschenberg, he had been aware of the German man's inner turmoil. The impromptu meeting had been arranged by Nancy Keeting, an embassy employee, who had told Palmer she had a "friend" with some very important information for his ears only. Palmer suspected Kirschenberg was more than a friend, and as he studied him, he wondered what such an attractive man saw in a woman like Nancy, whom he found devoid of any redeeming feature other than a meticulous attention to detail.

Palmer gestured toward a bottle of whiskey. "Drink?" he asked, trying to put Kirschenberg at ease. The German refused. "How about a cigar?" He opened a box on his desk and offered one to his guest. Again Kirschenberg shook his head.

"I believe I'll have one," Palmer said. He cut the end off the cigar methodically, then lit it, drawing on it hard as he scrutinized his visitor's face. He noted that the muscles in Kirschenberg's jaws were twitching incessantly.

"Well now," Palmer said with a smile, "I understand you want to let me in on something interesting."

"Yes."

"What is it, exactly?"

"I need you to act as a contact between me and the security man from the Israeli Embassy." The words poured out. "It's urgent."

John Palmer was surprised. He loosed a cloud of cigar smoke and bent forward, leaning on the desk.

"That's a rather strange request." He smiled slightly. "Can you explain it?"

"I have information that concerns the lives of certain important people in Israel." Hans Kirschenberg spoke almost in a whisper. "I know that you and your Israeli counterpart have a mutual interest in this kind of material."

"That's an interesting explanation." It was clear to Palmer that he had to take the German seriously. He shifted his position and leaned back in his armchair. "Why don't you go directly to the Israeli Embassy?" he asked.

"For two reasons," the German explained. "First, if I went there it could be dangerous for me . . ."

"You're being followed?"

"I think so. Secondly, I don't know anyone in the Israeli Embassy. I want to be certain I'm speaking to the right man. That's why I want you to act as the go-between."

Palmer narrowed his eyes, as if trying to focus more clearly. He was convinced the man was telling the truth.

"What's your motive for doing this? Ideological, or other?"

"Other." His meaning was clear.

"This information you have, is it firsthand, or hearsay?"

The German hesitated. Finally he decided to answer. "Firsthand."

John Palmer's manner remained unhurried. He had to find out the kind of pressure the man was under.

"Give me a couple of hours to check it out," he said, as if ending the conversation. "Call me in the evening. Say around seven?"

"Now," the German stated flatly. "And here. In your office. Seven is too late."

The tension he was under was evident on his face. John Palmer decided to test him no further.

"Okay," he said. "I'll see what I can do." He pressed a button on his intercom. "Call the Israeli Embassy please, and ask for Mr. Yaari. Tell him I'd be grateful if he could come over to my office right away."

Palmer looked at his visitor once more and noticed that the muscles of his jaw were still twitching.

Palmer's message reached Yaki Spillman while he was conferring with the El Al airline security officer in Paris. They were examining the new safety procedures worked out by Uri Cohen, head of the surveillance division of the intelligence services. Spillman had been alerted when John Palmer's secretary had asked to talk to "Mr. Yaari." This was a code name which the American was to use, when, in his judgment, it was better not to use Spillman's real name.

"We'll continue this later," Spillman said to the El Al man. "I have to go out immediately—an unexpected meeting."

When Yaki Spillman entered the spacious office of his American colleague and saw the stranger sitting there, he understood why Palmer had used his code name.

"This is Mr. Yaari of the Israeli Embassy," said Palmer as Yaki Spillman entered his office. He did not introduce Kirschenberg, a deliberate move on his part to show the German he would protect his identity. "Our friend has information for you."

"What kind of information," said Spillman, "and what do you want in return?"

Kirschenberg looked at the Israeli with undisguised mistrust; the man looked for all the world like a minor clerk. The German was relieved that Palmer had not given him his name.

"It's vital information . . . about an assassination plot." Spillman and Palmer exchanged glances. "For myself, I need to get away, far away. The United States probably. And I'll need money. A hundred thousand dollars."

"That's a lot of money," said Spillman. "Let's hear what you have to say." Once Kirschenberg began to talk, however, Spillman decided it wasn't such a large sum after all.

According to the German, he had been approached in Brussels in early May by a Libyan named Adel el-Magrabi. He had been given Kirschenberg's name by a "middleman" in Paris who specialized in assassins for hire. He described el-Magrabi as a man of about forty, average in height but very broad with a huge belly. The only other distinguishing features were piercing black eyes under thick brows that met in the middle. Shortly after their meeting, at which he was given a substantial payment, Kirschenberg was flown to Tripoli where he met el-Magrabi's superior, a man named Adam Ahmed. After two days of interrogation and discussion, the German discovered that there was a Libyan plan afoot to kill a prominent Israeli leader. This was to be his mission, although he was never given the name of the target. He was told to return to Paris and await further instructions. However, further instructions never came. Instead, el-Magrabi sent word that plans had been "postponed" and that he would be contacted when they needed him. In need of money, Kirschenberg had decided to contact Palmer.

"I'll need forty-eight hours on this," said Spillman when the German had finished his story.

"No," Kirschenberg replied. "Twenty-four hours at most. It's not your life that's in danger. Every hour is vital to me."

"All right," Spillman agreed. "Tomorrow, same time, same place."

Hans Kirschenberg stood up. He was sweating. The discussion had exhausted him. He stopped at the door and his fingers tapped nervously on the handle. "My name is Hans Kirschenberg, Mr. Yaari," he said. "If I didn't tell you, Mr. Palmer would, the moment I left."

Palmer's expression did not change. The Israeli smiled faintly.

"Thank you for your confidence," he said. "And let me give you some advice. If you think someone has put a tail on you, don't go home. And if you want more protection—a place and surveillance of any kind—you will have it."

The German's hand trembled slightly. "No need," he muttered. "I have a safe place."

It was six fifteen when Hans left the embassy. He looked around cautiously but found nothing to arouse his suspicions.

Nevertheless, he felt a strange disquiet. He hailed a taxi and took it to the center of the city, where he got out and turned quickly down a side street. A few minutes later, he flagged another cab and gave the driver Nancy Keeting's address.

When she arrived a few minutes after eight, she found him sunk in the large armchair where she had often spent hours watching television by herself, before he had dropped into her life. He too was watching the screen at that moment, his legs stretched out in front of him and his arms draped over the sides of the chair. He leaped up when he heard the door open.

"Hello, love!" she greeted him, her smile radiating happiness. She darted about him, twittering like a bird. In the past, he had needed her for her contacts at the embassy, and now he needed her for a refuge, but even so he felt a sudden desire to shout, to take her thin neck in his hands and squeeze it until it snapped. However, in his position, he had to control his impulses, so he endured in silence the unwanted attentions she lavished on him.

"Look, Hans," she cried gaily from the kitchen. "Aren't they wonderful?" She brought in a bowl filled with large, lusciously ripe peaches. He forced himself to smile and thanked her warmly. He was only dimly aware of her continuous and annoying chatter. From time to time, he nodded as if listening, but his mind was elsewhere. His feeling of unease grew. Doubts began to gnaw at him.

Nancy busied herself about the table in a burst of energy. She put out the silverware inherited from her parents, which she used only for very special occasions. She placed antique candlesticks at the center of the table, lit the candles, and turned down the lights. In the background, music drifted from the stereo.

"How lovely!" She stood for a moment and admired her handiwork. That was how her parents' table had looked. Now here she was with Hans. As they sat down opposite one another, her happiness knew no bounds.

The door to the apartment was opened so swiftly that Hans Kirschenberg did not even have time to spring out of his chair. The two young, dark-skinned, strongly built men who entered were well dressed. Behind them the bulky figure of a third man could be made out.

Even before they got to him, Hans Kirschenberg knew what was going to happen. The only thing he didn't know was the method they would select to kill him. Nancy sat rooted to her chair, her limbs frozen, her eyes wide in shock. Her mouth fell open as if she wanted to scream, but no sound came out.

Adel el-Magrabi glanced at his two bodyguards. They knew what to do. They took thin, strong nylon cords from their pockets and quickly tied the wrists and ankles of the German man and the American woman, and then tossed them side by side onto the couch. They gagged them with adhesive tape. Hans Kirschenberg did not even try to struggle. He knew he was doomed. His face was ashen and his watery eyes seemed to film over. He had accepted his fate.

The fear that Nancy Keeting felt increased to paralyzing dread. Never in her life had she encountered such terrifying people. With bulging eyes she stared beseechingly at the broad face of the fat stranger, who now sat down opposite them on the chair where Hans had been sitting just minutes before. Nancy was breathing in rapid bursts like a fish thrown onto land; her heart beat wildly.

Adel el-Magrabi regarded the bound man and woman with indifference. "I treated you well, Monsieur Kirschenberg," he said evenly. "Is that not so?" He paused as if expecting an answer from the gagged man. "I didn't care much for you. But neither did I dislike you," he said. "It was a business proposition. Both sides had to keep their part of the bargain—at different stages. I kept mine. You did not. But I have not come to judge you. You knew what would happen if you chose not to keep your mouth shut."

The Libyan selected a large peach from the bowl in the middle of the table. He took a knife and neatly cut even slices from the fruit; as though for his amusement, he carefully left a thick layer of flesh around the stone, which he put to one side. It looked like a wrinkled tennis ball.

He ate the juicy slices slowly. "You know, Hans Kirschenberg," he said, between bites, "our customs differ from yours in Europe. If we catch a miserable thief, we sever his right hand; a liar, his tongue. And if we find a traitor, we execute him. There are various methods. It depends on the nature of the treason."

Adel el-Magrabi did not hurry. There was no rush. He did not particularly enjoy what he was doing. It was merely a matter that required attention, and it had to be done his way. He took a napkin from the table and carefully wiped the corners of his mouth. Then he took another ripe peach and cut it as he had the first. The two young men watched him in silence. The Libyan pushed another slice into his mouth and chewed it slowly, savoring the sweet juice as it ran down his throat.

"Miss Keeting," el-Magrabi said in a low voice. He observed the formalities even in circumstances which for his listeners were desperate. "Allow me to express how much I regret your involvement in this undignified affair. But, madame, you know that in a road accident innocent bystanders are sometimes hurt."

A shiver ran down Hans Kirschenberg's spine. When he saw the Libyan holding the peach stones with their thick layers of fruit, he began to tremble with fear. The Libyan was playing with the two balls, looking from one hand to the other. Hans Kirschenberg realized what was to come next. He began to jerk about as if trying to break free of the nylon cords that bound his wrists and ankles so tightly.

"That's useless." The Libyan looked at the German without interest. He turned to Nancy Keeting. "I apologize, madame, that you have to participate in such an unpleasant affair."

Hans Kirschenberg's eyes seemed about to burst from their sockets. He strained his muscles with the last ounce of his strength, struggling in vain to break the bonds that cut deep into his flesh. His skin was torn and drops of blood began to seep out. Nancy Keeting still did not understand what was going to happen but her breathing grew heavier and her heartbeat became uneven. The choking sensation in her throat made breathing difficult.

One of el-Magrabi's two bodyguards went over to the stereo set. He turned up the volume until the music reverberated between the walls like the sound of great sledgehammers. His partner caught the peach stone that Adel el-Magrabi tossed to him. In a rapid movement the young man tore the tape off Hans Kirschenberg's mouth. The German tried to cry out but the thunderous noise of the music drowned the shout that burst from his throat. The peach stone was pushed in skillfully and forced down his gullet. The thickness of the flesh of the fruit caused the stone to lodge firmly in his throat, closing off the air passages.

Hans Kirschenberg began to jerk convulsively. The few seconds that it took were for him an eternity of endless and horrible pain. Nancy Keeting was now paralyzed with fear. Her vision became blurred. The men and objects in the room began to spin around her in a hideous dance. Her throat felt occluded even before the young man approached her, the other peach stone in his hands. The throbbing pressure she had felt in her chest increased until she lost consciousness.

The young Libyan stopped suddenly and bent over the still form of the American woman. Then he straightened up with an expression of surprise on his face.

"She's dead!" he muttered in amazement.

In Tel Aviv the second half of May was marked by the blooming of the brief Israeli spring. The heat of summer had not yet struck and the air was clear. In the headquarters of the intelligence service, Uri Cohen, chief of the surveillance branch, was scanning the reports his assistants had prepared on the events in Paris.

At forty-five, Cohen looked years older. His thinning hair and the paunch that called attention to his bowed shoulders gave him a worn-out look. Only his eyes had kept something of their youthful clarity.

He sat for several minutes without moving, studying the detailed report that Yaki Spillman had sent from Paris. He read it carefully a second time before taking out a file bulging with reports about the branch of the Libyan intelligence responsible for activating foreign agents. A plan to assassinate Israeli and Egyptian leaders accorded well with the background information he had already received. The Libyan ruler Mu'ammar Qaddafi had promised that any means could and would be used to strike at anyone attempting to bring

Israel and Egypt together. It now appeared that Libya had decided to act in areas other than the Middle East.

Cohen called in his assistants. The three weary men who entered and sat down had proved themselves in their work together over the years. To Cohen's left was Yitshaq Goldberg, who in the early 1950s had served in the Golani Brigade. He had risen rapidly through the ranks, and while he was deputy battalion commander, he had met Uri Cohen. The two men were the same age and had become good friends. Some time later, Uri suggested that Yitshaq retire from the army and join the security unit where Cohen was a young section head.

To Uri's right sat Avshalom Kedmi. Thirty-seven years old, Kedmi had long been one of the senior intelligence agents. He had been seriously injured six years before, when members of the "Popular Front" had made an attempt on his life. For a year he had undergone a series of operations and, since then, had been serving as assistant to the chief of surveillance.

Opposite Kedmi sat Yirmi Spector, at thirty the youngest of the group and the academic among them. A specialist in Middle Eastern studies, he was working on his doctorate. He had joined the branch shortly after completing his military service in the paratroops. The chief relied on these men for their knowledge, judgment, and loyalty.

"First, you've done good work in preparing the report on the Libyan plan," Uri said. "We've been through many similar situations in the past. Fortunately, we've never been forced to face the test. But one day there will be no choice." He smiled grimly. "In view of past experience, it's been decided to put us in charge of this operation, with assistance from all the branches, of course. This time it might be for real."

The men around the table remained silent. Cohen already had their comments in the margins of the document that lay before him.

"Right now we have all the questions and no answers," Uri Cohen said. "But, in view of our present internal political situation, one particular question bothers me. Who is the target the Libyans have chosen?"

He paused and then continued quietly, as though talking to

himself. "No doubt, they have a target. The question is, is it someone in the new government or someone from the previous one? It might just be a coincidence, but I'm struck by the proximity of Begin's election and the discovery of this business in Paris.

"The information the murdered German wanted to pass on might have concerned a plan that the Libyans decided to cancel. On the other hand, the plan could be in its earliest stages." Uri seemed to be asking himself a question. "What are the Libyans' motives at this point? Give me a motive and I might tell you who they've set their sights on."

Yitshaq Goldberg used the silence to clear his throat, as if preparing to speak. He leaned forward, removed his glasses, looked at them and replaced them. He looked like a professor beginning a lecture. "Since we don't know details," he suggested, "it's worth treating it as if the target were a member of the new government."

"I agree with Yitshaq," Avshalom Kedmi said. "If it turns out that the plan's been canceled, so much the better. But we should consider the plan from now on as if it's in its operational stage. And the members of the outgoing government are unlikely targets. It isn't logical."

"The Libyans' logic is different from ours," remarked Yirmi Spector cautiously. "Better remember that."

"Particularly Qaddafi's logic," Yitshaq Goldberg added.

"The classic method," Avshalom Kedmi pointed out, "is to liquidate a leader from one state and put the blame on another."

Uri Cohen had missed parts of the conversation among the three men. He was once again analyzing the handful of facts that had been sent from Paris.

"It's late," he stated. "I suggest that we stop now. At this stage, we won't enlarge our little team until matters become clearer. Until then, I don't want anything that has been said here tonight to reach anyone else. I hope to set guidelines for you tomorrow after I've checked them with Avital."

As the three men got up and left the office, the chief of surveillance glanced at his watch. It was two thirty. He picked up the various folders once again and began to study the material, this time making notes on a piece of paper. He wanted to present a clear picture to Avital Arnon, head of the security service.

Pierre de Maline, the fifty-two-year-old owner of a perfumery on the Champs Elysées, had had an interesting past. A native of Marseilles, he had belonged to a street gang in his youth, but he was lucky and never fell into the hands of the law. The Second World War uprooted him and he spent the war years in the uniform of the Free French under the command of General Charles de Gaulle.

After the war, various daring and quick-witted men with uncertain pasts managed to acquire respectable businesses. One of them was Pierre de Maline. His perfumery became a well-established operation. He lived above the store, on the second floor, and had set up a luxurious office from which he could observe his staff working below.

However, the perfumery served as a cover for far more lucrative business operations. De Maline was a conduit between underworld figures who had valuable property to sell and suitable parties who wished to buy. He also acted as the go-between for men who wanted someone killed and the hired executioners who were ready to do the job. He was an invisible force behind the scenes, but his occupation was not without its dangers. If a go-between failed or caused the ruin of one of the parties, it could cost him his life. The middleman served as an insurance policy for both sides: the hirer and the man hired to carry out the job. For this reason, he could demand huge sums and his cut was large.

From Pierre de Maline's point of view, the night of May 25th began with promise. A few days earlier, he had met Madame Audrey Fontaine, a young woman of thirty, who was seeking a husband of means. She was elegant and well-bred, a tall and willowy woman with a trim posterior that suggested pleasures yet to come. He had convinced himself that she would fall into his hands like a ripe fruit after a suitable courtship, during which he would display his wealth.

At six o'clock in the evening, Pierre de Maline called for Madame Fontaine at her apartment on the Boulevard Calvert. They dined at an expensive restaurant near the Place de l'Opéra. He was enjoying the evening; Madame Fontaine proved to be a lively and intelligent conversationalist with an excellent sense of humor. After dinner, they went on to the Olympia nightclub where they stayed until after midnight. The bottles of champagne had their effect. De Maline was in good spirits.

After he saw Madame Fontaine to her door, he returned to the waiting cab. It was about one o'clock when the taxi stopped in the Champs Elysées, opposite the perfumery. As de Maline headed toward his door, he suddenly was aware of strangers approaching him. He stepped back in alarm but was relieved when he recognized the broad figure of the Libyan.

"Monsieur el-Magrabi!" he called out in surprise.

The Libyan was an important client. He often required Pierre de Maline's services as a middleman, especially when the Libyans found it necessary to use European killers whose actions could in no way be linked to the Libyan intelligence. Nevertheless, his appearance was unanticipated, particularly at that hour. Adel el-Magrabi held out his hand, and the Frenchman grasped it. El-Magrabi's two bodyguards remained in the background, half hidden in the darkness.

"I hope that I am not disturbing you at this hour," the Libyan said slowly. "I have an urgent matter for you. Especially after the disappointment with the last person you recommended to me . . ."

It was the first time that a threatening note had crept into the quiet voice of the Libyan. The Frenchman waited, uncertain.

"You mean the German?" he asked in a low voice.

"Yes." The Libyan fixed him with a stare. "But I do not believe there is any need for us to continue talking in the street."

A feeling of unease came over de Maline. The news that the German he had recommended had failed the Libyan caused him concern. He was not a coward, but he well knew the fate of a middleman whose recommendations proved unsatisfactory.

He opened the door and the two men entered. El-Magrabi's two bodyguards remained outside. At the foot of the staircase to the second floor, de Maline stopped and politely gestured to his guest to precede him. The Libyan did so. The silent assent alleviated some of the Frenchman's fears. If the Libyan had intended to harm de Maline, he would not have agreed to climb the stairs ahead of him.

"When did you arrive in Paris?" he asked his guest, as the latter lowered himself into a comfortable armchair in de Maline's living room.

"Several hours ago. We reached an important decision today. Events occur rapidly in our world," he chuckled. "But it is late, monsieur. I have no desire to rob you of the remainder of the night."

"It is my pleasure to listen," the Frenchman said courteously, and settled into his armchair.

"You exhaust me, de Maline." The Libyan looked at him severely. "I do not like to fly around on airplanes to no purpose simply because you fail me with your recommendations. You fail me and I fail my boss. A chain reaction. He fails his superiors. And I run about like a mouse, back and forth." He clicked his tongue. "You, too, would not be pleased to find yourself in a similar situation."

"I have taken care of your needs in the past . . ."

"You earned a nice sum."

"I have never failed you. What happened this time?"

"The German betrayed me."

Pierre de Maline leaped out of his chair in fury. "I'll take care of him!"

The Libyan waved his hand in a gesture of dismissal. He gave an uncharacteristic laugh, perhaps because he was tired.

"No need." He inhaled deeply. "You can't take care of a dead man. And I do not accept your statement that these things can happen!" His heavy eyebrows came together over the bridge of his nose in a threatening glare. "Do you seek excuses in these matters?"

The Frenchman became more and more uncomfortable. He wondered if, after all, the Libyan did intend to harm him. "I meant to say that if I don't receive exact details, then a mistake can happen." He stopped and studied the Libyan's expression carefully. "I am sorry."

"We are all sorry."

"I am not the only one to blame." De Maline tried to defend himself. "You did not tell me what kind of an operation you had in mind . . ."

"True," the Libyan agreed. "Perhaps I do have a certain share in this failure."

Pierre de Maline relaxed. Obviously, the man opposite him had come to discuss a new deal.

"In the past you have been satisfied with my services," he observed quietly.

"Correct."

"I understand that you require the services of a man of extraordinary professional caliber."

The Libyan nodded his head in agreement.

"That is a different kind of operation, Monsieur el-Magrabi."

"I completely agree."

"Permit me to ask one question," the Frenchman said. "Is this connected with the settling of accounts between Arabs?"

The Libyan hesitated.

"No," he stated finally. "I must answer you so that you will know exactly which three men I require."

"Three?"

"Three." The Libyan looked at him coolly. "On the highest level. It concerns a political assassination."

Pierre de Maline looked up in alarm. He could not hide his reaction, even though it lasted only seconds. His eyes grew wide. He opened his mouth, then closed it.

"I am not sure that I'm the right man for an operation such as this," he said. The words seemed to spill out of his mouth before he could weigh their significance. Under no circumstances was he prepared to be a pawn in a foreign political plot. If the affair developed into an international outrage, he would be exposed. He wondered if there were any way out.

"No, monsieur. There is no way out," el-Magrabi said gently, as though reading his mind. "It is too late for ideas like that. Better avoid them."

The Frenchman felt trapped. "I see," he said. The sound of his voice amazed him. It was as if someone else were talking.

"Better get to work," the Libyan said. "Three men. The

best there are. Men who are prepared to take risks in order to earn millions. You will receive your full share too."

"How much time do I have?"

"Ha!" Adel el-Magrabi guffawed. He was overcome by tiredness. "What would you say, monsieur, to forty-eight hours?"

Pierre de Maline was slow to respond. The Libyans needed three professional killers quickly. They were ready to invest millions in the affair. This means, he thought, that they're planning to kill a world-renowned figure.

"I shall have to find out if the three are prepared to work together," he finally answered. "That takes time."

"They will not work together," the Libyan stated flatly. "Forty-eight hours!"

"It's impossible!"

The Libyan got out of the armchair and turned toward the stairs. Only when his thick, stubby fingers had grasped the rail did he turn his head. "De Maline," he said in a low voice, "if you knew that these were the last two days of your life, you would move heaven and earth, would you not?"

The threat was now out in the open.

The Frenchman's flesh grew cold. He made an effort to smile, but his face was twisted. In silence he accompanied his guest to the door. For some moments he stood, as though transfixed, and watched the Libyan walk away slowly, the two bodyguards at his side like menacing shadows.

Pierre de Maline locked the door and lowered the steel grill behind it. After setting the electronic alarm, he slowly climbed to the second floor. Try as he would, he could not think of more than two people who would qualify. One was Madame Jacqueline Charlotte, a member of French society. Because of her connections, no door was closed to her. She was the owner of a successful modeling agency as well as a cold blooded murderess whose method was death by poison. The other was a journalist, a specialist in terror, named Jorg Gibskopf. His method was detonating explosive charges kept in cameras and tape recorders, routine equipment for a journalist. Those two were capable of the job, de Maline estimated, and could be of use to the Libyan. They would also agree, since the Libyans were willing to pay huge sums. But where would he find the third?

The strain he was under found expression in the pounding pulse in his temple. His head felt like it was about to burst. God, he thought, this is the last time. No more. After this, he would get out of Paris altogether. He'd start a new life, perhaps in Monte Carlo. After all, he liked the sea and the sun. Monte Carlo would be enjoyable. He would have plenty of money, enough for years to come.

Monte Carlo . . .

Suddenly it struck him. Christ! Boncho lived in Monte Carlo; Boncho, his friend! He could solve the problem in a day. The Italian was involved in similar deals, but on a far larger scale. He wouldn't desert his friend in a time of need.

Feeling encouraged, Pierre de Maline went to the bar and filled a glass to the brim with Martel brandy. He drank and felt the warmth spread down into his stomach. He drank again and his spirits rose. He went to the phone and called the main office of Air France, which was open around the clock. He booked a flight to Monte Carlo on a plane that was scheduled to take off in six hours. It gave him time to take a short rest.

On Thursday morning, at five o'clock, the parting blast of the cargo vessel *La Mer* could be heard as she made her way slowly toward the harbor exit. In just a few minutes, she would slip out of the embrace of the port of Marseilles. She had been there for several days being loaded with a mixed cargo destined for New York. The rays of light signaling a new day began to spread over the harbor. The dirty waters now lost the magic glow granted by the darkness of the receding night. A light breeze wafted over the sea.

A young man standing on the quay watched the stern of *La Mer* for some time after she had sounded her last blast. Amid the cargo in her hold was a valuable shipment, whose dispatch to the United States the young man had handled. It included antiques stolen from archaeological sites recently uncovered on the border between Greece and Turkey. The American antique dealer, Alex Kraskin, had placed the order through the Italian from Monte Carlo.

The Italian had promised that he could find the right man to carry off the theft. The antiques were valued at close to a million dollars. In return for his labors, which had taken six weeks and involved certain risks, the young man had received $200,000. After paying the Italian his cut as middleman, and subtracting his expenses, $135,000 remained in his Swiss bank account.

The young man was far from satisfied with the work that the Italian had offered him during the past year. He wanted to retire in a few years, but it seemed that the Italian was having difficulty getting him a contract with a large enough profit. His last killing had been carried out three years before in Africa. One shot had eliminated a mad ruler, and the revolution had gone forward without further bloodshed. His price then had been $600,000. But times had changed. He let the Italian understand that he was willing to risk his neck only for sums much larger than those he was being offered. The Italian was waiting for an opportunity to offer him his big chance.

As the cargo boat receded into the distance, he turned and walked toward the parking lot. He started the engine of his green Alfa Sud and drove slowly toward the port gate. His small apartment was just a short drive from there. He would head for it and wait until a message came from the Italian.

That same morning, May 26, at eight o'clock, Pierre de Maline flew to Monte Carlo. Four hours later, an El Al Boeing 707 landed at Orly Airport. Among the passengers were Uri Cohen, chief of surveillance, and his deputy, Yitshaq Goldberg. When they left the plane, they drove off immediately in the direction of Paris. With them was Yaki Spillman, who had been waiting for them at the airport.

The two Israelis had been sent to Paris by Avital Arnon, head of the security service, to determine quickly if the Libyan plot was still operational, or if it had been connected with the outgoing government and was canceled following the election of Menachem Begin.

Four people seemed likely targets: Golda Meir and Yitshaq Rabin, the former prime ministers, and Menachem Begin and Moshe Dayan. Since these four were already under constant protection by the surveillance branch, it was possible to augment their guard without drawing unnecessary attention to the fact.

Yirmi Spector was put in charge of the direct control of the security units attached to each of the four political figures. Avshalom Kedmi was placed in charge of coordinating the general security operations. His division was set up to deal with the fact that the unknown assassin had two areas of operation: a foreign country that one of the four people was likely to visit in the near future, and the State of Israel. Until the situation became clearer, immediate steps had to be taken to prevent breaks in the security wall in order to prevent the killer from entering Israel, or at least to make it difficult for him to do so.

Avshalom Kedmi held a series of meetings with representatives of the various security branches. In Jerusalem, he met with the head of the special task force of the Israel police. At this meeting, it was agreed that the police would increase security checks on travelers entering by air or by sea, as well as those entering Israel from the Arab countries via the bridges linking Israel to Jordan.

At another meeting that Kedmi held, this time with the chief of operations of the Israel Defense Forces, it was agreed to reinforce the patrols and searches carried out by the army. Orders were also sent out to the navy to run sea patrols round the clock along the entire coastline. A similar order was sent down to the army units that patrolled the frontiers. They were told to report immediately the arrest of any suspicious person.

Instructions were also given to those in charge of ongoing security on the border between southern Lebanon and Israel, near the "Good Fence," which served as a permanent meeting place between the commanders of the Christian forces and the commanders of the Israeli units that were helping them in their defense against attacks by the Palestinian guerrillas. This was a region that would be easy for a foreign agent to infiltrate. Identical orders were handed down to the Defense Forces command responsible for the units that policed the Gaza Strip and Samaria and Judea. They overlapped instructions given to the army intelligence personnel who worked among the Arab inhabitants of the Arab territories.

Briefed on all this on the journey between Orly airport and Paris, Yaki Spillman reported that his efforts to track down Adel el-Magrabi in Paris had not succeeded.

"Why?" Uri Cohen glared at him.

Yaki Spillman laughed wryly. "For a very simple reason. The French services are still under pressure from above not to cooperate with us." He turned and looked at Cohen, who was sitting next to him. "But I did get a tip from Inspector André Cordeille of the French antiterrorist division that Adel el-Magrabi is somewhere in Paris."

"What else?"

"El-Magrabi," Spillman explained, "is the deputy of Adam Ahmed, who is in charge of the division responsible for activating foreign agents."

"At the moment, el-Magrabi is the only real lead we have," Uri said quietly. "We must get hold of the tail in order to reach the neck and break the backbone."

Uri was under a great deal of pressure. He and Avital Arnon had decided unilaterally to delay making any reports on their activities to higher-ups in government. It was a calculated risk. There was a danger of a serious leak if they widened the circle of those in the know. On the other hand, if something went wrong, there would be a high price to pay.

That evening Uri met with agents of Israeli security based in Europe to find out what they knew about el-Magrabi. Only two of them, Ze'ev Shahar and Motti Klein, had heard of the man, but both had come across him several times in the past, and Shahar had spotted him just a short while ago in Brussels.

"All right," said Uri. "You two have got your assignment. Find el-Magrabi. We know he's in Paris now. I don't care what means you use, as long as it's fast. Remember, you've got one advantage. You know him, and he doesn't even know you exist."

A short time later, Uri, accompanied by Yitshaq Goldberg and Yaki Spillman, arrived at John Palmer's house on the Boulevard Gabriel, near the American Embassy, to be briefed on what the American had been able to find out from his sources. Palmer told them about the special Libyan unit that had been set up to liquidate various political figures in the Middle East, the targets all selected by Colonel Mu'ammar Qaddafi.

"They are training two groups," the American explained. "One from the terrorist organizations of the 'rejectionist front' that will be active within Egypt. The other composed of foreigners. Perhaps one of these has been picked to strike at one of your people. The reason for a foreigner, I think, is that the Libyans are afraid that most of those active in Arab terrorist organizations are known to you. You will find it hard to keep track of a European, particularly if he decides to work outside the borders of Israel."

In Palmer's view, the German had been one of the foreign killers the Libyans had chosen to carry out these assassination attempts. From the information he had received, it appeared that Qaddafi's main objective was to strike at Egyptian leaders, in view of the mounting tension between Libya and Egypt.

"Let's assume for a moment," Uri Cohen suggested, "that the targets are Egyptian statesmen. Why did Hans Kirschenberg come to you in order to contact Yaki Spillman?"

"Money."

"Is that all?"

John Palmer smiled. "He could have tried to make contact with the Egyptian Embassy for exactly the same reason," he remarked. "Money has no smell. It doesn't matter where it comes from, an Israeli source or an Egyptian source. He needed a lot of money, and fast."

"Why?"

"In the course of the investigation I made," the American explained patiently, "I discovered that Hans Kirschenberg was in the process of applying for an immigrant's visa to the United States. Actually, Nancy Keeting had been helping him. He merely had to prove his financial independence. So let's assume that for that reason he was ready to take on an assignment from the Libyans. But something went wrong and he was dismissed. He suddenly finds himself in a corner. He needs money urgently. Lots of money. So what does he do?"

"Tries to sell his information."

"Exactly."

"Do you have any way of finding out if he did go to the Egyptian Embassy?" Uri Cohen was worried by the American's analysis of the situation. "The possibility of playing a double game would be in keeping with his character." He hesitated and then continued: "You understand. This might not concern us after all."

"Maybe," the American agreed. "But you have no proof of that. Better to accept the facts you have as solid evidence. As for the Egyptian Embassy, I have no way of checking. But it's possible that the Libyans really do intend to assassinate Egyptian leaders.

"I'm sure," Palmer added, "that you'll find a way to check the information. Meanwhile, I would continue to act with maximum care and vigilance."

"Is there any way of involving the French?" Yaki Spillman asked. "They have a good relationship with the Egyptians. What do you think?"

"It's a good idea," John Palmer smiled. "But I can't do it. You'll have to find your own way."

"What about your people in Cairo?" Yitshaq Goldberg suggested.

"That's complicated." The American seemed to reject the idea.

"We're working on foreign territory," Yitshaq Goldberg persisted. "It isn't easy, Mr. Palmer. Believe me."

"I do believe you." The American nodded his head. "But I'm also limited. I would suggest that you try and find a motive. If the Libyans do want to knock off one of your leaders, what's the motive behind it?"

"He's right, that Palmer," Uri told Yitshaq on their way home. "Give me a motive and I'll tell you how serious the German's information was."

Yitshaq Goldberg looked at him. "The American is playing a careful game with us," he stated.

"That's true." The chief smiled. "They are treading between us and the oil states like tightrope walkers. You really can't blame them. But he did throw out an idea in the end. We have to find a way . . ."

Uri went over the details of the conversation. The American was guarded. But there was nothing to stop him. He would find a way to the Egyptian intelligence and get the information he needed from them.

The next morning, before Uri's return to Tel Aviv, he was contacted by Yaki Spillman. He had just talked to Inspector André Cordeille of the French antiterrorist division; during the night, information had come in from Germany on Hans Kirschenberg. The dead man had been identified by his fingerprints as Heinrich Woltan, a one-time member of the Baader-Meinhof gang, wanted in connection with several murders. It would appear that after fleeing Germany he had become a paid killer.

"All of which," Spillman told Uri, "lends credence to the story he told me."

Uri sighed. It was obvious that if they had to contend with an anonymous killer working on territory he knew well, they were in trouble. They would be in a desperately defensive situation with only a slim possibility of responding in the right way. It was no secret that the chances of a cunning and daring killer, well trained in his profession, were better than the chances of anyone trying to stop him. Two main objectives still remained: to discover the Libyan plot and to determine who the Libyans had selected as their target.

Uri fervently hoped further investigation would show that the Libyans planned to launch assassins in Egypt. For a few minutes, he allowed himself to enjoy the comfort this possibility gave him, but when he pulled himself together, he knew that this refuge from his anxieties was a luxury that he could not yet afford.

On Saturday morning the postman stopped at the old gray house located near the harbor of Marseilles. When the young man who lived on the second floor saw him pass, he went downstairs and checked his mailbox, as had been his daily custom since he returned from his long trip to acquire antiques for the American dealer. He was expecting a message from the Italian, who had promised to provide him with work at the beginning of the summer. Today again the box was empty.

The young man shrugged his shoulders and turned to go back to his small apartment, one of several that he rented in various cities. From time to time, he changed apartments as other men change clothes. This one contained only an old bed, a table, and a chair.

He rarely left the apartment, and then only in the early morning hours when he went out for a walk to release the tensions that had accumulated like toxins in his powerful body. Occasionally he went to buy a few days' supply of food. Otherwise he sat by the window for hours at a stretch, looking out to sea.

This time he undressed and went into the small shower. He was extremely fastidious and was used to showering every few hours. His body was the instrument of his profession and he took care of it the way a racing driver takes care of his car; his life depended on its being in good condition. After a long while, he turned off the faucet, took a large towel, and dried off his body. Then he dressed and sat down once more on the chair next to the window and waited for a message from the Italian.

At noon the same day, the Air France plane from Monte Carlo carried a vastly relieved Pierre de Maline back to Paris. His old friend Boncho—Vittorio Angelo Massino, to give him his full name—had come to the rescue as he had so often during the war when the two had served together in the ranks of the Free French under General de Gaulle. A man of incredible daring and courage, Boncho had once said jokingly that he might become a professional killer when the war was over, and, in fact, that is exactly what had happened. At first he offered his services to the highest bidder, but over the years he began to branch out, planning art heists and procuring killers in return for a large cut of the fee. Now exclusively a go-between, he had no equal in the field. Which is why de Maline had turned to him as a last resort to locate the third killer he needed.

As soon as de Maline had arrived in Monte Carlo he made for the harbor where Boncho's yacht, the *Paedaeia*, lay anchored off the jetty. He was welcomed effusively by Boncho, a tall, handsome, vital man whose only indication of age was a slight graying at the temples. The Italian was quick to notice that something was wrong and led de Maline to his luxurious cabin where he poured him a brandy and gestured to a chair. "Come, spill everything," he said.

De Maline hesitated a moment, then said in a rush: "I'm in real trouble. I have to find the right person for a job, the best person there is. Frankly, if I don't find him, and fast, my head's on the block."

Boncho smiled slightly, but the smile was a cover for an inner contempt. What a fool, he thought. It disgusted him that this weary, frightened man was all that remained of the husky, daring youth who had been his comrade in arms in one of the most exciting periods of his life.

"It is a political matter?"

De Maline hesitated. "I think so."

Boncho was silent. He thought of the young man waiting in Marseilles for word on a new operation. He was the only person he knew who had the necessary qualifications.

"I might know someone," he said quietly.

De Maline's eyes lit up. "Someone good?"

"The best," the Italian stated flatly. "And if I say so, you can count on it."

Pierre de Maline let out his breath slowly and within seconds felt a sudden easing of tension.

"How do I make contact?" he asked.

"It's not easy."

"Why not?"

"First," the Italian stressed plainly, "I don't know exactly who needs him. Are you sure it's a political assassination?"

"That's my estimate."

"It's an expensive business."

"Money is no problem."

"My man will require a very substantial advance," Boncho observed. "You are not used to hearing sums like that mentioned."

"How much?"

The Italian was slow to answer. The man in Marseilles had said that for a political killing he would not be satisfied with less than several million.

"He will want half a million dollars," he said. "Just to negotiate."

The Frenchman's face flushed. His mouth fell open. "Are you serious?"

"You heard me, Pierre."

"That's a huge sum!"

"You're not dealing with an amateur," Boncho smiled. "You have to find the right man. Good. You have him. If they can't satisfy his conditions, you have still done your share. The rest is up to them."

Pierre de Maline recognized the logic of the Italian's words. Boncho was right. He would supply them with three names: Madame Jacqueline Charlotte, Jorg Gibskopf, and this third man. The negotiations were el-Magrabi's affair.

"All right," he said. "How do we do it?"

"I shall give you the number of a bank account in Zurich," the Italian explained. "If they mean business and manage to get that sum into the bank account, the connection will be made."

"Is that the only way?"

"There is no other." Boncho's face grew stern. "And let me give you one little piece of advice, Pierre. After this one, get out. Drop this business."

"What's wrong?"

"Everything's fine." The Italian poured more cognac into his glass. "But it's a dangerous game. You will have a good profit. However, if I were you, I wouldn't deal any more. You're not as young as you were. And you're over your depth."

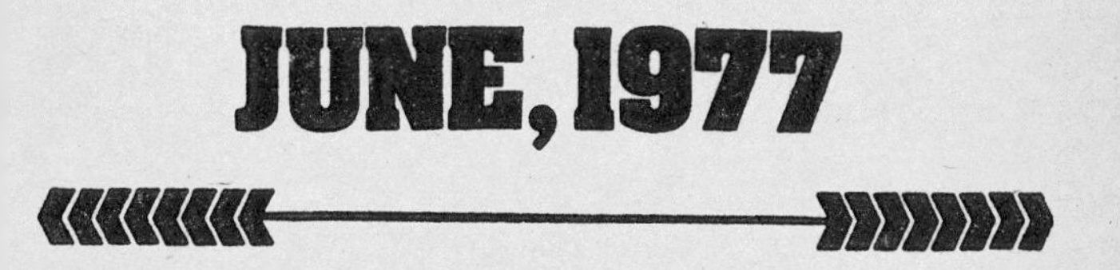
JUNE, 1977

On Thursday, June 2nd, a sealed envelope bearing a top secret classification was placed on the desk of the head of surveillance at the headquarters of the security service in Tel Aviv. It contained a detailed report from Yaki Spillman. The first part covered the outcome of further investigations into the murders of Hans Kirschenberg and Nancy Keeting. The second detailed the efforts of Motti Klein and Ze'ev Shahar to find Adel el-Magrabi: they had, in fact, succeeded in tracking him down and had tailed him until he left Paris for Tripoli.

Yaki Spillman had managed to obtain more details on the last days of the German's life. Investigators from the crime division had located his apartment in Paris and there they found his passport which indicated that on May 11th, Kirschenberg had arrived in Tripoli and spent two days there before returning to Paris. This was solid proof of his direct connection with the Libyans. Now there was a basis for the assumption that he had been murdered because of the three-man meeting that had taken place at the American Embassy. If this assumption was correct, the information he had wanted to sell was undoubtedly valuable.

From the report on Adel el-Magrabi, it appeared that Motti Klein and Ze'ev Shahar had done their work thoroughly. From the moment they had traced him to a small hotel not far from the center of Paris, they trailed him without let-up until he left the city. Their report included details of various meetings, with notes of the exact times and places, as well as sketches of the people whom he had contacted.

Uri Cohen put the report down. At first glance, except for the fact that he was always accompanied by his two bodyguards, the Libyan's movements had resembled those of any tourist with money in his pocket, enjoying what the city had to offer. He found it difficult to spot a single point that could link the visit of el-Magrabi to the case that was causing him sleepless nights. He looked through the papers again, then pushed them aside and went back to routine reports concerning the protection of Israeli embassies in South America.

After lunch in a small restaurant in north Tel Aviv, Uri returned to his office and once more began to look over Spillman's report. He carefully studied each of el-Magrabi's appointments. Only one meeting differed from the others. After midnight on a Saturday, the Libyan had paid a visit to a perfumery on the Champs Elysées owned by one Pierre de Maline. His bodyguards had remained outside a long time, waiting for him. Significantly, this was the only meeting when they did not accompany him. Suddenly Uri was struck by the lateness of the hour.

"Saturday night!" he said with a curse. The visit was reasonable—a tourist might go to a fancy perfumery in Paris to buy gifts for his wife in Tripoli—but the hour was not.

Soon afterward, a message was sent from his office to Spillman to check with police headquarters in Paris and with Interpol for information on a man named Pierre de Maline. At the same time, he asked for an answer by telephone as to whether for any reason the perfumery was open late on Saturdays.

At six in the evening, the missing piece came in, and the picture was complete. His suspicions were correct. The perfumery closed on Saturday night at seven o'clock. What, then, was the Libyan doing there so late?

When Uri Cohen reached his home in Ramat Hasharon, he found his soldier son there. Seeing the boy made him forget his troubles for a while. Gadi's appearance had changed. The boy in him was being worn away by his army training. His face had become mature, he was taller, and his shoulders had broadened. They sat down to dinner, which Shula, his wife, had taken pains to make special. Gadi left shortly before nine to take his girlfriend to a movie in Tel Aviv, and Uri switched on the television to watch the news. The major story had to do with the efforts of Menachem Begin to complete the formation of his government and submit it to the Knesset for approval. This was followed by an account of the growing tension between Libya and Egypt; foreign correspondents had reported large troop concentrations on both sides of the frontier.

At ten o'clock, the call came in from Yaki Spillman in Paris. His first contacts with the various security agencies regarding the Frenchman, de Maline, had yielded nothing. Uri thanked him and asked him to continue investigating. The nagging thought that they had missed something still disturbed him. He suggested that Yaki get in touch with other people in intelligence, including their American friend, John Palmer.

"This Frenchman is bothering you," Spillman stated.

"And you?"

"I don't know," Spillman admitted, "but it's worth checking again."

"I have the feeling that he was connected with the German."

"The go-between?"

"Maybe." He thought about what he was going to say. "He could be the go-between. It would explain the connection."

"Recruitment of new people," Spillman conjectured.

"Perhaps. That's why it's important to keep digging. Pick up any lead. We'll see where it takes us."

As yet they had nothing concrete. Although it seemed that there was a direct link between the dead German and the Libyans, Uri had no way of knowing if the Libyan plan was directed against Israel or Egypt. And in the absence of real evidence, his hands were tied.

* * *

As soon as the Libyans became aware that Menachem Begin intended to include Moshe Dayan in his cabinet, they were sure that Israel's secret negotiations with the Egyptians would continue. Intelligence chief Adam Ahmed once again received definite instructions from Mu'ammar Qaddafi: he was to act, and soon. His deputy, Adel el-Magrabi, had returned with the information he needed to set the plan in motion. They had an unlimited budget. Indeed, money had no meaning where the target was concerned.

And the Libyans had selected their target.

The discussion between Adel el-Magrabi and Madame Jacqueline Charlotte was short and to the point. An attractive woman of forty, Madame Charlotte proved to be as cold and calculating as a computer. She considered the offer and the conditions and, a day later, replied in the affirmative. That same day, she flew to Tripoli to seal the agreement with Adam Ahmed.

Jorg Gibskopf, the journalist, could not resist the huge bait either. He agreed in the course of his first discussion with el-Magrabi. A day after Madame Charlotte left Tripoli, Gibskopf arrived in the Libyan capital.

Now el-Magrabi had to deal with the third man. On Thursday, June 9th, he arrived in Zurich. All he had was the name of a bank and the number of an account. A short time later, he had settled into a hotel in the center of the city and, by then, had the name of the bank manager: Michel Jean Louis.

Louis, a man of sixty, was a widely respected banker. His position demanded unusual flexibility in dealing with the eccentricities of his clients, whose real identity in many cases was not even known to the management of the bank. However, el-Magrabi's visit to his office revealed that in one area Michel Jean Louis had no flexibility whatsoever, namely the disclosure of account holders' identities.

The interview had started off pleasantly enough. Adel el-Magrabi had introduced himself to Monsieur Louis's secretary as a potential client who was interested in making certain investments. Several minutes later, he was invited into the manager's spacious office with its dark wood paneling and valuable paintings. Louis rose and held out his hand across the antique desk. Although he was smiling, his eyes remained cold.

"I am happy to make your acquaintance, monsieur," he said.

"Adel el-Magrabi," the well-dressed Libyan supplied his name as he sank into the comfort of a deep leather armchair. Coffee was offered but he refused; his time was limited.

"I understand that monsieur is interested in some advice on investing money." Michel Jean Louis valued his Arab customers. The amounts they invested were worth taking pains over. "I am convinced that you came to us after verifying that we are one of the most efficient banks."

"That is so, monsieur," the Libyan replied evenly. "I am also convinced that you are open to a fair proposal, which, if you so desire, could interest you personally."

The bank manager studied the Libyan for a moment. "As to my personal interest, allow me to clarify that at a later stage."

The Libyan smiled. He appreciated intelligent men. "I wish to deposit the sum of half a million dollars to the account of one of your clients," he said. "I feel that the deposit of such a large sum of money requires the personal attention of the bank manager."

"That is an awkward matter, monsieur." The manager twisted in his chair. "As a rule, we do not accept deposits to the account of any customer without his express permission."

The Libyan smiled but made no comment.

"It is possible that you have made an error, that this is not the right bank."

"There is no error," the Libyan replied. "I have the man's account number."

"That will not help us." The bank manager removed his glasses and polished the lenses with care. "What you are asking is not done. Under any circumstances."

Adel el-Magrabi was a man of experience. "I understand what your problem is." He picked up the briefcase he had brought with him, placed it on his knees, and opened it. It was filled to overflowing with packets of dollars. "There are five hundred and fifty thousand dollars here, in one-hundred-dollar bills. I shall leave this briefcase with you. If you find that you are permitted to deposit the money in the account of your esteemed customer, fifty thousand dollars will remain in your hands. Please regard this as a token of my appreciation for your efficient service."

The bank manager became even more flustered. It was true that from time to time, in the course of special bank dealings, he had picked up substantial sums of money, but this cut was unusually large. He cleared his throat, trying to relieve the hoarseness that had come on him suddenly.

"What is the account number?" he asked. "Of course, I do not commit myself to confirming that he is, in fact, one of our customers."

"Here it is." Adel el-Magrabi wrote the number on a piece of paper and placed it on the manager's desk. "As I have said, monsieur, fifty thousand dollars are for you. Of course, it will be necessary for you to deposit the money in the appropriate account first. Afterward, when the account holder confirms acceptance, you will have to tell him how to contact me."

"I must study the matter," Michel Jean Louis said thoughtfully, and with his customary politeness, he accompanied his guest to the door of his office, where they parted with a handshake.

Adel el-Magrabi made his way back to the penthouse suite he had booked in the center of Zurich. There he waited, and at five thirty in the afternoon he received a call from Monsieur Louis.

"Monsieur," the manager said, "I am happy to inform you that the sum of money has been placed in the proper account."

"I am very grateful."

"Regarding the rest," the banker continued, "the moment I hear from the client, I assure you that your address will be submitted to him. But it may take several days."

"I understand."

"In that case, thank you once again," the banker concluded. "I shall be happy to cooperate with you in the future."

"I do not doubt it." Adel el-Magrabi smiled to himself.

The Libyan was under orders from Adam Ahmed to arrange the recruitment of the third man as quickly as possible. By now the other two certainly had begun to map out their plans without either knowing of the existence of the other. This mystery man, too, the one recommended by Pierre de Maline with such enthusiasm, would soon be similarly engaged.

Adel el-Magrabi was obliged to forego any visits to places of entertainment in the city, since the unknown man might try to contact him at his hotel when he was out. This unusual situation weighed heavily on his bodyguards. The two well-built young men were used to being constantly on the move. Now, forced to spend hours waiting, they began to show signs of restlessness. For that reason, during the day el-Magrabi put them on duty in turns so that one of them might enjoy the pleasures of Zurich while his comrade remained on guard. At night they stood guard together until midday; one of them remained with Adel el-Magrabi while the other stayed in the suite across the hall keeping watch along the corridor and covering the entrance to the elevator.

The waiting lasted until Friday, June 17th.

In the office of Michel Jean Louis the day began as usual. At nine o'clock Louis looked over various financial transactions. At nine thirty he drank tea with milk, no sugar; he had to be careful because of a slight diabetic condition. For the next fifteen minutes, he read the paper closely, giving special attention to the business columns. At nine forty-five, his secretary buzzed him. The manager pressed a button on the intercom.

"Yes?"

"A Mr. Ullstein is here. He wishes to see you."

"About what?"

"About a certain deposit made into his account."

Michel Jean Louis's pulse quickened. The message he had sent had reached the anonymous account holder. He wondered what this unknown man, who went by the name of

Ullstein, and whose account was half a million dollars richer, would look like.

"Send him in," the banker said in an unsteady voice as he put down the morning paper.

Several seconds later the heavy wooden door opened. The man who entered his office in no way fitted the image he had formed. He was about fifty years old, above average in height, with round shoulders. His small belly protruded beyond the flaps of his old jacket. His square jaws emphasized his sunken cheeks. His face looked gray, and stubble sprouted on his chin, attesting to several days' growth without a shave. He seemed to have come on a long journey. When he took off his battered hat, his disheveled hair was streaked with gray. His eyes were swallowed up behind the dark lenses of thick horn-rimmed glasses. He looked like a farmer from a remote village who had come to town to attend to his affairs. Michel Jean Louis was certain that there had been a mistake. Who would invest half a million dollars in this ragged gray character?

"Mr. Ullstein?" he asked the blank-faced visitor.

"Mr. Ullstein," the man concurred. His voice was rough. Hoarseness blurred the edges of his words. Nevertheless, the banker was convinced that his knowledge of the German language was perfect; it was the German of a peasant, but German nonetheless.

The man approached the large desk, his feet dragging in weariness. In one hand he grasped the handle of an old suitcase; its color was faded, but in the past it had been a bright blue.

In view of the man's unprepossessing appearance, the manager felt obliged to pursue the matter thoroughly. "Mr. Ullstein," he asked, "you do have an account with us?"

"I have." The man made an effort to straighten his head which was drooping somewhat. "I'm tired, sir," he added wearily.

"Excuse me." The bank manager had still not recovered from his surprise at the apparition before him. "Please, do sit down."

The man lowered himself slowly into the armchair, as if

slightly wary of the luxurious surroundings. He held up a piece of paper on which was written a column of numbers.

"This is the account number," he said. "I should like to know exactly how much money is in the account."

Michel Jean Louis examined the number and compared it with the one that he had marked on his notepad. The numbers were identical. It was amazing. The man *was* the account holder.

"I am pleased to make your acquaintance, Mr. Ullstein." The bank manager began to treat his mysterious client with respect. "But allow me to clarify one point. The rules of the bank require that we identify you. When you opened your account, it was through a lawyer's office in Luxemburg."

"I gave a note with my signature," the man mumbled tiredly.

"Would you therefore be kind enough to sign this paper?" The bank manager placed a form before him requesting a statement of the account. The man picked up a pen and wrote down the account number and signed his name below it in a firm hand. Michel Jean Louis called his secretary into his office and gave instructions to compare the signature on the form with that already on file in the bank. In the meantime, while awaiting the answer, he asked his guest if he preferred tea or coffee. The guest refused both, preferring to remain enveloped in silence.

When the secretary returned, he brought with him a confirmation of Ullstein's signature and a detailed list of the deposits made into the account. The statement showed a curious pattern of deposits and withdrawals. For the seven previous years since the account had been opened, very large sums of money had been deposited once or twice a year. Only a man who had property or a highly successful business could credit his account with such large deposits. But then the withdrawals were also large. Apparently the account holder periodically required large sums of money. Michel Jean Louis handed the statement to Ullstein.

"Until two days ago, there were two hundred and seventeen thousand dollars in your account. But you are no doubt pleased to observe that a sum of half a million dollars has been added." The banker smiled as though satisfied. "Hence, the sum at your disposal at this moment is seven hundred and seventeen thousand dollars."

The man did not bother to look at the details of the statement. His expression was still one of indifference.

"Who deposited it?" he asked.

"I made a note of his name and the hotel where he is staying," the banker replied immediately, holding a card out to his visitor. The latter took it, examined it closely for a few seconds, and then tore it to shreds.

"I trust that you are satisfied?" Michel Jean Louis asked.

"Do not ask me and I shall not ask you," the stranger replied evenly.

The banker was taken aback by the reply. "Perhaps you have some special instructions, Mr. Ullstein?"

"Yes," came the calm response. "I am closing the account. I want the money in cash: in dollars."

The banker was pained. "Are you dissatisfied with our service?"

"I am entitled to make use of my right to close the account," the man stated flatly, without troubling to answer the question put to him.

"Nevertheless . . . ?" the banker persisted. "We can offer you a whole range of investments bearing a considerable interest——"

"Don't give me all that bank jargon," the man interrupted. "The money. Here. Now. Do you understand?"

Michel Jean Louis realized that there was no further use in talking. He gave instructions that the sum marked on the margin of the account statement be brought immediately to his office. Ten minutes later, a small chest was wheeled into the room on a trolley that looked like a tea cart.

"Where shall I put the money?" the clerk asked.

"In the suitcase," the customer replied.

The clerk glanced at the bank manager, who ignored his look. Ullstein opened the suitcase, and the clerk began to pack it with bundles of banknotes.

"Do you wish to count it?" the manager asked.

The visitor shrugged his rounded shoulders in indifference. "It's your job to be accurate. I haven't the time."

It took only a few minutes for the money to be transferred to the suitcase. The man snapped the catch shut without troubling to lock it. He stretched his hand out across the desk top and picked up the statement of his account.

"I need this," he said, "it's mine."

When the manager tried to protest, the stranger simply ignored him. He carefully folded the sheet of paper and pushed it into his pocket. Then he turned and grasped the handle of the large suitcase. He seemed to have difficulty lifting it. Finally he steadied himself and moved toward the door, leaving the banker watching in bewilderment.

The moment Ullstein was gone, Michel Jean Louis phoned the Libyan. He felt obliged to inform him that a connection had been established with the unknown man. El-Magrabi was uninterested in the fact that the man had closed the account and had taken the money with him. He only wanted to know what Mr. Ullstein looked like. The banker carefully described the paunchy figure of the man and his "quite primitive" manners, as he put it.

Several minutes after noon, the telephone rang in the guest room of the penthouse where Adel el-Magrabi was staying.

He lifted the receiver. "El-Magrabi."

"The man you are expecting is speaking." The voice was masculine and pleasant. His French was fluent.

"When will you be here?"

"I am in the lobby. May I come up?"

"Certainly."

Adel el-Magrabi replaced the receiver. He told his body-guard to go into the adjoining room. He didn't want the stranger to know that there were bodyguards. He wanted him to feel at ease, comfortable in the belief that they were having their conversation alone.

A minute later he heard a polite tap on the door to the suite. When he went over and opened it, his immediate reaction was surprise. From the banker's description, he had expected to find a tired farmer, poorly dressed and about fifty years old. The man before him was the exact opposite of the colorful description given by Louis. He was tall and impressive in appearance.

"Monsieur el-Magrabi, I believe?" He held out his hand to the Libyan.

"Indeed. Monsieur Ullstein?"

The stranger smiled a dazzling smile.

The Libyan had not yet recovered from his surprise. The man who entered the room could have been older than he appeared, but he was tall, about six feet, perhaps more, and very erect. His face had a fresh look, his color indicative of a man in peak physical condition. A few flecks of gray in his neat moustache and beard were the only signs of age, nothing more. The gold-rimmed glasses matched his light hair which was combed carefully back, except for a lock that fell over his forehead. He was dressed tastefully in the latest fashion. The spring in his step and his ramrod-straight back hinted at a military past, almost certainly as a senior officer. The manner in which he grasped his black cane with its silver knob also bespoke someone in the habit of giving orders.

"I understand," the visitor smiled, "that Michel Jean Louis was quick to report to you about my coming to Zurich. Is that not so?"

Adel el-Magrabi laughed. "It is true, Monsieur Ullstein."

The man looked at him through his glasses. The lenses were gray, which made it difficult for the Libyan to determine the color of his eyes.

"I don't care for German names," he said. "For the purpose of our talk please call me by another name. Let us say, d'Astine. What do you think?"

"Very well, Monsieur d'Astine."

The Libyan felt rather uncomfortable. There was something disquieting about the behavior of the stranger. It was difficult to judge the character of the man; he appeared to be both deferential and disdainful.

"I trust that you are satisfied with the change that has occurred in your bank account." El-Magrabi studied the expression on the stranger's face anxiously.

"Please don't concern yourself with my affairs," the man replied with a faint smile. "I do not take any interest in your financial situation. As I understand it, we have before us an entirely different matter. The most I can do, with all due respect, is to thank you for the sum you have transferred to me in accordance with the instructions of your superiors."

Adel el-Magrabi's mouth fell open. "Monsieur!"

"Do not be surprised, my friend." The man looked at him haughtily. "You are only a messenger. You have been staring at me from the moment I entered as if to convince yourself that there has been no mistake."

"Well, to be truthful . . ."

"Keep the truth to yourself," the stranger said sharply. "I am the man. And do not busy yourself with matters you have not been asked to concern yourself with. You have established the connection with me. I am here. If you feel that I am not suitable for the project in which your superiors wish to involve me, you had best let that decision rest with Adam Ahmed."

The Libyan was dumbfounded. "You know Adam Ahmed?"

"In my business I have to know a variety of things, Monsieur el-Magrabi. My life has depended more than once on such knowledge. Now I propose that we get down to business." He ignored the Libyan's outraged expression. "The generosity you have displayed to me is attractive, but I am still not committed. What do you want from me?"

"It is an assassination."

The man laughed and stroked the ends of his moustache in amusement. "You surprise me. Please tell me something I don't already know."

"The target is a political figure."

"I gathered from the size of the advance payment that it was not a question of a neighborhood squabble." He massaged the silver knob of his cane with the palm of his hand. "Am I to take it that I shall have to obtain the details from Adam Ahmed?"

"I believe so," Adel el-Magrabi replied. He felt stupid. The man had thrown him off balance with his behavior and forceful tone. "You will have to travel to Tripoli. Adam Ahmed will discuss all the details and the conditions with you."

The man rose. "Well, we seem to have completed one stage."

"When will you arrive?"

"At the beginning of the week." He approached the door. "Either Monday or Tuesday. And allow me to advise you, Monsieur el-Magrabi, not to judge a man by his external appearance." His hand gripped the brass doorknob, and as if for his own amusement, he snapped it off without any visible sign of effort. He tossed the knob to the Libyan, who caught it hastily. "And always beware of estimating the capacity of a man by his age. My regards to your two watchdogs, the one in the next room and the one you have stuck in the room across the way." He laughed as he turned and left.

Adel el-Magrabi cursed out loud. No one had ever treated him with such contempt. As the Libyan went over their meeting in his mind, he came to the conclusion that this time they were dealing with someone far more professional than he had envisioned. Obviously, the unknown man was capable of changing his appearance as easily as a chameleon changed its colors. It was the only way he could explain the contrast between the old peasant who had turned up at the bank manager's office to claim the money and the urbane and handsome man who had been in his suite a short time before.

The Libyan wondered if the stranger knew what fear was. His manner had been overbearing and his impertinences stinging. Adel el-Magrabi swore again in fury. He rarely lost his temper, but the man had treated him like a worthless messenger boy. True, he was an emissary, but he did not feel unimportant. He had a talent for dealing with complex assignments that required intelligence and courage and he was accustomed to making others ill at ease. It suddenly struck him that the emotion the stranger had aroused in him was fear.

On Monday, June 20th, at four o'clock in the afternoon, all one hundred and twenty members of the Knesset gathered in Jerusalem. The galleries were filled to capacity with guests and distinguished visitors. Menachem Begin was about to present his cabinet and request a vote of confidence in the new government.

Prime Minister-elect Menachem Begin opened the debate.

"Our primary concern," he declared in a solemn voice, "is to prevent a new war in the Middle East. I call upon King Hussein and Presidents Sadat and Assad to meet with me, whether in our capitals or on neutral ground, either in public or outside public scrutiny, in order to discuss the establishment of a true and lasting peace in our area. Much blood, too much blood, Jewish and Arab, has been spilled in this region. Let us put an end to the bloodshed, which is hateful to us, and in sincerity and seriousness, let us sit together around the conference table."

A stir rippled through the gallery. Some of those present remarked that this was the first tangible evidence of the cooperation between Begin and Dayan. The Foreign Minister had long been known for his belief in negotiations among the warring states. His knowledge of Arabic and his childhood acquaintance with Arabs made such contacts easy and natural for him. In addition, those close to him claimed that Dayan's desire to negotiate with the Arab states was the one factor that had moved him to join the new government.

When the debate finally ended eight hours later, there was a vote of confidence, and the new government became an established fact. Menachem Begin was again called to the platform. The atmosphere was tense, almost electric, as the spare man dressed in a black suit walked slowly forward. His face was lined with weariness, but his spirit was elevated. His voice seemed controlled, as though he had succeeded in overcoming the emotions of this great moment in his life.

"I, Menachem, son of Ze'ev and Hassia Begin," the Prime Minister intoned, declaiming the Oath of Allegiance, "pledge as Prime Minister to be loyal to the State of Israel and its laws, to discharge faithfully my task as a member of the government, and to uphold the rulings of the Knesset."

In that instant, the curtain fell on the ruling power of the Labor party. A new era had begun. The Israeli people, who sat glued to their televisions and radios, sensed the special quality of this first change of party rule since the establishment of the state. The feeling was accompanied by some uncertainty, for no one knew if the new government would fare any better than the old in guiding the ship of state.

* * *

At that very moment in the center of Tripoli a stranger was relaxing in a hotel reserved for visitors who were not citizens of Libya. He was not yet aware that his own fate was to become bound up with that of a man who had just sworn allegiance to the State of Israel. He had arrived in Tripoli about an hour and a half earlier and had gone through passport control and customs. His Luxemburg passport bore the name Claud Boyer, aged fifty-two, profession: businessman. At the airport Boyer found a taxi driver whose Mercedes 220 took him rapidly through the main streets of the Libyan capital and within an hour, he was ensconced in a large suite on the fourth floor of the hotel.

He had just showered and dressed when the waiter entered with the two bottles of Coca-Cola he had ordered. Alcoholic drinks were forbidden in Libya. From a secret compartment in his suitcase, he took a flat bottle of Bacardi, a favorite of his, poured a little into a glass, and filled it with Coca-Cola. He stirred the drink with his finger and then stretched out in a deep armchair before taking the first sip.

He occupied himself by considering his situation. The Libyans were prepared to pay huge amounts to secure his services. At first, he had supposed that the target was an Arab leader in one of the neighboring countries. But after some deliberation, he rejected that idea; they didn't need him to kill an Arab. Any daring and fairly competent compatriot could do the job just as well. He reviewed the situation again. The amount of money that had been deposited in his bank account on the orders of the Italian from Monte Carlo indicated that the treasury of the Libyan state was probably behind the deal. Which meant that Mu'ammar Qaddafi had undoubtedly given his consent to an assassination that could send shock waves across the globe. But in any event, he concluded, there was no use trying to second-guess when the facts would be apparent to him in a very short time.

Twice before, he had wiped out prominent men in Africa and had then disappeared, leaving no trace. His method was tried and tested, and he was careful never to leave the slightest clue that might one day reveal his true identity, which even the Italian did not know. On occasion, he had been obliged to destroy several people in order to cover his tracks completely. These killings had not brought him any financial profit, but had been necessary to protect his cover.

His scrupulous attention to detail paid off. He was convinced, beyond any shadow of doubt, that none of the various police forces and intelligence services had an inkling of his true identity. The long roster of pseudonyms had served him well, and he took great pains to add new identities to the list, all of which required large sums of money. The apartments and houses he rented in various countries were expensive too. He needed money to maintain secrecy. His price was high, the highest ever paid to a hired assassin.

He looked at himself in the mirror. His shave was perfect. The skin of his face was smooth. He could once again paste on the moustache, the handsome moustache of Claud Boyer, the businessman from Luxemburg. A makeup kit lay before him. He did the work with quick and skilled hands. Claud Boyer was born again. Afterward, he hid the kit in another secret compartment in his suitcase. It was time to make the phone call.

The operator at the hotel desk gave him an outside line, and he dialed the number. A minute later he heard the drowsy voice at the other end.

"Hello?"

"Adam Ahmed?" Claud Boyer asked.

"Speaking . . . who is this?"

"Claud Boyer."

"Who?"

"The man you are waiting for."

"Oh! You have arrived!" It was evident that he was surprised. "When?"

The stranger suppressed a laugh. He knew that Adam Ahmed had sent men to the airport in order to spot him the moment he arrived.

"I am sorry that I made fools of your men at the airport," he replied in a conciliatory voice. "In the future, please don't do that. Allow me to determine the time at which we shall meet. If I conclude an agreement, I usually adhere to it."

There was silence as Adam Ahmed thought over what he had just heard. "Where are you now?"

Claud Boyer gave the name of his hotel.

"Good," came the reply. "In the morning, someone will come and pick you up."

"I am sorry," the man responded. "In the morning, I shall not be here. You are able to do what you like with your time; I decide what to do with mine. I require a conclusive discussion now. Tomorrow I leave Tripoli."

"You're a difficult man!"

"I am the man you need for a certain task. Forgive me for reminding you of that point."

"All right," Adam Ahmed conceded. "I'll send a car for you now."

An hour later, Claud Boyer found himself in the spacious office of Adam Ahmed, at the headquarters of Libyan intelligence. Four other men were present, among them Adel el-Magrabi, who was stunned when he saw Claud Boyer; the man was totally different from the ex-army officer he had met in Zurich.

"It seems that we shall never know exactly what you look like," he remarked.

"You do not have to know," Boyer replied. "That is precisely my intention. Neither you nor anyone else. Identity has no bearing on the matter at hand. The main object is to carry out the assignment."

Adam Ahmed smiled and presented him to the other men, whom he had obviously summoned from their beds shortly before. There was Yusuf Gabor, who was in charge of providing assistance to foreign agents; Jamil Ya'id, the planner of various subversive operations in foreign countries; and Ali el-Hamid, chief of the data-collecting bureau. All three, like Adam Ahmed, were in their late thirties.

Claud Boyer bowed his head as he shook hands with each man. He studied them as if sizing up their capabilities. They, in turn, watched him with worried interest. The reports they had received from Adel el-Magrabi on his meeting with the stranger had roused their curiosity. In the past, they had never had dealings with a man whose identity was unknown; a man who took care to prevent anyone from knowing who he was. They stared at him as if they had been duped. None of them had expected what stood before them now: an unknown businessman from Luxemburg. As he looked at the expressions on their faces, the stranger was aware of their consternation.

Adam Ahmed motioned all of them to sit down in the uncushioned carved wooden chairs. To his surprise, the stranger found his chair far more comfortable than it looked. After they were seated, a servant entered bearing a tray with cups of steaming black coffee.

Adam Ahmed looked hard at Boyer. It was difficult to judge his exact age. He seemed too old to be a daring killer, yet at the same time, the skill with which he had evaded the men posted at the airport was undeniable. "So, you are our man!"

"I am your man," Boyer said pleasantly. "My age, my state of health, and my sexual inclinations are my own affair. Even if you are not convinced that I am the best in my profession, you have no alternative. Here I am. Half a million dollars of yours is in my account. You really have no way of discovering anything about me. Is that not so?" he asked mockingly. "Jamil Ya'id has carried out a thorough investigation and has failed to find anything. Do you deny it?"

He looked at the man sitting next to Adam Ahmed. Ya'id lowered his eyes as if to confess his failure.

"And you, Yusuf Gabor," the stranger continued, "you have determined the size of the budget earmarked for the assignment that has brought us together here. As for Ali el-Hamid, he will provide us with details about the target. The target, of course, I don't yet know, but I will shortly."

They were clearly astounded. Boyer could tell that, although they tried to conceal their reactions.

Adam Ahmed's face grew cold. "You know many things, Claud Boyer. Perhaps too many."

Claud Boyer sipped his coffee. "There is no such thing as too many," he replied. "You are obliged to lay bare every detail connected with your work. I will be too. Every point in my mission has to undergo examination. Perhaps that is why I am here right now, after years of carrying out assignments, the risks of which are well known to you."

Adam Ahmed could not deny what he said. As he studied

Boyer, he compared him to the other two, Madame Jacqueline Charlotte and Jorg Gibskopf. Those two had something in common: they had created lives for themselves, each was well known in his own world. It was hard to imagine that either of them belonged to the strange and alien band of professional killers. But the man facing him had sprung out of nowhere. He had not established a base like the other two, and he jealously guarded the anonymity he had cultivated.

"Do you have any idea why we invited you?" Jamil Ya'id asked, placing his hands on his knees, awaiting a reply.

"It's very clear, sir." The man became serious. "You wish me to carry out the mission in such a way that no one will be able to prove a link between the act and Libya."

Yusuf Gabor smiled. "Assuming that is correct," he said, "what is your next deduction?"

"That the subject is a political figure."

"At what level, in your opinion?"

Claud Boyer took a deep breath. The Libyans were trying desperately to look like professionals, when in actuality they were rank amateurs. Their questioning nauseated him.

"Let us make the situation clear," he said. "Whoever the target is, your operation must involve a world-famous figure. You're pouring in money without limit, so it has to be with the approval of Mu'ammar Qaddafi. You can't jeopardize the project by using amateurs. You have already burned your fingers with unsatisfactory candidates. If I am not mistaken, you have also been obliged to destroy one of them."

"What are you talking about?" Adel el-Magrabi growled.

Claud Boyer looked at him with indifference. "Someone by the name of Hans Kirschenberg. Is that enough?"

He had riled them deliberately. It was necessary that he prove to them that any flaws could endanger their plan, whatever it was. Flaws were dangerous for him too. If professionals picked up his tracks through the Libyans' incompetence, he was endangering himself for no purpose.

Adam Ahmed decided to change the subject. "Well," he said. "I suggest we get down to business."

"One moment!" The stranger raised his hand, ordering Adam Ahmed to wait. "I don't want you to reveal the target until we have concluded all aspects of the agreement between us. I don't want to know any further details until it is clear that my demands will be met."

"We are ready to conclude the agreement," Adam Ahmed replied.

The stranger smiled. "Good," he said. "My fee is three million dollars. I have received half a million. When I complete the assignment, you must transfer another two and a half million to my account."

"You're joking!" Jamil Ya'id was shocked.

Ali el-Hamid, who until then had been listening carefully, shook his head sadly. "Everyone who deals with us," he said quietly, "believes that the golden finger of God has touched his shoulder . . ."

"I regret that this is your reaction." Claud Boyer was calm and cool. "I have a clear picture of your financial capabilities. If Carlos received a token appreciation of two million dollars for his game of kidnapping the oil ministers at the OPEC Conference in Vienna, whatever you are asking me to do is worth several times more. You ought to appreciate the modesty of my demands." His irony was stinging.

"It is worth your while to reconsider your demands," Ali el-Hamid said angrily.

The man with the straight back and bronzed face shook his head. "The time for bargaining is over. We each made our calculations before we met. You want me to undertake a killing that will make me the object of an immense manhunt. In order to assure my continued existence, I need money in my coffers and not in yours."

"This is entirely beyond our estimates," Adam Ahmed said emphatically. "It is a huge sum . . ."

Boyer pulled out his wallet. "Gentlemen, you were kind and gracious when you gave instructions to transfer half a million dollars to my account in order to awaken my interest. Now you claim that the sum which I demand is out of the question. My conclusion is that the basis for cooperation between us no longer exists. Permit me to return your retainer fee." He drew a bank check out of his wallet and placed it on the table.

As the Libyans looked in amazement, Claud Boyer rose

and walked calmly toward the door. "It is late." He smiled politely. "I will certainly have difficulty finding a car to the hotel. I trust that you can provide me with transport there."

He was a daring gambler, and they knew that he had won. Their budget was, in fact, unlimited. The aim was to strike the target, regardless of the cost.

Adam Ahmed got up from his chair. "Please. Kindly sit down again."

"I am willing to listen," said Claud Boyer, but he remained standing.

"I want to emphasize one point," Adam Ahmed explained. "If, for any reason, the target dies before you make your strike, you will not receive one penny more than the advance you have already been given."

Claud Boyer narrowed his eyes behind his gold-rimmed spectacles. He took in the comment but did not respond. He waited.

"One further point for clarification," Adam Ahmed went on. "The strike must be made within a certain period. In our view, you have several months to plan and execute it. If you accept these two conditions, the agreement is made."

Claud Boyer came back from the door. He walked toward the table, picked up the check, and tore it into small pieces.

Adam Ahmed sighed. "Well," he said, "it's settled." And both men sat down again.

"I am not sure that you need to know the background or the effect we want to create by this operation, which we all hope will succeed," Adam Ahmed said. "All you have to know is the name of the man."

"When you hear the name," Jamil Ya'id explained, "you will understand that the amount of assistance we can offer you is limited."

"Whatever the situation, I shall need intelligence information," came the reply.

"In that, we shall do our best," Ya'id stressed. "Your target is an Israeli . . ."

He stopped. It suddenly struck him that Claud Boyer's eyes were years younger than his overall appearance.

"The name?" Claud Boyer demanded.

Jamil Ya'id exchanged glances with Adam Ahmed.

"Moshe Dayan," he said.

Boyer's expression did not change. Then he smiled slightly. "Are you still haggling about my fee?" He shook his head. "It must be perfectly clear to you that after the killing I will be hunted for the rest of my life by the Israeli secret service"—he decided to needle them—"which you probably know is the best espionage service there is. I believe, gentlemen, that I will deserve every dollar I get from you."

A look of chagrin passed over their faces. Adam Ahmed exhaled slowly.

"You must remember the two conditions," he said. "You will not receive another cent if the man dies before you strike. Secondly, the time limit has to be observed. We shall determine the exact limitations later. It will be done through a communications system we shall set up between us."

"How?"

"At every Libyan embassy there will be a contact whose task it will be to provide you with information. This network already exists and is waiting to be activated. We shall provide you with the list before you leave Tripoli. You will have to memorize the names."

"Fine."

"You must also choose a name that we can give to our people." Adam Ahmed waited for his reply.

Claud Boyer was deep in thought. So it was Moshe Dayan. One of the best-protected men on earth. His name would figure in the headlines for a while, then disappear, then appear again only to disappear. He was like the legendary phoenix, that marvelous bird of myth that was a symbol of rebirth through death. The ancient Romans had believed that the bird set itself on fire and rose again out of its own ashes.

Claud Boyer smiled. "Phoenix," he said softly. "My name for this assignment will be Phoenix."

Adel el-Magrabi laughed out loud. "What is that supposed to mean?"

Claud Boyer straightened his back in a gesture of scorn. "You know, Monsieur el-Magrabi," he countered, "there are other interesting books of merit in the world besides the Koran; the New Testament, for instance, or classical mythology. I would advise you, if the opportunity presents itself, to broaden your knowledge."

Adam Ahmed looked sharply at Adel el-Magrabi, who flushed and shifted uncomfortably in his chair.

"Phoenix," Adam Ahmed agreed.

"Good." The stranger smiled. "That's settled. The moment the mission is completed, the full amount is to be put at my disposal. Here is the account number."

He gave a small card to Adam Ahmed, who took it and studied it.

"I see that you have changed your bank."

"I change many things quite frequently," came the answer. "That is my way, the one thing in my life that does not change."

It was four o'clock in the morning when Adam Ahmed drove Claud Boyer back to his hotel. When they reached his room, the Libyan handed him the list of his contacts in the embassies. He read the names through several times, then handed the list back to Adam Ahmed.

"So," Boyer said. "It is time for us to part." He accompanied Adam Ahmed to the door. "I assume that we will not meet again. Be sure to fulfill your part. I will take care of mine."

After Adam Ahmed left, Claud Boyer undressed. It was a warm night. The beads of perspiration on his face annoyed him and he wiped them off carefully with a towel. Since his plane was scheduled to leave early the next morning, there was no point in going to bed. He sat in an armchair by the window, looking out across the city until the rim of the sky began to turn crimson and the minarets emerged from the darkness of the fading night.

At six thirty, he boarded the plane for Paris. He was acutely aware of the weight of his assignment; he had to infiltrate one of the most efficient protective networks on earth. It was a challenge that exhilarated and stimulated him.

When his plane landed at De Gaulle Airport, he stopped at the washrooms and went in. In one of the cubicles, out of sight, he began to remove his makeup. Claud Boyer of Luxemburg departed this world forever. In his place was the quiet young man who lived in a modest apartment on rue de l'Amber in Montparnasse.

On Thursday, a small advertisement appeared in the Paris papers. A well-known perfumery on the Champs Elysées was for sale; its owner was retiring from business. A telephone number appeared at the bottom of the advertisement and with it the name of the owner of the perfumery, Monsieur Pierre de Maline.

A day earlier, his banker had informed him that $250,000 had been deposited in his name. It was the sum that Adel el-Magrabi had agreed to transfer to him if the deal with the three people went through. He was surprised at how quickly the Libyan had brought it off. Apparently he had already recruited the three people he had recommended.

Later that morning, several businessmen called to inquire about the conditions of the sale. There were only two: the firm price and that the sum be paid immediately. Callers agreed that the price was fair but asked if they could make payments in installments. De Maline refused and decided to continue to run the ad until a suitable buyer appeared.

He had promised Boncho he would disappear, although he did not understand why the Italian had insisted that he act quickly. Undoubtedly he had good reasons. But de Maline preferred to handle the sale of his business himself, among other things because it would save him the price of a commission.

From the time Pierre de Maline returned to Paris, Boncho's peace of mind had suffered. He had called the Frenchman a day after he left.

De Maline was surprised to hear his voice. "My friend," he said, "years go by without hearing from one another, and now, within several days, we see each other face to face and are talking over the phone from Monte Carlo to Paris."

The Italian gave a short laugh. "Pierre," he said, "what's happening with your plans to leave the vanities of this world behind?"

"It's all right, Boncho," the Frenchman promised. "I'm

settling everything. As soon as the big deal is completed, I'll quit."

The conversation ended with the Italian once again urging his friend to sell everything as soon as possible and get out of Paris. The feeling of unease that had disturbed Boncho was growing, especially since he had sent the message to Marseilles that the deposit to the numbered account in Zurich had been made. However, as the days passed and nothing happened, his anxiety receded.

On the evening of Sunday, June 26th, the Italian gave a midsummernight's party on his yacht. By ten o'clock, the party was in full swing. Motorboats plied back and forth from the jetty to the yacht. About a hundred guests were gathered around tables laden with excellent food and rare wines. An orchestra played in the background, the music reverberating across the water. Boncho circulated among his guests; two young girls, graceful as fauns and nearly naked, clung to his arms. He enjoyed the company of important people. Among the guests that night were several from overseas: an American senator, Edward Klinberg, and a British MP, John Quincey. The presence of these two minor statesmen among the gathering of actors, artists, and entrepreneurs lent a note of formality to the affair. These diverse connections were useful to Boncho's business interests, none of which were ever really discussed.

A few minutes after midnight, the Italian caught sight of a man who had climbed with agility up the iron stairway of the yacht. He looked about thirty-five and appeared to be very fit. Although he was slim, his shoulders were broad, and his muscles could be seen outlined against his white dinner jacket. His long thin face was tanned. The lock of brown hair that fell over his forehead lent a youthful look to his somewhat ascetic features. His eyes were gray but flecked with black, and his eyebrows were so light that at first glance he seemed to have none.

Boncho noticed the young man the moment he stepped on board. The two exchanged glances, and the new arrival smiled mockingly. That was all it took. Boncho knew at once that the one man he feared was aboard his yacht, and the stranger knew that the Italian would soon excuse himself from his guests and find his way to him.

Several minutes later, Boncho found an excuse to leave. Turning quickly, he slipped down the ladder to his cabin. Before he reached the room, he heard the piano. When he opened the door, he found his guest at the keyboard, playing serenely. On the piano lid was a tall glass of brown liquid. Boncho recognized the mixture: Bacardi and Coca-Cola, half and half.

The guest ignored him and continued to play. Boncho sat down in silence on the sofa, waiting for his visitor to finish the piece. The long fingers of the stranger moved quickly over the keys, then suddenly stopped. His hand reached out to the glass. He took a sip and only then turned toward his host.

"Hello, Boncho."

Boncho smiled. "I've been expecting you."

"I'm surprised that a man like you can make such a mistake . . ."

The young man got up from the piano stool and moved lithely across the room. Boncho continued to smile as the hand struck out like a whiplash against his neck. He was smiling even when the long fingers gripped the collar of his shirt and lifted him bodily off the sofa as though he were weightless.

"One day I shall kill you," the visitor said as he released the Italian.

He turned and went back to the piano. He paused and took another drink from the tall glass. "You know, Boncho, until today you have made no mistakes. I am amazed at the way you slipped up. One day I shall come back and finish you."

"I know." Boncho had no doubts about the stranger's threat. "But not today."

"True," the young man murmured. "This mistake may be rectified. But you heard what I said."

"I'm sorry. He is a good friend of mine," the Italian muttered.

"You make me want to cry!" the young man said with a sneer.

Boncho had realized his error the day after Pierre de

Maline had returned to Paris. He had also realized that the man who stood before him would discover the mistake in a short time and would confront him with it.

"We had an agreement and you broke it." The stranger sat down on the stool and ran his fingers over the keys. The notes sounded ragged. "In our business, whoever makes a mistake pays with his life. You're getting old, Boncho. You should leave the field. The day I make a mistake, I shall pay the full price." He continued to play, the music a sharp contrast to the harshness of his voice. "The difference between us is that I want to get out before I get hardening of the arteries: before I start making mistakes. I want to live quietly and peacefully. Not like you, Boncho. I need a pile of money in order to disappear forever. You are the only one who knows something about me. That is not good, Boncho." He turned his head and looked innocently at the Italian. "How is it that you, the cautious one, put another man into the chain? Why?"

"It was a mistake."

"A stupid mistake."

"True," the Italian agreed. He knew that the man playing the piano was right. Obviously, he had not been idle. Yet Boncho should have known he would discover the existence of de Maline, the other link in the chain. "You haven't been wasting time since I sent the message to Marseilles."

"You know me."

"Almost as well as you know me."

He had erred in helping de Maline simply because the Frenchman had needed him. It was difficult to find words to explain the phrase "comrade in arms," and he knew the young man would not understand the bond between de Maline and himself. Pointless to try to explain that. Better to take another tack. "Don't forget that you were pressing me for a big project. Well, this was the opportunity, and it was the Frenchman who provided it."

The fingers continued their skillful run over the keyboard. "You could have paid him off," he said. "Your soft heart was the lousy stumbling block."

"The day will come when you, too, will make a mistake."

"Perhaps." The visitor smiled. "I'll try to avoid it."

"What do you intend to do?"

"I have to talk to the Frenchman," the reply came. "We'll see then."

"Don't hurt him!" the Italian said, suppressing his anger. "Only if it's absolutely necessary to break the link."

The stranger made no attempt to reply. He continued to play for a minute, his head bent down in concentration, his eyes closed. He seemed lost in thought. Finally he roused himself from his revery.

"You're a fool, Boncho," he said quietly. "But nonetheless I respect you. It's a pity that you didn't know that de Maline was a bungling amateur. He came running to you for help after a fat Libyan scared him. You threw him a juicy bone because he was once a pal of yours." He got up from the piano stool and turned toward the door. "I'll try not to hurt him. But if I find he can endanger me, I'll solve the problem in my own way."

The message was clear. The Italian did not move for a long time after his visitor left. He would have phoned immediately to warn the Frenchman if he hadn't known that he would be risking his life. As it was, fear imposed silence upon him.

On Tuesday, at eleven o'clock in the morning, the unmarked car of the investigations department of the Paris police drove up to de Maline's perfumery. Inspector Jules Gourot got out and went into the large shop, which was crowded with customers. He approached one of the salesgirls and asked to see Monsieur de Maline.

Over the past few days he had been pestered by requests from the investigations department of Interpol. Interpol wanted information about Pierre de Maline. A routine check had indicated that he was an upright citizen and that he owned some property, but this did not satisfy Commandant Pasquine, who requested that a more thorough investigation be made. Giscard Noir, head of the investigations department, explained to Gourot that he thought the Americans were applying pressure. He showed him the paper that contained de Maline's advertisement for the sale of his perfumery. It afforded a good opportunity to see him and find out what kind of a man he was, and the meeting could settle the affair with Interpol.

Pierre de Maline came down from his office to greet the inspector. Jules Gourot introduced himself and asked if he could spare a few minutes of his time. De Maline suggested that they go up to his private office on the second floor. Once there, Gourot plunged in.

"Monsieur," he said, "I must be frank with you . . ."

"Is something not in order?" de Maline asked. It took everything he had to maintain his composure.

"That's exactly what we want to find out," the inspector said, twisting his mouth into the semblance of a smile. That morning the dentist had extracted one of his molars and his mouth was still numb. "Reports have reached us that some clever boys are trying to squeeze money from businessmen in this vicinity. The fact that you are selling out makes us wonder if it may be connected with these crooks. Have you been threatened, monsieur?"

Pierre de Maline laughed in relief. "My dear inspector," he said, once his laughter had subsided, "of course not! I am selling the business because after twenty years I am tired of running it." He tapped his chest and said proudly, "I am one of de Gaulle's men! It isn't easy to frighten a man like me, but all I want now is to enjoy life a little."

Jules Gourot was forced to admit that the man's explanation was convincing enough. He, too, had often thought about an early retirement. Once assured that there was nothing unusual about de Maline's actions, the inspector thanked him for his time and departed.

After the police officer had gone, de Maline took a deep breath and wiped the sweat from his forehead with a silk handkerchief. His tension was increasing. The inspector had been far too curious. If only he could get rid of the shop; his nerves were on edge after so many years.

He was, therefore, pleased with the telephone call that came that day. A businessman with a very pleasant voice announced that he was interested in purchasing the perfumery. A cash payment was fine. They arranged to meet at nine thirty that evening. De Maline explained how to reach the place and which bell to ring.

Promptly at nine thirty, de Maline heard the downstairs bell ringing. He hurried down and opened the two safety locks. The electric light illuminated the long, pale face of a man who, were it not for his well-cut summer suit, would have looked liked a tired clerk.

"Good evening, monsieur." De Maline held out his hand.

The man smiled pleasantly, took off his straw hat, and shook de Maline's hand limply.

"Soucier," he said. "Jacques Soucier." He followed Pierre de Maline, who switched on the large chandeliers so that the perfumery could be seen in all its beauty. It was a beautifully appointed place.

"It's a fine business," Soucier said after examining the premises carefully. He spoke with a distinct south-of-France accent.

"Among the best there is!" Pierre de Maline exclaimed. "Among the best! You ought to come during business hours and see Madeleine, Henriette, and Françoise running from customer to customer, nonstop! Oh!" He spread his arms wide. "What a sight!" He laughed. "It's a fine business, Monsieur Soucier. For anyone who wants to come to Paris and begin a new life, this is a rare opportunity."

"Oh!" The stranger seemed surprised. "You noticed that I'm not from here?"

"Of course." Pierre de Maline drew himself up with pride. "I have a good ear. When I come across someone from the south of France, I can tell immediately. Am I not right?"

Jacques Soucier smiled awkwardly. "You are right, Monsieur de Maline. I had thought that my accent wasn't quite so strong." He looked toward the wooden staircase. "May I have a look at the accounts?"

"Certainly," de Maline replied. "I won't sell you a pig in a poke. Come, let's go up to the second floor. All the books are there."

He quickly turned off the large chandeliers. The price of electricity was on the rise. Then he hurried to rejoin his visitor, who was slowly climbing up to his office. De Maline was in excellent spirits. He was sure he had a serious buyer. The man was observant and knew what he needed to know before he made his decision. De Maline sat down at his desk; the thin and tired-looking visitor sat across from him.

"Would you like to see our gross and net figures?"

"Yes," came the quiet reply. "But not from the perfumery, monsieur."

The blood drained from de Maline's face.

"What do you mean, monsieur?"

He found that he could not return the man's steady gaze. Fear stuck in his throat like a block of ice and left its mark on his face. It was his expression that was the deciding factor in determining his fate. Pierre de Maline's raw nerves betrayed him; he was a man who could not overcome his fear. At that moment the visitor decided that he owed the Italian in Monte Carlo nothing. De Maline was the weak link; he had to be removed from the chain. It would be too easy to squeeze information from this man.

"You know what I mean," he said casually. "I am the man whose petty cash account in Zurich was augmented by the half a million dollars you took pains to have deposited."

"You . . ."

The man nodded.

"What can I do for you?" The words rushed from his throat as though he were possessed. He was transfixed by the man's penetrating stare.

"Tell me the whole story," the stranger said, as he settled himself into his chair. "Don't omit a single detail."

Pierre de Maline spoke for a long time, with fervor, as if by talking he could be rid of his anonymous guest. He had the feeling that death lay in store for him. As though he thought that he might avert the sentence hanging over him by being accurate to the minutest detail, he told his story, overlooking nothing. The man opposite him did not move a muscle. His face was expressionless. De Maline was unable to gauge his reactions. Only when de Maline mentioned that he had received full payment from the Libyans for the three people he had recommended did the stranger's eyes light up.

"Three?"

"Yes," de Maline went on. "You and two others. That was to ensure that if one failed, the other two would continue. If the second failed, the third would remain. You understand, they took out triple insurance . . ." Suddenly he stopped and looked warily at the man. "But, monsieur, why am I telling you all this?" de Maline asked. "You know the details anyway. Each one has his part to play."

"True," the stranger agreed. "Nevertheless, tell me everything you know. I want to ascertain your part in the affair."

"I merely negotiated . . ."

"Go on." The words were somewhere between a command and a threat. De Maline's sense of fear increased and the words spilled out of his mouth.

What de Maline had to say surprised his visitor. It suddenly occurred to him that Boncho had known none of the details of the Libyan plan, and if he had not discovered it now, from de Maline, his ignorance might have cost him his life. There were three killers—himself and two more. The cunning Libyan bastards, he thought, as he listened to the stream of words.

Three contracts. Three killers, each of whom had been given the same mission. A common target. But none knew that the others existed. The Libyans evidently realized that at some point Israeli intelligence might get wind of their plan. Perhaps something had already been spilled to them. Possibly they know about the killing of the German. For that reason, the Libyans developed the three-killer idea. The Israelis would go after one of them and might even get to him, but there would still be two more, one of whom had a chance of striking the target. Particularly if the Israelis were less alert once they had succeeded in stopping one of the three.

"You see, monsieur," Pierre de Maline said excitedly, "it's a wonderful idea, isn't it? Three. Like the heads of the ancient hydra. One is lopped off, another immediately grows . . ."

While de Maline continued to elaborate on his role in the plot, the stranger pondered the striking metaphor used by the go-between. A hydra; surely there could be no better description. He felt a sneaking admiration for the Libyans whom he had previously scorned. All at once, he understood the significance of Adam Ahmed's strange remark: if, for any reason, the target died before he struck, he would not receive a single penny beyond the generous advance. The plan was very clever and had great chances for success.

Suddenly he became aware of the silence. Pierre de Maline had concluded his story.

"Is that all?" the stranger asked.

"Mother of God, do you think I've hidden anything from you?"

The visitor scrutinized him carefully. "Do you have any cognac?" His face remained expressionless.

"Of course, monsieur."

"Bring it," the stranger commanded. "And one glass."

The Frenchman returned with a bottle of cognac which he put on the table, pouring out a glass with a trembling hand. He offered it to the visitor.

"Not for me." The stranger waved him away. "For you. Sit down."

Pierre de Maline sat down obediently.

"Drink," said the man.

Pierre de Maline raised his glass. He cursed his trembling hand as drops of liquid dribbled down his chin and caught in the folds of flesh under it. He drained the drink at one swallow.

"Now tell me about the other two."

De Maline revealed everything he knew about Madame Charlotte and Jorg Gibskopf. "They are professionals," he said. "Believe me. They're good."

The man smiled. "They're all good, de Maline," he said. "Pour yourself another drink."

He had decided to treat the Frenchman mercifully; after all, the information he had given was vitally important. After a while de Maline's senses became dulled by the cognac, so that he felt nothing when the sharp blow to his neck brought everything to an end.

At nine fifteen the next morning, Inspector Jules Gourot was called to the office of his department chief, Giscard Noir. He had no idea what had caused the urgent summons. Customarily he reported to his chief either following a request for a personal interview or when he was called in for a dressing down; rarely was he invited for praise. As much as possible, Jules Gourot preferred to avoid meetings with the cold-eyed department head. Giscard Noir always made him feel very insignificant.

As the clerk opened the door for Gourot, Giscard Noir put down the paper he had in his hand and looked up. His lower lip was drawn down at the sides like a bulldog's.

"Come in and sit down, Gourot."

"Yes, sir."

The door closed. He sat down and waited as the department chief picked up the sheet of paper again. Gourot recognized it.

"This is your report from yesterday, is it not, Gourot?"

"Yes, sir."

It was the report he had written on his meeting with businessman Pierre de Maline, owner of the perfumery on the Champs Elysées. He wondered what flaw the chief had found.

"Is something not in order in the report?"

"Perhaps," came the reply. "There is certainly something not in order with de Maline."

"If you wish, sir, I can resume the investigation."

The department head looked at him as if he were a clown. "I doubt that you will succeed in meeting de Maline, Gourot," the chief mocked. "Half an hour ago, he was found dead. Stone dead, Gourot."

"How did it happen, sir?"

"According to the report of Inspector Montier, who was first on the scene, it seems that he had a drop too much. When he tried to go down from the second floor to the shop below, he slipped on the stairs and broke his neck." The department head put the sheet of paper down. "I suggest, Gourot, that you get over there. As you have already been there, you will be able to assist Montier. I want to know your findings. Call in the pathologist as well. Try to have a report on my desk by noon. There is no doubt that the people who were already interested in de Maline will increase their pressure on us now."

"I'll go at once." The inspector rose. "Is there anything else, sir?"

"That's all, Gourot."

At noon that day, the report was submitted to the chief. Gourot's conclusion, reached with the help of the pathologist, was that de Maline's death had been accidental. An empty bottle of cognac had been found in the office. De Maline had evidently fallen on the top stair, slipped, and somersaulted several times until his head struck the floor. His neck was broken in the course of the fall. At present, the body was being autopsied.

By afternoon, the report on the accidental death of the businessman was given to the newspapers and, at the same time, was submitted to the agencies that had been requesting information on de Maline over the past week. The communications officer at Interpol got in touch with John Palmer of the American Embassy that evening.

"The man was unlucky," the officer observed. "A drinker ought to be careful."

John Palmer thanked the Interpol officer politely and immediately called Yaki Spillman to tell him de Maline was dead. Spillman did two things. First, he prepared a report containing the facts surrounding the death of Pierre de Maline. That night the report went out to the headquarters of the security service in Tel Aviv. Then he called Motti Klein and Ze'ev Shahar and instructed them to find out whatever they could about the events leading up to de Maline's death.

Later, Spillman contacted his friend from the DST, the antiterrorist division of the French counterintelligence service, Inspector André Cordeille, and asked him to check on the routine investigations of the Paris police if anything new turned up.

At noon on Thursday, June 30th, Uri Cohen was the guest of Dick Coleman, the legal attaché of the American Embassy in Tel Aviv. The meeting took place in Coleman's office on the third floor of the embassy building on Hayarkon Street. Coleman's official title, "Attaché for Matters of Law and Order," was, in fact, a cover for his function as senior operative of the Federal Bureau of Investigation, coordinating the American police and espionage branches and their equivalents in Israel.

A man approaching fifty, Coleman had a long record of service. During the previous eight years, he had worked as legal attaché at various embassies. He had arrived in Israel at the beginning of 1976, and had succeeded in establishing a friendly relationship with the members of the security branch in Israel. His Israeli colleagues liked and trusted him.

Coleman welcomed Uri Cohen warmly. They were meeting to discuss security arrangements for Prime Minister Begin's visit to the United States. He was scheduled to fly there on July 14th for a series of talks with President Carter and various members of the administration. There was a fixed routine on the Israeli side and the American, and both knew their roles in the security precautions surrounding the visit of an Israeli official to the United States, or an American to Israel.

"Well, then," Dick Coleman said, "the arrangements are as usual. Only the faces change. Last time, Rabin; this time, Begin."

"It's not just the faces," Uri replied. "Carter's not Ford, and Begin certainly isn't Rabin."

Dick Coleman laughed. "True, true," he agreed. "But from the point of view of protection, I take it there are no changes from the norm?"

Uri Cohen stroked his chin thoughtfully and did not reply at once.

"Dick," he said finally, "we've done several jobs together in the past. Let me ask you something."

"Of course. Whatever you like," Coleman replied.

"Some of my colleagues think that I tend to be an alarmist. I mean, I see shadows on the wall when there is nothing there to cast a shadow. Is that your impression of me too?"

The American smiled. "As a matter of fact, yes. But let's face it—it's better to see a shadow that isn't there than to be shadowblind."

"I like that." Uri laughed and ran his fingers through his thinning hair. "Shadowblind." He looked at his colleague inquiringly. "In that case, let me throw you a long shadow:

a shadow over the routine security plan for our Prime Minister."

"What is it this time, Uri?"

"I see a shadow, and I can't pin it down." He rubbed the palms of his hands together nervously. "We have information, as yet not verified, that certain Arabs are planning to assassinate one of our officials. It could be Begin. It could be someone else. At this moment, we are faced with Begin's trip. I want to sleep easy, which is why someone has to persuade me that we've covered every possible angle."

The smile faded from Dick Coleman's face. The possibility of an assassination attempt had to be treated seriously.

"May I know more details?"

"Certainly." Uri rose from his chair and turned toward the large window which framed a shore crowded with bathers. Sailboats bobbed in the blue water not far from the coast. The colors were clear and almost too bright. Then he turned back to Coleman. "Yes, Dick. It's right that you should be in on this business. I need your help in checking security arrangements in the States. We haven't much experience in protecting someone from an assassination attempt. That's a fact."

Dick Coleman realized at once what Uri wanted. The ordinary arrangements, which consisted of Israeli security men plus members of a special American unit, trained to protect guests of the administration, would not be adequate. He wanted additional safeguards.

Uri Cohen's visit was longer than usual. At one thirty, the two men decided to eat lunch together at the embassy restaurant and then return to Dick's office to continue their discussion.

This time the American took his colleague's anxieties seriously, even though nothing was definite: political assassinations constituted a dark chapter in American history. One of the tenets of intelligence work was to leave no isolated fact or rumor unexamined, no matter how groundless it might seem.

"Actually," Dick admitted to Uri, as they were drinking coffee, "the chances of stopping a lone assassin are very slim. Our experience over the years has taught us that it's worth making every effort to block an attempt in its earliest stage."

"That's my opinion," Uri agreed. "I won't accept any other approach."

They continued discussing various details until three o'clock in the afternoon and agreed to meet the following day. As the chief of surveillance left the air-conditioned embassy, he was enveloped by a blast of afternoon heat. Summer had taken over. The day was unusually humid and he began to sweat at once. Tel Aviv was buckling under the heat. A city of stone and asphalt, it was a veritable hothouse in summer. Uri's car inched along in the traffic of the busy streets; only when he turned north into Ben-Yehuda was he able to put his foot down and let the small car accelerate. The slight breeze dried his sweat, but the humidity still was oppressive.

When Uri Cohen reached his office, he found on his desk among a batch of folders and documents requiring his immediate attention a report from Yaki Spillman in Paris. He tore open the envelope and read the contents quickly. He clenched his teeth in anger and smashed his fist on the desk again and again, until the pain lessened his fury.

Then he headed for Avital's office and burst in, not waiting to be announced. Avital, who was in conference with two of his senior assistants, stared at Uri in surprise.

"I'll be finished shortly, Uri."

"Avital!"

His voice was quiet, but his tone was not lost on the man sitting across the table. Avital Arnon realized that Uri was striving to control his temper; better not to test his patience at the moment.

"Something urgent, I see," he said.

"Yes."

"All right," the chief of service said dryly. He turned to his assistants and asked them to leave. As they were leaving, he considered how best to handle the man standing in such a barely controlled fury.

The discord between the two men had begun long ago. Uri Cohen had grown up in the intelligence service, whereas Avital Arnon had been given his post after a distinguished career in the army, in which he rose to one of the highest positions in the Israel Defense Forces. The two men differed totally in character and approach.

Avital Arnon, a man of proven experience in the field of espionage, approached his work like a calm and controlled surgeon. He demanded that those under him operate on the basis of facts and avoid assumptions, which in his opinion could lead to errors. Uri, on the other hand, was a firm believer in intuition. Although he based his work on an examination of the facts, his experience had taught him that instinct was the frame that held the picture together. Hence, the two were total opposites, in their natures, their approach, and their conceptions. Nonetheless, they had worked side by side for years, always trying to avoid the personal confrontation that could endanger their work.

"What's shaken you up?" Avital asked.

Uri Cohen put the report on the conference table. "Read it," he said. "It's from Spillman."

Arnon read the report through calmly. When he put it down and looked up at Uri, his expression was unchanged.

"I've read it," he said.

"Is that all you have to say?"

"What did you expect?"

Uri waved the report. "You apparently can't see what this means," he growled. "You always want facts. Well, then, here you have the facts. Two men whom we know to have been in touch with Adel el-Magrabi are dead. No more Hans Kirschenberg or Pierre de Maline. For God's sake! You ask me what I expect!" He rested his palms on the desk, his eyes bright with anger. "Perhaps I ought to ask you what I can expect from this attitude of yours?"

Avital Arnon was slow to reply. He reconsidered the situation. Perhaps Uri was right. Certainly he had produced facts. Up to this point, Avital had wanted Uri to slow down. From now on, he had to contend with the fact that Uri might be on to something. Avital took out a cigarette and rolled it between his fingers.

"What's your conclusion?" It was evident that he intended to ask questions rather than take a stand that might increase the existing tension between the two men.

"I have only one conclusion," Uri Cohen replied. "It's time to act. I know that you would prefer to adopt a wait-and-see position. But I am convinced that the time has come for us to make a move. In my view, the Libyans are already well advanced in their plan."

"It could still concern the Egyptians and not us."

"Can you prove that?"

"No." The answer was restrained. "And can you prove your version?"

"In a certain sense, yes." Uri dropped into a chair. "The German came to us. That same night he was liquidated. The go-between whose tracks we picked up was liquidated . . ."

"What you say proves only one thing. The Libyans are planning an assassination. You have no real proof that it's directed against us."

"I don't even want to concern myself with looking for proof at this stage," Uri said sharply. "My instinct tells me this is directed against us. We might miss the boat and the proof we get will be the target's dead body. Do you want to wait for that?"

Avital Arnon kept his temper. "Don't get excited and don't exaggerate," he said quietly.

"For God's sake!" Uri hit the desk with his fist. "This isn't a debate between us, Avital!"

His heart was pounding. He inhaled deeply, trying to calm down before going on. As long as he was responsible for the surveillance branch, he would not back down from his position.

"Neither of us has any experience in political assassinations. We both have a lot to learn. And for precisely that reason, we don't dare wait. Facts? Hell! First of all, I'm convinced that we have enough facts to get us moving. More facts can be uncovered. And if we don't move, no one will find them for us."

Uri fell silent. It was the quiet after the storm. To his surprise, Avital was in no hurry to reply. He lit a cigarette slowly and tossed the match into the ashtray. He exhaled smoke, all the while thinking, drawn in on himself. Uri watched him through narrowed eyes. Something has happened to all of us since the last war, he thought. We're cautious. We hesitate to take responsibility, afraid that we might jump in and find ourselves over our depth.

"What do you suggest?" Avital asked at last.

"First, I want a free hand to act as I see fit. Second, we have a man in Tripoli—we have to activate him."

"Impossible," Avital said quietly. "Can't be done."

"Why not?"

"It's been decided to call him in. You don't want to hold the man back after so many years of service there?"

"In view of the situation, there is no other way."

"Maybe."

"Avital." Uri fixed his eyes on his chief. "Believe me, I know what it means to keep an agent planted for an extended period of time. I know the meaning of every single extra hour. But we have no alternative."

"Let's leave it there," Avital said. "I'll check into the matter. What else?"

"We have to move quickly and intelligently," Uri explained. "We have one more source we know about: Adel el-Magrabi. Unfortunately, we have no idea exactly what he knows. The rest of our sources have been wiped out. Give me a free hand."

"What do you mean when you say a free hand?"

"I have an idea," Uri replied, trying to control his excitement. "I have to try it."

"What is it?"

"I'd like to suggest that you don't get involved in it."

An expression of amazement spread over Avital's face.

"Meaning?"

"If it doesn't work, it will be my failure," Uri explained. "I'll be responsible and I'll have to pay for it."

Avital Arnon smiled.

"I appreciate your thoughtfulness," he said, "but it doesn't work like that. As long as I'm sitting on top of the heap, the responsibility is mine."

"Ours!"

Avital knew in that instant that the tension between them had been dispelled.

"I accept your interpretation," he replied to Uri's correction. "Tell me what you're up to."

The plan Uri presented was extraordinary, original, and daring. The chief of the service listened attentively as he outlined it.

When Uri had his say, he scrutinized Avital's face. "Well, what do you think?"

"Put it in writing. I'll support it."

That night Uri met with Yitshaq Goldberg, Avshalom Kedmi, and Yirmi Spector to outline his plan to them. When the meeting was over and the men drifted out to the parking lot, they knew they were partners in an operation unlike any they had been involved in before. Kedmi's car was already moving toward the exit as Yirmi Spector got into his car and switched on the lights. Although he was very tired, he had a strange feeling of elation. Uri's plan to get Egyptian intelligence working for them through Avshalom Kedmi was both daring and frightening.

JULY, 1977

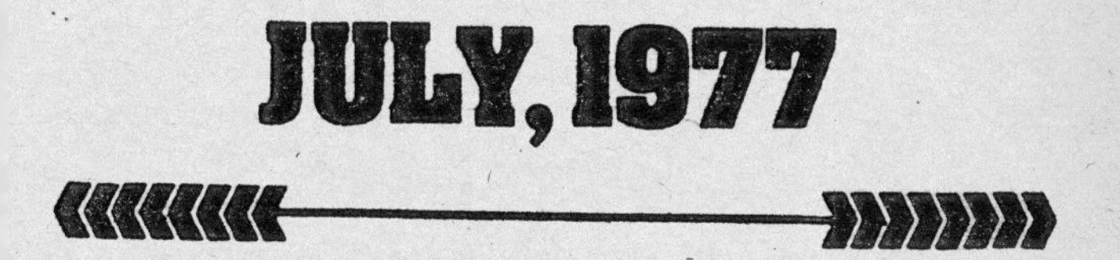

Avshalom Kedmi arrived in Paris on Saturday night, July 2nd. Long recognized as one of the best secret agents of the Israeli security service, he had operated in Europe for many years, hunting down the leaders of Arab terrorist organizations that had established command posts in various European cities. He was fluent in Arabic and familiar with Arab customs, having grown up in the city of Tiberias, which in those days had a mixed population of Jews and Arabs. Kedmi always worked alone; occasionally he would disappear for months at a time, severing all contacts with headquarters and surfacing only when his mission was completed.

He had been badly wounded on his last sortie in Europe, and, after a long convalescence, he had been transferred to Tel Aviv as senior advisor to Uri Cohen. This post left him chafing at the bit, longing for the day when he would be given a more active assignment. He missed the special atmosphere that surrounds an agent working on his own—a lone wolf. Now, at last, he had such a mission. Although it was limited, it had all the ingredients he had longed for.

No one was waiting to meet him when he arrived at Orly. No one knew that he was coming. From that moment he would decide when and how to contact the members of the security service if he needed their help. The mission required great daring and was fraught with danger. It might cost him dearly. But it was doubtful he would ever have another such opportunity in the future.

Philippe d'Astine took up residence once again in his small Paris apartment on the rue de l'Amber in Montparnasse. The other tenants on the block of shabby gray-fronted houses had not noticed that their young neighbor had been gone for several months, so no one paid any attention to the fact that the small fourth-floor apartment overlooking the narrow street was again occupied.

D'Astine had taken the apartment several years before. It was conveniently located and it allowed him anonymity. His neighbors kept to themselves; indeed, you could die and no one would notice until you began to stink. Philippe d'Astine stayed in the apartment whenever he needed a convenient and inconspicuous base in Paris. If he wanted to enjoy the nightlife of the city, he had only to go down the sloping street and turn the corner to find himself in one of several cafés or small nightclubs which exuded an atmosphere of false gaiety.

This time he spent the first few days holed up in the apartment in absolute solitude while he analyzed the information he had obtained from Pierre de Maline. Although he saw the Libyans as amateurs and unimaginative dullards, they had caught him by surprise with the originality of their plan—the "hydra," as de Maline had described it moments before his death. A hydra with three heads—all three of them professional, each working according to his own method. One of the three might well succeed in penetrating the defensive wall around the target. A woman and two men. None knowing of the existence of the others. But only one of them would win the prize—the first to hit the target. Madame Jacqueline Charlotte seemed the likeliest to succeed. No one would imagine that a woman of her social and professional stature had, as a secret occupation, killing for money.

D'Astine was not pleased with the setup. Had he not lucked into the truth, he would have found himself in a no-win situation. First he would have endangered himself, and then, at the last moment, he might have learned that the prize had been snatched from him. Ultimately he might have had to pay for the success of another. The Israeli security services would never give up the chase until they got results. They might uncover his tracks and become convinced that he was the killer. He would find himself always on the run, hounded for life, while the real assassin sat safely enjoying great wealth, secure in the knowledge that no one was after him.

On Sunday morning, he placed a call from a nearby florist's shop to the Italian's yacht in Monte Carlo. Although he did not give his name, Boncho recognized his casual voice at once.

"I'm sorry about our friend," he said.

"Was it necessary?" The note of bitterness was obvious.

"Yes," he replied quietly. "I found a bundle of raw nerves. One jab of the finger and he'd have spilled everything. I'm sorry."

There was a short silence. Then a slight cough. "I understand you want something."

"Yes."

"I'm listening."

"I need details on two people. Addresses. Exact occupations. Social activities. Weaknesses . . ."

"In brief, life histories, eh?"

"Exactly."

"Their names?"

"A woman in Paris. Owns a modeling agency. Jacqueline Charlotte."

"Oh-ho," the Italian replied in surprise. "She's one of the best!"

"And also in the profession."

"I didn't know." The Italian hesitated. "It'll take a few days. Who's the other one?"

"A journalist. Jorg Gibskopf. Lives in Copenhagen. Apparently wanders around a lot. Find out every detail, and if there is a possible link between them."

"All right. How shall I get in touch with you?"

"I'll contact you."

"I gather that you need the help of one of them."

"Possibly." Better to let the Italian think so. "You'll hear from me."

He hung up. While he waited for the information, he would take care of two other matters that required his undivided attention. He would spend time studying the personality of the Israeli, Dayan, and he would draw up a list of the various documents, disguises, and other items he would need during the coming months.

For years it had been his practice to use his free time preparing for the tasks ahead of him. He loathed amateurs who began to work only after they had a contract in their hands. This kind of activity done under pressure was disastrous. A professional dare not depend on the goodwill of counterfeiters for documents. He always had to be prepared. D'Astine had learned from the mistakes of others. He knew that the cumulative effect of even the slightest mistake was often ruinous. He had learned that a stolen passport could not be used too soon after its theft. At that moment, he had fifteen usable passports. He took care that at least two years elapsed between the time a passport or any document came into his hands and the time he used it.

If he were obliged to make use of forgers, he flew to South America. Since he did not operate in Latin America, there was no way to connect him with the excellent counterfeiters working there. Over the years, he had gathered a fine collection of passports, driver's licenses, birth certificates, marriage licenses, and diplomas from various institutes.

He was aware that he was excessively fastidious when it came to his profession, but he was determined to avoid failure. No detail was too small to merit attention.

After surveying his collection of documents, d'Astine was satisfied that he could change his identity rapidly. Now he turned to his second consideration—to find out everything he could about the man who was his target.

Early Monday morning an Egyptian student named Hamid Dingi appeared at the Egyptian Embassy in Paris and asked to speak to the military attaché, Aqid Asis el-Masri. He brought alarming news. The previous evening in a café in St. Germain des Près he had overheard a drunken argument between a Libyan and an Egyptian, during the course of which the Libyan had made a very thinly veiled allusion to a plot to kill President Anwar Sadat. Hamid Dingi had joined the discussion in order to find out more, and although he had gotten no details, he had seen the Libyan home and thus had his name and address.

Shortly after the student left, el-Masri called in the intelligence man, Mahmud Ashraf, and related the student's story. Both men agreed that the incident warranted investigation and should be handled quickly and efficiently.

The efficiency was felt by the Libyan that very night. He had returned to his apartment in the Latin Quarter a few minutes after midnight. As he bent to insert his key in the lock, he was violently pushed aside. Someone hit him on the head while another assailant quickly unlocked the door. The Libyan was thrust into the room, and two large men, whom he had never seen before, followed him inside.

"Who are you?" the Libyan asked as he backed away. Rigid with fear, he looked about wildly, seeking some way of escape.

"We ask the questions," the taller of the two men said. The Libyan immediately caught the Egyptian accent and his eyes widened in fear.

"What do you want?" he asked, his throat dry.

"Answers," said the Egyptian. He stood in front of the Libyan, who was shorter than he, and his fist flew out in a rapid movement. It struck the Libyan in the neck and he let out a choked scream. The force of the blow thrust him onto the bed. The second Egyptian joined the first and together they dealt him one blow after another. The Libyan howled in pain. At first, he tried to defend himself by covering his face with his hands, but it was useless. The two men knew exactly how to make use of their fists, and when they stopped, he was sobbing. Blood streamed from the gashes on his face.

The two Egyptians sat down on wooden chairs opposite the bed.

"You're going to talk, eh?"

"What about?" the beaten man mumbled. "What about?"

"You know, my friend, you know."

"I don't know. In God's name, I don't know . . ."

The pain was excruciating. He tried to get up, but a sharp jab in the pit of his stomach made him collapse backward onto the bed again, groaning in agony.

"Talk!"

"About what!" the Libyan sobbed. "Just tell me . . ."

"About Anwar Sadat, you dog!" The Egyptian bent over him and twisted his nose.

"I don't know much . . . Something . . . from my brother in intelligence . . ."

"The name of your brother in intelligence?"

"Adam Ahmed."

"His position?"

"I don't know . . . I swear I don't know . . ."

"What did your brother tell you?"

"They're working on some plan . . . To do with the president . . . That's all I know . . ."

They fired question after question at him. His answers did not change. It appeared that all he knew were hints. They struck him again in an effort to extract detailed information from him, directing their blows at his testicles, his ribs, his shoulders, his face, but he could add nothing. All he knew, he told them.

"Squeezed dry like a lemon," the tall Egyptian said to his companion. "Squeezed out."

His friend nodded and got up slowly. He looked scornfully at the man sobbing and groaning on the floor.

"Let's go," he said, and walked toward the door. They could still hear the Libyan's cries when they reached the street.

When the two agents had returned to the embassy and filed their report, Ashraf conferred with Aqid Asis el-Masri.

"I have no reason to doubt the information," Ashraf said. "We have to report it to Cairo and start to work at once. The Libyan madman is quite capable of dispatching assassins."

"So it would seem," el-Masri agreed. "I'll write out my report now. Put it with yours and in the morning, we'll send them by special messenger."

Mahmud Ashraf nodded in agreement. "I have one more suggestion. I'd like to hear your reaction. The Libyan may know more. Perhaps my two men didn't shake him up enough . . ."

"Meaning?"

Mahmud Ashraf paused for a moment. The idea was practical, but it could cause complications with the French authorities at some point. "Let's bring him in for further questioning at the embassy. How does that sound to you?"

"Why not?" el-Masri agreed. "He's our only source at the moment."

"In that case," Ashraf smiled, "we have a long night ahead of us."

When he left the military attaché's office, Ashraf ordered his men to return to the Libyan's apartment and bring him to the embassy at once. Half an hour later, they called him. He listened for several seconds before turning to el-Masri in frustration. "The apartment's empty," he growled. "The Libyan must have panicked and fled."

During the course of his third meeting in several days with Dick Coleman in Tel Aviv, meetings intended to wrap up details of the American and Israeli security measures during the Prime Minister's visit to the United States, Uri Cohen let a bit of information drop to the effect that Qaddafi had established a squad of killers and that his plan probably involved a series of assassinations including Arab as well as Israeli leaders.

When Coleman pressed him, Uri was noncommittal. "Well, if they succeed in getting Begin and Sadat . . ." he trailed off. "Listen, what's the point in dwelling on it. Anyway, Egypt's not my business. I've got my hands full as it is."

Recognizing the statement for what it was, Coleman laughed and replied, "Okay, Uri. I'll be your bridge. I don't know what your game is, but I'm ready to make a move."

They exchanged knowing smiles. Dick Coleman was well aware that he was allowing himself to be used by the Israeli, but he couldn't prevent it. Uri had managed to pull him into his corner. If something happened and it turned out that he had known of it in advance and had not reported to his bureau in Washington, he would find himself in a delicate position. Whatever the reason, Dick Coleman decided, Uri wants me to do this and I'm going to help him.

An hour later a carefully worded report was dispatched from the American Embassy in Tel Aviv to headquarters in Washington, D.C. The report mentioned as yet unverified rumors that Israeli espionage had information on a Libyan plot to assassinate the president of Egypt as well as other figures in the Middle East, including Israelis. That should get a lot of people off their backsides, Coleman thought.

Later that afternoon, Uri met with Avshalom Kedmi, who had just returned from Paris, his face a mass of bruises.

"They really worked you over," Uri said, looking at him with concern.

Avshalom Kedmi shrugged. He wanted to smile but the pain in his upper lip prevented him. "Yes," he agreed. "They know their business."

"Who covered you?"

"Ze'ev Shahar and Motti Klein were in the next room," he explained. "We made slits in the door. They saw everything that went on. If the two Egyptians had overdone it, they would have had a problem."

"Did the doctor examine you?"

"Yes, at the embassy."

"Is everything all right?"

"As you see." He shrugged his shoulders. "Blue marks on my face and a few more like them elsewhere . . . It's nothing. A few days and they'll be gone."

"Were they satisfied with what they got out of you?"

Avshalom Kedmi paused. "I'm not sure."

"What do you mean?"

"After we left the apartment, we stayed in the car to watch," he explained. "About an hour later, they came back."

Uri Cohen weighed the information. Clearly, the Egyptians had come back to get more information.

"What do you think?" Avshalom asked.

"They've swallowed the bait," Uri answered.

Their discussion was interrupted by the arrival of Yitshaq Goldberg and Yirmi Spector. Both men stared at Avshalom's face, but neither said anything. Uri filled them in briefly on the operation in Paris and on the various other measures that had been taken to put the ball in the Egyptian court. Within a short time reports of moves by the Egyptian intelligence service should begin reaching them.

Uri had just turned to a discussion of the security measures for Begin's trip when the door to his office suddenly burst open and Avital Arnon stood in the entrance, his face a study in barely controlled anger.

"I've read the report of your last operations, Uri!" he snapped. "Who gave you permission to activate agents?"

There was total silence in the room. Uri Cohen's face reddened, and he clenched his fists until the knuckles turned white. "We had an agreement!" he insisted.

"Agreement, hell!" The chief of the service leaned forward with his palms on the table, the upper half of his body bent toward Uri so that their faces nearly touched. "We had an agreement about your idea. Nothing else. I said that I'd view the matter sympathetically. You should have waited."

"I had no reason to believe that you would reject the plan," Uri replied angrily. "The ground's caving in under our feet. Let's stop these games of who's responsible and what's responsible . . . Are you worried? All right. I'll write up an official document for you stating explicitly that the decision and the responsibility are mine and mine alone! You're out of this. If something goes wrong, it'll be my head that rolls."

"That describes your position exactly!"

The two men glowered at each other, then Avital added: "But in the future don't forget that my head is also liable to roll."

"I'll remember," Uri said. "Incidentally, the man in Tripoli . . . you said you'd look into it, and I haven't heard anything yet."

"Come into my office when you're finished here."

As Avital Arnon turned to walk out, he stopped behind Avshalom Kedmi and his large hand fell gently on his shoulder.

"You won't get a medal for what you did in Paris," he said in a dry voice, "but if you need anything to ease your bruises, let me know." Without waiting for an answer he left the office, closing the door behind him.

When Uri entered Avital's office, Eli Rabhan was waiting there for him. Eli, who was responsible for activating field operatives in enemy territory, had been called in by Avital to discuss Hanania Siani, the man due to be recalled from duty in Tripoli.

"I understand, Uri," he said, "that you want the decision on the immediate recall of Hanania Siani overturned?"

"Yes."

"Why?"

"Siani has resources we don't have; he's been planted for so long in the Libyan intelligence branch. We can get hold of general information," he explained, "but not the details. Siani can get them."

"He's not in Adam Ahmed's division," Eli remarked.

"I know that. But if you send him the right instructions, he'll be able to get close to the source. Isn't that so?"

Eli Rabhan nodded in agreement.

"I know what it means, especially in view of his family circumstances, for Siani to stay out there for another stretch." Uri knew that this was what was bothering Eli Rabhan. "But I know him, as do you. Don't forget that I was the one who recommended him at the time. I'm convinced that if you explain how important it is, he'll agree."

Eli was slow to reply. It was a difficult decision. He had wanted to let Siani pack up and come home from Tripoli. The long years of absence and the separation from his family had been hard on him.

Eli drummed his fingers on the table and studied the face of the chief of the service. "How do you feel about it, Avital?" he asked.

Arnon smiled. "In the last analysis the decision rests with the two of you," he said. "But if you want my opinion, I tend to agree with Uri. It's hard to live with this fellow"—he stared at Uri Cohen—"but the problems he raises have to have a practical solution."

Eli got up and pushed his chair back. "All right," he said. "I'll deal with it."

After he had turned and left the room, Avital bent forward. He hunched his broad shoulders and leaned on the table, his head jutting out like a charging bull. "Satisfied?"

"That isn't the point," Uri replied seriously. "The question is whether we are taking all the necessary steps. I'm pleased that you're beginning to see eye to eye with me on some things."

"Someday we'll get rid of all the irritations that have cropped up between us."

"If you say so."

Avital Arnon could not suppress the trace of a smile.

"I've gone over your report. Even though you forced me to approve it retroactively, I confess I think you're doing the right thing."

"I never thought you'd get around to saying that," Uri said.

Philippe d'Astine had turned the apartment on the rue de l'Amber into a research library on Moshe Dayan. For days he had read everything he could find, including all the books the general with the black eye-patch had written. No detail was too small or irrelevant to be ignored, for who knew how it might fit into his assassination plan. As he read, d'Astine made notes on various aspects of Dayan's character, recording the attitudes, pastimes, and actions of the leader who was to be his target. He studied the character of the man as it emerged from the pages of books and articles, absorbing everything with a sharp and watchful eye. Only after he was sure he knew Dayan well would he decide how, when, and in what fashion he would move.

I couldn't have hit upon a better name than Phoenix, he thought during one of the breaks he permitted himself. It's symbolic of the target: the man arose and disappeared. He floated to the surface and then was lost from view again. Just like that mythical bird, his return to the public arena was always sudden and unexpected, as if he had arisen out of his own ashes.

The distant country where Dayan had been born was foreign to d'Astine. He had only heard about Israel, but had never been there. From Dayan's descriptions of the country at the turn of the century, it was a hard land, a terrain of rocks and deadly swamps, of burning sun and drenching rains.

The opening sentence of Moshe Dayan's book *Landmarks* taught him more about the character and history of the man than all the articles published in the international press. "My name, Moshe, was given to me in sorrow. It was chosen in memory of the first man who fell at Degania, Moshe Braski.

The young man who had come to the land from Russia and joined the settlement was killed by Arabs a year and a half previously. His grave was dug in the olive grove, the first grave in Degania."

Dayan's earlier books, *Sinai Diary* and *Vietnam Diary*, revealed an intelligent man with a clear and concise style and a sharp mind honed to analyze facts and draw conclusions. But it was in the last book, which described the story of his life, that the young man could follow the stages of Dayan's growth and development. Only after reading it carefully did he realize that behind the tough image of the man with the black eye-patch lay a man of poetic instinct who saw himself created out of the soil of his land.

As he read, a strange sensation came over d'Astine. He was slowly beginning to understand that the man he was stalking was very unusual and far different from any he had confronted in the past. This uneasy feeling remained with him as he read Dayan's description of his first visit as Minister of Defense to the Old City of Jerusalem, which had been liberated in the Six-Day War from Jordanian control.

In one of the corners near the Western Wall, which was a remnant of the ancient Temple of the Jews, Dayan found a cluster of delicate blue wildflowers. He picked some to bring to Rachel, the woman who was to become his wife. Later, on his return to Tel Aviv by helicopter, Dayan wrote, "I settled into a corner. Not because I wanted to sleep. I did not want to talk. I did not want to dissipate the visions and sensations of the liberated Jerusalem. There will never again arise a separation between us."

Strange lines, d'Astine thought. A man who was part of a city. A city that was part of a man. How does one grasp the nature of a man like that? How does one find a way to penetrate the wall of security that enveloped him day and night?

To his surprise, Philippe d'Astine found the solution in the chapters relating to the general's private life and his only pastime, archaeology.

In 1951, Moshe Dayan chanced upon some ancient pitchers from the ninth century B.C. in a small town he was visiting. For him it was yet another link joining him to the soil. He wrote, "When I find the shards of a vessel that has been broken but has remained in place, I collect them carefully. In the garden behind my house in Zahala, I have built a workroom where I keep glue and plaster for joining the fragments together, and acid to remove the layers of stone and lime that have accumulated and become adherent to them over thousands of years. On Saturdays and in the late night hours I open the paper packages, wash the broken pieces, and join them together. I do not participate in sports or other hobbies. Every available hour is devoted to antiquities. I enjoy physical work and I need many hours of solitude. Repairing the broken vessels, reshaping them into the form created by the potters and housewives three or four thousand years ago, gives me a feeling of creativity, and a sense of satisfaction like that which I experienced in my youth in Nahalal, when with my own hands I sowed, planted shoots and saplings, and helped the cows in the barn to bring forth their many young."

Philippe d'Astine placed the book face down. He got up and walked back and forth across the room, lost in thought. It seemed that here, in this passage, he had discovered something real that could help him. He returned to the table, picked up the book, and marked the passage with a blue pencil.

"Here is a possible bait," he murmured as though wishing to hear the sound of a voice reacting to what he had just said. "This is the trigger."

Suddenly he laughed a laugh of release. The thought that had flashed through his mind had begun to take shape. The details still had to be worked out, but he knew that he was on the right path.

A feeling of weariness came over him. His eyes were strained from the hours of reading. Fully clothed, he stretched out on the bed and fell asleep. He awoke at midnight and picked up the book and again read the passage marked in blue pencil. He continued reading, marking other passages that had a bearing on the first. He did this with suppressed enthusiasm, like someone on the verge of completing a complicated crossword puzzle. He fell asleep again in the early morning.

At ten he awoke and showered for a long time, as was his

custom. At eleven o'clock he went out to the flower shop at the corner of the street to call the Italian. He was forced to wait; a woman of ample proportions was conducting a loud conversation with someone. He waited patiently until the phone was free, then was obliged to wait even longer until he could get a direct line to the yacht. Eventually, he got through.

"Hello." The voice was Boncho's.

"Do you have it?" he asked.

"I have."

"I'm listening."

Boncho described at some length what he had discovered about Madame Jacqueline Charlotte. His people had done their work thoroughly. He relayed a number of details: her home address; her office address; her personality traits. Boncho stressed that the expertise and professional standards that had made her unique in the modeling world carried over into her other sphere of activity as well. It was a sphere in which she operated only occasionally.

"Is she lethal?"

"In every way," the Italian stressed. "Hardly anything is known about her."

"Is it possible to get her in bed?"

The Italian's sudden peal of laughter took him by surprise.

"Don't try it!"

"Why not?"

"She's a lesbian. She lives with a black model named Dorothy. An American. And lovely . . ."

Philippe d'Astine thought for a moment. "Do you know anything about the relationship between them?"

"That's no secret," Boncho replied. "It's unfortunate that the gossip columns don't interest you. You'll find material in abundance there. The American girl apparently likes men too. Which has caused some outbursts on the part of Madame. She once attacked a photographer who showed an interest in Dorothy."

"And what about Gibskopf?"

"A famous journalist in his field," Boncho answered. "An expert on terror. He's believed to have connections with circles close to various terrorist organizations. His real origins aren't known, but he wasn't born in Denmark. He also operates only occasionally, when the price is enormous. Madame Charlotte is known to use poisons. He's an expert in explosives. He keeps them in his equipment. Sometimes a camera. Sometimes a tape recorder."

"Is there any link between them?"

"No. At least, we haven't found any connection. They may have met one another. But neither has any idea that they have anything in common."

Boncho filled in more details on the journalist. His permanent base was Copenhagen. From there, he traveled across Europe. The Italian had the names of several journalists with whom he associated, and he mentioned the paper that served as his base when he was in Denmark.

"Good work," d'Astine said.

"Do you need anything more?"

"Yes." His voice was low, almost a whisper, but the Italian sensed the request was important.

"Use your connections with the different branches." The Italian knew that he was referring to various police forces, to Interpol and espionage headquarters. Boncho had reliable paid informers everywhere.

"What do you want to know?"

"If something leaks out, it will come to the attention of one of the branches," Philippe d'Astine explained patiently. "I want to know about it. It's important to me. I do not trust the Libyans' capacity for silence."

The Italian was quiet for a few seconds. "I ought to know the name by which you are known to the Libyans," he said finally. "If something leaks out, the name will also become known. It will make it easier for me to discover the leak."

"This time it's something unusual. Phoenix."

"Phoenix?"

"Yes."

"I won't forget it. Now, if you need anything more . . ."

"I'll be in touch with you soon. In two weeks, maybe longer. Are you staying in the same place?"

"I have no reason to move," Boncho said. "I'll be here."

When the quiet young man returned to his small apartment, he prepared a light meal in leisurely fashion. Deep in thought, he ate absentmindedly. He had a number of decisions to make before he could carry out his contract with the Libyans.

Again he was swept by a sense of weariness, as if he had completed some grueling physical task. His hours of long study had exhausted him. He removed his clothes and entered the shower. First he shaved and then he let the water pour over his body, all the while elaborating a plan of action.

After he got out of the shower, he closed the shutters, plunging the apartment in darkness; he stretched out on the bed, closed his eyes, and fell into a deep sleep. At five in the morning he awoke refreshed. He exercised for a while, enjoying the sensation of physical movement, then showered again and made some coffee. While he was drinking, he reviewed his passports and chose an American one. It bore the name of Jeremiah Austin, architect, aged thirty-seven. He examined the picture pasted in the passport. All he had to do was add a bushy blond moustache and a pair of horn-rimmed glasses. To soften the sharp outline of his jaw, he inserted soft plastic pads in the space between the flesh of his cheeks and his gums. As his sunken cheeks filled out and his jaws became rounded, his likeness to the photograph became perfect. The American architect was ready to meet the world.

The same day, at two twenty in the afternoon, an SAS aircraft landed at the airport in Copenhagen. Among the passengers was one Jeremiah Austin, a lanky, smiling American. His clothing was stylish but casual, after the fashion of young men. A Pentax camera was slung over his shoulder, and in his hand he carried a small leather suitcase. He went by cab from the airport to a small hotel in the center of the city where he took a room, after jovially presenting himself as a tourist who had come to discover the city of Hans Christian Andersen. Once he had settled in, he leafed through the telephone directory, looking for Jorg Gibskopf. When he failed to find a listing, he decided to call the offices of one of the newspapers that published the journalist's reports from time to time. The switchboard put him through to a secretary who informed him that Gibskopf was currently in Berlin and would not be back for several days.

"What a pity." His voice held a note of regret. "I've come

a long way and I had hoped to meet him." His voice was pleasant and friendly, and the secretary responded to it.

"Can I help you in any way?" she asked.

"Perhaps you can. Could you possibly give me his address?"

"Mr. Gibskopf doesn't have an apartment in town," the young woman replied. "He lives in a hotel."

That explained why he had not found the man's name in the telephone directory.

"I have a small parcel for him from a mutual friend," he said. "I promised to give it to Mr. Gibskopf. But I'll be only here for a few hours."

"Well, you can leave it with us, or at his hotel."

She gave him both addresses. He quickly memorized the name and address of the hotel.

"I gather that that's Mr. Gibskopf's permanent address in town," he remarked, as if it were an afterthought.

"Yes, he has a suite there."

Shortly thereafter Jeremiah Austin emerged from his hotel. He knew Copenhagen well. It was a city that left him cold. He found it dull and monotonous, but in any event he was not seeking entertainment on this occasion. Gibskopf's hotel was three blocks away from the one where he was staying. One minor problem remained: the number of the journalist's suite. Since he had no desire to attract unnecessary attention by asking too many questions, he decided to solve the problem in his own way.

As he walked along the street, he passed a bookshop and his eyes scanned the window. He caught sight of a pile of copies of the newspaper for which Gibskopf wrote. He entered the shop and for a few minutes browsed through the shelves. Finally he selected a book of tales by Hans Christian Andersen. As the salesman was carefully wrapping the book in brightly colored paper, the young American asked if he could use the services of their messenger to send a few newspapers to a friend who was staying in a hotel. As he was pressed for time, he would consider it a great favor.

"No trouble at all," the salesman said with a smile as he observed the sizable bill that the client had slid across the counter. "We're always ready to help."

He chose two papers; the salesman wrapped them in the same colored wrapping paper he had used for the book.

"Who is it for?" the salesman asked.

"Mr. Jorg Gibskopf," the American replied and gave the address.

"The papers will be delivered within two hours," the salesman promised. "Our messenger will take them when he goes out on his last round." He glanced at his watch. "They should be there by six."

Austin thanked him, and picking up the book of Andersen fairy tales, he left the shop.

He stopped at a small café not far away and took out the book of fairy tales. Because he knew the stories so well, he had no difficulty comprehending the text, even when he came across words in Danish that he did not know. At six thirty he paid his bill and left the café. Gibskopf's hotel was just around the corner.

It had an ornate, old-fashioned facade and was very popular with tourists. Jeremiah Austin looked around the lobby, then approached the information desk. The two clerks were occupied with a group of German tourists so he had ample time to check out the open mail cubicles. He spotted the flowery wrapping paper at once. The newspapers were in a pigeonhole that bore the number 302: Jorg Gibskopf's suite.

Pleased with his success, Jeremiah Austin returned to his hotel and ate dinner in the small and remarkably pleasant restaurant there. He concluded his meal with his favorite drink, Bacardi and Coca-Cola. At eleven o'clock he returned to the journalist's hotel. He entered the elevator in the company of two elderly ladies, tourists from North Carolina, who chattered to one another and exchanged smiles with him. The elevator stopped at the third floor, and he stepped out. He found himself in a wide corridor with a purple carpet on the floor and a ceiling paneled in dark wood. Room 302 was at the end of the corridor.

The young man walked purposefully toward it. The door had two locks: one had apparently been installed at the request of the occupant. The stranger took a short, steel sawblade from his pocket. The entire length of its serrated edge had been filed down. He began to work rapidly now. He pushed the tongue of the flexible steel into the upper keyhole. His fingers sensed the short steel points, feeling out the slots of the lock until they matched. The tongue of the lock sprang back and was trapped in its socket. Opening the lock on the door handle was easier. He pushed the handle down, and the door opened. He slipped quietly into the suite and locked the door.

One small light over the main door had been left on. Although the light was dim, it was adequate for him to see the room he found himself in. It was in perfect order. A nice place, he thought. Neat but with a lived-in quality.

His first priority was to check out the layout of the suite. He crossed the room quickly. To the right was the bedroom, which was also tidy. It appeared that Jorg Gibskopf was a man who liked order. To the left of the bedroom was a bathroom and shower. Opposite he saw a tiny kitchenette with a small refrigerator, a hot-plate, and some kitchen utensils.

On the far side of the room, there was a large window. Crossing to it, he found the cord of the heavy curtain and drew the curtain closed. Then he switched on the lights.

By the door to the bedroom stood a large bookcase jammed with hundreds of books: classical literature, modern literature, and a special grouping of books on politics and terrorism. Evidently, Gibskopf was a man of varied interests.

Austin approached the journalist's writing table. Except for the locked typewriter, it was bare. He sat down and began sliding open the drawers. The top drawer contained sheaves of paper. In the second drawer, he found the material he had been looking for. Pierre de Maline's information had proved accurate. There was a leather case and in it dozens of newspaper clippings arranged chronologically. They dealt with one figure: Moshe Dayan.

The young man smiled in admiration. How thorough Gibskopf was. A real professional, he thought.

From what the Italian had told him, he ought to find some explicit information on Gibskopf's method of operation. Boncho had said he used explosives that converted a camera or a tape recorder into a bomb. If so, the Libyans had been right to bet on him. As a journalist, he could gain entry almost anywhere without arousing suspicion, place a small and sophisticated bomb, and get away undetected.

In the bottom drawer of the desk, Jeremiah Austin came upon a diagram. It was a detailed plan for converting a tape recorder into a bomb. To accomplish his mission, all Gibskopf had to do was attend a press conference at which the Israeli Foreign Minister was scheduled to appear, place the tape recorder in with the recording equipment of the other journalists, and depart. According to the drawing, the timing mechanism was placed under the right-hand spool. Two minutes after the recorder began working, the small detonator would be activated, thereby triggering the plastic bomb packing in the case. A lot of people might get hit, but one of the first would be the target.

Austin found more recent clippings in the bottom drawer, reports on Moshe Dayan's movements. A news release to the effect that the Israeli Foreign Minister might hold a series of meetings with the ministers of the European Common Market was circled in red pencil. Austin smiled. So Gibskopf's arena was to be Europe.

Underneath these clippings he found what he had been looking for—a large package of photographs showing Gibskopf in the company of various people he had interviewed in recent years; Gibskopf with prominent men—heads of government, ministers, industrialists, men of letters, and philosophers of the New Left. Jorg Gibskopf's face appeared in every one of the photographs.

Austin studied the face. Gibskopf appeared to be about forty-five. He had a long, stern, heavily lined face. It was hard to judge the color of his hair. It might be a mixture of blond streaked with silver. His beard was so carefully trimmed and clipped that it appeared false. His expression showed determination, even obstinacy. He was tall and straight-backed, although his hips appeared to be quite broad.

The young man proceeded to memorize Jorg Gibskopf's features. One day soon, their paths would cross and he would have to recognize him at a glance, as if he had chanced upon an old acquaintance whose face was familiar even in a large crowd.

He replaced all the photographs carefully and put the

papers and leather case back in their place. He straightened up and inhaled deeply, as though trying to dissipate the tension that had built up in him. Only then did he glance at his watch. It was eleven thirty. Before he left the suite, he looked around once more to make sure everything was in place. Gibskopf was a very organized man and he would surely notice even the slightest alteration. Austin turned off the lights and crossed to the window to draw the curtain back to its former position.

He opened the door a crack and, looking quickly down the corridor, saw that it was deserted. Opening the door wider, he slipped out, and closed the door behind him. With the aid of the steel sawblade, he secured the two locks, and a few minutes later, he was making his way back to his own hotel.

The SAS plane took off for Paris at nine o'clock the next morning. The young man sat at the rear of the aircraft, his eyes closed and his mind concentrated on his next move.

Those bastard Libyans. He remembered that de Maline had described the Libyan plan as a many-headed hydra. Well, there were a few heads too many. He would lop them off until only one remained. His own. Three million dollars was too good a return to tolerate any obstacles.

As soon as the decision was made to seek help from the police forces and espionage services of various European countries, Avital Arnon added two more men to his staff: Assistant Commissioner Akiva Novik from the Israeli police force and Gad Erez from the intelligence branch. Bit by bit, information began to flow in through the combined efforts of these two men and the various members of the surveillance branch operating in Europe. The police and espionage services in Rome, Brussels, Amsterdam, Berlin, Paris, and London, which had more than once received extensive aid from Israel, were enlisted to help obtain information on European mercenaries. The instructions were clear: compile all available information on mercenaries known to be involved in political assassinations.

In Tel Aviv, a special headquarters was set up under Yitshaq Goldberg. He was empowered to call on any man or service in the Israeli intelligence community without going through regular channels. Speed was essential if the enemy was to be headed off.

As the lists of mercenaries came in from the various capitals, Goldberg went over them, eliminating the names of those who were clearly out of the running, leaving the others for further investigation.

One man on the list from Paris aroused Goldberg's interest. He was described as a Frenchman of Italian origin who frequently changed his name and place of residence. He had been under surveillance in connection with at least two political assassinations in the 1950s. However, there had been no real proof to back up the suspicions. Later, in the second half of the 60s, he was thought to have become a go-between, assigning the contracts he received in return for a substantial cut of the payment. Yitshaq Goldberg circled his name.

After Yitshaq Goldberg had finished checking the reports he called a meeting. The participants found themselves facing a large diagram mounted on the wall with the names of various suspects divided by areas of operation. The men listened attentively as Yitshaq spoke.

"I have no illusions that we are doing anything at this stage but scratching the surface, but there are a few things we do know. First, the Libyans tried to recruit a killer named Hans Kirschenberg, who for reasons that aren't yet clear, and maybe never will be, tried to sell us information and paid for it with his life. We know that Adel el-Magrabi needs a go-between to put him in touch with European assassins. It's our belief that in this case the negotiator was a Frenchman named Pierre de Maline. Unfortunately, we have no means of verifying this because he too is no longer alive. However, we do know that two days before his last meeting with the Libyans, de Maline flew to Monte Carlo. We still don't know who he met there, but we can make a few assumptions. One is that after the German had been murdered by the Libyans, they put pressure on de Maline to find another man, someone more capable and efficient. He might have heard about someone in Monte Carlo who would have been right for the job. We can't find any other reason for this sudden trip. We think it might turn out to be the key factor so far."

"I gather you have a suspect in mind," Uri said.

"Quite right." Yitshaq pointed to the diagram. "This man, whom the Paris police gave us a report on, aroused my interest immediately. We are dealing here with a man about fifty, possibly older. Up until fifteen years ago, he was thought to be active in the business of murder. As he got older and less fit, he apparently decided to retire. But the contracts kept coming in and he found he could carry them out by using younger men for the job. We don't know his present whereabouts. The tabs on him were lifted years ago. But de Maline flew from Paris to Monte Carlo. Why?"

He looked at the others as though expecting an answer, but they preferred to let him continue developing his theory.

"All right," he went on, "let's say that I'm de Maline. I have to get a professional killer quickly and I don't have the man I need. So what do I do? Obviously, I turn to someone else who's also in the negotiating business . . ."

Uri Cohen rose, walked around the table, and went up to the diagram. For a moment he stood examining the information on it. Then he went back to his chair and sat down. "Let's assume that I agree with your theory. What you're saying is that we might have another source to help us discover the identity of our killer?"

"Yes," Goldberg said quietly. "That is my conclusion." He opened his leather briefcase and took out a pile of typed sheets which he distributed among the group. "As you will see," he explained, "there are two sections here. The first contains the names of suspects who we believe should be investigated more thoroughly. The second category concerns the unknown negotiator. Each one of you has means and men. Get them working. And step up the pressure on your European contacts."

Uri Cohen stood up. "I have something to say before you go," he said. "As you know, we are working against the clock and we are working in foreign countries, where, for political reasons, we won't always find a sympathetic response. For that reason, we may be obliged to use unconventional methods. Feel free to do so."

* * *

For the last few days, Philippe d'Astine had rarely been in the apartment on rue de l'Amber. Since his return from Copenhagen as Jeremiah Austin, he had haunted the archives of various newspapers and journals daily, concentrating his attention on the gossip columns which detailed the doings of "high society." The name of Jacqueline Charlotte cropped up frequently.

Boncho's information proved accurate. Jacqueline Charlotte was a society woman in the broadest sense of the word. A vivacious and stimulating woman of great gregariousness, she moved in various circles of society. No doors were closed to her. In addition, she had special prestige in the French fashion world where she was regarded as the foremost expert in discovering and nurturing the best models. Until recently, she herself had been one of them. Photographs of her revealed a woman of great charm and sensuality.

Reading between the lines, d'Astine found thinly veiled clues to her private life. One of the columns remarked that if modeling agencies had not existed, Madame Charlotte would have had to invent them in order to insure herself a stable of young and beautiful lovers.

In some of the more recent weeklies, he found photographs of her in the company of a beautiful black model, an American named Dorothy Brown. She was described as a rising star whom Madame Charlotte was developing; her success was assured as long as Madame Charlotte saw fit to give her special attention. In a gossip column, he found a reference to an argument between Madame Charlotte and her top model. Madame Charlotte had fiercely opposed Dorothy Brown's involvement with a man whose name was not mentioned. The column was hinting that the two women shared a love nest.

The newspaper articles had given Philippe d'Astine an idea. The Italian had given him the address of the modeling agency as well as of Madame Charlotte's home. The rest would be easy.

Cairo in July is stifling. It is like a huge furnace emitting blast after blast of suffocating heat. Like the heat, the tension between Egypt and Libya had risen and intensified. Colonel

Mu'ammar Qaddafi's outbursts about secret attempts to bring a rapprochement between Egypt and Israel never ceased. His attacks increased after three men were arrested in Egypt on suspicion of having been sent by Libyan intelligence to assassinate President Sadat.

Meanwhile, reports arrived from Paris and from Washington that the Libyans were mounting an assassination attempt against Sadat, using foreign mercenaries. The report from Paris was most convincing; it came from both Aqid Asis el-Masri, the Egyptian military attaché, and Mahmud Ashraf, the intelligence representative. The report from Washington was much more low key. It simply spoke of rumors that had as yet to be verified.

Fariq Ariz Urabi, the head of Egyptian intelligence, reported these developments to the Minister of War, Abdul el-Ghani Gamassy. In the course of their conversation Urabi told the Minister of War that he had already sent out an order to his agents in Paris to track down Adel el-Magrabi for questioning.

Following this meeting, additional orders went out from the office of the Minister of War to the intelligence branch. Throughout the early evening, information and instructions were transmitted to representatives in various regions of the Middle East, Europe, and the United States. The Egyptian intelligence machine had moved into high gear.

Israeli and Egyptian agents spread out across Europe almost simultaneously. Their objective was to find Adel el-Magrabi.

In Washington, a representative of the Egyptian Embassy contacted a senior member of the Middle East desk of the U.S. State Department. The American official was told that Egypt wanted to know the Americans' source on the suspected assassination attempt so that they could evaluate the information.

After lengthy discussions in Washington among American officials, instructions were sent to Dick Coleman in Tel Aviv. The next morning Coleman contacted Uri Cohen and explained the situation to him. Uri returned to the headquarters of the security service, and, after a consultation with Avital

Arnon, it was decided that the Americans could tell the Egyptian representative their source was an Israeli.

On Wednesday night, July 13th, a message arrived in Tel Aviv that brought Yitshaq Goldberg to his feet. A rumor had been picked up that a bank manager in Zurich had received a sizable sum from an Arab for negotiating the deposit of a huge sum of money to the account of an anonymous client. The report, which might once have seemed no more than entertaining gossip, hit Goldberg head on and he rushed to Uri Cohen's office. Uri read the report and then looked up:

"Adel el-Magrabi!"

"Right," said Goldberg. "He's the one who made the deposit to the mercenary's account."

Shortly thereafter, a cable went out to Paris instructing Yaki Spillman to send Motti Klein to Zurich to verify the story and get additional details.

Ordinary people see the fashion world as glamorous, faraway, and unattainable. Actually, its inhabitants—the models, designers, clothing manufacturers, photographers, and buyers —toil and sweat as though engaged in hard labor, but from a distance the sweat turns to glitter. It's a closed world, difficult to enter and, once there, hard to leave, although careers can plummet overnight. Only the best, those with particular talent and luck, stay the course, often clinging by their fingertips to the ladder of success.

Paris, traditionally the leader of high fashion, had, in recent years, found a fierce competitor in New York. For the first time, American designers rebelled against the dictates of Parisian fashion, branching out on their own. Nonetheless, there were still American models who believed that it was necessary to launch a career in Paris in order to succeed in the United States. One of these was Dorothy Brown, a beautiful black woman who came to Paris from Chicago. She was tall and slender with a delicately curved body and a café-au-lait skin. She carried herself in such a way that she seemed to float rather than walk.

Her face was strikingly beautiful, with high cheekbones and large almond eyes. Dorothy had been born in Chicago's black ghetto. She never knew her father. Unable to contend with more responsibility in the face of growing poverty, he had left home when she was a week old. Her mother accepted his departure with indifference and resignation. Over the years, she and her five children had been supported by welfare, and had been sustained by her trust in the Almighty, to whom she offered hymns hour after hour. Then, one day, she lost her reason. Taking three-year-old Dorothy in her arms, she walked to the local church and sat down on the steps. Ignoring the falling snow, she sat singing hymns and hugging the freezing child to her.

Dorothy would have frozen to death had not the local priest passed by. As it was, she came down with pneumonia and was sent to the city hospital. Her mother was placed in the state insane asylum.

When Dorothy was five, her mother died. She was passed from one institution to another, with occasional stays in foster homes. Her life among her own people was hard, for her skin was lighter than theirs. They would stare at her and then taunt her, saying that white blood flowed in her veins. She never knew to whom or where she belonged.

At fifteen she was suddenly transformed from a tall gangling girl into a young woman of rare beauty. It was then that she discovered men—or rather, that they discovered her. She was seventeen and working in the photography department at Field's when a professional photographer spotted her. He told her how beautiful she was and offered to take pictures of her. She agreed. From the moment that her photograph appeared in a small monthly journal, she became obsessed by the desire to become a model.

She appeared in occasional fashion shows and from time to time photographic assignments were arranged for her by an agency. Had she stayed in the States, she would probably have attained success eventually, but she was impatient. She came to believe that if she went to Paris she would be discovered there and that, then once known, she could make her way to the top in New York. So she saved her earnings and in the summer of 1976, she left for France.

No one had told her, and she certainly had not asked, but summer in Paris is a dead season for models. Her money ran out in no time. By fall she had only a few dollars left, and she was beginning to be afraid. The street offered the promise of a living if she was willing to prostitute herself.

Innumerable times she knocked at the doors of modeling agencies, waiting for hours only to be rejected. She escaped in daydreams, in which she had arrived and was rich and successful. Meanwhile, it grew colder. The remaining leaves drifted slowly down, the branches bent by gusts of cold wind that reached into her very marrow. Her days in the seedy hotel where she lived were numbered. The proprietor had already told her several times that she must pay or move on.

One morning, in a café in St. Germain des Près, she met a petite French model named Jeanette who lacked neither ideas nor the means for survival. When she could not make a living modeling, she supplemented her income on the street without any pangs of conscience. Jeanette appeared to Dorothy like a ray of light. She noticed the look of hunger in the bright eyes of the tawny-skinned girl and offered her coffee and a roll.

"Listen, Dorothy," she said suddenly. "At Madame Charlotte's agency they're looking for a black model for photographs of next season's bathing suits."

Dorothy shrugged her shoulders wearily. "I don't stand a chance."

"At least give it a try," Jeanette urged. "You're beautiful. Like a black panther!"

Street words, Dorothy thought. She closed her eyes in utter fatigue, wishing only to slip slowly and easily into an unending sleep.

But Jeanette was persistent. In a flash she decided to take on this strikingly beautiful black girl as a personal challenge. If she herself had no chance of success, at least she could try to do something for Dorothy. Almost by force, she dragged her to Madame Charlotte's.

A number of black models were already waiting there, women from all over the world—the States, Brazil, the Virgin Islands, and Africa, and most were as hungry as Dorothy for food and success. Jeanette cast an appraising eye over the beautiful young women and concluded that not one of them was in the same class as the black woman she had brought with her.

Shortly before one, they were shown into the inner office, a vast, opulently carpeted room decorated with priceless works of art. Madame Charlotte's secretary tried to stop Jeanette from entering with Dorothy, but she walked past with authority.

"I'm her manager!" she said deflantly. "She's the model you're looking for!"

Madame Charlotte sat in a lucite chair, looking as if she were suspended in space. At forty-two she was still beautiful, with flaming red hair that accented the whiteness of her skin, and huge, catlike green eyes which widened as they came to rest on Dorothy. She slid out of her chair and circled the black girl twice before speaking. When she did, her voice was low and throaty, with just a trace of hoarseness. "What is your name?"

"Dorothy," the girl replied, feeling ill at ease. "Dorothy Brown."

"And who is this?" Madame Charlotte pointed to Jeanette.

"I am her manager!" Jeanette interjected quickly.

"I want to employ your girl," Madame Charlotte said. Even as her words registered, the room began to spin for Dorothy—more the result of hunger than anything else. Jeanette quickly came to her side, supporting her until her head was clear.

In the beginning, Madame Charlotte treated Dorothy as if she hardly existed. She gave her occasional small jobs but continued to treat her with a coldness verging on disdain. It was a calculated approach. She allowed Dorothy to earn a living, but she made sure she had no illusions that she was a success.

The winter was unusually cold. One day, when Paris was blanketed in snow that had been falling for hours, Dorothy was called to the agency. Madame Charlotte had selected three girls to be photographed on location in Spain for one of the fashion magazines. Dorothy was one of them. Jeanette was informed gently, but firmly, that she would not accompany Dorothy on this trip.

Only when she was installed in a luxurious hotel in Barcelona did Dorothy realize that Madame Charlotte's room was next to hers and that there was a connecting door between them. It made her anxious, since she had heard disquieting rumors about love affairs between Madame Charlotte and other women. Dorothy dragged a heavy chair across the room and pushed it against the door. That night she heard the door knob turn, but the weight of the chair prevented the door from opening. In the morning Madame Charlotte treated her with excessive coldness. When they returned to Paris, Dorothy was paid, but in the ensuing weeks she did not receive a single booking. Jeanette decided to see Madame Charlotte to find out what was wrong. When she returned from the meeting, she was ill at ease.

"What happened there?" Dorothy wanted to know.

Jeanette hesitated, trying to choose the right words.

"Well, Dorothy," she said after an embarrassed pause, "she's in love with you."

"What exactly are you trying to say, Jeanette?"

"She wants you," Jeanette replied. "The way a man would."

Dorothy stiffened defensively.

"She can go to hell!" she said furiously. "Do you hear, Jeanette?"

"I hear," she answered. "But you're making a mistake. She can turn you into a top model. What will it really cost you? Getting yourself felt up a bit? I'd keep on whoring if I knew that getting fucked would get me nearer to the top." She put her arms around Dorothy. "Listen, it wouldn't do me any good. I don't have your qualities. But you can make it there. To the very top. So what if you have to sell yourself a little? What do you care?"

Dorothy did not hear Jeanette's last words. She wrenched herself away and ran to the bathroom. She vomited until she was bathed in sweat and her whole body shook.

Two months later she was starving. A short time after that, she was ready to try the street, to get in bed with the first man who chanced along. Only then did she submit to Madame Charlotte. Shortly thereafter Dorothy moved into Madame Charlotte's large apartment on the sixth floor of a luxurious building on the Boulevard Victor Hugo.

By spring, Dorothy began to long for the company of a

man. In her spare time, while Charlotte was traveling or occupied with business at the agency, she would wander about the narrow streets, seeking diversion. Not far from where she lived, she discovered a small, dimly lit bar that had a jukebox with old jazz and ragtime records. The music appealed to Dorothy and she began to frequent the bar. Sometimes there would be live music when someone came in who could pick out melodies on the old piano that stood in the corner.

By mid-July, when her desire for a man was at its peak, she met someone in a bistro whose look seemed to electrify her body. Frightened by the intensity of her reaction, she did not return his gaze. But the next day she went back to the bistro, and he was there, sitting at a table. This time she looked at him. His face was long and thin, and although in the darkness it was hard to see him clearly, he appeared to be young and handsome.

The following day, she went to the bistro again. She was wearing her favorite outfit: a bright shirt with a pair of faded jeans. Once her eyes had become accustomed to the darkness, she saw several men sitting at the bar, but the young man was not among them. Two tables away she saw two young lovers who sat with hands intertwined in silent rapture.

Dorothy Brown went to the jukebox and placed a coin into the slot. The gruff and rasping sounds of Louis Armstrong overtook her as she sat down, her long legs stretched out in front of her, the upper part of her body hunched forward against the table, her head resting on the palms of her hands. The waiter placed a Pernod in front of her and disappeared as wordlessly as he had come. The notes of Armstrong's magic trumpet hung in the air and, mixed with the warm, hoarse voice, elicited in Dorothy memories of her childhood. The trumpet wailed forgotten sounds of joy and sorrow, hope and despair.

Dorothy raised her head just as the stranger entered the bistro. She noticed his tall body moving lithely like a dancer's. He passed her, then paused and smiled like an old friend before he moved on. It seemed to her that at any moment he might turn back and join her. Just like that, he would say her name—"Hello, Dorothy"—and she would say nothing. Or perhaps she would smile.

But instead he sat at another table, although he kept looking at her. She closed her eyes again and once more rested her head between her hands. The sounds of Louis Armstrong faded and were replaced by the whispering voice of Nat King Cole. Again sounds from the past. Suddenly, the record stopped. Something was wrong with the jukebox.

Dorothy looked up in annoyance as the waiter approached the machine and struck it with his hand. He hit it again to no effect, then shrugged his shoulders helplessly.

"Sorry," he announced into space, as though addressing his words to everyone present. "It happens sometimes. What can I do?"

Dorothy picked up her glass and sipped the Pernod slowly. The silence that fell after the music stopped disturbed her. The chatter from the bar resumed; to block it out, she closed her eyes. Suddenly there was music again, as though the jukebox had started up at the point where the melody had been broken off. But the sounds were of a different quality, a different intensity. The tones were richer and more passionate, although the timber of Nat King Cole's voice was missing.

Dorothy opened her eyes. The stranger was sitting at the old piano, his shoulders inclined forward slightly, as if to protect his extended arms. He ran his hands expertly over the keyboard. His mastery of the piano was absolute.

As he played, Dorothy studied his face. His sunken eyes and fine, chiseled jaws gave him a severe look. It was a face of a hungry wolf. She picked up her glass and moved toward the piano. She stood there, resting her arms on the piano and looking at him. Her glance took in his hands. His fingers were long and powerful and they moved rapidly over the keys. Occasionally he stopped to take a drink with one hand while he kept playing with the other. She knew that he was directing his music at her, wanting it to form a bridge between them. Finally, he raised his head, looked at her, and smiled. His eyes were fascinating.

"Hi!" he said quietly. "My name's Gregory. Gary to friends."

There was no mistaking his accent. He was an American.

"I'm Dorothy," she said. "Where are you from?"

"Forest Hills." He smiled again and she saw his white, even teeth. She noticed the tiny lines around his eyes when he smiled. He wasn't as young as she had thought. As he continued to play, they explored each other with burning looks. As she watched his fingers move over the keys, Dorothy felt as if his hands were moving on her body. In a flash, she realized she wanted him desperately. He was a man and she was hungry to be with a man again. He was virile and handsome and would be able to release her from Madame Charlotte's confining bonds. The thought made her quiver with excitement. He saw her shiver and stopped playing.

"Are you cold?"

"I'm tired." She was almost whispering. "But go on. Please."

Her mind was racing. The timing was perfect. Charlotte was out of town and would not be back until late that night or early the next morning. During the past month, she had gone on several short journeys and she had not seemed to want Dorothy with her. She had been strangely preoccupied and not like herself.

An hour passed while Dorothy and Gary sat talking. From time to time they ordered another round of drinks, Dorothy a Pernod and Gary a Bacardi and Coca-Cola. He told her about his travels in the States and Europe, amusing stories that followed one after the other, like links in a long chain. His company warmed her heart.

"What about dinner?" he asked. Quite naturally, as if he were a good friend, he took her hand in one of his and covered it with the other. His touch was very gentle, but she could sense his strength.

"Why not," she said.

Outside it had grown dark. The heat of the day had begun to wane. They found a small restaurant nearby. Their order was modest: a salad, cheeses, and a bottle of chilled wine. They talked about home. From a distance, their country seemed precious and sorely missed.

"I'm already looking forward to the day I can go home

again," Dorothy admitted. Her eyes filled with tears. "Maybe I'll go home at the end of the summer. To stay, I mean. Always . . ."

"What's happening?" he asked.

"Madame Charlotte, my boss, is planning a trip in September and October, from coast to coast, with a new fall and winter collection," she explained. "We'll be in New York, Washington, Detroit, Los Angeles . . ."

She failed to notice the look in his eyes. This piece of news was of vital importance to him. It meant that the Frenchwoman was planning to strike the target in the United States. In the past few days, he had taken to reading the daily papers every morning. He knew that the Israeli Foreign Minister, Moshe Dayan, planned a visit to the United States at the end of the summer. An article that appeared in *L'Aurore* had stated that the exact date of the visit would be determined after Prime Minister Begin arrived in the States on July 14th. He had already decided to fly to New York and follow the Prime Minister's route, New York-Washington-New York. It was a golden opportunity to check out the security arrangements of the Israelis and the Americans. What Dorothy had just told him meant he must act immediately.

Nothing in his external manner revealed his inner concentration. He ate a piece of cheese with great deliberation and slowly sipped some wine.

"America is the only place to live," he said. "One day I shall settle down there permanently."

"What do you do?" she asked.

"Oh!" He smiled and waved his hand casually. "Precious stones. Diamonds. I'm not a merchant. I'm an intermediary. I fly from place to place looking for a good deal. When I find it, I make a connection with a merchant in the States. If the deal comes off, I get a fat commission."

He spun a pleasant tale for Dorothy. Its very vagueness was convincing. Even as he aroused her interest, all the while, he was thinking about Madame Charlotte. He wondered if Jorg Gibskopf and the woman were on his level. Either way, he would have to clear the arena of rivals, no matter what their competence.

It was growing late. He had spent a long time with Dorothy and was sure that the groundwork had been laid for making love. Her desire was evident. The moment to act had come.

A smile played over his lips.

"What are you thinking about?" she asked.

"I was going to suggest that you come with me," he said.

She opened her eyes wide.

"Where to, Gary?"

"Anywhere that I can have you tonight."

Her lips parted. She longed to cry out that she wanted him to the point of madness, that she needed a man to take her, to free her from Madame Charlotte.

What a sweet revenge on Charlotte! She would spend the night making love with this man in Charlotte's bed. The smell of his body would chase away the odors of the French-woman's perfumes. Her heart beat wildly at the thought. The blood raced through her veins, heating her body to a fever.

As she opened the door to the spacious apartment on Boulevard Victor Hugo, a shiver of an intoxicating passion ran through her. The wall sconces cast a dim light on the expensive drawing room filled with works of art. The man looked around him admiringly.

"It isn't mine," she explained. "It belongs to the woman I share the apartment with. But don't worry," she added hastily when she noticed his inquiring look, "she won't be back until morning."

He did not ask any more questions. He had all the time he needed. Dorothy was standing opposite him, her body quivering. She waited for him to make the first move before surrendering. His approach was a blend of charm and tenderness. They quickly found themselves stretched out on the large bed in Charlotte's bedroom. Their clothes were shed in haste, as each gave way to the uncontrolled passion that overtook them.

Their first kiss was passionate evidence of their needs, and from the first touch of their tongues they knew they were well matched. His tongue traced its way around her ear, then slipped down over the hollows of her slender throat and onto her upright nipples.

He moved down over her firm belly and buried his head between her long legs. She moaned in ecstasy. His tongue and fingers played over her body, triggering her into a throbbing response. The storm of passion robbed them of their senses. They moved together, their lithe bodies blending into a single unity. Slowly and rhythmically, with a gentle touch, the man prepared the way for his entry.

Dorothy was overcome. Her senses had not misled her. She felt the power of his body, of his thighs. Her hands caressed the back of his neck, and with clasped fingers, she drew the upper part of her body toward him. Her breasts pressed against his chest. He entered her, and she groaned like an animal. Again and again, the explosion of passion was expressed in violent thrusts. She lost control, and a sob burst from her throat. Her body shuddered, and she sank her teeth into his shoulder. With a single act, he wiped out the months with Charlotte. In that moment, even as he lay over her passion-wracked body, his hands closed around her throat. Dorothy opened her eyes, trying to understand. The pressure of his thumb was lethal. In the haze, she could still make out the form looming over her before it receded and she sank into oblivion.

When he left the building, he walked quickly, keeping close to the wall, until he reached the far corner where his small car was parked. He got in, started the engine, and pulled out, coasting down the incline of the boulevard. A hundred and fifty feet from the building he parked his car among those of the residents and slid down at an angle that enabled him to watch the apartment building. A passerby would not have noticed him.

At four o'clock in the morning, as dawn was breaking, a taxi drove up and stopped at the entrance to the building. A tall, elegant woman emerged and a minute later disappeared through the doorway.

The waiting man started the engine and the car nosed its way out of the parking spot, merging in a moment with the traffic along the boulevard. In a short time he reached Montparnasse and his apartment on rue de l'Amber. After locking his door, he went to the telephone and dialed the central Paris police station.

"Investigations department, please," he requested in a low voice.

Several seconds later a police officer answered. "Good morning, sir. What can I do for you?"

He gave as his address the building in which Madame Charlotte lived. He said he had at that very moment been wakened from sleep by angry voices coming from the neighboring apartment, which belonged to Madame Charlotte. Then he had heard a woman scream. He thought he should call the police. As the policeman asked him his name, he gently replaced the receiver, ending the conversation. He was very tired, but he had almost no time. His plane for New York was due to take off in three hours.

Within an hour Madame Charlotte would be arrested on suspicion of murdering her lover. Many months of custody lay ahead of her. She might be acquitted. She might not. In any event, she had been taken out of the running. Now there were only two. Himself and Jorg Gibskopf. When he returned from the States, he would find a way to eliminate the journalist too.

On the morning of Thursday, July 14th, Ben Gurion Airport was the scene of the first farewell ceremony for the Prime Minister of Israel, Menachem Begin. He was about to leave for the United States as the guest of President Carter.

Long before the convoy of cars bearing the Prime Minister and his entourage had reached the airport, security personnel had been reinforced in the airport and surrounding areas. Green-bereted policemen from the Border Patrol strengthened the security on the periphery, and additional policemen were brought in to augment the security checks on anyone entering the airport during the morning hours. Plainclothesmen from the surveillance staff of the security service and El Al airlines were stationed at various points.

At ten minutes to seven the convoy of vehicles drew up in front of the terminal. The Prime Minister and his wife, surrounded by members of their entourage, were welcomed by waiting Cabinet members. Begin waved toward the large crowd of onlookers, many of whom called out their good wishes for the success of his first state visit abroad.

Scores of journalists and television and radio commentators from Israel and other countries were waiting inside the terminal building where a short press conference had been scheduled. The Prime Minister was relaxed and calm, more like someone who had been in a position of leadership for a long time, not just a few weeks.

Although his words were delivered with restraint, he took a firm stand. The future of the Geneva Conference would be one of the main points of discussion in his talks with the President of the United States. Moreover he was prepared to present comprehensive proposals to President Carter that could lead to the signing of a peace treaty between Israel and the Arab states. "Within the framework of these talks," the Prime Minister said, "I shall propose the termination of the state of belligerency and the adoption of permanent borders between Israel and her neighbors."

The press conference ended at seven thirty and the Prime Minister left the terminal building and was driven to the steps leading up to the waiting plane. After the national anthem, "Hatikva," had been played, the Prime Minister took leave of his colleagues and, together with his wife, ascended the stairs to the plane.

Many of the surveillance personnel who were to act as a security guard for the Prime Minister during his trip were already on board the jumbo jet, among them Avshalom Kedmi.

In Libya, Adam Ahmed was becoming increasingly anxious. Already rumors about "special operations" were being bandied about by members of the intelligence branch. Adel el-Magrabi, Ahmed's senior assistant, had alerted the Libyan embassies and legations abroad, particularly those in the Middle East, Europe, and the United States, to be prepared, when the time came, to provide intelligence data to a woman and two men whose code names were Charles, Hans, and Phoenix, respectively.

Libya was flooded with foreign agents. Tripoli had become one of the biggest spy centers in the Middle East and Africa, and many countries had agents operating there. The majority were Egyptian, but hundreds of others, many members of Egyptian and Libyan families, helped to collect information.

On July 14 several significant events occurred.

Senior Egyptian agents were alerted to find out all they could about a Libyan plot to assassinate political leaders in Egypt and Israel. According to Washington, the information had come from an Israeli esponiage team during an investigation of a Libyan plot to assassinate one of their leaders. The Egyption Minister of War informed the Americans that, as a sign of gratitude to the Israeli intelligence service, Egyptian agents would pass on, via an American intermediary, any new details they found that affected Israel. The Egyptians, of course, expected that Israel would act reciprocally if and when they had additional information involving Egypt.

Then, on the afternoon of the 14th, Libyan intelligence received a message from its embassy in Paris. Madame Jacqueline Charlotte, a well-known figure in the fashion world, had been arrested on suspicion of murdering an American model, Dorothy Brown. Adam Ahmed summoned Adel el-Magrabi and instructed him to leave immediately for Paris to find out what had happened and just how Madame Charlotte had been implicated.

The third event involved an Arab of Palestinian origin named Hamid Mashawi. On that day, he received a cable from Amman informing him that his uncle was gravely ill and that he was requested to return immediately to receive his blessing before he died.

Many years before, Hamid Mashawi had immigrated to Bahrain, where he had been employed as production manager at one of the large oil companies. A year later, he was offered employment in Libya. The salary was good and he was able to send some of his earnings to his family in Amman as well as maintain an apartment in Brussels where his wife lived and raised their two small sons. Twice a year, Hamid Mashawi traveled to Brussels where he spent a long holiday with his wife and children. In addition, he made occasional short visits to his family in Amman.

Mashawi was fluent in several languages, among them Hebrew. Word of him reached the ears of the Libyan intelligence service in 1971, and after checking him out, they offered him a job as an analyst of Arabic and Hebrew newspapers published in Israel. The offer was attractive and after some initial hesitation, he accepted it. The following year, in recognition of his talents, he was given additional responsibilities.

In view of his uncle's terminal illness, Mashawi requested a special leave. His superior, who liked him, granted it on the spot, and Mashawi immediately cabled his family that he would be on his way to Amman the following day.

On that same July 14th, a certain Jim Campbell was driven from Kennedy Airport to the Filmore Hotel on 29th Street. The Filmore is a convenient location for someone needing temporary residence in New York at a reasonable price. Its proprietors take pains over its upkeep although the services are those of a second-class hotel. Its clientele consists mainly of suburbanites who, for various reasons, are obliged to stay in Manhattan for a night or two. Some choose the Filmore because it is inexpensive, others because it is convenient, still others because it allows them to preserve anonymity.

The hotel is located in an area that even its inhabitants would describe as dreary. It is surrounded by dingy shops, lofts, and warehouses with here and there a small restaurant or a bar that has a nocturnal atmosphere even during the daylight hours. The residents of the neighborhood keep the police precinct hopping day and night, for a large percentage of them are drug addicts or drunks. Out-of-towners who stay at the Filmore tend to use taxis coming and going.

New York was a city Campbell was familiar with, and he knew that a room could usually be had at the Filmore at any hour of the day or night. The reception clerk gave him the key to room 427. When he stepped out of the old elevator that had creaked its way to the fourth floor, he turned left and passed along a curved corridor. When he reached his room, he was well satisfied. It was a corner room and from his window he could see across to 28th Street.

He decided to spend his first night in New York watching television in his room until the early hours of the morning. He undressed and stepped into the shower; for a long time he let the water run over his body, enjoying the sensation. When he was through showering he spent some time studying his face in the mirror. There was nothing remarkable about his looks. His straight chestnut-colored hair merged naturally into the long sideburns he had pasted on. They softened the outline of his cheekbones and the sharp angles of his jaw line. It was now the face of Jim Campbell, aged thirty-three, a musician from Pennsylvania, an ordinary young American in every way.

He switched on the television set and stretched out on the bed. He did not change his position for hours. By midnight, in the midst of a talk show, he decided he had had enough. Nothing had changed over the years since he had first seen the program: the same faces, the same jokes, the same opinions. He slid from the bed and switched off the set.

Hamid Mashawi arrived in Amman on Friday morning, July 15th. One of his cousins had booked a room for him in a hotel in the center of town. He managed to rest for a few hours before the telephone operator called to tell him that his cousin had come for him. In keeping with the custom of his family, Hamid Mashawi wore a gray summer suit and put a kaffiah with a black band on his head.

His cousin Abdalla Mashawi was waiting for him in the wide lobby, which was crowded with tourists. They embraced for a long moment; they had not seen each other for many months.

"Welcome, Hamid," Abdalla said.

Hamid studied his cousin's face sadly. "I am sorry to hear of the illness of our uncle," he said.

His cousin grew grave. "All is in the hands of God," he said, "and we accept His verdict."

After an exchange of questions and answers on the health and circumstances of other members of the family, the two young men turned and went out through the hotel exit. Abdalla's car, a bright orange Mercedes 220, was parked a short distance away.

When he saw it, Hamid smiled. "Life has treated you well, Abdalla. That's an expensive car."

Abdalla grinned. "For us it is easy, but in our neighbor Israel, only a rich man can purchase a car like this."

He opened the door and slid behind the wheel. His cousin got in beside him and closed the door. The car moved forward, slowly merging into the flow of traffic on the main street. Now they could get down to business.

"I hope," Hamid said, "that you have a good cover for me. A genuine sick uncle. Recently the Libyans have begun to suspect everyone. It's impossible to tell when my turn will come."

Abdalla chuckled. "Don't worry. If we had not already thought of everything, we would not have called you."

Hamid glanced at him. "You mean that you are postponing my return."

Abdalla nodded. "There is a reason for the postponement."

"There is always a reason." Hamid Mashawi's voice contained no trace of bitterness. He had simply stated a fact. "I had hoped that this time it would be over."

"Is it difficult?"

"Particularly for my wife," Hamid said quietly. "She's tired. Belgium gets on her nerves. Everything gets on her nerves—seeing me only once every few months, having to look after the kids, never knowing if she's going to see me again. You know, there are quite a few Israelis in Brussels. She dare not have any contact with them. She's a devout Muslim."

"I know."

Hamid Mashawi grinned. "How long is it this time?"

"Not long, I hope. You can send your wife and kids back home whenever you like."

"You're joking!"

"I mean exactly what I say."

The man from Libya took a deep breath. "What is it this time?" he asked, after he had regained his composure.

"We have solid information that a special section has been established in Libyan intelligence." Abdalla watched the traffic in front of him. "It is headed by Adam Ahmed. You know him, don't you?"

"Very well."

"Their aim is to torpedo the contacts between Israel and any Arab states that are willing to enter into negotiations."

"Egypt?"

"Egypt, for example."

"What do you mean, torpedo?" Hamid Mashawi asked.

"According to our information there is a plot to kill one of our people on the one hand and the Egyptian President on the other." Abdalla studied Hamid's face. His expression was serious. "As the first stage, you have to check the details of the plot and report to us as soon as possible . . ."

"And the second stage?"

"No less difficult than the first. We hope you will succeed." Abdalla passed a large truck. "We have no idea who the paid killer is. We assume he's a European. Do you know someone called Adel el-Magrabi?"

"Yes. Why?"

"He's the Libyans' procurer. He must know who the killer is. What's your relationship with him?"

"Friendly."

"Well, that's it," Abdalla said. "If you can manage to carry out both stages at once, so much the better. Eli Rabhan has asked me to stress that you not put yourself in any danger of being discovered. Act carefully, and the moment you finish, make yourself scarce and get home immediately. That's all."

Although the car was air-conditioned, Hamid Mashawi was perspiring. His face glistened as if it had been doused with water.

"Are you nervous?" Abdalla asked cautiously.

"Go to hell," Hamid replied. "It's a strange feeling to know that the end is in sight. That I've finished my mission. That I can go home, and be with my wife and kids, and shout from the rooftops that my name is Hanania Siani and not Hamid Mashawi. Wouldn't you be nervous?"

"I would."

"That's what's happening to me." His eyes filled with tears. As if to mask his outburst, he pulled a handkerchief from his pocket and wiped his perspiring face several times. "You know, sometimes you get the feeling that they've forgotten you out there. That they've stuck your name in some computer and the current has stopped. You feel that you hardly exist . . ."

Abdalla put a hand on the man's narrow shoulders. "No one has forgotten you," he assured him. "Here, I'm the proof."

Hamid Mashawi smiled. "You can't help the doubts. The hesitations. The loneliness. You can't even involve your wife because she's far away in a relatively safe place. You live constantly with the feeling that any moment someone will blow your cover in spite of everything. A chance word and it's the beginning of the end . . ."

It was evident that the incredible tensions he had been living under had built up in him. Up to now he had, in large part, determined his activities, which had mainly involved gathering information on members of the pro-Qaddafi "rejectionist front." This time his mission was clearly defined, and it was perhaps the most dangerous he had ever had to face.

At two o'clock in the afternoon Abdalla drove his cousin Hamid back to the hotel, where they parted with a firm embrace.

"Take care of yourself," Abdalla whispered. "We'll see to the wife and kids. Don't worry."

Hamid Mashawi stopped in the broad entranceway and turned to look back at the orange Mercedes speeding away. Abdalla had to get to the Allenby Bridge before dark if he was to reach his home, which lay in the west.

At eight o'clock that morning, Jim Campbell awoke in the Filmore Hotel. He exercised for ten minutes and then showered and shaved. When he emerged from his hotel he was wearing a short-sleeved, sky-blue shirt and a pair of worn jeans. He made his way to a cafeteria near 29th Street. He placed a cup of coffee, two rolls, a small bowl of cream cheese, a pat of butter, and some orange marmalade on a tray and found a vacant table near the door. For the most part he found simple American food a welcome change from the rich European fare, although even there he was usually Spartan in his eating habits.

He could already feel the rising heat of the day when he

left the cafeteria. The city was in the midst of a heat wave. At Lexington Avenue he turned uptown, moving at a leisurely pace in the midst of the rushing throng. A quarter of an hour later he reached the Concord Hotel, which was where many visiting Israelis stayed. He decided to make his call from a public phone in the hotel, since it would be difficult to trace.

He found a vacant booth, closed the door and dialed the operator. He asked to be connected to the Libyan Embassy in Washington, slid the necessary coins in the slot, and within seconds was put through.

"Good morning. Libyan Embassy."

"Would you put me through to Mr. Jarbil, please?"

"Immediately, sir."

A moment later a man's voice answered; it was not Mr. Jarbil, but his secretary, who informed him that Mr. Jarbil would be in the office in about half an hour. Could he take a message or a number for Mr. Jarbil?

"No," the young man replied. "I'll call again in half an hour."

"What name shall I say, sir?"

Jim Campbell hung up without answering.

He looked at his watch. It was nine forty. Mr. Jarbil likes to sleep late, he thought, then shrugged his shoulders indifferently. He was aware of the customs of the people of the East. He crossed to the newsstand and bought a *New York Times*, then noticed there were foreign papers and asked if the French papers had arrived yet.

"Just a moment," the vendor replied. "They've just been delivered."

"Good," Campbell said. "I'll take *Le Monde*."

The vendor bent over and lifted a large bundle of newspapers. With a rapid movement he severed the thick nylon cord and, spreading the papers on the counter, pulled out a single copy.

Moving to an armchair in the lobby, Jim paged quickly through *Le Monde*; he found what he was looking for on the second page. There were two pictures, one of Dorothy Brown and the other of Jacqueline Charlotte. The caption read: "Love Affair Between Two Top Models Ends In Murder." From the first lines of the report, it was clear that the affair had sent shock waves throughout the fashion world. Madame Jacqueline Charlotte, the reporter wrote, had been arrested on suspicion of murder but had denied having any part in it. According to her, she had returned to her apartment in the early morning hours and found Dorothy dead on the bed. Half an hour later the police had suddenly appeared. When asked why she herself had not called the police immediately, Madame Charlotte answered that she had been in a state of shock. Questioned as to the nature of her relationship with Dorothy Brown, the suspect said that the American model was being promoted by her. The reporter went on to give the police version of the events as well. They stated they were aware that the relationship between the two women went farther than ordinary friendship. At this stage the investigators believed that the motive had been jealousy. It was possible the American woman had been involved in a love affair with an unknown man which had aroused a violent reaction in her famous friend. The report ended with the comment that the investigation would undoubtedly be lengthy. Madame Charlotte had engaged the services of two first-class criminal lawyers, but it was likely that she would remain in custody until charges were brought, if, in fact, they were brought at the end of the inquiry.

Campbell folded the paper and laid it aside, then opened *The New York Times.* His eye was caught by the large picture of Menachem Begin. The major part of the front page was devoted to coverage of the first hours spent by the Israeli Prime Minister following his arrival in New York the previous day. The inside pages also dealt with Begin's visit, and here he found what he wanted: an agenda of Begin's appointments while he was in New York.

He finished reading *The Times;* he now had all the details he needed. When the phone booth became vacant, he entered and placed his call to Washington. This time he had more luck. Mr. Jarbil had arrived.

"Who am I talking to?" the Libyan wanted to know.

"Phoenix," came the reply.

There was a stunned silence.

"Would you repeat that, please."

"Phoenix," came the sharp reply. "And I won't say it again. You know who I am and what you have to do for me."

"I have received instructions," the Libyan replied. "We shall try to do——"

"You will try!" interrupted the stranger. "You will do!"

The Libyan hesitated. The man's aggressiveness angered him, but he decided it was prudent to be polite. The instructions from Tripoli had been clear: provide full assistance, whatever the cost.

"Yes, sir," he said. "What is it you want?"

"I need exact details of the schedule of the Israeli Prime Minister."

Jarbil was shocked. "But that is not your man!" he interrupted.

There was a pause and then the voice resumed with great patience. "I know exactly who the man is, and I know exactly what I need. I have to learn their program. Do you get it, Mr. Jarbil?" Fortunately Jarbil did not have to see his derisive smile.

"Yes, sir." He took a deep breath.

"Then kindly move that fat ass you're sitting on," the stranger said coldly, "and get me the information. And don't sell me any stuff you are not certain of."

"Of course, sir."

"When shall I call again?"

"Tomorrow."

"Too late, Mr. Jarbil," he broke in. "You will do it today. Is that clear?"

"All right. Try to contact me this afternoon. No later than five."

"I'll be in touch with you, Mr. Jarbil. You can depend on it."

And with that, he hung up.

The telephone conversation simply confirmed his contemptuous feelings toward his employers. He abhorred amateurs. The man responsible for espionage at the Libyan Embassy in Washington sounded like a spoiled child who thought that he was doing his job simply by being at his desk.

The exact schedule was essential. At some stops, the Israeli

Prime Minister would keep his distance. At others, where the number of onlookers would be small, the security detail would be increased. Campbell knew a good bit about the operational methods the Americans used to protect foreign dignitaries, but his information on the way the Israelis worked was limited, and he did not want to be caught off guard.

Once he had an accurate schedule, he could pick one or two stops where he would be able to mingle with the crowd. He needed to study and memorize the faces of as many of the security men, both Israeli and American, as he could. He was aware that the Americans and Israelis had security people who operated without contact with the regular team. It would be difficult to spot them, even with an observant and trained eye. Therefore, he would have to act as if he himself were constantly being watched.

He left the Concord Hotel and began walking toward Madison Avenue. A bit of information that he had gleaned from clippings he had collected in his apartment in Paris was becoming central to the plan forming in his mind. In an article that described Moshe Dayan's hobby, he had read that when the Israeli was in New York, he always visited one of the better-known antiquarian shops on Madison Avenue.

More than once, Dayan had treated his personal safety casually, particularly when it came to the subject that fascinated him—archaeological finds. Jim Campbell had decided that he must find a weak spot in the security chain through which Dayan could be induced to slip away from his guards, if only for a short time.

The last section of Moshe Dayan's book *Landmarks* had left a permanent impression on the young man's mind. In it, Dayan described how, after he had resigned as Minister of Defense, he used his first day as an ordinary citizen to make a trip to the Negev, to the valley near Beersheba. In one of the turns of the valley, he came upon the entrance to an ancient cave, which in his judgment had been inhabited thousands of years before by his forefathers. He drove his car to the edge of the high cliff and, tying a rope to the fender of the car, he climbed down it to the level of the entrance to the cave. He crawled into the cave on all fours and inside found what he wanted. All around were strewn earthenware and stone objects, from fragments of lamps to an axehead fashioned from a flint smoothed by the waters of a stream.

"A family dwelt in this cave two thousand years before our father Abraham," Moshe Dayan had written. "They did not read or write. Sometimes they drew on the rocks. They decorated their earthenware pots with lines of red, dark red and warm! This was their home. Here they lived. They wandered back and forth, in the Negev and Sinai. Now I had crawled in and entered their dwelling. All the films showing the wonders of distant worlds did not equal this visit, this sojourn by the fireplace. Now the fire was out. But I did not even have to close my eyes in order to light it once more and see the flaming coals, a woman bending forward stirring the pot for her family. My family."

This passage now inspired the young man's plan of action. He had to create such a cave, an enticing trap, into which he could lure the Israeli with archaeological bait. The antiquarian shop toward which he was heading on Madison Avenue would serve as the setting for the plan that was slowly formulating. In the meantime, he would study the security staff and learn the route between New York and Washington. The schedule for the Foreign Minister would be similar to that now being followed by the Prime Minister.

The heat intensified, but he maintained a steady pace. The bustle on Madison Avenue increased as he moved farther uptown and the small unfashionable shops gave way to prestigious art galleries, dealers in precious stones, boutiques, and antique shops.

Although he walked on the shaded side of the street, the flashes of sunlight reflected from passing cars, showcase windows, and the sides of some of the new buildings were blinding. In an optician's window he saw a pair of sunglasses that he liked, thin silver-plated steel frames with lenses that grew lighter or darker depending on the intensity of the light. They were rather expensive, but, deciding he needed them, he went in and bought them.

The area where he was walking was one he was familiar with. From the optician's it was a ten-minute walk to the antiquarian shop. He made no attempt to hurry. Window shopping was a pleasant relief from the problems that occupied his mind.

The antiquarian shop dealt chiefly in objects from the ancient East, those civilizations that had formed the cradle of modern civilization. He passed slowly in front of the store window, looking first at the objects for sale and then beyond, into the store itself. There were a number of ancient vessels from Egypt, Syria, Palestine, Greece, and Crete. If indeed the plan were feasible, this place would be an ideal trap. He would have to come back and examine it more closely, then make his decision.

When he reached Fifth Avenue, he found a large bookstore and went in. First he paused in the section on Jewish literature where he found a volume on the history of the Hassidic movement. He took it from the shelf and went across to the section on archaeological literature. Two books caught his attention; one was a book by Henry Frankfurt, *Art and Architecture in Ancient East*, the other by Leonard Woolley, *The Art of the Middle East*. He purchased all three.

His next stop was the office of a realtor where he discussed renting a house, something in the suburbs. The realtor mentioned a house in Scarsdale, which was a neighborhood he happened to know. The house, he was told, stood on a hilltop on an acre of land. The rent was $1,300 a month. He took it, sight unseen, and paid in advance for three months. He needed a house as a permanent base. It would also serve as a refuge for some time after the killing. Scarsdale was hardly an area where one would think to look for an assassin.

With the keys to the house and his books firmly in hand, he took a cab to a car agency. He explained to the salesman that he wanted a used car in good condition, and several were shown to him. Among them was a light gray 1976 Ford. He checked it thoroughly. The car had traveled only 19,000 miles and it was in excellent condition. He paid $2,600 in cash.

"Please have it washed and check the oil," he told the salesman. He left his books on the front seat. "I'll come back this afternoon to pick it up."

It was now almost two o'clock. He found a small restaurant nearby and ordered a Bacardi and Coke, which he followed with a whole lobster, a baked potato, and a salad. While he ate, he mapped out his plan of action.

The operation that lay ahead of him was completely different from any killing he had carried out in the past. It had always been his custom to prepare several getaway routes from the country where he was working. This time, things would be different. It was obvious that minutes after the hit, seaports and airports throughout the United States would be sealed off. There would be close searches at every bus and train station and on all the interstate highways. New York would be combed from end to end. Therefore, he had to be prepared for a long stay. From that point of view, he could not have found a better place than the house he had rented. From Manhattan to Scarsdale was at least an hour's drive during the rush hour, but the moment he got back to the house, Jim Campbell would disappear forever and a new character would emerge.

The house had another advantage. It was located in an area of wealthy homes. Every one of them was secluded, and the neighbors took little interest in one another's activities. At most, just for the record, there might be a superficial check, but the investigation would be focused elsewhere.

The waiter brought him a pot of coffee. He drank two cups, taking his time, and decided to place the call to Washington. There was a pay phone in the passage leading to the rest rooms. He dialed the number and asked for Jarbil. He was put through immediately. He smiled to himself. The man had evidently been waiting for him.

"Hello?"

"It's me," he said. This time he did not mention his name. He was sure that the Libyan knew it, as well as the sound of his low voice.

"Oh!"

"Did you get what I wanted?"

"Yes, sir."

"I'm listening."

The Libyan spoke for several minutes. He had up-to-date

information on the Prime Minister's itinerary for the next three days, at which time he was scheduled to fly to Washington for his meeting with the President.

"In two days I will be able to fill you in on details of the visit to Washington," Jarbil said. A note of self-satisfaction had crept into his voice.

"Mr. Jarbil." He lowered his voice until it was a whisper. "You have learned to read English, have you not?"

The Libyan was taken aback.

"Of course!"

"So have I, Mr. Jarbil." His voice became thin, almost hissing. "Like you, I have read this morning's *New York Times*!" He inhaled deeply, making an effort to moderate the contempt he felt toward the Libyan. "I do not require your valuable time to read the paper. Do you understand, my good man? I need information that cannot be picked off the pages of the newspapers. What you read there is a simple mixture of accurate and erroneous information. It's a smoke screen sent up by the man's security staff. Your task is to clear away the fog."

"I understand. But . . ."

"But nothing!" He spoke harshly. "You have an excellent opportunity to practice. Like a dress rehearsal. Don't miss that opportunity, because I personally will come looking for you, Jarbil. Do you know why I am still alive?" He gave a short laugh. "Because I have always taken care not to rely on amateurs!"

"I am sorry." The Libyan tried to interrupt. His voice was quavering.

"Being sorry is useless. Just do what I tell you to do. You have connections in Washington. Use them. If necessary, grease some palms. If you can't do it, inform Tripoli that they have planted a weed in your embassy!"

"Mr. Phoenix!"

"Without names!" The whisper was sharp. "I ask you again. Can you do it, or can't you?"

Dazed, the Libyan paused.

"Yes," he said at last. "Of course, I can."

"Then better remember that my life may depend on the information you produce. I don't like failure or someone who causes me to fail. So try not to find out what I am capable of."

"I will remember," the Libyan muttered.

"And now find out something important for me."

"Certainly. What is it?"

"About the Lubavitch Rabbi. Did you get that?"

"Who is that?"

"Anyone who wants to have dealings with Jews," he replied with derision, "ought to learn something about them. There's a newspaper item that our man intends to visit the Lubavitch Rabbi. It says that the visit is tentatively scheduled for Sunday evening. Check it out. I want to know exactly when."

"I'll check on it. When will you call me?"

"Tomorrow."

"But tomorrow is Saturday. I was planning a trip . . ."

"Forget about your weekend vacations! You work when I work. We'll fix our schedule now. Okay?"

"Yes."

"Every day, between ten and twelve noon, you are to be in your office, next to your lousy telephone!"

"Sir!" The Libyan was offended. "Watch your tongue, please!"

"Quiet," came the reply. "You don't have to like me or my style. You just have to do your work, and do it well. Without mistakes. Be certain not to give me a reason to come after you. Right?"

"Right, sir."

"Now you're sounding better."

Idiot, idle amateur, he thought angrily as he hung up. If the Libyan turned out to be as ineffectual as he seemed, he would break off the contact and get the information on his own.

At four thirty, he picked up his car and drove downtown. The car ran well. He felt the surge of the powerful engine and was reassured: he could rely on it. He drove fast and skillfully, like one well acquainted with the city. A few minutes after five he parked the car a few blocks from Washington Square.

For an hour he wandered through the stores in the area and bought the items he needed. A large suitcase was his first acquisition. It was intended to hold his makeup kit, the wigs, a black cloak, and broadbrimmed hat. At another store he bought a pair of faded gray trousers. He rounded off his shopping at a liquor store and a supermarket, buying enough food and liquor to last him for some time.

It was dusk when the gray Ford drew up outside the Filmore Hotel. He parked the car and locked it, then went into the hotel and up to the fourth floor where he collected his clothes and toiletries, packed them and checked out.

He drove out of the city, and at about eight thirty reached Scarsdale. He found the house easily; the area was just as the agent had described it. The house, which had been built in the late thirties, was a two-story structure that was centered on a broad hilltop surrounded by trees whose green boughs hid it from the eyes of the occupants of the neighboring homes. The lot was large compared to the others in the area.

The private driveway wound through dense shrubbery and trees before it reached the entrance to the house. He ran up the wide outside stairs and quickly unlocked the door. To the right, he had been told, he would find the main switch. His hand felt its way along the wall until his fingers touched the switch and light flooded the broad entrance hall.

He went over the house thoroughly, first checking the various exits and entrances. He was relieved to find that the doors locked securely and were fitted on the inside with bolts. Next to the central heating room in the basement was a large area divided into two sections. In one was a workbench with various tools that he could make use of when the time came. He returned upstairs and passed from the large kitchen to the dining room, and from there to the spacious living room with its adjoining library.

On the second floor were four bedrooms and two bathrooms. He decided to use the bedroom that overlooked the front of the house since it had the added advantage of an adjoining bathroom with a shower.

His tour completed, he went out to the car and brought in his suitcases, the package of books, and two cartons containing food and liquor. He unpacked the suitcases and carefully hung his four summer suits in the closet. After he had set his toilet articles out in the bathroom and put his shirts, underwear, and socks in drawers, he opened the false bottom of the suitcase. Inside lay various forged documents and fifty thousand dollars in fifty- and hundred-dollar bills. Cash was essential since he did not have an American bank account. He placed the bundle of money in a plastic bag which he taped under the top of the toilet tank. He replaced the packet of documents in the suitcase and locked the false bottom.

Now he turned his attention to various items he had purchased that day. He opened the large suitcase and placed the packages, as they were, in the closet. He put the makeup and wigs in a separate drawer, examining each item carefully.

Now he could relax. He undressed and stepped into the shower, letting the water soothe away the weariness that had accumulated during the long hot day. Bit by bit, the sense of exhaustion began to recede and by the time he had dried and dressed, he felt energized again. He went down to the kitchen and busied himself for a while with the food he had bought, putting it in the freezer or the refrigerator and stocking the cupboard shelves.

With a tall glass of his favorite drink in hand, he returned to the bedroom. He put the glass on the night table and, propped up on two pillows, stretched out on the bed and began to read. First he studied the book on the Hassidic Jews. The extraordinary world that unfolded before his eyes fascinated him.

Later, he skimmed the archaeology books. He already had some knowledge in the field. On more than one occasion he had carried out robberies at archaeological sites for certain collectors so eager to enrich their collections that they were willing to go to any ends to obtain a rare find. This time, however, he was looking for a particular period in history so that he could find within its confines the rare vessel that a genuine collector would be prepared to travel far and wide to obtain. If he was correct, his quarry might be such a man. If he could appeal to Dayan's collector side, he would be able to penetrate the security that surrounded him and lead him to a trap in an area that was under his control.

He drank the last of the Bacardi and found he was overcome by fatigue. He put the book aside and fell into a deep, untroubled sleep.

That same Friday evening, Yitshaq Goldberg and his wife Yael were just settling down to a quiet evening at home watching television when the doorbell rang. Yael stood up. "I'll get it," she said; a moment later Yitshaq heard Yirmi Spector's voice, and, damning his bad luck at another evening of leisure lost, he rose to greet him with a handshake and a quizzical look.

Yirmi read his glance and laughed: "Don't worry. Everything's all right," he said, "but I have some messages for you." The two men went into the small study and Yirmi described his meeting in Amman with Hanania Siani. "It's the same Hanania," Yirmi said, "but he's tense. I think it's essential to bring him home after he gets what we need. He wants his wife and children brought back from Brussels now."

"We'll take care of it," Yitshaq promised; as soon as Yirmi left, he called Uri Cohen.

"I'd like to talk to you about this in person," Uri said. "And I have some things to discuss with you anyway. How about popping over here with Yael?"

Yitshaq knew from past experience what "popping over" to Uri's meant: the two wives would go off to talk while the two men discussed business. It would not be a social evening.

"Is it urgent?"

"Fairly," Uri said curtly.

"Okay," said Yitshaq, bowing to the inevitable.

Half an hour later, the two men settled down to talk in private. Uri let Yitshaq fill him in on his meeting with Hanania Siani before turning to his news.

"An hour ago a report came in from Yaki Spillman," he explained. "Motti Klein made an important find in Zurich. He got in touch with our friend and through him managed to locate the bank where the large deposit was made. Half a million dollars it was."

"That's a pile of money!" Yitshaq Goldberg interjected.

"It shows that the Libyans are evidently determined to achieve their objective, whatever the cost. It seems that they already found their man several days ago, maybe even weeks ago."

"Is there any chance of getting information from the bank?"

"I think so." Uri nodded his head. "We have several people in Zurich in key financial positions. They won't hesitate to put pressure on the bank manager, a man by the name of Michel Jean Louis."

"What can he give us?"

"An address. A post office box. Something of the sort," the chief said. "Good God, the bank manager has to tell someone that a huge sum of money has been deposited into an account!"

"Assuming for the moment that things will turn out as you hope," Yitshaq said, "what next?"

"That's your problem; mine as well." Uri drew a glass of tea toward him and took a drink. "You see," he explained, "on Sunday I'm flying to the United States to check the security arrangements in Washington. I have told Spillman to maintain contact with you. So from tomorrow morning, be in the office to start things moving. If you have to do anything while I'm away, check with Avital Arnon first."

"All right."

"There's one more thing you'll have to deal with while I'm gone." He looked thoughtful. "There has been a decision to work in cooperation with Egyptian intelligence."

"Through the Americans?"

"Exactly," Uri replied. "They have agreed to relay information to us on condition that we give them any information that has a bearing on Sadat's safety."

"Meaning that at this stage the Egyptians also have nothing definite?"

"So it seems," Uri agreed. "They have made some arrests, apparently members of the rejectionist front who infiltrated from Libya to carry out an attack and were caught. But they have no idea that Qaddafi might use European assassins."

Yitshaq Goldberg studied Uri's face for a moment. A number of questions had been turning over in his mind, causing him disquiet. Finally he spoke up. "What are your feelings about it?" he asked. "Who are they aiming at? One of us?

The Egyptians? And if it is us, who is the target? I don't think it's Begin. They know that he's a sick man. They also know that he won't compromise. So where do we stand?"

"You know the answer," Uri grinned, "and so do I. Begin is out. He's an extremist and, as such, suits the Libyans because of his views. That leaves only one man: a man who from the point of view of the Libyans and the rejectionist front is very dangerous. A man whom a lot of people regard as the one person who's trying to set up a dialogue. Do you agree?"

"All right. It has to be Moshe Dayan."

"That's my view," Uri said grimly. "Dayan is the Libyans' target."

They fell silent again, each man lost in his own thoughts.

"Suppose for a moment," Yitshaq suggested, "that cross examination of all of our sources proves you right. Where will the Libyans' man move?"

"He has three arenas. Three geographical zones. Here Europe. And America." He felt a wave of tiredness come over him and suppressed a yawn. "It's a bad business. We go into the ring with both hands tied and only our brains to go on. We are dependent on the goodwill of foreign police forces and espionage services." He closed his eyes for a second, then blinked to push away the trace of weariness. "You see, I don't think that he's been operating in Israel. He doesn't know the country. He can't ensure his getaway. So what's left? Europe or the States. I think that he will learn the schedule of the Foreign Minister and try to strike at a moment and in a place most convenient for him."

"To hear you tell it, he's the worst enemy you've ever had to face," Yitshaq observed.

Uri gave a faint smile. "I have to act like that. So do you. We all do." Uri grasped Goldberg's arm. "Haven't you been aware that in the last few days we've been dealing with an unknown man whose existence is nevertheless acknowledged. We know that he exists somewhere. We know that every hour he is taking another step forward. Do you understand? We have to start acting like him from now on. To think as he thinks. To react as he reacts. To live as he does."

"We still have no idea who he is." Yitshaq frowned. "Under the circumstances, how can we be expected to do what you are suggesting?"

Uri rubbed his eyes. "We have no choice," he said. "At some point a link will break, and when it does, we have to be there."

Jim Campbell was awakened at a quarter to five that Saturday morning by the sun shining into his spacious bedroom. The chirping of the birds in the tall trees surrounding the house sounded strange and distant to his ears. It took him a few moments to absorb the special calm that enveloped the large house. The extraordinary quiet was broken only by the whispering of the leaves in the wind and by the songs of the birds.

Slipping out of bed, he went over to the open window and inhaled the scents of the new summer day. The thick foliage of the closely growing trees obstructed his view of the other houses situated on the far side of the flat hilltop.

At five thirty he went out for a walk. He wanted to explore the hidden pathways that crossed the lush hill. When he reached the center of the rise, he heard the fierce barking of dogs among the trees. He stood rooted to the spot, waiting to catch sight of them. Suddenly they bounded into view; two fine Alsatians, a male and a female, whose gray fur shone with dewdrops. The pair had evidently been released by their master to race among the trees.

They stopped about thirty feet from him, their ears pricked up and their heads tilted to one side, as though examining the stranger who had invaded their early morning kingdom. As he moved toward them, their bodies grew tense and they growled threateningly, revealing sharp fangs. He smiled. He liked Alsatians. He pursed his lips and made a thin whistle-like sound, barely audible to human ears. The dogs heard the faint, friendly whistle clearly and their suspicious growling stopped. He took another step toward them. They did not move, but the tension was evident in their posture which indicated their readiness to spring. When he finally came within arm's length, the male began to bark loudly and the female bounded down the hill; the male leaped after her, waving his bushy tail. Within seconds, both dogs disappeared, but the echoes of their barking rang behind them.

Campbell returned from his walk; once back in the house, he washed and shaved, and then prepared breakfast.

It was eight thirty when he left the house again. The heat was already beginning to become oppressive and he had a long drive ahead of him. He was headed for Eastern Parkway in Brooklyn, to the neighborhood where the venerated Jewish leader, the Lubavitch Rabbi, lived. A strange people, he thought as he drove: a prime minister comes and seeks out a meeting with some religious leader in a run-down area of Brooklyn. From the knowledge he had gleaned the day before in the book on the history of the Hassidic Jews, he knew that the Rabbi, Menachem Mendel Shneurson, was seventh in the dynasty of Masters of the Hassidic sect of Habad, a sect that had grown up in Poland two hundred and fifty years earlier. The Lubavitch Rabbi was a man of great influence among Jews. From the moment he assumed leadership, he retained his power until his death, and all over the world, there were separate communities of his followers ready to do his bidding at a moment's notice.

From the few details he had managed to glean on the personality of the religious leader, he understood why the Israeli Prime Minister might seek a meeting with him. The Rabbi was believed to be a miracle worker, a man of outstanding spiritual powers. He was, moreover, a man of vast education, a scientist who had gained academic honors from German, Russian, and French universities. His amazing grasp of science had given him a reputation among prominent scientists all over the world. His followers lived their daily lives in accordance with rules and regulations determined by him. None of them could conceive of making any major decision without first requesting his advice and blessing. What the Rabbi ordained became law.

Once in Brooklyn, Campbell parked his car and bought a copy of *The New York Times* from a nearby newsstand. He walked back to the car, scanning the headlines about Begin's visit and looking at the photographs. One news item attracted his attention. It concerned the unprecedented security network that surrounded the Prime Minister. The report emphasized that not for many years had there been such a large number of security men as were now participating in the present visit. The reporter noted that these highly trained men were equipped with sophisticated communication and surveillance equipment in order to protect the important guest from the Middle East. A round-up of Prime Minister Begin's schedule in New York included mention of his visit to the Lubavitch Rabbi on Sunday evening.

Campbell started up the engine and thirty minutes later, the gray Ford approached the Brooklyn neighborhood that Begin was to visit. Even at a distance, the driver sensed there was something strange. The huge area, populated mostly by Orthodox Jews, looked deserted. It was the Sabbath. Only a few people could be seen walking in the narrow streets. Most of the residents were in synagogue at that hour. No vehicle was allowed to enter the area from the eve of the Sabbath on Friday until sundown of Saturday. Jim Campbell parked his car and went on foot, passing men and women who looked as if they came from a different time and a different world—eastern Europe, perhaps, around the turn of the century.

He continued to walk down the peaceful streets propelled by a sense of curiosity that was almost detached from the reason for his visit. His eye was caught by occasional passersby, dressed in black like eternal bridegrooms. He studied the way they walked and was struck by the strange urgency that seemed to drive them, as if they were hurrying to some hidden refuge. He observed the position of their heads, pushed slightly forward, as if their minds were weighed down by thoughts linked to a world beyond. Aware that he must seem an obvious stranger, he too began to walk with a sense of purpose so that he might seem one of them.

The stores were shuttered, the restaurants closed. It was as if an invisible curtain had descended and cut the district off from the busy life that went on just a short distance away. The street where the Rabbi lived had an atmosphere of holiness, as if here was to be found the center of the universe.

Shortly before noon, Campbell left the district and, not far from where he had parked his car, found an open restaurant. It had a pay telephone although it offered no privacy since the phone was not in a booth. He spoke to the operator in such a low voice that she was obliged to ask him to repeat the number he wanted several times. Finally he was connected with the Libyan Embassy.

"Mr. Jarbil, please," he said to the operator on duty, and after a short pause, he heard the voice of the Libyan.

"It's me," Campbell whispered. "Speak briefly and to the point."

On the other end, he heard the heavy breathing of the Libyan. "The meeting with the Rabbi's been changed," Jarbil said.

"To when?"

"Monday. In the morning. After that, he flies to Washington."

He considered the information. It sounded feasible. The schedules of some of the meetings could be changed, but not the official meeting with the President. The first meeting between the two leaders had been set for Tuesday. If so, the Prime Minister's meeting with the Rabbi would apparently be the last of his engagements in New York before he left for Washington.

"Has the information been verified?" he asked.

"Yes," the Libyan answered in an agitated voice. "Verified one hundred percent."

"All right. We'll see."

He hung up. There was no point in a lengthy discussion. The Libyan had seemed positive.

He returned to his house in Scarsdale at three o'clock in the afternoon and went down to the basement where he spent some time examining the tools he had found there. The variety pleased him. His plan was beginning to take shape. There were several possibilities. One involved the use of an explosive charge detonated by the voice print of the target or by his smell. But he still had time.

He spent the afternoon and evening carefully reading the books on archaeology. He again lingered over the illustrations that appeared in Leonard Woolley's *Art of the Middle East*. His intention was to locate some vessels, rare specimens, one of which would serve to bait the trap.

* * *

On Saturday, close to midnight, Motti Klein returned from Zurich to Paris; the minute he got in, he headed for Yaki Spillman's apartment. Although it was just a temporary residence for the Spillmans, Yaki's wife had done her best to make it seem like home. The walls were covered with scenes of Israel, and ceramic pots, the work of Israeli craftsmen, stood in one corner of the living room.

Motti described his trip to Zurich and remarked on the cooperation of their friends there. He confirmed the report that Adel el-Magrabi had been the depositor of the half-million-dollar deposit and then added: "But the real pay-off was that the banker, Michel Jean Louis, had the number of the post office box where he sent the credit note confirming the deposit." He handed over a slip of paper.

Yaki looked at it and said in surprise: "Monte Carlo!" He thought a moment and then said, "Strange, according to your description, a shabby-looking old man with a marked German accent showed up at the manager's office. Then a well-dressed man speaking perfect French, giving the appearance of a retired army officer, came to el-Magrabi's hotel. What's the connection? And how does all this tie in with a post office box in Monte Carlo?"

The next day, Sunday, Spillman called John Palmer, hoping against hope to find him in the city. Luck was with him and at ten in the morning the two men were conferring at Palmer's house.

"Right now the most important lead we have is the number of a post office box in Monte Carlo," Yaki said.

Palmer looked up. "The post office box where the credit note from the bank was sent?" he asked.

"Exactly."

"That's a good piece of information," John Palmer said, with a note of admiration.

"But not enough," Yaki went on. "We have no contacts in Monte Carlo to help us find out who holds the post office box. You do have connections. Your representatives are on excellent terms with the senior officials of the principality."

He handed Palmer a piece of paper. The American took it, looked at it, and placed it in front of him on the table. Then he leaned back again in his armchair.

"I'll deal with it," he promised. "But it might take a day or two. I doubt that I'll find anyone at home on Sunday. In any case, I'll give it a try."

"I'm very grateful, John." Yaki Spillman stood up.

The American pulled himself out of his chair and turned to the door.

"By the way," Palmer said. "I have something for you. It might not mean anything, but yesterday we received more findings on the death of de Maline."

"What's the conclusion?"

"Just as you thought. Murder. A powerful hand-chop broke a vertebra in his neck. Whoever the unknown killer is, one thing is certain. You're dealing with a man of extraordinary physical strength."

At five o'clock on Monday morning, July 18th, the occupant of the house in Scarsdale was taking his morning stroll. A cool breeze wafted through the tall trees and the light of day was still hidden in the shadows of the receding night that played among the interlacing branches and shrubbery. Once again he heard the sound of barking and the pair of beautiful Alsatians emerged from the bushes. As before, they stopped a short distance from him. He sounded his thin whistle and the animals seemed to relax. This time he took some slices of sausage from his pocket. He dropped one slice in front of him. The male did not move, but the bitch came over and sniffed tentatively. Then her tongue flicked out to gather up the bite that the stranger had thrown to her.

He whistled again and the male pricked up his ears. This time the man threw down two pieces of sausage, one for each of the dogs, and started to walk toward them. They did not move; they only lifted their heads, eyeing him warily. He threw more slices and the dogs quickly jumped forward to devour them. Now he was standing just a few feet from the animals. He held two more pieces of sausage in his hand, but he did not drop them. The animals waited. Then the female began to move toward him. At the same moment, the male succumbed. The man whistled once again, and the dogs fed from his hand. This time he was able to stroke their necks as they ate.

A minute later, the dogs darted away among the trees, barking joyfully. Suddenly they bounded back and ran in a circle around the man. He bent toward them, and they let him pat them. They ran off again and, with a zigzagging run, were lost among the trees and bushes, the sound of their barking fading behind them.

Jim Campbell had spent all of Sunday at home, watching television and trying in general to distract himself after his long period of concentration. On Sunday night, he had rechecked the equipment he would need the following morning. He would have little time to spare. Just applying his makeup would take a long time and require some care. He would have to allow for the stifling heat, since he would be standing for hours in the street opposite the Rabbi's house, unprotected from the sun.

At nine o'clock he had climbed into bed after setting the alarm clock for four in the morning. Proper rest was essential in his line of work.

By morning, as he walked back from his meeting with the Alsatians he felt the positive effects of his twenty-four-hour rest. Back at the house, it was now time to attend to his disguise. He ran his finger over his cheeks several times, then massaged some drops of oil into his face, rubbing back and forth to soften the skin. For two hours he worked on the disguise. The beard consisted of tens of crinkly brown hairs, interspersed here and there with gray, which he glued painstakingly to his face piece by piece. The depressions under his high cheekbones and the bold angle of his jaw disappeared under the thickness of the beard. He applied the long sideburns with the same patience, first attaching them to the roots of his natural hair, and then pasting them alongside his ears until they intermingled with the beard. He used a touch of makeup to lend the grayish skin color of a man who does not expose himself to the sun.

He examined his face in the mirror and then looked once more at the features of the man whose picture in the book *The History of Hassidism* was his model. It was a good likeness. He checked his makeup job in a strong light, since it would have to stand the test of brilliant daylight. He ran his hand over his beard in a gesture characteristic of the Jews he had observed in Brooklyn. Satisfied that his appearance was authentic and that he could easily merge with the crowd, he set off for Brooklyn.

Today the neighborhood where the Lubavitch Rabbi lived seemed to have changed its appearance as though by the magic wave of a wand. The man in the gray Ford noticed many police officers in patrol cars along the main thoroughfares leading to Eastern Parkway. Although it was still early, the security and police guard in the neighborhoods surrounding the Rabbi and his followers was very much in evidence.

At the crossings police were already controlling the flow of vehicles and people who wanted to reach the area where the Israeli Prime Minister was due to visit. The crowd was far greater than Campbell had expected. He decided to park the car near the spot where he had left it two days before. As he locked the car and put on his black hat, he stroked his beard again, partly in imitation of the people in whose midst he was, and partly to make sure it was still securely pasted on.

As he began walking toward the street where the Rabbi lived, he was surprised to find himself being almost carried along in a crowd of hundreds of men of all ages hurrying to the same destination. The nearer he got, the denser the flow became, as still more men emerged from their homes or businesses. The crowd was swollen by many worshippers who had just completed their morning prayers; with prayer shawls still about their shoulders and prayer books under their arms, they now poured out of the synagogues to merge with the surging mass.

The sun beat down upon the narrow sidestreets packed with members of the Hassidic community. Campbell was pleased to see that he did not arouse any curiosity. He looked just like everyone else. His step was hurried, his broad shoulders hunched slightly forward, his bearded face tilted downward in the posture characteristic of those who spent many hours each day poring over sacred books.

A phalanx of gleaming police cars and motorcycles was parked in close formation. The police officers looked on in wonderment at the stream of humanity that flowed past, as though funneled into a channel that led to the house of the

Rabbi. Campbell, in the midst of the crowd, was pushed along as the stream of Hassids moved forward. He was surrounded by a babble of languages—a mixture of English and Yiddish with some Hebrew thrown in. It was a strange world he found himself in; a world he had heard about but whose reality had not existed for him until now.

The street where the Rabbi lived was choked by dense crowds. Police officers struggled to keep a section of the street open so that the convoy of cars with the Israeli Prime Minister and his entourage could come through. The spectators were perspiring under the weight of their heavy clothes and the intense heat of the day. They stood, planted in their places, and swayed like waves of the sea, ebbing and surging. They were waiting to see their Rabbi in his moment of glory, when even the Jewish Prime Minister came to do him honor and hear his words of wisdom.

Jim Campbell inched his way step by step. His aim was to get as close as possible to the courtyard of the Rabbi's house so that he could use his Pentax camera. He had to succeed, for the Prime Minister's security staff, both Israeli and American, would be the same as those protecting the Foreign Minister when he visited the United States. Campbell had to record and then memorize their faces. Until he completed his mission, he must live like one expecting to be trapped. He therefore had to learn to recognize his hunters.

Aping the tactics of the crowd around him, Campbell pushed and shoved, elbowing his way to a better position. Soon he found himself standing close to the Rabbi's door.

Security men were already there, positioned along the front of the house. From the apartments and buildings opposite, other security men watched the milling crowd. Jim spotted two on distant balconies observing the throng through binoculars. It was easy to identify them. Their external appearance was different from others in the vicinity, and their faces betrayed concern and tension as they scanned the swarms of people milling in the street. Campbell judged that an efficient communications system was at work passing information along to security personnel unable to have a view of the entire area.

The heat and humidity were dreadful. Unused to dark heavy clothing in the middle of summer, Campbell felt his entire body awash with perspiration. Even those around him who were accustomed to heavy clothes at all times of the year seemed to be sweating like he was.

Campbell sensed the growing tension and expectancy as the mass of people waited impatiently. The sun was high in the sky when a rumor that Begin was approaching ran through the crowd. The convoy, which consisted of four cars, moved along slowly, walled off by a line of policemen and young Hassids. A patrol car came first. The second car contained security men, and in the third sat the Prime Minister and his aides. More security men were in the fourth car, which brought up the rear.

The murmur of the crowd became a roar as the door of the Prime Minister's car opened, and the slight, bespectacled man appeared, smiling and waving. From all sides came a tumult of greeting in English, Yiddish, and Hebrew. To Campbell's ears, the confusion of languages sounded like a waterfall, the roar of a cascade. As the Prime Minister of Israel, surrounded by security men, began to move toward the house of the Rabbi, many of the onlookers pulled out cameras.

Jim Campbell began taking pictures too, inconspicuous now among so many others enthusiastically taking photographs. He took his shots effectively, focusing his lens not on Begin but on the security men around him. Shot after shot, from above, from below, from the side, all the movements of the men were caught, every face engraved.

Suddenly a strange quiet fell. It was as if an order had been given to the crowd to restrain itself and suppress the flow of emotions. At the front of the house, which bore the number 770, the short figure of the seventy-five-year-old Lubavitch Rabbi appeared. A single gesture on the part of the elderly sage, whose face was ringed in a silver beard that descended to his chest, had stilled the crowd. As he had emerged from his house to welcome his distinguished guest, the shouts gave way to whispers. But when Menachem Begin walked toward the Rabbi and the two men embraced, the whispers grew to a roar.

During all the excitement, Jim Campbell continued to use his camera with its special lens. From his point of view, the events had exceeded his wildest expectations. He had never thought that all the members of the Prime Minister's special security unit would be gathered together. He was certain that some of them were mingling with the crowd and would be difficult to spot, and it was possible that some were disguised as he was. But in any case, he now had pictures of most of the security men.

He was pushed aside and trapped in the crowd as the journalists moved forward. Again the Rabbi raised his hand and the silence fell. He gave words of greeting in Hebrew and Yiddish. Campbell knew no Hebrew, but his German was good enough so that he could understand the Yiddish words as the Rabbi offered a blessing. He spoke quietly, but the silence was so profound that every word could be heard clearly. The crowd seemed frozen in place.

Only after the Rabbi and his guest had entered the house to talk in private did the crowd begin to disperse. Jim, too, began to move away, still casting observant glances on the chance of catching one more face worthy of being photographed.

Before he left Brooklyn, he drove into an alleyway and parked. Rubbing oil into his face to loosen the glue, he began to remove the sideburns and beard. By the time he reached Manhattan, the Hassidic Jew had been transformed into a clean-shaven gentile.

In Tel Aviv, Tuesday, July 19th, was drawing to a close; nonetheless many of the members of the surveillance branch were still in their offices at the headquarters of the security service. During the afternoon many of them had switched on their radios to hear reports of the first meeting between the President of the United States and Prime Minister Begin.

At six o'clock in the evening a telephone call from Paris came through to the office of Yitshaq Goldberg. Yaki Spillman reported that with the help of their American friend they had managed to obtain the name of the man who held the mysterious post office box in Monte Carlo.

"What is it?" Yitshaq asked.

"Vittorio Angelo Massino," Yaki said. "He was on the list the French originally sent in as suspects."

Yitshaq's pulse raced. "There's our missing link," he said excitedly. "The weak link."

"I thought you'd be pleased," Yaki said.

"Where will you be if I need you in the next hour?"

"At the embassy. I'll stay around."

Immediately after the call, Yitshaq had his secretary bring him the file of suspects. He opened the folder and began to read the information that they had amassed on Massino.

Vittorio Angelo Massino, known as Boncho, had been born in Italy in 1921. He arrived in Paris at the beginning of 1938 and, shortly after the German invasion of France, he disappeared. Later, he surfaced as an outstanding soldier in a commando unit of the Free French forces under General Charles de Gaulle. He was known to be a relentless killer when it came to the soldiers of the retreating German army. By the 1950s, he was under surveillance by the French police on suspicion of carrying out killings for large sums of money, but investigators were unable to gather evidence against him. It was later believed that he had become a fence for stolen art and artifacts and that he also negotiated murder contracts. He had left France in 1961, and shortly afterward the files on him were closed. At present, his whereabouts were unknown to the French.

Yitshaq drew a deep breath. This was the turning point they had all been waiting for. It was a pity that Uri was in Washington, he reflected. Avital would be making the decisions now. He picked up the inside line and dialed Avital Arnon's office.

"It's Yitshaq. There's been an important development. I'd like to consult with you."

"Come ahead," Avital replied.

Yitshaq found the chief somewhat weary at the end of a long day that had already merged into night. The lines on his face seemed deeper and he looked unshaven and aging. The large ashtray in the center of the table was overflowing with cigarette butts. The fresh cup of coffee before him attested to the fact that his day was far from over.

Avital looked up as Yitshaq closed the door. "Is it something substantial?" he asked.

Yitshaq grinned. "I think so," he said. "Do you remember that I suggested that de Maline had traveled to Monte Carlo to meet another go-between working in his field?"

"You thought at the time that he might have been one of the men on the list of suspects the French sent in," the chief said slowly, his eyes intent on Goldberg's face. "Someone whose tracks they had lost . . ."

"That's it exactly," Yitshaq placed a sheet of paper in front of Avital. "Well, we have his name—Vittorio Angelo Massino."

"What's the connection?"

"First, we discovered that the credit note on the half million dollars deposited in Zurich had been sent to a post office box in Monte Carlo. Motti Klein went to Zurich and put a bit of pressure on the bank manager. We got the number of the post office box. Then Yaki Spillman went to John Palmer for help. This morning Spillman got the name of the post office box holder from Palmer. Vittorio Angelo Massino."

Avital was galvanized into action. He instructed Yitshaq to contact Spillman and have him send Motti Klein and Ze'ev Shahar to Monte Carlo to find out what they could about Massino. He would bring Uri Cohen back from the States, leaving Avshalom Kedmi in charge there.

It was the moment both men had been waiting for—the moment that comes in every investigation and marks the turning point, when the possibility of a solution comes into view.

At noon on Wednesday in the Israeli Embassy in Washington, Uri Cohen told Avshalom that he was leaving at once for Monte Carlo. He instructed Kedmi to return the next day to New York with the Prime Minister as planned and escort him back to Tel Aviv. Then he filled him in on Motti Klein's findings in Zurich and added: "It seems we're dealing with a master of disguise, a man who knows how to erase his tracks, not just cover them. But one thing is clear: the Libyan plot is well advanced. Two hours ago I met our contact. The Egyptians told him to tell us that their agents in Libya have confirmed the existence of a special assassination headquarters headed by Adam Ahmed. But the Egyptians are as much in the dark as we are as to who Qaddafi's target is. And we're not likely to get any more information from that quarter."

"Why not?" Kedmi asked.

"We have military intelligence reports that the situation between Libya and Egypt is on the verge of exploding. If that happens, I doubt that their agents can be bothered with what would then be a minor issue."

"Which would leave us alone on the stage," Avshalom remarked.

Uri patted his aide on the shoulder. "We'd be alone in any case."

Among the cheap clothing stores on West 42nd Street was a photography store belonging to an aged Jew named Selig Auster. The seventy-year-old owner was a widower, the father of three grown sons who had thriving businesses of their own in California. He had refused to close his small shop and join them for fear that giving up his livelihood would hasten his end. Because the shop was more than just a living for him, he provided better service than his competitors, and at a lower cost.

Early Tuesday morning, a young man had brought him a roll of film to develop. He promised to have the prints ready by the following afternoon. To his surprise and pleasure he found, as he developed the film, that the photographs were of the meeting between the Prime Minister of Israel and the Lubavitch Rabbi. Consequently, when the young man entered the shop at four o'clock Wednesday afternoon, Selig Auster welcomed him warmly. "Nice shots," he said. "You a reporter?"

"Yes," the young man replied with a smile. "I gather you recognized the event."

The old man smiled back. "Is it possible not to recognize Begin and the Rabbi?" He placed the developed film and the prints on the counter. "Two such men! Ah!"

The young man examined the prints carefully. They were very good.

"You're a Jew, aren't you?" he asked.

"And what a Jew," the shopkeeper laughed. "Believe me, from the days of Solomon and David."

Hearing that, Jim Campbell decided to change his plans. He had intended to ask Auster to enlarge the faces of the security men in some of the photos. But this man was a Jew. If he were at all suspicious, he would not hesitate to act.

He thanked the old man for his fine work, paid his bill, and left the small store quickly. Nearer Times Square he found a photography store owned by a black, and entering, he asked for a set of enlargements of each of the faces circled in ink.

"I want them as soon as possible."

"Like when?"

"Tomorrow."

"That's a special order, sir," the black owner explained. "So it's a special price."

The young man nodded. "That's all right," he said. "As long as the results are good."

When the young man left the store, he headed back to the parking lot where he had left his gray Ford.

Adel el-Magrabi had arrived in Paris on the instructions of Adam Ahmed. His task was to get information on the events that had led to the arrest of Madame Jacqueline Charlotte. However, he had been unable to discover any details beyond those already published in the press. All he could report was the simple fact that Madame Charlotte was definitely out of the running.

El-Magrabi was unaware that his movements were being watched by French agents. A few days before, Inspector André Cordeille of the DST, the antiterrorist division, had been informed by his agents that el-Magrabi was in Europe again. His Israeli colleague, Yaki Spillman, had alerted him to the possibility that the Libyans were planning a coup in Paris, and Cordeille was aware that both Egyptian and Israeli agents were trying to find el-Magrabi, whose name was well known to the inspector. On the face of it, there was no valid reason to prevent el-Magrabi from entering France, and even if there were, the politicians would veto any such attempt.

The policy of the French government was to maintain friendly relations with the oil states at all costs. Cordeille, who felt very differently, as did most of his DST co-workers, had been unable to do more than put a permanent tail on el-Magrabi and request that the Libyan's movements be reported directly to him.

El-Magrabi had decided to spend a few days in Paris indulging in some personal pleasures before returning to Tripoli and the heavy hand of Adam Ahmed. He felt entitled to a small reward for the diligence with which he had applied himself to his tasks.

There was a small nightclub in St. Germain des Pres that was a favorite spot of his. A blond-haired Swedish stripper named Mona, who worked there, had caught his attention. He had met her for the first time on his last trip to Paris and had found himself obsessed with the desire to have her.

On his first night in Paris this trip, he had stayed at the club until the early hours of the morning, but to his disappointment, Mona had rejected him. She was busy, she explained. The next night he had made another attempt, and again she turned him down politely with a smile. These rejections merely served to excite him even more.

Now he decided he must have her whatever the cost. It was hard for him to say what it was about her that set his blood on fire, but the very thought of the Swedish girl was enough to make him break out in a sweat. He set out for the club, his pockets loaded with money; only a patron with an open hand and a pocket full of bank notes was welcome there.

Adel el-Magrabi and his two ever-present bodyguards arrived at the club at eleven o'clock. The Libyan was determined to spend that night in Mona's bed. However, enthusiasm at being in Paris had dulled the sense of caution of the three Libyans and they did not observe the four DST men following them. The French agents were adept at trailing, and they had been instructed to keep track of el-Magrabi until he left the country. When el-Magrabi and his bodyguards entered the club, the DST agents remained outside at four observation points which permitted each of them to watch the entrance to the club and at the same time to maintain eye contact with one another.

In the last twenty-four hours, the men of the DST had become aware that others as yet unknown to them had succeeded in tracing el-Magrabi and were close on his heels wherever he went. Indeed, so intent were these others on their quarry that they did not notice that they themselves were being followed by Inspector André Cordeille's men. The inspector had ordered his agents to lie low as long as their intervention was not called for.

El-Magrabi was received warmly by the manager of the club, and he and his bodyguards were quickly seated at a table between the bar and the small stage. About thirty men and women were in the club. Before the stage show began, slides of naked men and women in various sexual positions were shown on a screen. Then precisely at midnight the spotlights played on the small stage. In the center a young man and a young woman appeared naked. Adel el-Magrabi knew the various stages of their act very well. For him, released as he was from the asceticism of Tripoli, this sensual paradise was an experience that fired his senses and intoxicated him. He felt his penis growing hard.

He took a long drink of cold water. The caresses of the young couple increased the tension in his testicles. He thought of Mona and his fervor grew. Hot with desire, he took out his handkerchief, spread it out, and placed several ice cubes in its center, then tied the ends and slid the handkerchief around the back of his neck, on his forehead, and over his burning cheeks to cool them. He was in a storm of impatience, waiting for the appearance of the striptease dancer.

At one o'clock her turn came. Adel el-Magrabi ran his tongue over his dry lips. He concentrated his stare at the center of her voluptuous body. Her fine, round bottom rotated on its axis, as if there were a small, powerful engine in that ripe posterior that moved every other part of her luscious body. Her blond hair tumbled down and hid her soft shoulders with locks that flew out like snakes.

"Daughter of hell," the Libyan thought. "Daughter of the devil."

She raised her body upward in erotic gyrations. Her hands

slipped over the upper part of her body, caressing huge breasts whose nipples stood out as if in defiance. From there, her hand slid down onto her genitals and then up again over her flat belly. Adel el-Magrabi's breathing was heavy as he watched her long fingers pinching her nipples that stiffened with the contact. In his burning imagination the Libyan saw those same hands playing at the opening of his trousers, slipping onto his erect penis. Again he drank cold water in an effort to douse his lusts.

At that moment, the spotlights went out and Mona was swallowed up into the protective darkness. When the dim lights went up again in the club and the sounds of the cool music replaced the pounding beat that had accompanied the stripper's dance, the Libyan began to breathe regularly, moderating the force of his pulse which had been racing out of control. He waited for Mona to join him at his table, as she had finally promised she would the night before.

But Mona did not appear. Instead, the manager of the club approached his table and placed a small envelope before him.

The Libyan looked at it in surprise. "What the devil is this?" he asked.

The manager smiled appeasingly. "Madame Mona has sent this with her kindest regards."

The Libyan pulled a hundred-franc note out of his wallet and handed it to the manager, who thanked him with a slight bow. After the manager had turned and gone, the Libyan opened the envelope. Inside was a brief note written in badly spelled French.

I would prefer not to be seen leaving the club with you. Wait for me at my home. The key is under the mat. Mona.

Below these lines the address was written in a careful hand.

Adel el-Magrabi glanced at his bodyguards. "We're going," he stated.

They went out into the cool night. Mona's apartment was not far from the club, to the right at the second corner, in the middle of a winding alley paved with cobblestones. El-Magrabi walked quickly, his heavy belly swaying before him. His breathing came in short bursts to match the pounding of his heart. The two young men hurried after him, wondering what was happening, for he had not troubled to tell them. El-Magrabi stopped only when they neared the entrance to the apartment.

"I am going in here," he said. "You wait outside. Madame Mona will come soon."

The bodyguards glanced at one another. So that was it. The fat man was planning to devour some forbidden fruit. They remained standing on the opposite side of the street as Adel el-Magrabi crossed over and went up the steps of the old two-story building. He found the key under the doormat and bending over, inserted it into the lock and opened the door.

He was met by an impenetrable darkness. He pulled a lighter from his pocket and snapped the small lever. As the flame sprang up, he was struck a stunning blow that sent him reeling backward even before he could call for help. He felt another blow at the back of his neck and knew that he was sinking into unconsciousness.

A minute later the door opened a second time. The two bodyguards, frightened and bruised, were pushed inside by four burly men who entered behind them. Together with their two comrades who had been waiting inside the apartment for el-Magrabi, they numbered six. Their commander crossed to the telephone to report the capture of Adel el-Magrabi.

The long, persistent ringing of the phone in the house of the intelligence officer eventually awoke his servant. When asked where his master was, he replied that he had left an hour before for the Egyptian embassy.

At that moment, Mahmud Ashraf was presenting a rapid briefing to Muhammad Hafiz Ismail, the Egyptian Ambassador to France. In accordance with a priority instruction from Cairo, the intelligence representative was ordered to brief the Ambassador on the events of the last twenty-four hours which had brought the military situation on the Egyptian-Libyan border to a head. The message was quite simple: Egypt was about to attack Libya. Therefore, the order had gone out to all intelligence personnel to brief their ambassadors so they could prepare the information campaign they would have to launch in the countries to which they were accredited.

As the briefing was nearing its end, the outside telephone standing on a shelf near the Ambassador's desk buzzed. Muhammad Hafiz Ismail lifted the receiver and listened for a few seconds, then held the receiver out.

"It is for you," he said.

"Thank you, sir." Mahmud Ashraf took the receiver and spoke his name.

"Sir, this is Azin."

"Something new?"

"The Libyan is in our hands."

"Everything in order?"

Azin chuckled. "Fell into the trap like a ripe fruit," he answered. "He's just a bit shocked by his welcome."

"Wait for me. I'm coming at once." The intelligence officer replaced the receiver. His brow was furrowed as he reflected on the plan that had just succeeded. From the moment his men had discovered the Libyan, he ordered them to find a way of getting him without the use of weapons. It was Azin who had chanced upon the object of the Libyan's interest at the nightclub, and hence, the idea of using the stripper as bait had been born.

The Ambassador looked at Ashraf inquiringly. "Is everything in order?" he asked.

Mahmud Ashraf responded with a calm smile. "No, sir, on the contrary." It was necessary for him to keep the Ambassador in ignorance. "There has been a development which, if successful, will cause all of us satisfaction. But in the meantime let me conclude the briefing, for I have an urgent matter to attend to."

Ashraf left the embassy quickly after making his farewell to the Ambassador and once again apologizing for awakening him.

It was two thirty when his car turned into the narrow, winding alley and stopped at the house where el-Magrabi was being held. The events that were taking place inside that house had had no effect upon the street, which was quiet and peaceful. It appeared that everything had gone according to plan. Azin could be relied upon. It was true that he was known to have a hot temper, but he always adhered to instructions and brought his missions off.

Mahmud Ashraf parked his car near the house, which had been rented by his predecessor. It served as a convenient headquarters for various intelligence operations. The small apartment had been used many times for various interrogations. The walls and doors had been soundproofed so that a shout or scream of pain could not be heard by people outside.

Ashraf knocked twice at the door, one knock after the next, as though he were impatient. The door opened. Like the master of the house, Ashraf threw the door wide open and entered. Only then did he stop in stunned amazement.

The scene before him was far from what he had expected. On the low sofa sat three men, badly beaten. In the center was Adel el-Magrabi, whom the intelligence officer recognized immediately from Azin's descriptions. On either side sat his bodyguards. From the expression on their faces, they were still dazed. Opposite six men stood in a row, their hands clasped behind their heads. They were his men. In the center of the row stood Azin, his eyes half-closed. His face was flushed with rage.

Both groups, the Libyans and the Egyptians, were under the guard of eight men dressed in civilian clothing. Opposite them, in the center of the room, a comical-looking man sat on a chair. He was so short that his feet did not reach the floor. Judging by the lines of his face, he seemed to be about fifty or sixty years old. Although his wrinkled face was pinched and sharp, his large eyes held an expression of permanent childlike wonder.

"Welcome, Monsieur Ashraf," the little man said pleasantly. "Please come in, and if you don't mind, close the door."

The intelligence officer did as he was told, then turned and took several steps into the center of the room. Suddenly, he was swept by rage.

"What is going on?" he roared.

"Monsieur." The short man smiled calmly. "I beg of you. In a moment I shall clarify the situation for you. In reality, it is not you who should be angered. I should be the angry one. I do not like it when undesirable acts are plotted in our beautiful city."

Ashraf's rage mounted. He tried in vain to control it. In situations like this, he became subject to a slight stammer. The contortions of his tongue brought in their wake still more fury.

"Who are you?" he bellowed.

"I am not deaf, Monsieur Ashraf." The small man slipped off his chair. He was a head shorter than the well-built Egyptian. In other circumstances his appearance would have brought a laugh to the lips of the Egyptian intelligence officer, but not when he had absolute control of the situation. He strode forward. "Permit me to present myself. I am Inspector André Cordeille from the DST. I hope, sir, that in spite of the fact that we have not met before, my name is not unknown to you."

So: this was André Cordeille, Mahmud Ashraf thought. The name of the veteran French officer had reached his ears many times, but never in his wildest moments would he have imagined him to look like the man before him.

As if catching the meaning of Ashraf's incredulous glance, Cordeille said with a smile, "I can assure you that I am he. But this is certainly not the most fitting place to have a friendly conversation so that we may deepen our acquaintance, which this time is not by chance. With your permission, and in spite of your diplomatic immunity, allow me to invite you and your men to drink a cup of coffee at my office in rue Susa. Shall we go?"

He turned, then paused when he heard the curses the Egyptian officer showered on his men.

"There is no cause to blame them," he said gently. "I am the one to blame. You see, Monsieur Ashraf, we also have professionals. We knew of the arrival of Monsieur el-Magrabi, and we discovered how anxious you were to get to him. I believe that we must clarify that point and then part as good friends. Shall we not?"

The Libyans and Egyptians were taken in separate cars to the DST headquarters and the investigation was continued there. El-Magrabi was placed in one room, his two bodyguards in another. The Egyptians were separated into three rooms: in one were Azin's five men, in the second was Azin himself. Mahmud Ashraf was taken into Cordeille's office and left to cool his heels.

Inspector Cordeille interrogated the Libyan bodyguards and then the five Egyptians. He preferred to begin with the small fry before moving on. Only after he had finished with them did he enter the room when Azin was held. Threatened with deportation, Azin quickly passed the buck to his superior, Mahmud Ashraf. The questioning of Ashraf finally produced an admission that he believed el-Magrabi was involved in a plot to harm Sadat. André Cordeille reserved his main attack for el-Magrabi, suggesting that other agents awaited him and that simply by alerting them to his release, Cordeille could assure the Libyan of certain death. When he confronted el-Magrabi with complicity in a plot to kill Sadat, the Libyan seemed thunderstruck; his black eyes opened wide. Then he began to laugh.

"You know so much, Inspector," he said, "but not everything."

"True," the investigator agreed. "But I know that the Egyptians and Israelis are pursuing you. If you fail to give me the information I want, I can tell them your whereabouts and one of the wolves will pounce on you."

Frightened by this repeated threat, the Libyan responded. "I can tell you one thing and one thing only. Otherwise I am a dead man in Tripoli. It has nothing whatsoever to do with Egypt. That I swear is true."

Cordeille shrugged his shoulders. "We shall see," he said as he turned and left the room. Entering his office he found a somewhat subdued Ashraf. "Well, Monsieur Ashraf, I believe that you and your men are free to return to your homes. And I am free to assure you that whatever the Libyan plot may be, it has nothing to do with your president or any Egyptian for that matter." As he waved the Egyptian out of his office, he asked an assistant to send el-Magrabi in.

When el-Magrabi entered the room, Cordeille did not offer him a seat. In a flat voice he said, "My men will take you and your two bloodhounds to your hotel where you will collect your belongings. From there they will take you to the airport and will guard you until the flight to Tripoli takes off. And make sure that our paths do not cross in the future."

Once he was alone, André Cordeille sat down to write a report on the night's events. In it, he stated that in his view the Libyans were planning to assassinate a high-level Israeli politician. He recommended that his findings be submitted at once to the appropriate Israeli officials.

The lively barking of the Alsatians reached Campbell's ears even before he had left the large house for his morning walk. When he opened the kitchen door, he found that this time the dogs had been bold enough to approach a short distance from his back steps.

He smiled. The friendship between himself and the two beautiful animals was growing deeper. They trusted him. He gave a low whistle and their ears picked up the friendly sound. The male raised his head and growled; the female broke into a run and circled her mate, standing again by his side and looking at the man. He took some sausages from his pocket and held them out to the dogs. They approached him and took the food from his hand.

He stroked their necks gently and lightly patted their backs. When he turned to stride off between the trees, the dogs bounded after him. He began to lengthen his stride until he broke into a run with the dogs leaping joyfully after him and barking. Finally, the dogs came up to him and encircled him several times as though asking his pardon for their departure; then they broke into a run toward the slope of the broad hill. He watched them for a few moments and saw them bounding toward their home.

It was the morning of Thursday, July 21st. At eight o'clock Campbell drove away from his house, heading for the city to collect the enlargements of the faces of the security men that he had ordered the day before. When he reached Times Square, he parked the car in a lot and walked east. On the way, he stopped for breakfast.

He reached the photography store at nine thirty. The black owner welcomed him warmly. "Everything is ready, sir," he said, and spread the twenty enlargements before him.

Campbell examined the faces carefully. The work was not flawless but the results were adequate enough for his purpose.

"Something wrong, sir?"

"No," he said. "They're fine. What do I owe you?"

"Sixty dollars."

The young man glanced sharply at the shopkeeper. "That's a little excessive."

"It was a special order," was the firm reply.

"Very well. Wrap them up." And he placed three twenty-dollar bills on the counter.

After he left the shop, he began to reflect on Alex Kraskin, the dealer in art and antiquities. In Marseilles he had handled the shipping order for the smuggled artifacts and he remembered the addressee's name well. He wondered if Kraskin would answer his needs. Alex Kraskin. He turned the name over in his head.

He needed a quiet place to think things through. But first he decided to walk up Madison Avenue to check out the antiquarian shop again. His plan was beginning to take definite shape. He could begin now to refine the details.

Madame Charlotte's arrest on suspicion of murder had raised many doubts in Boncho's mind. He felt sure there was more to the affair than was indicated in the press. Although he had never met the Frenchwoman personally, he had learned much about her as a result of the request made by the young man. She was known for her cold-bloodedness, her ability, and her silence. It was unlikely that this calculating woman would allow herself to become implicated in a simple case of murder.

He also reflected a great deal about Pierre de Maline. The Frenchwoman and the Frenchman both shared similar fates, although it was true that the one merely had a noose around her neck whereas the other one was dead. But in one way or another, both of them were connected with Phoenix, who was the only person on earth who aroused naked fear in Boncho.

His disquiet grew; it gnawed at him and disturbed his well-being. He continued to follow his usual routine on the yacht anchored some distance off Monte Carlo, but he became more cautious. He had never trusted the young man, for he knew that if he—Boncho—were to become an obstacle Phoenix would not hesitate to destroy him. He instructed his crew and various on-shore informants to be especially alert to any strangers taking an interest in him or his ship. To date, nothing had been reported to him.

On Thursday evening, he had had an appointment with two businessmen in his cabin. One was a well-known diamond merchant from Antwerp, the other an Englishman who dealt in stolen gems. The latter was seeking a buyer, and the Italian had found him one. The deal was concluded at the meeting. Boncho's share came to $25,000, a nice cut. In an expansive mood, he invited his guests to dinner at one of the exclusive restaurants in Monte Carlo.

After an extraordinary meal that lasted until quite late, Boncho drove each man to his hotel and returned in his Mercedes to the large parking lot near the broad quay of the yacht basin. He parked his car and, getting out, glanced around to check out his immediate surroundings, as had been his wont of late. He strained his ears to pick up any unusual noises. Strains of music wafted across to him from the large cafés and mixed with the gentle sounds of the breaking waves. Reassured, he turned and walked rapidly toward the motorboat that awaited him. Dino, one of his crew members, a taciturn man of about forty, had been there for some time and stood up when he saw the Italian approaching.

Boncho jumped lightly off the quayside into the motorboat.

"What's new, Dino?" he asked as he sat down in the seat.

"Charlie was here," the man answered.

"Charlie? The Englishman?"

"Yes. From the Bristol Hotel."

The Italian's body immediately grew tense. Charlie was one of the waiters who had frequently benefitted from his generosity. He was also one of those whom he had asked to keep his eyes and ears open.

"Did he leave a message?"

"Yes. Some strangers have been asking questions about you."

"Where are they?"

"At the Bristol. They arrived yesterday."

"Where is Charlie?"

Dino smiled. "I took him to the boat, boss." He tossed a cigarette butt that had almost scorched his lips into the black waters. "I knew you'd want to talk to him." Dino started the motor. The regular beat of the steel body on the waters matched the pulsing rhythm of the Italian's heart. Something was happening. Maybe he would have to do something. He emitted a groan. Old age was creeping up on him. In his youth he would not have hesitated to take on even a messenger of the devil. But he knew that inside his youthful exterior there was an aging man whose powers had decreased and whose courage was not what it used to be.

Charlie, the waiter, was waiting for him on the top deck. Boncho hurried him down below to the seclusion of his cabin.

"What's up?" the Italian said abruptly.

"Two men turned up at the hotel yesterday and booked a room facing the harbor," Charlie said. "Both about thirtyish, average height, sort of. Well built. One of them fair-haired—reddish. The other black curly hair. They asked about you."

"What language did they speak?"

"French. Spoke it fluently."

"What did they want to know?"

The Englishman thought for a moment. "Everything," he said. "They asked questions like the fuzz. Not like anybody just taking an interest. They spent a lot of time walking around. Like they were killing time. Or maybe waiting for someone."

The Italian went across to the bar and poured himself a glass of brandy. Charlie's eyes narrowed. He could have sworn that the yacht owner's hand was trembling as he raised the glass to his lips.

"I hope it's worth something . . . what I've told you . . ."

"Yes, yes," the Italian muttered and drew some money from his wallet. The Englishman slipped it quickly into his shirt pocket, and, closing the door carefully, ran lightly up the wooden companionway. Dino was waiting for him on deck. Ten minutes later the motorboat slipped alongside the large jetty and stopped. It was one o'clock in the morning. The quay was in darkness so the waiter did not notice the two figures standing between two small craft near the spot where the motorboat had tied up.

"That bastard Englishman," Motti Klein muttered.

"Our cover's blown," Ze'ev Shahar said somberly.

"Perhaps we ought to contact Spillman to hear what he has to say."

"What can he do?" Ze'ev said with a curse. "Tell us he's sorry we got shafted?"

When Uri Cohen arrived at the Bristol the following morning, he found Motti and Ze'ev sitting by the window facing the sea. One look at them told him that something had misfired.

His face grew grave as they reported their findings. It was clear that the Italian was a key figure, one who could shed some light on the identity of the killer. "All right," he said. "Where is he now?"

"Good question," Ze'ev said. "His ship was anchored out there." He pointed out to sea.

"*Was* anchored . . ."

"By the time we got up this morning, at six," Motti explained, "he had already sailed."

They looked intently at Uri. He moved away from the window and sat down. His brow was furrowed and his gaze fixed in concentration.

"You have to look on the bright side of every setback," he said finally. "The departure of the Italian is undoubtedly connected with your investigation. I don't know what he found out about you, but he panicked. That means he is up to his neck in this business, one way or another."

"What do we do now?" Ze'ev asked.

"You go back to Paris. You'll have your hands full. I'm going home. We'll start a simultaneous search. We'll get hold of this Boncho, whatever the cost. We'll stick our people in every corner—merchant shipping, the navy, the air force. The Italian has to drop anchor somewhere in the Mediterranean. And when he does, we'll find him."

The longer Campbell stayed in the house on the hill, the more certain he was that his choice of Scarsdale as a temporary residence had been inspired. It was completely quiet and peaceful and one could live for months on end without anyone bothering to take an interest or even sense his presence.

For the past few days he had occupied himself with the photographs. To double-check the effectiveness of his shots, he spent time hunting through the files of the agencies of press photographers in Manhattan. Presenting himself as a member of the editorial board of a Dutch weekly, he obtained dozens of photographs of the Prime Minister and the security personnel who surrounded him.

On Friday, he spread all the photographs in front of him and made a careful comparison. After several hours, he concluded that he had apparently succeeded in photographing most of the security staff. His next step was to memorize their faces so that when he encountered them, he would be able to recognize them at a glance.

Saturday morning, he drove to Manhattan. For several hours he shopped for food, stocking up enough to last him for several weeks in case he was obliged to remain in the house in Scarsdale. He had avoided making purchases at the large shopping centers in Scarsdale where every new face aroused curiosity. Here in Manhattan there was not the slightest chance that someone might recall that on a certain day a stranger had been in.

In the afternoon he decided to telephone Alex Kraskin, the dealer in art and archaeological finds. He had obtained the number of his house in Connecticut. When he called, a man's voice answered: "The Kraskin residence."

"Good evening," Campbell said. "I would like to speak to Mr. Kraskin."

"Who shall I say is calling?"

His answer was quick. "Philippe Montier," he said. His English was flawless, but this time he was careful to add a French accent to it.

"Please wait a moment."

A minute later he heard the voice of the servant once more.

"Mr. Kraskin says he does not know the name . . ."

"Then kindly tell Mr. Kraskin," he said patiently, "that Philippe wishes to convey regards from a mutual acquaintance in Monte Carlo."

This brought results; a new voice answered the telephone.

"Kraskin speaking." The voice was slightly hoarse as if the speaker were nervous. "Who are you?"

He decided to take a hard line with the millionaire.

"It is not important who I am," he said. "I'll be at your home in an hour and a half."

"But——"

He interrupted the dealer. "I said in an hour and a half. I am bringing with me personal greetings from Massino."

This time the reaction was different.

"I'll be expecting you," the man replied. "I am looking forward to hearing how our friend Vittorio Massino is."

"I had no doubt that you would be, Mr. Kraskin." He put down the receiver.

After attending to his makeup to give himself an older and more respectable air, one that suited the character of a foreigner who had come on business, he put on a summer suit, took his black cane with its silver knob, and climbed into the gray Ford.

Alex Kraskin's house was impressive; it was situated at the top of a hill with lawns stretching down to the shore of a private inlet of the ocean. The sun was setting as the gray Ford approached the large wrought-iron gate, which was still open. The private road wound through huge trees up to the entrance to the house. The last rays of daylight illuminated the carefully tended lawns and flowerbeds, the province of a team of gardeners. Alex Kraskin's enormous wealth was evident at every turn.

The winding road veered to the right, parallel to the entrance, then continued to form a wide ellipse around the vast beds of summer flowers. On the right, a short spur of the road led to a wide area for parking cars. Montier parked his car and got out. Swinging his walking stick, he turned toward the impressive entrance and ascended the six stone steps. At the door, he pushed the pointed tip of his cane against the large doorbell. From where he stood, he could hear the bell resounding through the house. A moment later, the door opened.

An elderly butler, immaculately dressed, stood before him. The butler inspected the visitor and approved of what he saw—a European man of affairs, perfectly dressed in a well-cut blue summer suit that set off his flaxen hair, lightly touched at the temples with gray. His face was pleasant without being handsome and his moustache was trimmed in the old-fashioned way.

"Mr. Montier?" the butler asked.

The man nodded.

"Mr. Kraskin is expecting you, sir," the butler said.

A moment later, a tall, rather fleshly man came toward him. Alex Kraskin's shoulders were so broad they seemed about to burst from his jacket. A short, thick neck supported his flat, coarse-featured face. He looked more like a retired wrestler or football player than an art dealer. A healthy tan emphasized smiling gray eyes, the only feature that softened the expression of a face that otherwise bore the stamp of violence.

As Kraskin shook hands, he looked carefully at the stranger who had all but forced himself upon him. Although the smile never left his fleshy lips, the laughter disappeared from his eyes as they scanned Montier questioningly. The quiet voice with the metallic ring still resounded in his ears, a voice whose controlled menace had caused him misgivings. Certainly the dignified man who stood before him now bore no relation to the impression Kraskin had formed from the brusque voice on the telephone.

Alex Kraskin led Montier into the spacious library and closed the door, then waved his guest to a chair. Montier sat down, his hands resting on the silver knob of his black cane.

"A friend of Vittorio's, eh?"

The stranger smiled softly. "I am his friend," he said, "and Vittorio's friends are my friends."

"Well, then, my newfound friend," Kraskin said, "who are you and what do you want from me?" Kraskin found something inherently unpleasant about the well-dressed stranger sitting opposite him.

"I admire your directness." Again Kraskin heard that metallic ring. "Who I am is of no concern to you. As to what I want, I have need of an artifact, some ancient work of art. I want something extremely rare. Something priceless."

Anger flooded the art collector. "Why are you so certain you will get that from me?" he asked.

"Because if I do not," the stranger smiled charmingly, "Interpol will hear the little song I have to sing about a bill of goods. And a copy of this song will soon be sent to the FBI."

Although the dealer was a heavily built man, his movements were nimble and surprisingly fast. He leaped from his chair and sprang at the man. Montier's reaction was lightning swift. The walking stick swung in his hands; like a conjurer, he spun it in his fingers so that the large silver knob struck out while he held the other end between his fingers. The knob smashed into Kraskin's kneecap. The force of the blow threw him off balance. A groan of sudden pain erupted from his throat. His leg felt paralyzed. He hopped on one foot, his arms stretched out, trying to steady himself. Just then, the silver knob was jabbed into his chest, and he was thrown backward. He slumped into the armchair, powerless.

The man opposite him remained seated, calm and relaxed, his hand again resting on the knob of the menacing cane. "Do not be violent, Kraskin. Control yourself."

Kraskin, still doubled up from the sharp pain in his leg, felt a sudden stab of fear. "I don't know what you're talking about," he said.

"Then I'll refresh your memory," the man said evenly. "There was a shipment of stolen goods from an archaeological site. It was sent to you at the beginning of the summer from Marseilles." He gave a thin smile when he saw the dealer's eyes widen in alarm. "And in this house there hangs a very beautiful painting by Cézanne. From the year 1890. You and I know how it got into your hands. Or perhaps you would like me to remind you about the stolen Rembrandt you sold in London last April for close to a million dollars? Oh, I can sing a whole opera about your dealings, Mr. Kraskin."

"Okay," Kraskin said. "What exactly do you want?"

"An Egyptian or Palestinian piece dating from 2000 to 1000 B.C."

Kraskin considered his situation. He had no choice but to comply. "Look around you," he said finally. "Take what you want."

The stranger smiled. "Mr. Kraskin," he said graciously,

"there are some fascinating pieces here. I admire every one of them. But as I have told you, my friend, I am looking for something rare. Something that a genuine collector would be prepared to risk his hide to have."

"This is all I have."

"I do not like to be lied to," came the reply. "Although I can certainly understand why you might do so. However, as a generous host you should offer to show me around your cellar. What do you say?"

The dealer clenched his large fists until the knuckles turned white. He pursed his fleshy lips and deep wrinkles spread from the corners of his mouth to his heavy, square jaw. He got up and limped toward the narrow door set into an alcove between the wide bookshelves. First he slid aside a panel secreted between the rows of books. Behind it was a row of buttons controlling an alarm system. He pressed one of them. Only then did he put his hand on the handle of the door, which moved silently on its hinges and opened. A bright fluorescent light shone into the library. On the far side were wide, green-carpeted steps.

The Frenchman followed his unwilling host. Halfway down into the cellar, it already seemed as though they had entered an antique dealer's premises. There were Egyptian and Canaanite sarcophagi, slabs inlaid with ivory, breathtaking bronze sculpture from Akkad and Assyria, fascinating dishes from Ur of the Chaldees, from Persia, Egypt, and Greece. Some were of pure gold. In one corner on a low table were spread treasures found in the Pyramids: necklaces, bracelets and clasps fashioned of gold and precious stones.

"That's it," the dealer said dryly. He leaned his full weight on an Egyptian chest. His knee hurt. From the way in which the stranger examined the antiquities, Kraskin realized that he knew exactly what he was looking at. "I hope you find what you're looking for." The irony was bitter.

Philippe Montier cast a glance in his direction. "I am sure I will," he said. For some minutes he sorted slowly through the mounds of priceless objects. Finally his eyes fell on what he wanted.

On a stand made of inlaid wood lay a small carved ivory box from the thirteenth century B.C. The lid of the box was of bronze with a silver cobra twisted on it. The cobra's eyes were two small pieces of inlaid shell. It was a beautiful object; one that had been found decades earlier at a site at Megiddo in Palestine.

His hand caressed the box. "I'll take this. And I do appreciate your kindness."

Kraskin maintained a stony silence as he accompanied Montier to the front door of the house. When he had started the engine of his car the visitor glanced back. Alex Kraskin was still standing in the doorway, glowering in impotent rage.

It was dark when Montier reached his house in Scarsdale. He stopped the car in front of the entrance. He left the small parcel on the seat until he had removed the fake license plates from the car and replaced the originals. Wiping the dirt off his hands with a rag, he took his cane and the small parcel and entered the house. Once upstairs he undressed and went into the bathroom where he wiped the makeup from his face. Philippe Montier disappeared as though he had never existed. He washed the rinse from his hair under the shower and, shortly after, went down to the kitchen again. He took a cold bottle of Coca-Cola from the refrigerator and poured some into a tall glass that contained Bacardi.

Now he was ready to examine the ivory box. The box was some 3,000 years old, dating from the time of the Exodus, the time of Moses. No knowledgeable antique collector could deny its uniqueness. The ivory inlay was the work of a craftsman as was the bronze lid. The cobra writhed on it as though alive, retaining its gliding life as at the moment when the unknown artisan gave it its final polish.

After feasting his eyes, the young man began making preparations to photograph the box. He placed it on the table and stood a thick piece of cardboard covered in silver foil against the wall to form a background. He brought two lamps from the living room and placed them on either side of the table to dispel the shadows thrown by the box. Then he stood the Pentax camera on its tripod, focused, and began to photograph. He took a number of shots.

When he had finished, he wrapped the box, this time in a towel, and inserted it in a plastic bag. He then opened the freezer and began removing the frozen foods, piling them on the table. When he reached the bottom, he placed the parcel in the freezer and piled the food packages on top of it until it was hidden from sight. If strangers were to break into the house while he was out, the likelihood of their discovering this treasure among the frozen food was slim.

Now it was time to begin telephoning. He had the numbers of two well-known collectors. The first was not home, but the second answered his call. He introduced himself as a European collector interested in acquiring antiquities from estates. He was lucky. The collector, a man named Arnold Schwartz, told him about David Hirshkowitz, a well-known collector in Flint, Michigan, who had died the year before. Some of his collection had already been donated to various museums while the collector was still alive; now his widow was selling the remainder.

As he waited for the operator to put through the call to Flint, Michigan, he was struck by how lucky he was. The number was busy on the first try, but on the second, the line was free and he heard the pleasant voice of an elderly lady. Once again he presented himself as an art dealer, interested in those pieces of the collection that were being offered for sale. He said that Arnold Schwartz, the Los Angeles collector, had advised him of the sale.

"I'm so sorry," the woman apologized, "but most of the items have already been sold. The few pieces that are left aren't very valuable."

"I'll be in Detroit tomorrow on business," he replied patiently, "and I'd be happy to see whatever is left. There might be something to interest me. Would you have any objection to my visiting your home tomorrow?"

"You'll be very welcome," Mrs. Hirshkowitz said and gave him directions on how to reach her house from the airport. By the end of the conversation they parted like old friends.

Now he took up the Manhattan classified directory and looked carefully through the list of firms that developed and printed film. He found several businesses that were open seven days a week, twenty-four hours a day. An hour and a half later he reached the city and left the film to be developed and printed. It would take two and a half hours and was far from cheap, but when he returned to Scarsdale at two fifteen in the morning, he had several excellent enlarged pictures of the antique box.

On Sunday, at four thirty in the afternoon, his taxi stopped in front of a house in one of the exclusive neighborhoods of Flint, Michigan. He told the driver to wait for him. Mrs. Hirshkowitz welcomed him warmly. His appearance appealed to her. He looked like a man in the prime of life, tall and slim, with a graying beard that added to his charm.

"Mrs. Hirshkowitz," he said, "it is a great pleasure to meet you."

"It's my pleasure, Mr. Gregory." That was the name with which he had introduced himself. She led him into the living room. "I do hope that you haven't made such a long journey just to come here."

"Oh, no," he replied. "As I told you, I am on a business trip, and this takes me only slightly out of my way. It's a delightful detour."

"Thank you," she said with a smile. "I understand how you feel. I lived by the side of a collector for many years and I know what collecting means, particularly to someone who is absorbed in it like my David was." She smiled again. "David found nothing in life to equal this passion."

She went over to the fireplace and pointed to a man's portrait hanging there. "That was David, Mr. Gregory." She looked at it affectionately. "He was a wonderful husband and a good father to his children," she said in a low voice. "We all feel his loss . . ."

This conversation was the introduction to the welcome she had prepared for him. He drank tea with her and ate some cake that she had baked. Only then did she show him the few remaining pieces of a collection that had been recognized as one of the most important private collections of ancient eastern artifacts. He studied them and settled on a small bronze box.

"It isn't particularly valuable," she said, looking at him inquiringly. "There are many like it. A simple box, isn't it?"

"My experience has taught me," he explained, "that every item has a buyer."

She laughed. "I hope you aren't buying it just for my sake."

"Why would I do that?" he asked in surprise.

"Because you feel that you've taken up my time."

"Never," he replied. "I bought it because it appeals to me. But I do have one request to make. I need a statement from a lawyer that I acquired this box from your late husband's collection."

"But today is Sunday," she said. "All the offices are closed."

"Perhaps one of your acquaintances?" he asked.

Her eyes lit up. "Why, of course!" she said. "I'll call one of my friends right away. I'll explain the situation to him. He'll certainly be willing to do it for me."

She arranged a meeting with her lawyer, explaining to him that her visitor had come from New York and had to return there at once. Gregory bought the box for $750 and took his leave. He gave the waiting taxi driver the lawyer's address and by six in the evening the driver deposited him there. The lawyer was waiting in his office for him.

"A request from Mrs. Hirshkowitz justifies opening my office even on Sunday," the lawyer observed.

"I really appreciate it," the client said. "I'm sorry to have taken you away from home, but I want you to know that you will be well compensated.

"In that case, we'll both be satisfied," the lawyer said with a laugh. "Mrs. Hirshkowitz tells me that you have purchased an antique box. She said that you need a notarized statement that the item is from David's collection. Am I right?"

"Quite right." The client opened a folder and took out the photographs of the box he had taken from Alex Kraskin. "Mrs. Hirshkowitz was kind enough to give me a photograph of the box. You can simply endorse the other side with a statement that it was purchased from the private collection of David Hirshkowitz."

The lawyer looked at the picture. "I know nothing about these things," he said, "but this looks very handsome."

"I think so too," the client agreed.

The lawyer picked up his pen and wrote several lines to the effect that the box, which appeared in the photograph, was from the collection of the late David Hirshkowitz, citizen of the town of Flint. Then he signed the statement and stamped his seal over the signature.

The entire transaction took ten minutes. Two hours later, Gregory was sitting on a plane headed for New York.

On the morning of Monday, July 25th, Prime Minister Menachem Begin's visit to the United States came to an end. He regarded the trip as a success; he had achieved the desired results both with President Carter and the senior government officials and with the leaders of the American Jewish community.

During their talks, Carter and Begin had agreed that the search for peace must be continued and that war in the Middle East had to be avoided at all costs. During the talks, the name of Moshe Dayan was frequently mentioned as one who was active in secret discussions between representatives of Israel and Egypt.

During his long return flight to Tel Aviv, Begin prepared a detailed report to submit to the members of his government. Separately, he made notes on issues that he would raise only in the talks with Foreign Minister Dayan.

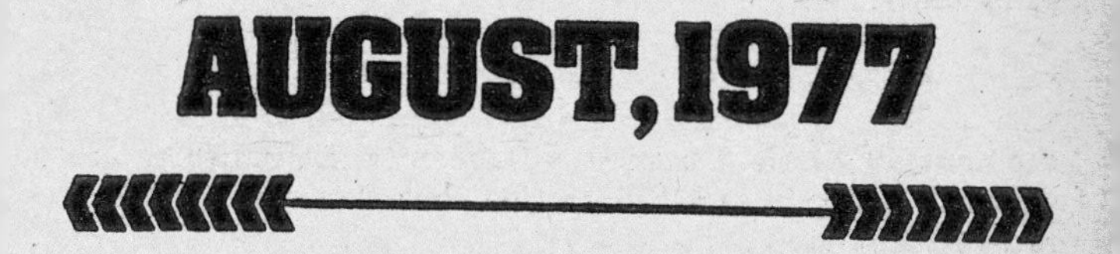
AUGUST, 1977

On Monday, August 1st, at midday, Jack Stone's law office near Lincoln Center was still very busy. Founded in the mid-thirties by Jack's father, Irving, the firm had gained a reputation over the years for representing Jewish interests in New York and elsewhere. The Stone family was known for its Zionist ties, and therefore many Jewish organizations put their trust in the firm. A Zionist atmosphere prevailed in Jack Stone's private office, where photographs and drawings of Israel and her leaders were prominently displayed.

The old man entered the outer office, stooped-over and taking slow steps, as he supported himself with a silver-handled black cane. He hobbled toward Mabel Freedman, Jack Stone's personal secretary.

"Mrs. Freedman?"

She raised her head and looked at the old man.

"Yes, sir," she answered. "Can I help you?"

"My name is Willy Miller," he said. "We spoke this morning on the telephone." He spoke quietly and his speech was weary and slow, reflecting his advanced years.

The secretary glanced at the lawyer's appointment book. "Yes, of course," she said. "You made an appointment with Mr. Stone for twelve. Correct?"

"Yes, yes," he agreed. "Twelve o'clock."

Mabel Freeman looked at her watch. It was almost twelve, but Stone was still tied up with his previous appointment.

"Wait a moment, please," she said and stood up to help him into a chair. The old man bent over, wheezing a little, and sat down laboriously.

"Old age creeping on, young lady," he said, somewhat embarrassed.

She gave him a warm look and returned to her desk. The old man watched her as she worked. From time to time he pulled a creased white handkerchief from his dark overcoat, coughed the way old men do, and wiped his thin lips, then replaced the handkerchief in his pocket.

It was twenty after twelve when the door to the inner office finally opened and the client emerged, followed by Jack Stone. Stone, a man in his forties, had a remarkably intelligent and sensitive face. He hurriedly approached the old man, who had pulled himself up with much effort from the chair and was now steadying himself on his black cane.

"Mr. Miller?"

"That's been my name for seventy-three years," the old man said with a smile.

"I'm very sorry to have kept you waiting," the lawyer apologized.

"Young man," the older man replied, "at my time of life I have already stopped attaching any importance to the passage of time." He chuckled. "I still attach importance, however, to getting things done properly."

"Well, our firm excels in that," the lawyer said briskly.

"I have checked you out, Mr. Stone," said the old man, giving him a shrewd look.

"Oh, really?"

"I belong to a generation that has all but disappeared. My generation was very distrustful. We are used to checking on every single point."

The lawyer was amused. "And what have you decided, following your inquiries?" he asked.

"I'm here!" the old man said. "There's no better answer than that."

Jack Stone winked knowingly at Mabel Freedman. These old Jews, he thought, smiling to himself. They really do belong to a dying world. Despite that, he liked and respected them. They had approached him more than once with strange requests, but they were always open-handed. It was rare that he had to argue about the fee for his services.

Jack Stone's inner office was vast. On the wall behind his desk were photographs of himself with prominent Israeli leaders and certificates attesting to his activities in the United Jewish Appeal and other Jewish organizations. He led his visitor to an easy chair opposite his desk.

"Well, Mr. Miller," he said, sitting down in his own chair, "I'm at your service."

It appeared that old Willy Miller had a question. His cousin David Hirshkowitz had passed away a few months before. His will, of which his cousin Willy was executor, had one special section dealing with the fate of his valuable art collection. All the terms in that section had been met, except for one, for which the good services of Jack Stone were needed. One rare piece of the collection remained—a box, and David Hirshkowitz had wished to send it to his friend General Moshe Dayan whom he had admired and respected for many years because he was, among other things, an archaeologist and well-known collector.

"Everything clear so far?" the old man asked.

"All clear," the lawyer nodded. "How can I help?"

"Well, sir," the old man wheezed again, trying to shake off a slight hoarseness. "My life is coming full circle, and I don't have the time left to handle everything I have to do. I have to travel to Europe this summer to close up my business there. Eh!" He waved his hand in dismissal. "Everything closes up, young man. Everything." The old man's mind seemed to wander and he appeared to have lost his train of thought.

"Yes." Jack Stone decided to help him. "We were talking about the will . . ."

"Oh!" The old man shook himself out of his revery. "The will. Yes. Well, it's like this." He paused, thinking how best to phrase it. "On Madison Avenue there is a well-known antiquarian. Have you heard of him?"

The lawyer's patience was beginning to wear thin. "There are several dealers there. Which one do you mean?"

"There's only one Charles Cottner," the old man said with a knowing smile. "And you've certainly heard of him."

Jack Stone had never heard of Charles Cottner, but he preferred not to admit ignorance of this trivial fact.

"Well," the old man continued, "my cousin wrote in his will that since he knew that Mr. Dayan had connections with this shop, he would like Charles Cottner, who is regarded as an authority in archaeology, to provide a certificate that this piece is an original and send it to Mr. Dayan. In that way the two things could be done together. Don't you think so?"

"Certainly!"

"So that's why I would like you to write to Mr. Dayan about this gift and tell him that he can collect it from Charles Cottner's shop when he comes to the United States. Of course I'll have to know when Mr. Dayan is coming to America in order to make sure the item reaches the dealer in time for Mr. Dayan to get it."

Jack Stone decided to curtail the explanation, which seemed likely to take up his entire lunch hour.

"As I understand it, Mr. Miller," the lawyer said tightly, "you want my office to handle the correspondence both with Mr. Dayan and with Cottner. Cottner will certainly ask something for his services and for the certificate on the piece. Right?"

The old man's face lit up. He was pleased. "You got it right. Very good," he agreed with the lawyer. "That's just what I want."

"And how will Mr. Cottner be able to authenticate the item and issue a certificate if he doesn't see it before it reaches him and Mr. Dayan arrives to pick it up?"

"A good question." The old man looked at him shrewdly. "Here. Have a look at this."

He pulled an envelope from an inside pocket of his jacket. He opened it with a shaky hand and drew out a photograph, which he placed before the lawyer.

"You see? This is it!"

The lawyer picked up the photograph and looked in amazement. "That box is incredible. The work is exquisite. It must be worth a lot of money!"

"A fortune!" the old man agreed. "That's why I won't let it out of my hands until Mr. Dayan gets here. Now you understand? I'm not willing to take any risks."

"Will an expert be able to authenticate the box from a picture?" Jack Stone wondered.

"In this case, the answer is yes," Willy Miller explained. "Look at the other side of the photo. There's a verification statement from my cousin's family lawyer in Flint. And don't forget that my cousin's name is known to Mr. Cottner."

Jack Stone turned the photograph over and read the lines on the other side carefully. The lawyer in Flint had indeed confirmed that the object was an archaeological find from the collection of the late David Hirshkowitz.

"That should certainly be satisfactory." For his part, the matter was settled.

"You might need another photograph or two." The old man placed two copies of the photograph on the desk. "Attach the original to the letter to Mr. Dayan. One copy you'll have to send to the dealer. One you can have as a memento, if you like, Mr. Stone."

"I appreciate it," the lawyer thanked him. "All we need is your address in the event we need to notify you about anything connected with the execution of this part of the will, and also so we can let you know when Dayan will be coming to Cottner's so you can bring the box there."

"I'll have to give you two addresses," Willy Miller said, "one to my house here in Scarsdale and the other to my address in Paris. You'll have to send out two copies of every letter."

Stone rapidly jotted down the addresses and below them listed instructions to Mabel Freedman on the handling of Mr. Willy Miller's affairs.

"Everything will be taken care of, Mr. Miller," he declared.

"I appreciate that, Mr. Stone. Now"—Miller pulled out a battered leather wallet—"what do you figure the fee for your services and the certificate from the dealer will come to?"

The lawyer thought for a moment: the dealer would certainly ask two to three hundred dollars; his work and the time spent on the letters should be worth a few hundred dollars.

"I'd estimate a total of eight hundred dollars."

"What!"

Now the arguments begin, Jack Stone thought wearily. "Let me explain how I arrived at this figure."

"No! No need! That wasn't what I meant." The old man smiled. "All I meant to say was that in my day we had to work months to earn that much. Well, Mr. Stone, times have certainly changed and maybe money has lost its value. Don't you think so?" Without waiting for a reply he put a wad of hundred-dollar bills on the desk. "I don't like checks," he explained. "I've always preferred cash. You'll find a thousand dollars there."

"A thousand?"

"Mr. Stone." The lawyer caught the note of irony in the old man's voice. "I've taken up a lot of your time on a minor matter. You're a well-known lawyer. Let me express my appreciation in this way."

"But I can't take money I haven't earned."

"No, Mr. Stone," the old man insisted. "Maybe you'll need an extra couple hundred dollars? Or give them in the name of Willy Miller to the Jewish Appeal."

The lawyer gave in. "Okay."

The old man pulled himself slowly out of his chair. He stood close to the desk and held out his hand. "Thank you, Mr. Stone." Jack Stone clasped the frail hand carefully. "Once you let me know when Mr. Dayan is due at the shop, I'll see to it that the box gets there the same day."

"Rest assured, I'll take care of everything, Mr. Miller."

The lawyer accompanied his aged visitor to the door of his office and, as soon as he had gone, called Mabel Freedman in and dictated two letters. One was addressed to the office of Foreign Minister Moshe Dayan in Jerusalem, the other to Mr. Charles Cottner, owner of the antiquarian shop on Madison Avenue.

"Put this photograph with the verification from the lawyer in Flint with the letter to Mr. Dayan," he told his secretary. "The second photograph goes to Cottner."

"What about the third one?" Mabel Freedman asked.

"That one?" He smiled. "Have that one framed, Mabel. We'll keep it as a souvenir."

The old man was making his way up the street by the time Mabel Freedman was back at her desk typing the letters.

His meeting with the lawyer had been very satisfactory. He was certain that no one involved would question any transaction handled by a lawyer like Jack Stone.

In Paris, at three thirty in the afternoon, a long, thin envelope stamped in red "Secret—For the Archives," was placed on the desk of Inspector André Cordeille. The inspector found it shortly before four o'clock when he emerged from a lengthy meeting with the chief of the DST. Settling down, the little man eased into his chair, shoving himself back until he was comfortable, which left his feet inches off the floor. He picked up the envelope and slit it open with the blade of his penknife. A wave of anger flooded over him as he discovered it contained his own report of his interrogation of Adel el-Magrabi. On the margin of the report someone had instructed that it be filed in the archives, an order that showed a complete disregard for his conclusion, which had contained a request for permission to bring his findings to the attention of the Israeli Embassy in Paris.

His jaw set in silent fury, he sat motionless for a few minutes, thinking. This time he was not going to let it pass.

He picked up the envelope containing the report, folded it, and placed it in an old briefcase in which he took work home. He slipped off the chair and left his office. He decided to make his call from a public telephone in a small café in the rue Susa.

He crossed the street quickly, moving with rapid steps because of the shortness of his legs. There were only a few customers in the café. He descended the stairs leading to the lavatories. The telephone was in the passageway. He inserted a coin and dialed the number.

A girl's voice answered. "Good evening. Israeli Embassy."

"Good evening," he replied. "Monsieur Spillman, please."

"One moment, please."

He heard the trill of the internal telephone; someone lifted the receiver.

"Hello, Yaki. It's André."

"André!" It had been a long time since they had spoken. The cool official attitude of the French government toward

Israel had obliged them to call a halt to their frequent meetings. "It's good to hear your voice."

"I have to see you, Yaki," the inspector said quietly.

"Urgent?"

"Yes."

"Where?"

"The usual. The entrance to the House of the Madonna."

"When?"

Cordeille looked at his watch. "In half an hour. All right?"

"Fine."

The entrance to the House of the Madonna was a code name used by the Israeli and the Frenchman. In the past, when they had wanted to exchange information outside regular channels, they had been in the habit of meeting at the entrance to the Louvre, which housed Leonardo's famous "Mona Lisa."

When Yaki Spillman arrived, he found Inspector Cordeille waiting. They shook hands warmly.

"Good to see you, Yaki."

"It's a pity we don't manage to meet more often," the Israeli said. He looked at Cordeille's drawn face. It was evident that something was troubling him. Cordeille opened his battered briefcase and, taking the envelope from it, held it out to Spillman.

"Take this," he said. "Find yourself a quiet corner and read what's inside carefully. We'll meet here again in half an hour."

Yaki found a convenient bench, sat down, and took a newspaper from his briefcase. Opening the paper in front of him, he took the envelope from his pocket and drew out André Cordeille's report. With bated breath he read about the Egyptian attempt to kidnap Adel el-Magrabi and extract information from him on the suspected assassination plots. He read Cordeille's conclusion that the Libyans intended to kill an Israeli leader and noted that the inspector's superiors had relegated his findings to the archives.

When Yaki returned to the Louvre, André Cordeille was waiting for him. In silence, Spillman slipped the envelope into the Frenchman's hand, and Cordeille quickly slid it into his briefcase. Then they turned and began to stroll casually along the walk leading to the museum.

"Thanks, André," Spillman said.

A wry smile spread across Cordeille's face.

"I don't have to tell you how much I appreciate what you've done," Spillman went on in a low voice.

"I knew that you were aware of the affair," the inspector said.

"More than that, André," the Israeli said. "We too were trying to trap Adel el-Magrabi. But the Egyptians got to him first."

"Your good luck," Cordeille said half-jokingly, "or I would have had to receive you in my office. I doubt that in that event the matter would have ended as quietly as it did with the Egyptians and the Libyans."

"I understand," the Israeli muttered bitterly. "After all, we are not Arabs . . ."

"I'm sorry, Yaki." The inspector felt uncomfortable. "We don't decide policy. You know that."

"I know," Spillman agreed. "Unfortunately I cannot thank you officially in the name of my government. But you know that when the day comes we will know how to express our appreciation."

"Au revoir, my friend," Cordeille said, his spirits suddenly lighter than they had been for months. "Au revoir. Hopefully, the day will come when we'll be able to meet openly again." He shook Spillman's hand briefly and then was quickly lost in the crowd.

For the last few days Jim Campbell had been engaged in studying the area around Charles Cottner's shop on Madison Avenue. He had already passed the antiquarian's shop many times. Now it was time to learn in detail every corner and every intersection in the area. He had to know the getaway routes from the place once he had hit the target. The heat was fierce, but he ignored the sweat pouring off him; his mind was concentrated on memorizing dozens of facts, every one of which was important to the plan he was so meticulously formulating. Back in Scarsdale, he made notes and listed landmarks on a small pad. He learned the variations in traffic from the early morning hours to the late evening and studied the parking zone opposite the dealer's shop on Madison Avenue.

On the third day of his study, he prepared himself for a visit to the shop itself. This time he disguised himself as a young academic. With unkempt hair and a pair of thick horn-rimmed glasses on the end of his nose, he dressed in plain, faded clothes and carried a small cloth bag stuffed with newspapers and journals.

He reached the shop at noon. Inside, he evinced great interest in some jars that had been unearthed at a dig several years before on Crete. These vessels, which dated back to the Minoan civilization, were incredibly delicate, consisting of a fine, thin shell on which the drawings had been preserved almost intact. The questions he asked impressed the dealer's assistant with his knowledgeability, and he was permitted to examine closely various items that interested him.

The shop occupied three floors. The top floor contained antiquities whose monetary value was moderate. The more expensive items were located in the basement, which was protected by an electronic surveillance system and the scanning eye of hidden cameras connected to a closed-circuit television system.

Business was conducted on the ground floor, which was fully visible from the street, separated only by the large showcase windows. He examined the windows, which were made of shatterproof glass. The two swinging doors of the entrance were similarly fitted with unbreakable glass. The distance from the door to the counter was about twelve feet. A distance of six feet separated the counter from the rear wall where dark wooden shelves held ancient vessels from various periods and civilizations.

The young man spent about a quarter of an hour inside the shop, long enough to study the area but not so long as to cause suspicion. This was to be his only trip to the place before his final visit. He thanked the dealer's assistant for his help and information, and left.

He returned in the afternoon and studied the parking zone on the opposite side of the street. The distance from the zone to the shop was about sixty feet. His next problem was to find a way to be assured of a parking place. It was important since the car was to be his base of operations.

It was only rarely that parking places became vacant in the area. The local businessmen usually left their cars by the parking meters. Every hour they would send out an employee to put a quarter in the meter. Clearly, if he wanted to park in the zone opposite the shop he would have to arrive early in the morning.

He spent Friday on extensive trips to various gun shops, examining different weapons. He had a specific weapon in mind.

A salesman in one of the stores tried to joke with him. "It sounds like you're looking for a weapon against elephants, not a regular rifle; you want a gun that will blow open an elephant's head with one shot."

"You know," Campbell replied, "I think you're right. Let's say I was planning a safari in Africa. And let's say that I wanted to hunt elephant. What do you think would be the most effective gun? One that would really smash their skulls?"

"There must be an answer to that question somewhere," the salesman observed.

"Can you find me the answer?"

"Well, I can try."

The salesman opened a drawer under the counter and took out some catalogues. He paged through them for several minutes and after some time spotted what he was looking for.

"Here's the one you need!"

He put the catalogue on the counter and pointed to a new model of a hunting gun. The explanation caught the young man's attention: "This suction action gun will stop an elephant and penetrate a tank." The young man picked up the catalogue. The weapon was a Mossberg model ATP 500-6. The bore of its wide barrel, which was about fifty centimeters long, was twelve millimeters. The magazines of the semiautomatic rifle contained six rounds. The explanatory notes said that the rifle was also effective for riot control, and for this purpose, it fired cartridges containing tear gas. The recommended range was between sixty-five and one hundred feet. The special steel coating of the bullet that projected out of the cardboard wrapping was capable of blasting concrete.

"What do you think?" the salesman asked.

"An interesting rifle."

"Listen," the salesman said, "I'm a specialist on guns. This is something extraordinary."

"Can I see it?"

"I'm sorry, sir," the salesman apologized, "but we don't usually keep guns like that in stock. There isn't much demand . . ."

"Why not?"

"You can see what it's recommended for," the man explained. "Only a few people can find any justification for spending such a large sum of money on it. Then there's an additional problem . . ."

"A problem?"

The salesman smiled. "You need a special license for that gun because of its multiple uses."

"I see."

He looked at the photograph again and at the drawings of its different parts. The rifle solved the problem that had been troubling him.

"Where can I see a rifle like this?" he persisted.

The salesman shrugged. "I don't know," he replied.

The man took out his wallet and withdrew a fifty-dollar bill which he placed before the salesman, who looked at it and said politely, "But I'll try to find out, sir."

He picked up the bill and slipped it into his pocket, then looked through the store's directory and dialed the company that supplied the Mossberg rifles. He talked for a minute with someone on the staff of the main office in Manhattan, then thanked him and replaced the receiver.

"Well?" the customer asked.

"You'll have to go to the agent's warehouse in New Jersey," the salesman said, writing out the address on a piece of paper which he handed over. "And, by the way, as far as I know, they also have a shooting gallery there for testing the weapons, so they'll be able to show you the gun in operation."

"Thank you very much." The man folded the paper carefully and put it in his shirt pocket. "I hope that with this rifle I'll get my elephant."

The salesman smiled. "Good luck, sir," he said. "And if you ever need my services, you can always find me here."

Campbell reached the large warehouse in New Jersey in about an hour and a half. It was located in a commercial and industrial area. The information he had received in Manhattan was accurate. The marketing manager confirmed that they had Mossberg 500 rifles in stock.

"These are excellent guns," he said confidently. "You can't find any better than these for a real safari." He picked up the rifle and held it out. "See how easy it is to carry. Its suction action reduces the kick to a minimum and increases the power of the shot. Its bullets are tremendously powerful. If you ask me, that's what you want!"

"Can I test it out?" the young man asked.

"You really interested?"

"Yes," he replied. "I'm opening an arms store in Boston. I want to sell special models."

"In that case, you can have a private demonstration." The salesman took a box of bullets off one of the shelves. "Jerry!" he called to one of his helpers. "Take the gentleman to the shooting gallery. He wants to check the Mossberg in action."

Jerry was a tall young man with terrible acne. His face was covered with suppurating lesions. He gripped the rifle and picked up the box of cartridges, then began walking, pointing with the rifle to one side of the upper floor of the large warehouse. The customer walked behind him until they reached a pair of large metal doors. Jerry pushed the right-hand door open with his shoulder. It swung on creaking hinges, and the young man followed him.

"Hold this," Jerry said, handing over the rifle and the box of cartridges. With his free hands, he locked the heavy doors, then took up the rifle and the bullets again. They went down a wooden staircase into a large hall that was illuminated with long strips of neon lighting. The shooting stands were about six feet from the wall against which they stood and the targets were set eighty feet away.

"I'll show you first," Jerry said. He chewed gum relentlessly, his mouth twisting rhythmically. "It's got two strong points. In spite of the extra power, it has hardly any recoil, and it keeps its range of accuracy."

Jerry handled the gun expertly. His grip and the steadiness of his legs placed slightly apart revealed a wealth of experience in handling firearms. He demonstrated the rifle twice—the first time for single shots, which he did with the magazine empty.

"If you know how to use this gun," Jerry explained to the customer, who stood watching him in silence, "you can fire it easily from different positions, including some that you can't manage with a regular rifle. For example, firing from the hip. The recoil is very slight and the deflection in this position is almost nil. Wait till you see the results with bullets."

He put the rifle on the long counter that stretched the length of the firing positions. Then he turned and walked to the far end of the gallery, where he placed a wooden board in front of the regular target. On the base of the board, which projected out like a tongue, he placed two heavy sandbags. Then he returned to the shooting stand.

"That board is an inch thick," Jerry explained as he loaded the magazine. "Now watch what happens."

The result was impressive. The special bullet, which came out of a thick cardboard shell and looked like a miniature rocket, pierced the wooden board as though it were thin paper.

"Of course, when this gun is used for riot control," Jerry explained as he handed the rifle to Campbell to examine, "you use different bullets. When the bullet fires and hits the target, a container of tear gas is discharged."

Jim Campbell examined the weapon carefully. It was an easy gun to carry and hold. With a gentle movement, he swung the gun and aimed it at the wooden board. His finger squeezed the double-action trigger lightly, almost lovingly.

First he fired a single bullet along the firing lane. The rifle responded perfectly to his pressure. Its designers had obviously given its construction some thought. A few seconds later he squeezed the trigger twice. One shot came after the other, with a fraction of a second between each. The echo of the double shot sounded like a strangled blast, like a cork bursting from a bottle.

"Hey, man!" Jerry was amazed. "You're no stranger to these toys, huh?"

Campbell smiled and lowered the rifle. It was the weapon he wanted.

"How d'you like it?" Jerry asked.

"A great gun," Campbell replied and pulled a fifty-dollar bill from his wallet. "There's enough here for the bullets we used. The rest is for you."

"Say, thanks." Jerry was impressed. "But you sound as if you aren't buying. Why not, man?"

"Jerry"—Campbell patted the young man's shoulder—"I don't have time to handle the papers for the license. Another time maybe."

As he turned to leave, Jerry's voice caught him at the door. "You know, it's an expensive rifle."

"I know, Jerry."

The young man seemed to hesitate. "You don't like paperwork, huh?"

"No."

"You willing to pay a little more?"

"Depends how much."

"You need shells too, don't you?" Jerry looked at him sharply.

"Yes. But not the regular. For riot control."

"How many?"

"A dozen. A few more, maybe."

"Listen." Jerry came up to him. "The gun and a box of twenty-four special bullets for a grand. Okay?"

"That's a lot of money." He seemed to think for a moment. "But you know that, Jerry. Okay. You and I have a little deal going. How will you set it up?"

Jerry smiled broadly. His eyes gleamed. "No problem, man," he said. "No one will notice that one is missing."

"How will I get it?"

"No problem." Jerry stroked the rifle. "Three times a week, I guard here at night, huh? Tonight it's my turn. Say you come at eleven?"

Campbell looked searchingly at Jerry's face and suddenly understood when he saw the young man's pupils: Jerry was an addict.

"You need money?"

Jerry did not answer, he just continued to smile.

"Okay. It's none of my business how you use your money. I'll be here at eleven."

"Come from the other end of the street," Jerry said in a low voice. "There's another door there that leads to this gallery. It'll be open. Just push. I'll be waiting for you here."

As he was leaving, Campbell stopped to talk to the sales manager. He said he was impressed with the gun and remarked that he would be back again in the very near future.

By Friday, August 5th, the picture was clear. The report from Paris, based on information delivered by Inspector André Cordeille, was confirmed by the Egyptians as well. Through the Americans, Egyptian intelligence had informed their Israeli counterparts that Libya was indeed plotting the assassination of a high-level Israeli leader.

At noon on Friday, a code letter from Hamid Mashawi, the Libyan intelligence agent who was also known as Hanania Siani, was received at the headquarters of the security service, by way of Amman. Avital showed the letter to Uri, who read it with barely controlled excitement.

"Just as I thought," he said, after he had finished reading.

"Yes, you were right," Avital agreed. "The Libyans' target is Moshe Dayan."

At two o'clock that afternoon, the senior staff of the various departments and sections were gathered together to be briefed by Avital Arnon and Uri Cohen on the plot to kill Dayan. The plan of action was outlined.

"We will need to establish a special headquarters," Avital stressed, "a headquarters divided into three sections: protection of the target in Israel, protection of the target in Europe, and protection of the target in the United States. These three sections will be responsible to the chief of the surveillance branch."

The men shifted their gaze from Avital to Uri Cohen.

"I want to stress," Avital went on, "that this time we

shall operate on a system of double-checks. One network will deal with the sifting of every crumb of information. The second network will check the activities of the first network and all the information that it collects. It is our assumption that the killer will make a mistake at some point. Our job is to catch his error in time.

"At present, we are engaged in a search for a private vessel which we know is somewhere in the Mediterranean. The ship underwent certain modifications in Genoa and then sailed in our direction. The owner of the ship, we believe, can assist us in uncovering the identity of the killer."

When the meeting had concluded and everyone had left, Uri Cohen slid back the screens that covered the maps hanging on the wall. The first was the map he wanted. It covered the Middle East and the Mediterranean Sea. The last report on the ship had come in from Genoa. The *Paedaeia* had changed color. The yacht had berthed only one day in the Italian port and had then set sail for Greece. She had been repainted gray. And her name had been changed: now she was called the *Massina*. It had been a psychological mistake on the part of the Italian not to discard a name similar to his family's, Massino. It appeared that Boncho still did not know exactly who was trying to catch him, but from the changes he had made on his ship, it was clear that he was afraid.

Uri Cohen looked at the map. The Italian would be able to find refuge in the Greek islands for only a short period. Information on him had been widely transmitted. His whereabouts would be known in several days, and then perhaps things would change.

The man called Jim Campbell returned to New Jersey that night. A few minutes before eleven, the time he was to meet Jerry, he drove through the deserted neighborhood. It was an area of warehouses, garages, and factories. Since there was no reason for anyone to be there at night, the police patrol car seldom made the rounds.

Campbell stopped his car, waited three minutes, and, at eleven o'clock exactly, got out of the car and locked it. He walked slowly, his keen eyes taking in the deserted surroundings. The night invested them with an atmosphere of menace. He turned a corner and found the iron door in the building which Jerry had described to him. He grasped the handle and slowly pushed the door open. The hinges creaked a little as the door swung inward, and he stepped quickly inside, closing the door behind him. He descended a staircase illuminated by the dim rays of a weak bulb that hung in the center of the sloping ceiling. When he reached the door to the shooting gallery, he found that it too had been left unlocked. The neon strip lighting shone at the far end where the firing positions were. Jerry was standing there, leaning against the long counter, on which lay a well-wrapped package.

"Hey, man." Jerry straightened up. "You're right on time."

"Always."

"Close the door behind you."

Campbell did as he was told and moved toward Jerry.

"Everything taken care of?" he asked.

"When Jerry does something, then it's taken care of." The young man patted the package. "You got here the big uncle and twenty-four kids. Enough, huh?"

"A whole family. Show me."

Jerry was surprised. "Don't trust me, huh? You one of the suspicious ones?"

"Let's have a look," Campbell said in a low voice.

Jerry smiled. He stuck a fresh piece of gum into his mouth and untied the knots of the cord around the package. Campbell examined the rifle and the box of shells.

"Just like you said, Jerry. Tie them up again."

Jerry grinned and began to wrap the package. The man took out his wallet, which was stuffed with bills, and carefully counted ten bills of a hundred dollars each. He held them out to Jerry. "Count them. A thousand exactly."

The young man with the scarred face held out his hand and took the notes.

"I'm sure it's okay." The grin never left his face. His jaws worked ceaselessly on the chewing gum. "Hey, man. You don't need the big uncle for elephants, right?" He wiped the smile off his face and put the bills into the hip pocket of his trousers. "You're not out for that. You're going to hunt something else, right?" He seemed oblivious of the tigerlike eyes on him.

"Jerry." His voice was soft, almost friendly. "After this pleasant meeting of ours, better forget each other. When I get the elephant, I'll send you a photograph of it. Would you like that, kid?"

The hint of a threat did not deter the young man. He spat the gum out of his mouth. "In color, huh?"

"You have a sense of humor, Jerry," the man remarked. "That's useful when you're standing on two healthy legs. Better keep them that way."

The gleam that flashed in the strange eyes of the man did not frighten Jerry. He remained standing calmly where he was, his hand stroking the package.

"Hey, that's good. A sense of humor!" He laughed. "But I want more photographs."

"What of, Jerry?"

"Of greenbacks. What do you say?"

"What I say doesn't count." The man smiled suddenly. "It's what you say that counts. How much would you want, for example, for your green collection?"

Jerry liked that answer. "Listen," he said. "I could tell that I could do business with you."

"How much?"

"What do you say to another two grand, huh?"

The man stiffened. The sum the young man had requested suddenly clarified everything. His cockiness could only be explained by the fact that someone else was in on this with him as a partner. Someone who at that very moment might be nearby, covering the kid with the scarred face. If he had asked for a little extra, it could have been a private last-minute venture, but the large sum meant he had a hidden partner.

"How do you calculate the extra, Jerry?" He kept his voice level while he strained to hear any suspicious sound.

"Simple, man." Jerry felt at ease. "Another grand for me and a grand for my brother."

"You have a brother?" His eyebrows rose questioningly.

"Not a brother exactly," Jerry grinned. "But like a brother."

Campbell caught the sound of footsteps behind him.

"I imagine that he's coming to collect his share?" he asked almost inaudibly.

"Man," Jerry pointed behind him, "he doesn't have to come. He's already here."

Campbell turned slowly. Twenty feet from him, a hulk of a man appeared. He was about twenty-eight, perhaps thirty, of Latin origin. His face was misshapen and marked, as though it had taken many blows. It was the face of a professional boxer who had always lost in the ring. His short neck rose from massive shoulders that seemed about to rip his short-sleeved shirt. The upper half of his body was enormous, but his muscular legs were short. He smiled, revealing two front teeth blackened with decay.

"I'm his brother," he said in a rasping voice.

"A nice family," Campbell said. "Brothers from a different mother or father, eh?"

The harsh features on the man's flat face twisted. He had not liked that remark. He took a step forward, then another, until he was standing opposite Campbell, towering over him by a head.

"Wipe your face on your ass!" he shouted. His eyes were bloodshot. "You can scream as much as you like. No one'll hear your fucking screams when I break your neck!"

Jerry was scared. He had not wanted things to get violent. He hurried over to the two men.

"Listen, hunter," he said to Campbell. "It's not worth messing with Speedy. Pay and get out. Otherwise, Speedy'll give you a new face, or the pigs might want to know what someone like you wants with a nice Mossberg. Huh?"

They were both right—Speedy when he said that no one would hear shouts coming from the soundproof room; Jerry when he said that the police would be glad to lay hands on someone trying to get hold of a Mossberg illegally.

"Okay," he submitted. "You'll both get what's coming to you."

He moved like greased lightning.

His actions were well thought out. He dealt with Speedy first. His knee jerked up and smashed into the huge man's balls. Then the pointed toe of his shoe shot out and struck a blow at Speedy's kneecap; he completed the movement by bringing the sole of his shoe down hard on the boxer's toes.

The three hammerlike blows, dealt one after another, with precision and no warning, elicited a noiseless scream from Speedy's throat. At the very moment that he doubled up in agonizing pain, his face met a pistonlike fist. The blow shattered the bones of his face, which turned into a fleshy pulp, oozing blood. He lost consciousness even before his heavy body slumped to the wooden floor.

Jerry had not moved. His limbs felt paralyzed. His eyes widened until the pupils seemed ready to burst out of their sockets.

"Hey, man," he whispered in a terrified voice. "We were only kidding."

Campbell smiled. "I know, Jerry," he said. "But you should know that I never kid."

Jerry tried to call out. The scream materialized in the depths of his chest, rose to his throat, and froze there. The chop from the man's palm, flat as an axe head, struck his neck and broke several vertebrae. He sank to the ground, his eyes wide, white froth bubbling at the corners of his mouth. A second blow smashed into his throat. Blood welled up out of his open mouth as he choked to death.

Campbell turned to Speedy, who lay writhing on the floor, and drove the toecap of his shoe into his temple. It was the coup de grace. The heavy body rolled over. The legs continued to twitch for some seconds before they stretched out still; a last grunt sounded as the heart stopped.

The man drew a deep breath. His pulse was slightly more rapid than usual. He picked up the package containing the rifle and the bullets from the counter and left the same way he had entered.

August has been a turbulent month in the Mediterranean since the beginning of time. The sea is changeable throughout the month. Sudden, unpredictable storms descend upon it with no prior warning. The fury rages for a few days, until the storm blows itself out and disappears. Then calm reigns once more. The sea takes on its blue and green colors again; its movement is steady and its swell regular. Suddenly a new storm erupts out of nowhere and sends the rollers crashing down from the horizon, while the howling wind beats the waves into frothy whirlpools.

There is no way of foretelling the capricious moods of the Mediterranean. Its nature is at one with the people who populate its shores—difficult to predict. The sun here is almost painfully bright. The azure sky, pure at the center, turns yellow toward the rim. The blues and greens of the sea are bold and strong. In the distance white-capped waves dance lightly or are driven by the winds of a gathering storm.

The *Massina* was a proud and sturdy craft with a structure suited for long voyages on the Mediterranean. Although her low lines did not allow her to contend with storms in the Atlantic, the rough seas of the Mediterranean were not capable of causing her harm.

The Italian handled her well. While he seldom sailed out of the comfortable harbor of Monte Carlo, sea-going was not an alien occupation for him. Vittorio Angelo Massino was an experienced sailor. He enjoyed short voyages, generally for the amusement of his guests, but he never liked spending many days at sea, especially not when the trip was without aim or purpose.

It was fear that drove him now; cold fear of the unknown. He did not know who it was that had taken such an interest in him, but his intuition told him that whoever it was, dogging his steps, was connected in some way with the man whom he now called Phoenix. At this point, what he wanted was time. He had to gain time. Days. Perhaps weeks. In the meantime, things could change. Perhaps Phoenix would complete his mission and the hunt would end. Perhaps Phoenix would fail—he couldn't quite imagine this, but it was still a possibility. That too would mean the end of the chase. Maybe not. Perhaps he would be caught in some narrow trap that awaited him God knows where. He had no idea of the identity of his pursuers, but they apparently knew all they needed to know about him.

For the last few days he had been sailing around the Greek islands. The sea there was perfectly calm. The last of the storms had been left behind as he sailed among the small islands that basked in the sun like grooved shells.

His crew was perplexed. Ostensibly they were on a holiday cruise, but the Italian's behavior was far from relaxed. His good humor had vanished and he was given to outbursts of violent swearing at them. His raw nerves cast a pall over the small craft, and the men moved like shadows to avoid his wrath.

The Italian had gone into seclusion. He held his tongue and kept his secrets to himself. His various occupations had made him cautious and distant toward those with whom he had no reason to exchange words. Although he was possessed of great vitality and charm, he was always careful not to reveal too much of himself to anyone. Lately, however, his longing for a sympathetic ear had increased, but, being subject to pursuit, he knew that talk could bring his ruin. Therefore, even when the ship dropped anchor and the crew went ashore in shifts to amuse themselves for a few hours, he elected to stay aboard, waiting for his men to return so that he could cast off on the next lap of this strange, aimless voyage.

If the days were long, the nights were even longer. The Italian was accustomed to sharing his bed with the beautiful women who crowded the beaches of Monte Carlo. Now his nights were lonely, with long hours for reflection and moments of fear that came out in bursts of cold fury. Occasionally his heart palpitated and his pulse accelerated to almost twice its normal rate.

Times without number his thoughts turned to the murderer with whom his life was bound up. From the moment they had started working together, something had told him that the day would come when he would have to pay the full price. A reckoning would be due for the fine profits he had made on his supply of contracts to Phoenix. At times in the past, he had reflected that the young man himself might someday harm him. Perhaps when he came to the conclusion that he, Boncho, was unnecessary or dangerous because he knew too much about his true identity. He had never imagined that strangers would seek him out because of his connections with the young man. But it had apparently happened. He was trapped with no escape.

For hours he lay stretched out on a canvas deckchair letting the rays of the burning sun sear his lined face. The sweat flowed and a thousand unanswered and unanswerable questions filled his mind. He wondered who the murderer's target was. Who the victim would be. Clearly this time it was different from anything in the past. Some project whose ramifications went beyond the measure of his experience, possibly involving forces vaster than anything he had encountered in the past.

At times he found himself cursing Pierre de Maline for not having troubled to give him any hint of what the affair was about, even though, at the time, he had not wanted to know. Then he would feel sorry, and be overcome with remorse at having damned his dead comrade. It was possible that Pierre de Maline had not known what the matter involved. He was to blame, not de Maline. He should have been suspicious when such huge sums of money were paid for the services of one man. If he had sized up the situation correctly, he might not have gotten involved.

He continued to torment himself. Perhaps he should have found out more about the murderer. But he had adhered to his golden rule, to know only what he had to know and nothing more, never to go beyond that boundary. Now he was torn by doubts. Over the years he had garnered certain details about the killer, but even to him the strange man still remained an enigma. In his lifetime he had known many hard and dangerous men. He himself had been one of them once. But none of them was in any way like the killer who now called himself Phoenix.

He remained for hours at a time staring at the coast of the islands opposite him, his arms resting on the polished wood rail. At such moments, he felt like one whose brain had stopped functioning as an independent unit, his entire being focused on the scene before him. He watched his shadow dancing on the rippling surface of the sea, a shadow devoid of substance, containing nothing but a gnawing fear.

Sailing around the islands was merely a postponement of the end. He was certain that sooner or later he would have to pit himself against the strangers who sought him out. Today. Tomorrow. Perhaps the day after tomorrow.

On Sunday morning, he heard a tap at the door of his cabin. He straightened up, his hand in his pocket where he kept a loaded Beretta.

"Who is it?" he asked.

"Dennis, sir."

The tension eased. "Come in."

A quiet Dutchman, Dennis was a first-class professional of forty-five who served as the ship's engineer and was responsible for purchasing equipment. He was short and slim, his reddish face covered with rust-colored freckles.

"We're having some engine trouble, sir," Dennis explained in a quiet voice. "I think that one of the pistons is faulty."

"What do you suggest?"

"Repair it immediately," the Dutchman said. "If we put it off, the job will be just that much more difficult."

"Where can it be done?" the Italian asked.

"In Piraeus. It's the nearest port from here. There are mechanics there."

"How long will it take?"

The Dutchman shrugged, having no exact answer. "Maybe half a day, maybe more. It depends if they find more problems."

"There's no other alternative?"

"No, sir."

He wanted to shout, to swear, but then he weighed the situation rationally. The engine had to be in first-class condition. With some luck, he could get out of Piraeus in a few hours. He disliked big harbors. Someone might be waiting for him there. He was not convinced that repainting the yacht and changing her name had prevented her from being identified, but he had no alternative.

"All right, Dennis," he said at last.

The following morning, the purple dawn revealed a sea stretched taut as skin with tiny waves running before the soft, cool breeze as the night passed into a new day. A few hours later, the *Massina* reached the port of Piraeus and by seven o'clock the yacht had slipped alongside the quay and was tied up. The Dutchman went ashore immediately to get a new part for the piston and find a local mechanic who could help him. He returned about an hour and a half later, accompanied by a burly Greek.

Boncho went on deck when the two mechanics began work. Before him lay the colorful Piraeus dockside. Cargo ships and tankers, some of them berthed near the quays, some anchored farther out, stood prominently among a variety of smaller vessels that were tied up along the docks in the port area. In among the working boats, pleasure craft rode at anchor. The *Massina,* whose luxurious surface had been carefully stripped and camouflaged in Genoa, sat anonymously among these ships. Only an experienced sailor could pick out the lines that marked her as a luxury vessel.

Stevedores, fork-lift operators, and port officials mingled with the fishermen and sailors, and their cries and shouts blended with the noise of the ships' horns on vessels sailing out to sea or others announcing their entry into the harbor. The heat of the day increased, burning off the morning chill.

The Dutchman came on deck and reported to Boncho that the job would take at least until the early afternoon. Since they had to remain berthed until the work was done, the Italian decided to go ashore. He longed to feel the dry land under his feet after so many days aboard ship.

He climbed down the rope ladder hanging against the side of the vessel and jumped lightly onto the thick, heavy wood planks of the quay. First he stood and breathed in the peculiar smell of the port. The same smell had reached his nostrils on the deck, but here it had a slightly different quality. He felt good, released from pressure. First he strolled slowly, looking around him. Even if he had wanted to, he doubted that he would be able to spot a stranger following him. He shook off his concerns and began to walk with a spring in his step toward a café by the port gates.

Zevik Brill was the second officer of the Israeli cargo ship *Tapuz,* which was anchored about 600 feet from the main quay. The small cargo vessel was on the last leg of a voyage that had lasted seven weeks, carrying mixed cargo to United States ports and picking up others there. On her way to her home port, Haifa, she had to make several calls in the Mediterranean to unload cargo and take on others intended for Israeli markets.

Piraeus was the last port of call on her voyage. The crew was returning to the ship, which had lain for a day and a half off the Greek coast. At one o'clock in the afternoon the ship was due to weigh anchor and sail back to Israel.

Outwardly, the short, thin officer with the tanned skin and black hair looked no different from any local sailor as he walked along the quay toward the motorboat that was waiting to take him out to the *Tapuz*. Had he not remembered the cable that they had received two weeks before while at sea, he might never have stopped in his tracks, as though struck by thunder. The skipper, Yigal Simkin, had called the ship's officers to his cabin and had read a message that had arrived from the Zim shipping offices. The cable had contained the description of a boat that the security services urgently wished to trace. The description, which had been given in general terms, had emphasized the low lines of the vessel's gunwales and the dark brown mahogany of the wheelhouse. The craft was named the *Paedaeia*.

True, the ship tied up before him differed in name and color, but two important details were identical to the description given in the cable. The gunwales were low and the wheelhouse was built of dark brown, highly polished mahogany.

Zevik Brill pulled a pack of cigarettes from his pocket. He took one out and stuck it in the corner of his mouth. When he tried to strike a match, he had to cover it with his hand, turning his head in the direction of the ship. A slight breeze prevented him from lighting the cigarette. He tried again, until he succeeded. This gave him an opportunity to study the ship and commit her name to memory—the *Massina*. Zevik Brill slowly blew out a stream of smoke. The resemblance between this vessel and the one described in the cable was amazing. Of course, he might be wrong, but either way, he would report this ship to the captain the moment he got aboard the *Tapuz*.

As soon as he arrived on deck, the second officer hurried to the captain's cabin. Yigal Simkin, a young man of thirty-three, with a slight protruding paunch that contrasted to his thin, youthful face, listened with great interest to Zevik Brill.

"The similarity is striking," the second officer stressed, "although the colors and the name are different. Maybe we've received more details meanwhile?"

"No," the captain said, "we haven't had anything more. But they might have changed the name of the ship and the color. That's possible. It's a ship on the run. Maybe they don't know this at home. Let's check right away."

The communications officer of the *Tapuz* was told to contact the company offices and transmit a description of the suspect ship to Haifa. At the same time, the captain told Brill to keep a constant watch on the vessel and to report regularly what was taking place on her decks. The message to the company offices went out at nine thirty. The reply came in at eleven fifteen, and Captain Simkin called the ship's officers to his cabin immediately.

"Gentlemen," he said after they had entered, "we are delaying our exit from this port. We have had new orders from Haifa. The ship sought by the security services, the *Paedaeia,* is berthed here in Piraeus under the name *Massina.* It looks as though we will have to hold the fort until the security people can get here. According to the cable, they should be taking off from Ben Gurion Airport at this very moment, which means they'll be here in two hours' time."

It was nine in the morning at Kennedy Airport. The young man was dressed in a light suit and carried a new suitcase. His plane was due to take off in an hour. He leaned against one of the public telephone booths opposite the Air France departure lounge, waiting to call the Libyan Embassy in Washington. By now, the procedure was familiar—first, the voice of the telephone operator, then the respectful voice of the Libyan, Jarbil. "Jarbil speaking."

"You haven't heard my voice for quite some time," the man said dryly.

The Libyan recognized the voice of Phoenix immediately. "No, sir . . ."

"Let's not waste time, Jarbil. Just listen."

"Yes, sir."

"Start working. On a certain day at the beginning of September, the Israeli is arriving here. Your communications people in the Foreign Office should know within a week the exact date of his arrival. Clear?"

"Clear."

"That's all I want to know at this point," Phoenix emphasized. "The day he's due to arrive."

The Libyan breathed so noisily into the receiver that the stranger removed it from his ear for a moment.

"All right. When will you be in touch?"

"In one week. Prepare the material: the day he is to leave and the day he is to arrive. And do not force me to use expressions I dislike, such as 'move your fat ass.' Eh, Jarbil?"

"There will be no need, sir."

"Well, that's good, Jarbil. You learn fast."

The moment the call had been cut off by Phoenix in his usual abrupt way, the Libyan dictated a coded message for Adam Ahmed. His instructions were to report any communications, with details of the conversation and any follow-up action he had to take.

In spite of the loss of Madame Charlotte, who was still under arrest, Adam Ahmed was convinced that the operation would succeed. From the reports he had received from the embassy in Washington, it seemed clear that Phoenix had decided to do the job in America, whereas the report that came in from the embassies in Paris and Brussels convinced him that Gibskopf was moving into high gear and intended to make his strike in one of the European countries which the Israeli Foreign Minister was scheduled to visit several weeks hence.

Recently he had been permitted to augment his staff at the special headquarters. He selected eight men from the branch, each of whom had some knowledge of the State of Israel. One of them was Hamid Mashawi, who was an expert in analyzing information published in the Israeli press. Adam Ahmed hoped he could clarify news on the expected travels of Moshe Dayan as well as any items hinting at the continuation of the secret negotiations between Israel and Egypt.

Ahmed had observed a number of vulnerable areas in the Israeli press. The newspapers often reported specific details of important events that were about to take place. Moreover, the press published various rumors, many of which, it transpired, were facts, but their publication as rumor was made in order to evade the security censor's scissors.

Hamid Mashawi had turned out to be effective in his new task. He was helpful and pleasant, and, in a matter of days, had become an integral part of the special team, as if he had been working with its members for many months.

Mashawi was willing to work long hours, day and night. He asked only that the work be interesting. As time went on, his counsel and advice were sought, and doors began to open to the Palestinian. Adam Ahmed made a mental note that when the day came, he would remember the Palestinian and give a concrete expression of his appreciation.

Avshalom Kedmi and Yirmi Spector reached the Israeli cargo ship *Tapuz* at one fifteen in the afternoon.

As soon as they boarded the ship, the first officer came forward to greet them and introduced them to Zevik Brill, the second officer, who had spotted the yacht *Massina*. Brill pointed the vessel out to them and the two men studied her through binoculars. "It looks like the *Paedaeia* all right," said Avshalom with satisfaction. He turned to the first officer: "I need to speak to the captain at once." Time was essential. At any moment the yacht might weigh anchor and sail out to sea, and there were still details to take care of. Leaving Brill above-decks to keep an eye on the *Massina,* Avshalom and Yirmi followed the first officer to the captain's cabin. Captain Yigal Simkin was ready for them.

"We have the uniforms. And a first-rate boat, fast and powerful, with two strong searchlights. Plus two Uzis and a few revolvers."

"We'll need two navigators and two additional seamen. Four of your men altogether. Oh, one more request. It would help if one of the men you're giving us knew some Greek."

"No problem," said Captain Simkin. "You can take Dario; he's fluent."

By the time the sun was beginning to set, the team on the *Tapuz* was ready to move.

* * *

It was nightfall when the repair on the *Massina*'s engine was completed. Disturbed that Boncho had not yet returned, Dennis went ashore looking for him. He strolled along the streets, entering bars, cafés, and nightclubs, scanning those present to see if Boncho was among them. Finally he found him, stretched out across a table in a nightclub, his head resting on his arm in a drunken stupor. Dennis had to shake him to waken him.

"It's you," Boncho mumbled, his voice hoarse, his tongue thick.

Dennis bent over him. "Sir, the ship is ready. We can sail." He took hold of the Italian's shoulder. "Come on. Let's go."

Boncho was bone weary. "Go where?" he said with a bitter laugh. He tried to rise and would have stumbled and fallen were it not for the quick hand of Dennis, who gripped his arm. Boncho steadied himself and began walking carefully toward the exit. He stopped outside the door and, turning to Dennis, said, "You don't know who they are, do you?"

"Who do you mean, sir?"

"Never mind, never mind. Don't worry. We'll outwit them."

A short distance from the port gates, the Italian doubled over and began to vomit. When he finally straightened up, his face was pale and bathed in a cold sweat.

"That helped," he said in a whisper. "Now I feel better." In all the years Dennis had worked for Boncho, he had never seen him like this. When they reached the *Massina*, the Italian managed to climb to the deck unaided. "Cast off," he muttered. "I'm going below."

Dennis gave the orders immediately, and at ten o'clock the yacht began to move toward the harbor entrance. The large orange moon flooded the smooth surface of the sea with pale light. The sounds from shore faded until only the regular pulsations of the engine and the rush of the water as it fell away from the bow could be heard. As soon as they left the anchorage of the large ships beyond the harbor, Dennis fixed their course for Rhodes. If the Italian decided to change direction, he would do it himself, in a few hours' time when he had shaken off the effects of his binge.

Dennis took the first watch himself. He preferred the night to the day watch, for at night he was freer to let his imagination take wing. His revery was interrupted by Atar, the cook, who came up to the wheelhouse, bringing a can of cold beer.

"Nice night," Atar observed. "Where to this time, Dennis?"

"Rhodes. Ever been there?"

"No." The cook paused a moment, then decided to share his thoughts. "Listen. This is a crazy trip. We're passing nearly every port. Maybe we'll reach one of the harbors of Israel. I've never been there . . ."

"You're a Jew, aren't you?"

"Yes," Atar admitted. He smiled shyly. "You know, Dennis, I even have family there. I can hardly remember them. They fled Morocco to Israel. My father took us to Marseilles."

"Who knows," Dennis answered. He took a long drink from the can of beer. "Maybe we'll even get there. You could look for your relatives."

They fell silent, lulled by the quiet murmur of the sea and the distance. He took a cigarette from a packet of Gauloises lying on the compass chart. Atar flicked his lighter and held the small flame to the tip of Dennis's cigarette.

"Do you see what I see?" he asked the Dutchman.

"That ship?"

"Yes," replied Atar. He sounded anxious. "She's been running parallel to us for a long time."

They looked hard at the dark outline of the ship. It sailed at a speed identical to that of the *Massina*. A distance of about seven hundred feet separated the two craft.

"Have a look and see what's going on there," Dennis said.

The cook took the binoculars that hung on the bulkhead, focused the lenses and trained the glasses on the strange boat. With a slow gesture he lowered the binoculars.

"It's hard to see anything too clearly, but it looks like there are men in white uniforms."

"It could be a Greek coast guard ship," the Dutchman said. "Anyway, go down and tell the boss."

Boncho came on deck cursing. "For God's sake!" he shouted from the deck before he had even started climbing to the wheelhouse. "Can't you handle it yourself?"

"Sir." Dennis pointed to the strange ship. "She's been with us too long."

Boncho lit a cigarette. He blew out a cloud of smoke and looked for some minutes at the ship, which continued to follow a course parallel to his own. The Dutchman was right. She was sticking to them.

"Close in on her," the Italian ordered. "When you get to within a hundred feet, I'll switch on the searchlight. We'll have a look at her from close up."

His voice was controlled now. He tried to suppress the fear that had again come over him. The drunken stupor had vanished, and he was once more caught in a web of doubts that generated a nagging fear. In five minutes the distance between the two vessels had narrowed. Boncho turned the searchlight toward the strange ship and pushed the switch.

The harsh ray of light shot out for a thousandth of a second and hit the upper deck of the unknown ship. Boncho caught a glimpse of men in white uniforms just as two beams of powerful light from above the command cabin of the ship turned on him, swallowing the ray of light from his own boat and dazzling him with their brightness.

"Heave to for coast guard inspection!"

The Greek words called out through a megaphone came across to them clearly, but apparently the speaker thought that the crew did not understand Greek since he repeated the order in English, with a foreign accent.

"What shall we do, sir?" Dennis asked.

"What can we do?" the Italian fumed. "They have the right."

"We left Greek waters a few minutes ago," Dennis persisted. "We don't have to stop."

"What do you propose we do?" the Italian jeered. "Let them fire on you and then ask for explanations? Slow down!"

Dennis obeyed, and a short time afterward the two vessels reduced speed, the distance between them now some fifty feet. The man with the megaphone called out once more. "We are coming aboard for inspection!"

It was evident that the captain of the Greek vessel knew what he was about. He maneuvered his craft expertly alongside the Italian's ship until he was three feet from it. At that moment, four men in sparkling white uniforms leaped from the boat. Two had submachine guns slung over their shoulders. The other two had revolvers strapped around their waists. The moment the Italian's eye caught the outline of the submachine gun, he knew his hour had come. He recognized the weapons. They were Israeli Uzis. The trap had snapped shut.

His immediate reaction was to step back, but he stopped himself. There was no point in trying to react. The four men had their weapons in hand. The man who had spoken Greek ordered all the members of the crew on deck to identify themselves.

"Don't move!" he ordered first in Greek and then in heavily accented English.

He and his companion, who held the second submachine gun, stood with their legs apart, ready to fire. The other two, revolvers drawn, were making a rapid search of the confused crewmen. They found Boncho's gun and relieved him of it, then went below to round up the other members of the crew to join their mates on deck. Meanwhile, two men dressed in civilian clothes came on board. The older of the pair, a slim, wiry man with a rather long face and smouldering eyes, turned to the Italian.

"Vittorio Angelo Massino." It was a statement rather than a question.

"I am he," the Italian admitted with great effort. His pulse was racing. Although the situation was clear to him, he felt strangely relieved. This stage of the chase had ended. His instincts had not betrayed him. He had been pursued by powerful forces.

The two men with revolvers emerged from below decks with three more crew members; the trio was obviously afraid—one of them was unable to stop trembling.

The man who apparently commanded the group turned to the two holding revolvers and spoke to them in heavily accented English.

"Is that all of them?"

"Yes."

"Take the crew below to the dining room. Not him, though." He pointed to Boncho. "He's staying here."

Dennis rebelled. "If he's staying here, we're all staying!" he said with courage.

The commander of the party smiled. "We don't want to have to use force," he said quietly. "Don't be smart. Now get below."

Dennis started to answer, but the Italian stopped him. "Go below with the others," he said. "I'll stay here."

Reluctantly, Dennis joined the rest of the crew and went below, leaving the four strangers and the Italian on deck. The man in command turned to one of the men carrying a submachine gun. "The ship's under your command, Zevik." Then he turned to the men waiting on the other ship. "Cable that we're on the way home," he called out.

"Good luck!" came the reply from the other ship as she began to move away from the Italian's yacht.

In his spacious cabin, Boncho began to behave like a host. He discovered to his surprise that now that something had finally happened, his fear had left him. The anticipation of something unknown had placed a heavy weight on him which he had tried unsuccessfully to slough off. Now that what he had feared was at last taking place, he concentrated on how to find a way to extricate himself from his predicament. He cast a glance at the two men.

"Would you like something to drink?" He turned to the older of the two.

"No, thank you," the stranger said politely. "But if you want something, please go ahead."

"Would you, perhaps?" Boncho turned to the other man and studied him. He was tall and handsome with fair skin and calm eyes set deep beneath heavy eyebrows.

"Not now," Yirmi Spector replied. "Later perhaps."

"Very well. *I* will have one." He laughed. "After the quantity I drank today, a small glass to wash out the gut won't do any harm. Do help yourself if you change your mind."

He opened the door to the liquor cabinet and took out a bottle of brandy. After pouring himself a glass, he sat down in his chair, waiting for the next move from the two strangers. They exchanged glances and sat down opposite him.

"Well now," he asked, "who are you?"

"At this point," Avshalom Kedmi replied, "it's worth your

while to save your questions for later. Let us do the talking now." His voice was low, but something in the way he spoke gave the Italian an unpleasant feeling. This man sitting opposite him, looking at him calmly with intense black eyes, could turn out to be far more dangerous than many others he had known.

"We have no interest in you per se," Avshalom went on, "any more than you have in us. But we want to know everything you know about a man who has an account in a bank in Zurich."

The knot in Boncho's throat seemed to expand, almost choking him. That damned Phoenix!

"I don't know what you're talking about," he answered. He tried to get a grip on himself. He hoped that they would not notice the trembling of his hand as he replaced the glass of brandy on the low table beside his chair.

"All right." Avshalom smiled gently. "I'll take the trouble to explain to you what you do know. Half a million dollars was deposited in Zurich to a certain account. The credit note on the deposit was sent to a certain post office box in Monte Carlo. The post office box is held by a certain man. That man is Vittorio Angelo Massino, otherwise known as Boncho."

The Italian became wary. These men had some information. But better wait. He still had time.

"Now listen." The man opposite seemed to have boundless patience. He addressed the Italian like a teacher talking to a pupil. "Don't waste my time with wild tales. If you like, I'll see to it that records at Interpol in France, Holland, Belgium, England—just for starters—are reopened. Certain people would be interested to know that the answers to their questions can be found with Vittorio Angelo. We would be happy to inform them where he was."

"I don't know what you're talking about."

"I'm talking about your involvement in crime. The thefts of works of art. Antiques. Diamonds. I'm talking about a whole batch of murders with a thick layer of dust accumulating on the records, which we can clear off with one puff. What do you say?"

Boncho remained silent.

"You have nothing to say?"

"You're inventing things."

"And you're behaving like a fool." Avshalom got up and poured himself a glass of brandy. "Well, Boncho. What's it to be? A friendly chat, or the other way?"

Boncho hesitated. "I tell you I don't know what you're talking about."

"What made you run from Monte Carlo? Charlie, the Englishman? Or maybe some woman was waiting for you at Genoa? Perhaps you wanted to surprise her with the new look of the yacht? That's why you had her dressed in new colors. And changed her name from *Paedaeia* to *Massina*. Eh, friend?"

The Italian remained silent. He tightened his grasp on his glass and took a drink from it, then hastily lit a cigarette.

"Listen, man," Avshalom said. His expression had become cold. "Let me explain, simply and clearly, just where you stand. Your friend received a fat wad of money, some of which came to you as a negotiating fee. Your friend has contracted to hit a very important person. If this man makes the hit, I personally will slit your throat. Now do you understand what I mean?"

"What man are you talking about?"

"At this point there's no need for you to know," Kedmi replied. "I just want to know every detail that can help us to find your pal as soon as possible. We want to know everything about him that you know about him. Even the smell of his sweat. Everything. Clear?"

"I have nothing to say," Boncho stated obstinately.

"You will have. You'll be surprised what a sweet nightingale's song will come out of your throat."

At that point in the conversation, Yirmi began to rise from his chair. A movement of Avshalom's hand stopped him and he sat down again.

"Listen, Vittorio," Avshalom said, his voice barely audible. "It's no good trying any of the tricks that you know so well. I prefer a talk that will get good results for us and for you. You quake when you think of your friend. You know he'll come looking for you, like he came after Pierre de Maline. He'll get you, too."

The Italian's heartbeat again accelerated as if he were in a mad race.

The two men opposite him knew certain things that were serious as far as he was concerned. They knew more than he had at first surmised. They must belong to an organization that had vast sources of information. Still, his fear of Phoenix was greater than his fear of them.

"Leave me alone," he muttered. "Who are you anyway?"

"We're Israelis," Kedmi said. The Italian's lips felt dry. So he was in the hands of the Israeli security service. The noose was already around his neck. He knew now where the ship was going.

"You understand your position, Vittorio?" The Israeli took a deep breath. "You're scared out of your wits by one wolf. We can send hordes of mad wolves after you. We'll finish you off slowly. Piece by piece." He paused. "You're not stupid. You know that after your friend accomplishes his mission, he will have to wipe you out too. You're the only one who can put the links together. He'll have to run for his life because we'll never let go. But by then you'll be dead. Right now you have a chance to save your life. Cooperate. We'll get him. Then you'll be free to go. You haven't met us, we've never heard of you. That's the best deal you can get. We're your life insurance."

Boncho stared at the faces of the strangers. The words had the ring of logic and sincerity. He knew that. The circle had closed. They had the advantage. In any case, he was in their hands. They were also right about Phoenix. Phoenix would not hesitate for a single second to strike him down.

"Can I have another drink?" he asked.

"You're the host. We're only visitors," Avshalom said with a smile. He knew then that the Italian had reached a decision.

Boncho picked up the bottle and filled his glass to the brim. He took a long swallow and then poured another.

"How long will you hold me?" he asked.

"You'll be free the moment we finish with your friend," Avshalom said.

"Where will I be held?"

"I promise you full protection and in comfort."

"In Israel?"

"Yes."

Boncho took another drink from the glass. "All right," he muttered. "What do you want to know?"

Avshalom looked at Yirmi and felt an easing of tension.

"Everything you know," he said. "Do you have some paper?"

The Italian stood up and, opening the middle drawer of his inlaid wooden desk, took out a pile of stationery and placed it on the desk. Yirmi drew his chair across to the desk. He took a pen from his pocket, poised to write.

Boncho began to speak hesitantly, as if trying to choose the right words. "I am what is known as a negotiator. Nothing more. A negotiator in various businesses. I made the acquaintance of the man you are looking for many years ago. I was then looking for someone to carry out the theft of an expensive painting from the collection of a certain Belgian industrialist. I had received an excellent recommendation on him. I was told that he was a first-class professional. A clean worker who left no traces. No criminal past. No identity, if you like. No one has his fingerprints."

"What is his name?"

Boncho smiled.

"I was afraid you would ask that," he said quietly.

"Why?"

"You probably will not believe me, but I don't know his real name."

"But you call him by some name!" Avshalom exclaimed.

"That's true," the Italian agreed. "Every time by a different name . . ."

"What do you mean?"

"As I have said," the Italian persisted, "from the very start he behaved like a ghost. He frequently moved to different addresses. He assumed a different name for every operation. He had a new name for every operation."

"What do you call him now?"

"Phoenix."

"Phoenix?"

Avshalom leaned forward. He fixed the Italian with a piercing look. "Phoenix," he said. "Does that have any significance?"

"I don't know," Boncho admitted. His unease was growing. It was proving difficult to convince these people. "But that is the name he chose for this affair. Phoenix."

In the ensuing silence the two men sat and looked at him. He felt the sweat trickle out of his pores. "This is not a man who can be described in ordinary terms."

"What do you mean?"

"He is a professional—a man who does not make mistakes." He groaned. "I know what you are thinking. But I am telling you the truth. Let me explain." He pulled out his handkerchief and wiped off the beads of sweat. "I also do not know how he entered our profession. I know nothing of his past. I don't know if he is French. Maybe he's Belgian. I don't know. He might even be a Jew. You must understand. He speaks many languages flawlessly." The Italian interrupted himself to light another cigarette. "But the name he chooses for himself does have some significance. At least, I think so. You see, he's an actor. He is a disguise and makeup artist. He lives as if he inhabits a giant theater where he constantly changes his role. It's always a different performance or a different mission. And each time he leaves not a single trace behind. It's as if he is consumed . . ." His eyes flashed.

"Go on!" the Israeli urged.

"You see, he's like the phoenix, that ancient bird . . . The one that burns itself up and then is reborn from its own ashes!" He was gripped by excitement. "Perhaps after this operation he means to disappear. For good. To finish with his profession and then to be born again, in a different place, with another name, a new life . . ." He laughed harshly. Now he knew why the man had selected that name for himself. And he knew too that without doubt Phoenix would reach him and destroy him before he erased his last character.

"I don't think there's a man alive who can tell you that he has seen him twice. Twice in one form, that is . . . Perhaps only one man."

"Who's that?" Avshalom asked.

"Me." The Italian stubbed out his cigarette. "I have seen him as he is . . . I guess that's what made me decide to co-operate with you. I realized that he would have to come and kill me at some point."

"You fear him," Yirmi observed quietly.

Boncho stared at him. "Yes." He breathed heavily. "He is the only man who can make me afraid . . ." He took out a cigarette and lit it. He made no attempt to conceal the tremor that passed through his hands.

"I know what it is to destroy a man. What it is to murder. I have done that too in my time. I have also known professional murderers. Men who live by murder. But I have never known anyone like him. For him it is just a business. He is a butcher. But instead of animals, he slaughters human beings. He's a cold-blooded perfectionist. A living computer. He makes no mistakes . . ."

"There is no man who does not make mistakes," Avshalom interposed.

The Italian lifted his hand and then let it fall. "Perhaps. But I am not aware that he has ever made a mistake."

"He has already made one," Avshalom stated. "That's why we are here with you."

"That was not his mistake. That was someone else's." The Italian laughed a little. "Someone else made a mistake. Perhaps I made it. But not he."

"That remains to be seen." Avshalom stood up and crossed over to the porthole. The sound of the sea could be heard through the darkness of the now fading night. In an hour it would be morning. "Listen, Vittorio, describe him to us. Tell us what he looks like. How he talks. Try to recall everything. If he has any special mark. The color of his eyes . . ."

Boncho thought a moment and then began to talk. "He's about thirty-four years old. Maybe thirty-five. Taller than you." He pointed to Avshalom. "But you two have the same physique. He is extraordinarily strong. You know"—the hint of a smile played at the corners of his mouth—"I once saw him take a key, place it in the palm of his hand, and shape it into a ring. As if by magic . . . His skin is fair. He has long hands with unusual palms. They are very narrow and his fingers are extremely long. Like the fingers of a pianist. He also uses them to play . . ."

"What?"

"The piano. He likes the piano." Boncho drank again from his glass. "His face is also one you can't forget. There's something wolfish about it with its long shape, sharp jaws, and high cheekbones. His eyes are like tiger's eyes, deep-set. He has a narrow nose, especially the nostrils . . ."

By sunrise, Yirmi Spector had twenty-five pages of notes containing every detail about Phoenix the Italian could remember: how he spoke; how he walked; his gestures; his disguises.

When dawn cast its light through the porthole of the cabin, the Italian fell silent. Now, more than ever, he wanted to shut his eyes and sleep. His brain felt blocked; if he could just have a few hours of sleep.

"I'm tired," he said heavily.

"You can sleep now," Avshalom said. "My friend will stay with you."

After the Italian had crossed to the couch, Avshalom left the cabin. He too was overcome by fatigue. In a few hours he would again interrogate the Italian to clarify a number of contradictory points in his amazing story, a story that he could not digest all at once. Boncho had had far more to tell than he had expected.

When he came up on deck, the sunlight shimmering on the water was almost blinding. He had to blink for several seconds before his eyes adjusted to the dazzling brightness. The sun's rays shone on the blue sea from horizon to horizon. The bright patches of light gave the impression of masses of silver and gold dust scattered over the smooth surface of the sea.

Avshalom looked at the high wheelhouse. "What's new with you, Zevik?" he called across to the second officer.

Zevik Brill was in great spirits. "A fine morning and a lovely ship! Everything's in order, Commander," came the answer as the prow of the yacht sliced through the calm surface of the sea on its way to Haifa.

* * *

PHOENIX

The Bayswater district of London, to the north of Hyde Park, harbors all sorts of characters from the fringes of London society. Each one has his own tale and some have unusual occupations best kept secret from the probing fingers of the law.

Freddie McKnight was a character, even by Bayswater standards. To date, his life had three major chapters: his youth in one of the slum areas of London, the Second World War where he had excelled in a division that dealt with chemical warfare, and a glorious period when he was a lecturer in chemistry. He was known as Dr. McKnight then. In addition to his contribution to the academic world, he was a senior scientist in a respected firm.

He had married his secretary, Mary Grant, a woman much given to debauchery. It took several months before the tales began to reach his ears. Gradually he learned that Mary was known in the company as "Mary Mattress." She was an expert in sensual pleasures and would part her legs for any man who desired her, and there were many who did. A tiny woman, her shapely body was powered by insatiable sexual desire. To her credit, she had truly believed that her marriage to the short, quick-tempered Scotsman, who was so absorbed in his research, would relieve her constant need for fulfillment. But, as it turned out, her lust was overwhelming, and so she continued to enjoy two worlds—those of wife and harlot.

Dr. Freddie McKnight was captivated by her charms and closed his ears to malicious gossip. When he finally opened his eyes, he discovered that his private Mary was common property. It enraged him, and he beat her, again and again.

When Mary was hospitalized following a particularly bad beating, Freddie was sentenced to a short term in prison. Afterward, he was dismissed from his job. Mary, however, remained with him, and he had no desire to leave her; she was the only person in his life for whom he had any affection.

Although the rift had healed, Freddie began spending long hours in the pubs and soon took to gambling. Before long, his savings had dwindled to nothing. It was just at this point that Mary showed herself to be a firm woman with a will of iron. She urged him to open a business of his own as a consultant in his profession. Freddie, however, proved incapable of freeing himself from his gambling habits; he needed money, lots of money. The solution lay in various shady deals. He began to supply materials to thieves whose specialty was cracking sophisticated safes or robbers whose method it was to gas the occupants of the apartments they entered. As a supplier to the underworld, Dr. Freddie McKnight had found a way of ensuring a living.

On Wednesday, August 10th, at the same time that a certain yacht which Freddie knew nothing about was making its way to Haifa, the telephone rang in his laboratory on the ground floor of an old house tucked away between two hotels. He picked up the receiver.

"Freddie here."

"McKnight?"

"Yes. Who's this?" he asked abruptly.

The man ignored the question. "I've gotten on to you after a few recommendations."

Freddie caught the tone of the stranger's voice at once.

"Only recommended people come to me," he said wryly. "What do you want?"

"Would it be possible to talk to you in private?"

The man was evidently being cautious and did not want to go into details over the phone. Freddie was used to such conversations. He had acquired a reputation among professionals and they never betrayed him, nor he them.

"Yes, it's possible," the chemist agreed.

"Shall we say, within the next hour?"

"I'll be here. Do you know the address?"

"Yes."

At midday, Freddie heard the quiet knock on the iron door of the basement. He got up from his chair and went to open the door. A slim young man with broad shoulders stood at the entrance. His hair was blond and combed back, with a part that began above his right eye. His blond moustache curved down around the corners of his mouth toward a sharp chin. Freddie was sure he was Irish.

"Nice day, isn't it, Dr. McKnight?"

Indeed, he had a marked Irish accent. The well-dressed young man smiled and walked into the large laboratory. He looked around him, peering with interest at the various pieces of equipment and the cupboards stocked with chemicals. Freddie followed him in.

"How can I help you?" he asked.

"We'll talk about it directly," came the reply.

But it appeared that the young man was in no hurry. He wandered about the laboratory as if it were his private domain. Freddie followed him in astonishment.

"Is it my services you want, or my premises?" he asked sarcastically.

"I was just looking to see if the McKnight laboratory really deserves its fine reputation." The young man fixed the Scotsman with a searching look. "Impressive setup you have here."

"So they say," the chemist agreed. "I hope you find what you want."

"I need professional assistance."

"Everyone who comes to me says that."

"I want something that will satisfy my needs."

"I also want to satisfy my needs," the chemist mocked, "and not with words." He made a gesture as if feeling banknotes with his fingertips.

The Irishman laughed. "You won't be left short."

"Well, then, my friend, what's your problem?"

He phrased his questions in general terms. One never knew if someone who came was a policeman sniffing about.

"McKnight," the young man continued to smile, "there's no need for you to worry. I don't belong to Scotland Yard. All right?"

"I didn't say . . ."

"But you thought it!"

This time it was Freddie who laughed. The Irishman was sharp, and he liked him.

"Very well," he said. "You talk. I'm listening."

"You make gases . . ."

"Perhaps."

The man pulled up a chair and sat down, setting a brown Samsonite briefcase at his side. He shook his head as though to discuss the chemist's noncommittal answer.

"You were in the British army in the Second World War," he said.

"Who wasn't?" McKnight looked at him with interest.

"Not everyone did what you did."

"What do you mean?"

"You worked in a special research unit on the development of gases. Now isn't that a fact, McKnight?" The stranger continued to smile pleasantly.

"You've been doing some research on me."

"It's been done."

So that was it. The chemist was certain he had made no mistake. The young man belonged to the IRA.

"Are you interested in gases?" he asked.

"We . . ."

"Yes, of course. All of you."

It was evident that the young man wanted to make it clear that he belonged to some organization. His hints reinforced the chemist's assumption. The lurking fear that the man might be connected to the investigation section of Scotland Yard was now dissipated.

"You haven't given me an answer yet, McKnight."

"What gas is it you want?"

"Nerve gas."

Freddie was aghast. The shudder that passed through him was not lost on the young man with the round, ruddy-colored cheeks and the tigerlike eyes.

"That's a lethal gas," Freddie muttered.

"We know."

"More deadly than lightning!"

"That doesn't answer my questions."

"It depends what you're asking, laddie."

Freddie McKnight felt he had to be careful. The man wanted something that the chemist had only rarely handled. This time it obviously involved human life, which was not to his liking. The young man seemed to read his thoughts.

"We're talking about the liquidation of a certain man," the young man said calmly. "Don't let your conscience trouble you, McKnight. It's one of our own people that we're settling accounts with. He collaborated with the bastards . . ."

"You have other ways."

"Leave that to us." The young man smiled again. "You'll have a nice payment, Freddie."

"What is it you want exactly?"

The man pushed his hand into his trouser pocket and took out a large hunting shell. He held it out to the chemist.

"Do you recognize that?"

"A hunting cartridge, but a much larger caliber than usual."

"Correct," the man agreed. "Open the cardboard casing. But do it carefully enough that you can put the shell back in so that no one can tell it has been opened."

Freddie examined the cartridge. He went to his bench and took up a sharp, narrow chisel. With an expert hand he made a cut around the base of the cardboard, which adhered to the broad copper cartridge whose diameter was as large as a quarter. He put the chisel down and pulled the brownish cardboard covering off, revealing a tiny rocket. Its head was fashioned into a hard steel ball, and its body, including the wings, was made of aluminum. He carefully detached the steel head from the aluminum body and inside found a glass tube containing liquid.

"That's a gas for riot control," the Irishman explained.

"I see."

"Well?"

"You want me to exchange this tube for one containing nerve gas," Freddie muttered. He looked up and stared at the smiling face of the Irishman.

"That's exactly the idea, Freddie."

"It's not an easy matter," the chemist observed.

"That's why I came to you, Freddie. You'll solve the problem."

"An expensive problem," Freddie hesitated. "I have to get the material from somewhere . . ."

"You'll get it."

"It'll cost a lot of money."

Freddie did not take his eyes off the healthy face of the blond young man. The ends of his moustache emphasized the smile fixed on his thin lips.

"Don't let the money worry you."

"How many cartridges like this do you need?"

"Eight."

"No small number. You can kill a lot of people."

"How much money do you want, Freddie?"

Freddie thought for a moment.

"Two thousand quid," he said, with an effort.

"We need this, Freddie." He stressed the word "we." "And we'll pay what you ask. All I ask is that it be ready in ten days. What do you say?"

"It'll be ready."

"It's good to do business with you, Freddie." The man picked up his briefcase and opened it. He took out seven identical cartridges and put them on the bench. "With the one you opened, this makes eight exactly. How much money do you need now, in advance?"

"Half."

"Here you are then."

The Irishman took an envelope from the case and drew out a wad of banknotes. He counted them and put them on the bench by the cartridges.

"A thousand," he said. "And a thousand when I come back."

"All right."

The man caught the note of hesitation in the chemist's reply.

"Something bothering you, Freddie?"

"You spoke about killing one man." Freddie shrugged his shoulders. "Perhaps it's none of my business. But you ought to know that with that many bullets you can kill a lot of people."

The young man grinnned. "Freddie," he said finally, "we usually check the material in our hands. That's all."

"I understand."

"Well, then, I'll get in touch with you to fix the day and the time." He locked the briefcase. "I hope to do business with you in the future."

Freddie McKnight remained silent. The young man turned toward the door, then stopped and looked around. His grin had disappeared and his expression was grim.

"No tricks, Freddie," he said in a cold voice. "We don't like anyone who doublecrosses us. You wouldn't like what we do, either."

Freddie felt a sudden wave of fear. "I'm on the level. Absolutely on the level."

The smile returned to the stranger's mouth as he left the basement, closing the door behind him.

That evening, when Freddie was sitting down to a meal with Mary, he put a small envelope by her plate.

"What's that, Freddie?" she asked.

"A little present for you," he said with feigned indifference. He watched her as she picked up the envelope and opened it. Her face lit up when she saw the five hundred pounds.

"Wonderful!" she cried excitedly.

"You buy whatever you want with it, darling."

Mary came around the table and placed a resounding kiss on his cheek.

"I knew that one day you'd do good business!" she said, kissing him again. "New customers, love?"

Freddie was pleased. "Yes," he smiled. "New customers, Mary."

He did not let her in on his doubts. Her face shone with happiness. And he did not want to spoil it, although he knew that her questions would be sure to come. Mary hurried to the kitchen and returned carrying a bottle of red wine which she had kept for a special occasion. She hummed as she poured the liquid into two glasses. Freddie would go far yet, she thought contentedly. One day they would be rich.

"To your success, darling!" she said, and raised her glass.

"To our success, Mary."

They drank the wine, and as Mary put her glass down, she asked, "Who are the new customers?" He tried to put her off. "It's not important. Pour me another glass, love." He knew what was coming.

"Freddie!" She was surprised. He always let her in on the general details. She picked up the bottle of wine. "Who are they?"

He squirmed in his chair. "Irish."

Mary's mouth opened in horror.

"Oh, no, Freddie! Not Irish!" Her voice was tremulous. "It'll end badly, love."

"What's wrong with the Irish?" he exclaimed. He was losing his temper.

"You daren't get involved with the IRA," she replied. "They're murderers . . . just murderers."

Freddie McKnight's face had become flushed with anger. He struck the table with his fist so that the wine splashed from the glass in front of him.

"For Christ's sake!" His voice was tight. "I'll do business with the devil if need be. How do you think I've been providing for you these last years? From church contributions?"

She backed away. "I don't want this money, Freddie." Her voice shook. "You daren't help murderers, and I don't care what their reasons are . . . I don't want any part of it."

Her eyes filled with tears and she wheeled around and left the dining room, leaving Freddie alone with his anger and disappointment.

From the moment the yacht *Paedaeia,* alias *Massina,* had entered the port of Haifa, there had been a shift in the activities of the surveillance branch. Boncho and the crew had been housed in comfortable quarters under a strict guard, and a twenty-five-page report on the interrogation of the Italian had been circulated. Now Israeli intelligence had a new name to work with: Phoenix. It was a name that gave them no rest—the name of an unknown but professional assassin who had killed in the past and left behind not a single mark of identification.

"This Italian Boncho worked with him for years?" Avital asked after reading the report.

"Right," Uri replied.

"It's hard to believe that he has nothing more concrete to tell us."

"I know it," Uri replied. "But I believe he's telling the truth. And more to the point, so does Avshalom and he's spent a lot of time questioning him. Moreover the polygraph tests back him up."

"Well, then," said Avital. "What do we have to go on at this point. What *do* we know about this killer?"

Yitshaq Goldberg took over. "First, we have a name. Real or not real, this is already more than we had. Phoenix. A man about thirty-five. Around six feet in height, weighing between one hundred and fifty-five and one hundred and sixty-five pounds. Wide shoulders, long arms, and unusually narrow palms. He has a long face, a prominent forehead, gray eyes flecked with brown. His nose is short and straight with narrow nostrils. His lips are thin also. He has a sharp jawline and therefore his chin is especially marked. His hair is light and straight, with no signs of thinning. He appears to be left-handed, but he has trained himself to write with his right hand too. The man is an expert in all types of weapons and explosives. He is a master of several methods of self-defense and unarmed combat. He speaks five or six languages and is fluent in all of them, with no foreign accent. The background of Phoenix is unknown; his past is a mystery. He seems to have had a wide general education and is particularly adept at the art of disguise. We might call him a quick-change artist. He uses forged documents and after a certain length of time destroys them and acquires others. In recent years, he has been engaged primarily in the theft of art works and antiques and in the assassinations of political figures. According to his agent Massino, Phoenix is fearless. And ruthless. The Italian describes him as a human robot. The man has an inexhaustible supply of patience and tenacity. He acts only after he has thoroughly studied the target and his background. He seeks perfection and avoids error. He constantly doublechecks everything. The Italian emphasized that in the years of their working together, he cannot recall a single instance in which Phoenix failed." Yitshaq stopped speaking and looked at the tense faces of his listeners.

"One more thing," he added. "I've asked Dr. Carmi to come in. I gave him a transcript of the interrogation. He'll try to have some conclusions for us tomorrow." Dr. Rafael Carmi, a well-known Tel Aviv psychiatrist, had assisted the security service many times in the past in character analysis. His views had frequently proved to be accurate, and in consequence his opinions were often sought.

"Good," said Uri. "Given the description the Italian supplied, I suggest we also try to do a composite on the face of Phoenix. Of course, we know that he changes disguises frequently, but we now have some base to go on. Once we get a composite face we can send it to the police and intelligence services in Europe and the United States. And we can make up composites using various disguises as well."

When Rafael Carmi met the next day with Uri Cohen and Avshalom Kedmi, he had some very definite impressions. "First off," he said, "I think you are dealing with a psychopath. He's obviously a man of the highest intelligence; a man who always operates analytically, no matter how complex the situation. I think that at some point he becomes totally identified with his mission—to such an extent that he cannot separate himself from it. That means he comes to believe that he is fighting for his very survival, and for that reason he must not fail. The concepts of life and death probably have no meaning for him, at least not in the way that we understand them. In my view, murder for him is simply a question of removing a problem that disturbs him. Nothing more. He does not see himself as a murderer. He simply eliminates all obstacles on the path to his target. The complex process begins, as I have said, at the moment he becomes identified with his objective."

"Dr. Carmi," Uri asked, "if I were to ask you to try to pinpoint a weakness in him, could you?"

The doctor lit his pipe and smiled at Uri. Then his face took on a grave expression. "One of the obvious qualities of Phoenix is the meticulousness with which he operates. It's a very highly developed quality. You might see it as a fastidiousness bordering on insanity. He has to be satisfied that every step he undertakes is perfectly executed . . . But life is not like that. Life is a series of errors and imperfections."

"Meaning?" Avshalom leaned forward, his interest suddenly aroused. "Where is the weakness?"

The doctor spread his hands questioningly. "I don't know what to advise you, Avshalom," he said. "I don't know where you are in your operations with Phoenix. But precisely because his personality requires perfection, if you come up against something that does not arouse suspicion, that sounds right, that has no flaws, that quite simply seems perfect, at that point precisely, I would pause and begin to ask questions."

"All right," said Avital after Carmi had left. "You all know your assignments. From now on, we're wrapping Dayan in a security screen every moment he's in Europe and the United States. In a few days we'll have Dayan's schedule. Every event, public or private, must undergo the closest scrutiny by us. I repeat: *every* event, no matter how minor. We have to be on the alert for Phoenix—and ready to spot any mistake he might make."

At five o'clock in the afternoon, on the day after the deal with Freddie McKnight had been concluded, Phoenix was among the passengers on a plane that took off from Heathrow Airport for Monte Carlo. He leafed through a copy of *Le Monde* until he found what he was looking for—a short piece on the investigation into the slaying of the American model by Madame Charlotte. The investigators were now convinced that the owner of the modeling agency had killed her lover. The postmortem had revealed traces of semen in the body, which led investigators of the criminal division to believe that Madame Charlotte had been driven by jealousy to commit murder. According to the police reconstruction of events, while Madame Charlotte had been out of Paris on business, the American model Dorothy Brown had taken advantage of her absence to engage in lovemaking with an unknown man. The investigators believed that Madame Charlotte had surprised them, and after the strange man had fled the luxury apartment, an argument ensued culminating in the killing of the black woman. Although Madame Charlotte claimed that she knew nothing of the murder, her claims sounded hollower and hollower.

The young man put the paper down. He was in excellent spirits. The investigation was going exactly as planned. Now only one hydra head still remained to be dealt with: Jorg Gibskopf. The time to lop off that head was approaching.

From now on, he would have to destroy any trace of his existence. Anything connected with his past would have to be eliminated. He had to be certain that Israeli security would not be able to track him down one day. He knew that after the completion of his mission they would never abandon the pursuit, even if it were to last for years. He had to cover his tracks, to obliterate them totally.

The assassination of the Israeli would be his last operation. He could have enough money so that he could live as he chose anywhere in the world. He wanted a peaceful life. He would create a new person; he was an expert at that. But until that moment came, he had to act with the same degree of caution and meticulousness as in the past.

He wondered if any inkling of the affair had gotten through to the Israeli secret service. The meeting he planned with the Italian would clarify that point. That was the reason he had told him to use his connections to keep track of developments in the police forces and special departments throughout Europe. As long as he needed his help, he would not harm the Italian. He would destroy him only in the last stage of his mission.

He did not trust the Libyans. He knew that even if they found out that the Israeli secret service was aware of the plot, they would not inform him of the gravity of the situation for fear he might back down. He could trust the Italian, however. He was the last remaining link connecting him to the past.

It was when he arrived in Monte Carlo that he realized his plans had gone awry. The *Paedaeia* had disappeared, and no one knew where it had gone or why. Phoenix knew that the Italian made short voyages at frequent intervals, but he was always careful to leave a message for him at the post office near the harbor. Normally the message would state when he intended to return. Since the post office was closed for the day, he was obliged to spend the night at a hotel. The following morning, his visit to the post office increased his concern; the Italian had left no message.

This was the first time that the connection between him and the Italian had been severed—a fact that caused him anxiety. The lack of certainty disturbed him. It was at such points that he lost control. He had no spare time to look for the Italian. Something serious must have happened to cause Boncho to sail without notice from Monte Carlo. He felt anger welling up inside him. He would have to live with danger for a while, until he had the opportunity to locate Boncho. One always paid for a mistake. If he had killed the Italian for making the error of introducing Pierre de Maline into their arrangement, he could have saved himself unnecessary complications now.

There was nothing left for him to do in Monte Carlo, so at noon he flew to Paris. Several hours later, he found himself at the entrance to the house in rue de l'Amber. He took out his pen and wrote on the mailbox beneath the name Philippe d'Astine, the name Willy Miller. Then he went up to his small apartment and passed the first days there destroying any items that could endanger him after he abandoned the apartment.

He made bundles of the clothes and suits he no longer needed and sold them at the flea market. The documents, newspapers, and books connected with Moshe Dayan he tore into shreds and spent several hours burning them laboriously in the bathroom and flushing the remnants down the toilet. From various secret places he took out piles of forged papers and passports, examined them, and determined which he would still need. The majority he destroyed. Those that were left he secreted in the false bottom of his suitcase.

Four days later, he was satisfied that the apartment contained only the items he needed. At noon that day he found a letter in his mailbox to Willy Miller from the lawyer in New York, Jack Stone. As agreed, the lawyer wrote, he had sent the original letter to the house in Scarsdale and the copy, in accordance with Mr. Miller's wishes, to the Paris address. The lawyer noted that his letter to Moshe Dayan had been sent. The moment a reply was received from the Foreign Minister he would contact Mr. Charles Cottner, the antiquarian, and ask him to attend to the drawing up of the certificate and the arrangements for getting the antique box to Dayan. He would then be able to report when the Foreign Minister planned to visit the antiquarian's shop so that Miller would know when to send the box to the dealer.

Phoenix destroyed the letter after he had read it. He decided to remain in Paris two days longer and then fly to London for his last meeting with Freddie McKnight. He took advantage of those two days for rest and reflection. He needed to reconsider the steps he had taken from the moment he began his mission. He was certain that the Israelis had had a hand in the mysterious disappearance of Boncho. Even assuming that they had the Italian, he thought, they would find it difficult to extract any information that could endanger him. Boncho could give them a general description, but his evidence might merely increase the Israelis' confusion. The Italian was unable to point to him and say, That is the man. The Israelis were still searching for an unknown factor. He smiled to himself as he hit upon the way to solve the problem. This is the answer, he thought. They are looking for a murderer, and they shall have one.

In his mind's eye, he saw the journalist Jorg Gibskopf. The idea had begun to take shape on his flight from Paris to London on the morning of Friday, August 19th. The decision was made. As soon as he finished his business with the chemist in London, he would go to Copenhagen. From then on, he would tail Jorg Gibskopf until the time came to trap him.

Phoenix arrived at Freddie's laboratory at Bayswater at ten o'clock. He knocked at the iron door and waited. The chemist's face took on a look of astonishment when he opened the door.

"Hello, Freddie," the young man said cheerfully.

"You said you'd call me before you came!"

The Irishman smiled and stroked the ends of his blond moustache. "There's been a change in plan," he said. "Aren't you going to ask me in?"

Freddie McKnight stood aside as the man passed him and entered. He held the same case in his hand.

"Are the cartridges ready, Freddie?"

Freddie hesitated. "They will be ready," he said.

"What's that supposed to mean?"

"I mean," said Freddie, "that you'll have to wait for a few more hours. If you come back this afternoon, you'll have them."

The stranger smiled. His eye fell on the cartridges lying in a row on Freddie's bench and he knew that McKnight was lying.

Freddie McKnight had indeed been surprised by the Irishman's unannounced appearance. For the last few days Mary had not left him alone. She demanded that he cancel the job, no matter how he had to do it. "Those mad Irish," she said tearfully. "You and I daren't get involved in any way with those madmen in Belfast." She gave him no rest. That morning she had even threatened to go to the police.

Freddie had left the house in a rage. On his way to the laboratory he had been unable to shake her words from his mind. Once in the laboratory the awareness came over him that Mary was really right, that he had to find a way to back out. He decided to put the stranger off and gain a few hours' time. By then, he would manage to contact the police.

Now the Irishman crossed to the bench where the shells lay.

"They aren't ready yet," the chemist said in an agitated voice.

The man examined the cartridges carefully. Although an untrained person might not have discerned that someone had cut slits into their cardboard casings, his keen eye saw the spot where they had been resealed.

"They look ready to me," he said evenly. "You know, Freddie, there's one you might not have touched, but the rest are ready."

"It's just the opposite!" Freddie swallowed the bait without realizing it. "One's ready. The rest aren't . . . I've told you . . . I need a few more hours to make up the solution . . ."

"All right," the Irishman laughed. "You know what we'll do, McKnight. I bet you five hundred quid that I can pick out the one that's ready. Here, look."

He began to switch the cartridges around with agile hands. His long fingers were amazingly nimble. He worked like a conjurer doing a trick as Freddie looked on in astonishment.

"You see, Freddie. Now every cartridge is in another place. Right?"

Freddie did not reply.

"You see how I take out the right cartridge," the man said gaily. His fingers grasped one of the cartridges and lifted it out of the row. "This one!"

"That's right," Freddie said anxiously. "The rest aren't ready yet . . ."

"In that case," the man said, placing the cartridge he held apart from the others, "let's open one of them up and see what's going on inside."

Before the chemist could react, he had picked up one of the shells and had begun to draw it out of its casing. Freddie McKnight was terrified. He leaped up and grabbed the young Irishman's arm.

"Look out!" he shouted.

The cheerful grin disappeared from the Irishman's face. "You were lying, Freddie, weren't you?" His voice was almost a whisper. "All the cartridges are ready. Why did you lie, Freddie?"

Freddie was afraid. Unconsciously he took a step backward. His heart began to beat wildly and his face grew pale.

"I didn't mean . . ."

"I asked why, Freddie."

The Irishman's face was suddenly impassive, as if he were almost indifferent.

"It was because I don't want to go through with the deal." Freddie's tongue was heavy. "I don't want any part in killing people."

"Your conscience has got to you? Just like that? In a split second?"

"Call it what you like. Here," the chemist begged. "Take your money back." He took another step backward. "Look," he said, panic-stricken now. "Let's forget everything. If you forget you were here, I swear to you I'll forget you were ever here . . ."

The tigerlike eyes caught McKnight's gaze and held it. "You know it can't end like that, Freddie."

Freddie felt paralyzed. The strange calm of the man induced boundless terror in him.

"I know . . . But . . ."

"Freddie," the man came toward him, "there's no point in discussing it any further."

"Here's your money!" Freddie cried in terror. "A thousand pounds . . ."

Freddie's hand never reached his pocket to take the money from his wallet. The blow from the Irishman's fist struck him on the temple and he sank to the floor unconscious. The man bent down and removed the wallet. He drew the banknotes from it and pushed them into his pocket. Then he replaced the wallet in Freddie's pocket and went across to the bench, where he collected the cartridges and put them in his briefcase.

Freddie McKnight lay stretched out on the floor, his eyes closed, his breathing heavy. The man gripped him by the shoulders, lifted him, and slung him onto the high stool next to the workbench. The upper part of his body lay across the bench. The man took a bottle of flammable liquid from one of the cupboards, opened it, and poured the contents over the head and shoulders of the inert man, then placed the empty bottle next to the Scotsman's head. A packet of Freddie's cigarettes lay on the bench. He drew one out and, moving away from the bench, lit the cigarette and, after drawing on it several times, threw it onto the bench. In a moment, the whole surface of the bench was in flames. The chemist's head and shoulders were engulfed by wild tongues of fire.

He was on his way to the airport when the fire brigade responded to a call to a burning cellar in Bayswater. By the time detectives were called in to examine the charred body of the unfortunate chemist, Phoenix was awaiting his flight to Copenhagen. No matter what the results of the investigation, no one could link him with the disaster that had occurred in Dr. Freddie McKnight's small laboratory. He was not even thinking about McKnight anymore. His mind was now occupied with the Danish journalist, Jorg Gibskopf.

* * *

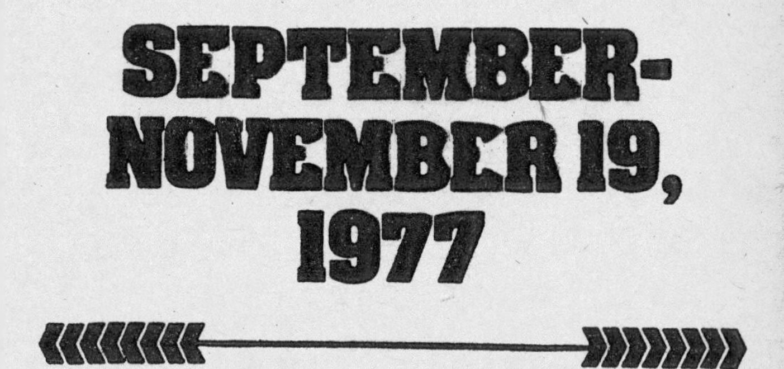
SEPTEMBER-
NOVEMBER 19,
1977

At ten twenty on the morning of Thursday, September 8th, Jorg Gibskopf made contact with the Libyan intelligence agent in Paris. They had had only one prior conversation a few weeks before, at which time Gibskopf was told that Tripoli was demanding that he move soon, by the end of the summer at the very latest. This time Gibskopf had a request.

"I have details on the departure of the Israeli," Gibskopf said in a low voice. "He is leaving on the fifteenth on a direct flight to Brussels. The following day he will arrive somewhere in France. He has a meeting, on which I have no details. I need them."

The request did not surprise the Libyan. This was the second time it had been made of him. A day before, the other assassin, known only as Phoenix, had called and had also wanted to know details on the forthcoming Paris visit.

"We have tried to find out," the Libyan told Gibskopf. "As yet we have no idea where it will be or with whom he is meeting. But he's expected to reach Paris from Brussels on the sixteenth at the latest. From Paris he goes on to the United States. The first meetings in Washington have been fixed for the nineteenth."

When Jorg Gibskopf completed his call to the Libyan, he returned to his table in a café in the Latin Quarter. At forty-six he was a handsome man, tall and slim and well-built. Were it not for the flecks of gray in his beard, which was trimmed like a Viking's, it would have been hard to guess his age.

Although he seemed the prototypic Scandinavian, Gibskopf had been born in Germany. Orphaned at the end of the Second World War, he had joined his mother's father in Denmark. Although to all intents he was a typical Danish youth, in one respect he remained profoundly German: in his heart he kept alive the belief in a master race and he awaited the day when history would reactivate the progress of the Aryan people, a progress that had been interrupted.

In 1956 he volunteered for the French Foreign Legion, and from there it was a short step to a career as a mercenary in Africa, participating in the bloody battles and coups that accompanied the birth of the emerging African nations. For the first time in his life, Jorg had a taste of money and the flavor intoxicated him. He became a specialist in assassination.

At the end of 1965, Gibskopf returned to Europe. The winds of change had blown across Africa; many mercenaries had been captured and executed. He had accumulated enough money to get out and begin a new life. Thanks to his experience as a soldier of fortune, he found a new vocation. He wrote a series of articles on the ways in which mercenaries were recruited and how they had operated in Africa. To his surprise, he discovered he had a talent for journalism. With the rise of international terrorist bands, his name became famous as a leading commentator.

But journalism was not that lucrative, and when he was approached by an ex-comrade to liquidate a Nigerian leader, the money was too tantalizing to reject. For the first time he used his profession as a journalist as a cover for a death-dealing operation. It proved a remarkably successful union. He hired out only at rare intervals, for he realized that the less he used his special gifts, the greater the chances of success and the higher the fees.

When Adel el-Magrabi had approached him through Pierre de Maline, the money was right and the challenge—particularly given his politics—irresistible.

As a journalist, Gibskopf had access to various Paris news

offices and wire services, and in the last two days he had learned that, although the Israelis were deliberately spreading false information about the schedule of their Foreign Minister, he was in fact coming to Paris before going to the States and that he would hold a press conference. Gibskopf had a booby-trapped tape recorder, ready for action. The explosive charge would destroy anyone within a range of fifteen feet. All he had to do during the conference was place the machine near the Foreign Minister and activate it. By the time it exploded, he would be out of range.

When Gibskopf left the café near the apartment he had rented in the Latin Quarter, he did not know that Phoenix was close on his trail.

The pursuit, which Phoenix had begun in Copenhagen, had continued to the very door of the small apartment in the Latin Quarter. It had required no special effort on his part, other than the need to change his disguises at frequent intervals. More than once he found himself standing only a few feet away from the journalist, who had no inkling that he was being followed.

He had had numerous opportunities to kill Gibskopf, but he stuck to the plan he had devised. He was in large part influenced by the strange disappearance of the Italian. It was his assessment that Boncho had been forced to run because he had realized that the Israelis had caught on to him. The more Phoenix thought about it, the more he was convinced that the Israelis were aware of the assassination plot and were trying to discover the unknown killer. In the interim, they had managed to get to the Italian. But no matter how their investigation progressed, they could have no idea of the Libyan plan to activate several assassins against the same target. They would therefore be seeking only one.

It was on the basis of this assumption that he constructed his plan for the fate of Jorg Gibskopf.

From the moment the journalist had arrived in Paris, Phoenix had tailed him constantly. Once he discovered Gibskopf's apartment, he was satisfied; it meant he could allow himself a brief rest. He was certain that the Dane had selected the French capital as his arena. His telephone conversation with the Libyan intelligence agent in Paris had strengthened this conviction. Furthermore, he had a good idea of Gibskopf's plan to make use of a tape-recorder with an explosive device. This method meant that the journalist had to be located a short distance from Moshe Dayan, an opportunity that would probably arise during the course of a news conference.

Professionally, he admired Gibskopf's plan. It had a good chance of succeeding, but it could be dangerous for its perpetrator. Even if it worked, the journalist could well be caught up in a round of interrogations, and all his escape routes would be blocked—two unnecessary risks. Without doubt, the man was extremely courageous.

Phoenix had been on his feet for thirty-six consecutive hours. When he saw that the journalist had returned to his apartment he knew he could take a short break. He drove back to his apartment in rue de l'Amber in Montparnasse and, a few minutes later, he had fallen into a deep sleep. He slept for fifteen hours.

When he awoke, he was completely refreshed. His first move was to take a shower. For a long time he allowed the stream of water to run over his body. Then he shaved and dressed, drank a pot full of coffee and prepared a sandwich. After he had satisfied his hunger, he went to check his mailbox. He found a letter waiting there from Jack Stone. The lawyer wrote that on September 2nd, a reply had been received on behalf of Foreign Minister Moshe Dayan. Dayan's secretary had thanked Stone for his letter and had noted that Mr. Dayan was extremely interested in the antique box. However, it would be impossible to schedule a visit to Cottner's shop until he had arrived in the United States. The lawyer wrote that he had advised Mr. Cottner of this development and Cottner had already expressed his willingness to handle the exchange. Stone suggested that Mr. Miller remain in touch with him and that he would be informed, without delay, as soon as they knew the day when Dayan would pick up the box.

The young man answered Stone's letter at once, thanking him for his efficiency and telling him that he was planning to return to the United States within a few days and could contact the lawyer immediately upon his arrival. When he finished the letter, he signed the name "Willy Miller" in a spidery hand.

Monday, September 12th, was chosen as the day of action. Yitshaq Goldberg was to fly to Paris while Avshalom Kedmi and Yirmi Spector prepared for their flight to the United States. The final preparations for the visit of the Foreign Minister had been completed at the meeting that had taken place on Sunday between Uri Cohen and Dick Coleman at the American Embassy in Tel Aviv. Dick Coleman had already been informed of the latest series of discoveries. His findings were sent to Washington and it was decided that an additional check of the joint Israeli-American security measures would be made.

Hundreds of copies of the composite pictures of Phoenix were sent to the American security staff at airports, seaports, and railroad and bus stations throughout the country. Scores of agents were ordered to put close tails on men suspected of being connected with Arab terrorist organizations or of being possible accessories to an assassination attempt.

Similar operations were set in motion in Belgium and France where the seriousness of Dayan's visit was recognized. Representatives of the two governments undertook to provide as much assistance as possible to the Israeli surveillance branch.

The schedule of the Foreign Minister was completed. He was to depart on Thursday, September 15th, on a flight to Brussels. The following day he was to travel to Paris. He would remain there one day and then fly to the United States. On Sunday, he would stay in New York and meet with various senior members of the Israeli delegation to the United Nations and of the Israeli Consulate. On Monday, September 19th, the Foreign Minister would arrive in Washington and would stay there two days, holding a series of meetings with the President, Secretary of State Vance, and the Advisor on National Security, Professor Brzezinski. Dayan would also meet with the Vice-President that same day. In the evening, a ceremonial dinner would take place at the home of Israel's Ambassador to the United States. On the second day of the visit to Washington, the Foreign Minister would have a breakfast meeting with staff members of the *Washington Post*. This would be followed by a general press conference. At midday, a meeting was set with members of the Senate Foreign Relations Committee. Another meeting would be held that evening with senior political correspondents of the American press. On Wednesday morning, the Foreign Minister would end his visit with a meeting with Jewish Congressmen and would then fly to New York.

In New York, meetings had been arranged with the foreign ministers of West Germany, Holland, Denmark, and Sweden, as well as with the leaders of American Jewry. The hours for Dayan's newspaper interviews and television appearances on the NBC and CBS networks had also been determined. Then on October 9th, after a tour of various American cities, Dayan would fly to Montreal for a meeting with the local Jewish community in that city. From there, he would go back to New York, and the following day take off on his return journey to Israel.

This was one of the most complex itineraries that the men of the surveillance branch had had to contend with. The last few days prior to the start of the tour had been marked by feverish checks at the security service headquarters. The route and the various meetings were scrutinized innumerable times. First, Uri Cohen's men studied the various public events. These were divided into two types: meetings with members of the Carter Administration and officials of other countries, and meetings with the leaders of the American Jewish community. The series of meetings Dayan was to hold with the press and the appearances he was scheduled to make on the television networks were to be handled separately. Here meticulous checks on every person who was likely to be anywhere near the Foreign Minister were necessary.

Yirmi Spector made good use of his time in Jerusalem. He extracted a great deal of information from the Foreign Minister's secretaries and from the chief of the bureau. He observed that in the last twenty-four hours further meetings had been crammed into the Foreign Minister's timetable, involving people that the men of the surveillance branch had not yet been able to check out. Among other things,

Yirmi noted that Dayan was due to visit an antique shop on Madison Avenue.

"I know the place," Uri observed, "and I don't see any special problem. Dayan has been there several times before—it's a man named Cottner, if I'm not mistaken."

"Yes," Yirmi affirmed. "That's the owner's name. But there's another party involved this time."

"Another party? What do you mean?"

Yirmi drew a copy of the letter from his briefcase and handed it to Uri, who looked at it and passed it on to Avital Arnon.

"The name Jack Stone is also known to me," Uri said. "If I'm not mistaken, he's active in the United Jewish Appeal."

"It looks all right," Avital remarked, and returned Jack Stone's letter to Yirmi.

"Anyway, we'll do another check," Avshalom advised. "It's a meeting that has only just been arranged. We'll put it with the list of things to be checked out in New York."

During the discussion, the special tasks in Europe and the United States were finally defined. Yitshaq Goldberg was asked to pay special attention to Dayan's arrival in Paris, a matter on which there was a total blackout.

"Dayan's flight to Brussels on Thursday is actually a decoy," Avital explained. "He will, of course, meet various people to justify the statements in the papers that these are routine meetings between our Foreign Minister and Belgian statesmen. But the main issue is the meeting that will be held secretly in Paris, which no one knows anything about. As far as anyone knows, Dayan will officially still be in Brussels."

Avital studied the faces of his men; they sensed he had something important to say.

"I say what I'm saying now because I believe you ought to be aware of it," the chief of the service said. "It looks as though something serious is afoot on the political level. After various contacts, it has been decided to make use of Dayan's trip to the United States to hold a meeting in Paris with another party, the Egyptian Ambassador Hafiz Ismail."

"That's exciting," Yirmi exclaimed.

"You haven't heard everything yet." Avital waited a few

seconds. "I said that the Egyptian Ambassador will be party to the meeting. In fact, he will be the host, and there will be two guests—Moshe Dayan on our side, and on the Egyptian side, Muhammad Hassan el-Tuhami, the Deputy Prime Minister of Egypt."

"That means that Sadat is taking the idea of negotiations seriously," Avshalom observed.

"So it seems," Avital confirmed. "I have decided that we should be aware of this move, particularly as we are involved in it," he went on. "Further developments can be expected. In the course of the coming months a heavy burden will fall upon us. Therefore, we have to rid ourselves of the Phoenix affair as quickly as possible. These developments also shed some light on the Libyan motive for attacking Dayan."

"When is the meeting due to take place?" Yitshaq asked.

"On Friday night." Uri placed his hand on his shoulder. "The following day Dayan will continue on his way to New York. Only after that will the embassy in Paris publish an announcement that the Foreign Minister came to Paris from Brussels on a short visit between flights. All clear so far?"

Yitshaq indicated with a nod that he had understood.

"As we have said, Yitshaq, this is your main mission, in addition to activating the security people to prevent an attack." Uri turned to Avshalom Kedmi. "The matter under your command is more complex. You have a long list of activities, personalities, places. Start with a thorough check of them the moment you arrive in New York. Does anyone have any questions?"

There were questions, mostly points to be clarified. Uri took pains to answer in detail each question put to him.

"Before we conclude," Avital stated, "I want to add a few words. From our point of view, every stage in Dayan's tour poses a security risk. If and when it becomes clear to us that there is a problem anywhere, you are fully authorized to alter the route, even if that means making a major change. Uri will be on the trip and will be present at all the stages. We will be constantly in touch. I want to wish you all good luck. I am sure you will give this operation everything you've got."

He extended his hand and the men rose one by one and shook his outstretched hand in turn.

The following day Yitshaq left for Brussels where Motti Klein and Ze'ev Shahar awaited him. An hour later an El Al plane took off for New York; among the passengers were Avshalom and Yirmi.

On Thursday, September 15th, a special El Al flight, number 1317, took off from Ben Gurion Airport at nine twenty in the morning. On board were Foreign Minister Dayan, his assistants, his advisors, and his personal security staff. Their destination was Brussels.

For the last few weeks, Jorg Gibskopf had been relaxing, a fact that gave him a great sense of satisfaction. It was as if his past experience had seasoned him, and he was still as competent as he had been in his youth.

However, a few days before Dayan's arrival in Brussels, Gibskopf had begun to feel a tremor of uncertainty. Up to that point he had no reason to feel he had taken on a mission that was beyond his capacity. But as the hour approached, Gibskopf's anxiety intensified. He tried to ignore it, but he knew that it was the beginning of a fear the likes of which he had never known before.

He had decided to delay his attack until the day Moshe Dayan was scheduled to fly to Paris. Meanwhile, he would take the time to familiarize himself with the faces of the security personnel in Brussels so that when he got within range of Dayan to place the deadly tape recorder near him, he could make sure that they were unaware of him.

As a journalist, he had many sources of information, among them newspaper offices throughout Europe. So it was that in the course of exchanging information with his Belgian colleagues at various newspaper offices, he picked up information on the itinerary of the Israeli Foreign Minister. His best source turned out to be the office of one of the major newspapers in Brussels where information came in to the editorial offices from the moment the Foreign Minister arrived in that city. In their photograph files he scanned the pictures of the Foreign Minister and his entourage and easily spotted the faces of the Israeli security men.

The following day, Friday, at five o'clock in the afternoon, the reporters suddenly had nothing more to file on. All at once there was a blackout on Moshe Dayan. No one knew where he was, and although rumors flew, a veil of secrecy had fallen. Jorg Gibskopf heard various theories, but the one that troubled him most came from a reporter who insisted that he had learned that Dayan had stepped up his departure from Brussels to Paris, and might also advance his departure date for the United States. No one took this claim seriously, except Jorg Gibskopf; it fitted in with information he had already received that the Israeli Foreign Minister was due to fly from Paris to New York on Saturday.

His decision to wait at the editorial offices of the Belgian paper for any further developments paid off. A reporter came into the office with a story that reinforced Gibskopf's hunch. He claimed that he had managed to follow Dayan's car, which had gone out onto the main road linking Brussels to Paris. However, a second car, apparently containing Israeli security men, had spotted him and had prevented him from continuing the pursuit. The Foreign Minister's car had disappeared, so he could not say for sure that the Israeli was actually heading for Paris.

Gibskopf wasted no time. He was at the airport in an hour. The plane for Paris was due to take off in ten minutes. As he waited for his papers to be checked, he did not notice a tall young man with long hair moving among the passengers behind him. The young man carried a guitar over his shoulder and held a small bag in his hand. The tails of his checked shirt hung out over his scruffy jeans. His dirty feet were encased in tattered leather sandals. And, through sunglasses with narrow, silver-plated frames, his eyes were fixed on Jorg Gibskopf.

At eight o'clock the floodlights that permanently illuminated the facade of the Egyptian Embassy in Paris were suddenly doused. Inside the building were the Ambassador, Muhammad Hafiz Ismail, and Muhammad Hassan el-Tuhami, the Deputy Prime Minister of Egypt. With them were two advisors and a special security team that had been flown in from Cairo. The regular embassy staff had all been sent home.

Shortly after the floodlights went out, six Israeli security men arrived, including Motti Klein and Ze'ev Shahar. Yaki Spillman remained as a communications link at the Israeli Embassy in rue Rabelais. Motti and Ze'ev were introduced to the commander of the Egyptian security staff, and together they checked out all the arrangements. Afterward, they joined two Egyptians positioned at a lookout post across the street near the impressive Dreyfus Bank.

A few minutes before ten, two cars bearing regular license plates drew up at the embassy building. By the time the first had stopped, the two Israeli and the two Egyptian security men had already hurried across the street. At that moment the second car stopped. The doors opened quickly and a medium-sized man with a black eye-patch over his left eye emerged from the first car. He was immediately surrounded by security men who flanked him in a solid wall. While the group was making its way rapidly toward the entrance to the embassy, the advisor to the Foreign Minister climbed out of the car and hurried toward the building.

The last man to get out of this car was the chief of the surveillance branch, Uri Cohen. He watched until the Foreign Minister had disappeared behind the wide doors of the embassy. Then he nodded to Yitshaq Goldberg, who got out of the car that was following his, and they both turned toward the entrance.

While the secret meeting was taking place at the Egyptian Embassy, an anonymous phone call came in to DST headquarters for Inspector Cordeille. Alerted by Yaki Spillman that Dayan was in Paris, he had stayed late, checking out the reports that had come in over the previous twenty-four hours from various security sources who had seen the composite drawing of Phoenix and thought they had leads. To date, their tips had come to nothing.

The first words of the anonymous caller electrified Cordeille.

"Hello, Inspector. I understand you're looking for someone. I think I can help you. You see, I know who he is." The low rasping voice stopped short.

"Yes," said Cordeille. "Go on."

"I know who is going to hit the one-eyed man. Does that interest you, Cordeille?"

"I'm listening." He tried valiantly to control his mounting excitement.

"The man you want is named Gibskopf . . . Jorg Gibskopf

. . . 34 rue de St. Pere in the Latin Quarter . . . second floor . . . right-hand door . . . you'll find everything there . . ."

"Listen," said the inspector rapidly, "I get a lot of tips—none of them worth a damn. How do I know yours is any different?"

He heard a scornful laugh on the other end of the line. "I don't lie, Cordeille. But I'll give you another hot lead. The general is in Paris at his very moment." Cordeille's pulse began to race.

While he had this unknown informant on the line, he decided to go for the clincher. "You've given me one name—but he's known by another. Give me that one."

There was a very long silence. Then the voice said slowly, "What name are you talking about?"

"If you know it," Cordeille went on incisively, "it would mean that your information was correct."

"Let's assume that I know. What then?"

"I'll give you the first letter. You give me the last. Is it a deal?"

It sounded as though the line had gone dead.

"Are you still there?" Cordeille said loudly.

"Yes." The stranger was hesitant. "All right. We have a deal. Tell me the first letter."

André Cordeille breathed deeply. He felt a slight pain in his chest. The tension was getting to him.

"The first letter is P."

It seemed to Cordeille that he had to force the words from his throat as if they were obstructing his breath. He waited for an answer. Every fraction of a second seemed like a year.

"The name ends," the stranger said in a barely audible whisper, "in X." The line went dead.

Moments later, Cordeille placed a call to Yaki Spillman.

"Get Dayan out of Paris without delay! Get him out the minute that meeting is over!"

"What's happened?"

"Phoenix . . ."

"You've found him?" The astonishment was evident in Spillman's voice.

"We're hot on his trail," André Cordeille said. "Get Dayan out of the city and spread a smokescreen. If anything happens, I'll let you know. I think this is it. I think we've found him!"

Uri took a moment to digest Cordeille's news, then quickly contacted the embassy press officer. "I want you to issue an official embassy announcement immediately," he said. "For immediate release in all the media. Say that the Foreign Minister has been obliged to postpone his trip to Paris and will arrive tomorrow, in the afternoon. He will hold several meetings here, and in the evening will meet journalists at the airport before he flies to the United States."

Sixty-seven-year-old Georges Roget had been the concierge at the house on rue de St. Pere for the last nine years. Roget, a wounded veteran, had been a concierge for many years. He and his wife Madelaine did not have many wants, so their small wage and the apartment they got free allowed them to live a satisfactory life.

The couple went to bed at ten thirty in the small bedroom next to the kitchen. Georges Roget tended to sleep badly, but he was so tired that night that he thought he would drop off in a few minutes. Madelaine was already asleep and he was just about to drop off when the persistent trill of the bell made him bolt up. Cursing the unknown caller, he climbed out of bed.

"Just a minute! Just a minute!" he called irately. When he opened the door, with a few more ripe curses ready on his tongue, he was taken aback. Five strange men stood there, four of them young and well built; the fifth, who stood in front, was older, about fifty-five, and extremely short. His face was pinched and lined. Georges Roget was frightened.

"Who are you?" he asked.

"Relax, monsieur," the small man said, showing his badge. "Inspector André Cordeille."

"Is something wrong?" The concierge's voice betrayed his anxiety.

"Everything is in order," said the short man with a smile. "Do you have a tenant here by the name of Gibskopf? Jorg Gibskopf."

Roget breathed deeply. "The Danish journalist?" He had begun to regain his composure.

"Yes."

"There's nothing wrong, I hope?"

The inspector ignored the question.

"Give me the keys to his apartment," he demanded.

"At once. At once, Inspector."

As Georges Roget turned to enter his apartment, the five men followed him in. They waited until he returned with the keys which he handed over to Cordeille.

"I apologize for the disturbance," the inspector said with a pleasant smile, "but I have to remain in the apartment with one of my men."

Georges Roget could not hide his agitation. There was something wrong, after all.

"But, Inspector, sir . . ." He tried to protest.

"Don't make too much of a fuss, Roget." The little man turned toward the door with three of his men. The fourth remained in the room. "Go back to bed and everything will be all right."

The apartment consisted of two rooms. One of them was the journalist's bedroom. The second was a large living area. It was clear that it was not a permanent residence. There were only a few suits in the closet and a collection of books on the wide bookcase. The inspector's men made a complete search of the apartment. They opened the cupboards and took out everything. They turned the mattress over and searched the bathroom. They even went through jars and canned goods on the kitchen shelves, checking them one by one.

"Strange," André Cordeille murmured. "Strange . . ."

Although the information given him by the anonymous caller was startling, it had sounded accurate to him. Cordeille, alone of all the DST men, knew the code name of the assassin, Phoenix. No one else was aware of this detail. But the anonymous informer knew. He cast a glance around the room. He walked through the apartment again, checking the work of his men. They knew their business. Only when he returned to the living room did his eye fall on the bookcase. It had not yet been examined.

"Take out the books," he ordered. "All of them!"

The removal of the books on the tightly packed lower two shelves revealed nothing, but a medium-sized tape recorder was found behind the books on the third shelf. The man who found it was standing on a chair.

"There's something here," he said. "It's a Sony."

"Take it down carefully," the inspector said.

The man on the chair obeyed. The tape recorder was taken down and placed on the table where André Cordeille examined it. It looked like any other tape recorder. He picked it up, as though checking its weight.

"Something wrong with it, Inspector?" the man asked.

"Yes," Cordeille muttered. "Its weight. Almost double."

He stroked the item as though trying to discover through his fingertips what he could not detect with his eyes. His finger lingered on the button that released the cover of the reels. He threw the catch and the cover sprang up.

"That's it!" André Cordeille whispered.

His fingers delicately grasped the right-hand reel of the magnetic tape. Holding his breath he lifted it from the spindle until it came free, and placed it to one side. The hands of the timing device lay revealed before him. One press on the button and the innocent tape recorder would turn into a deadly bomb. All his doubts were eliminated. The information passed on by the caller was correct.

They now had only to wait for the return of the tenant.

Jorg Gibskopf had arrived in Paris at eight fifty. The slovenly young man was not far behind him. He had tracked the journalist like a bloodhound. First, Gibskopf had gone to rue de St. Pere where he stayed until ten o'clock. He had washed and shaved and changed clothes, then emerged to walk to a nearby café, where the young man followed him. He saw the journalist sit down at one of the tables and give his order to a waiter.

It was the moment the young man had been waiting for. He went to call André Cordeille from a nearby nightclub. The conversation had gone exactly as he had expected it would until the moment when he was astounded by the cunning inspector who demanded to know his code name; with that, all doubts about the strange disappearance of the Italian were removed. The fact that the Frenchman had known the name could be traced only to Boncho. Phoenix was now certain that his anxiety had been justified. There was only one conclusion. The Israelis had caught the Italian and had made him talk. Their next step would be to call for help from foreign security services. They had apparently even submitted their information to all the services. It was possible that at that very moment feverish activity was taking place in the United States as well.

After the phone conversation he crossed to the bar and ordered his favorite drink: Bacardi and Coca-Cola, half and half. He leaned on the bar and drank slowly from the tall glass, his thoughts centered on the conversation he had held with the French inspector. The fact that the Italian had fallen into the hands of the Israelis and had cooperated with them was now confirmed. The plan that began to develop when he discovered that the Italian's yacht had vanished without trace, and he realized that the Israelis knew of his existence, was the plan he must now follow. An alert was out for him in Europe and the United States. The solution lay in his seeing that the Israelis got what they wanted, so that he could get what he wanted. They would have Phoenix, and he would be left alone to complete his mission. He took a last sip, then pushed the glass away and walked out into the dark street.

At that moment, Jorg Gibskopf was finishing dinner. Somewhere in the cafeteria a radio played a selection of songs; the husky, melancholy voice of Edith Piaf filled the air, but Gibskopf was too deep in thought to notice. Only when he heard the news announcer did he shake himself out of his revery. The announcer stated that the Foreign Minister of Israel had postponed his visit to Paris and would now arrive in the capital at noon the following day where he would remain for several hours. Following meetings with officials of the French foreign ministry and members of the press he would leave in the late afternoon for the United States.

The announcement pleased Jorg Gibskopf. Now he could figure out when the Israeli was to hold his press conference. He had two options. The first was to join the French journalists who were to meet with Dayan for an exclusive interview. Because of his close connections with various French journalists, he could get himself included. The second option was to get close to Dayan during his airport news conference. Dayan was not in the habit of evading meetings with the press so it was unlikely that either interview would be cancelled.

Gibskopf left the cafeteria and passed the hours until one o'clock in the morning at the AP wire service and at two newspaper editorial offices. The fact that the announcement on the radio had been issued by the Israeli Embassy strengthened his belief that the embassy was screening Dayan's presence in Paris, probably for reasons of security. Now he was certain that Dayan would continue to the States from Paris. An embassy spokesman had said that the Foreign Minister would meet correspondents at the airport at five in the afternoon.

Jorg Gibskopf was weary. It was time to return to his apartment to rest. The following day would be long and tiring for him. On the way he stopped at a café for a cold beer which eased his tiredness a bit. When he arrived home at ten minutes past two, the street was quiet. The darkness softened the sharp angles of the old buildings. The neon lights advertising the bars and restaurants were almost all out. From time to time a private car passed by or a truck carrying produce to one of the shops in the quarter. When he reached the entrance to his house, he pulled out a bunch of keys and opened the main door. The house was quiet, the tenants long since asleep. As he climbed the stairs slowly to the second floor, the old wooden staircase creaked a little, disturbing the silence.

He yawned expansively as he opened the door to the apartment, but as he did so, the yawn froze and a look of shock spread over his face, for, at that instant, the lights went on. His glance quickly took in four strange men. Three of them were standing next to him. The fourth, a thin man with short legs, was sitting on a chair next to the table. Gibskopf's eyes scanned the room wildly and caught sight of the tape recorder in the center of the table. His first seconds were dazed and confused. He did not know what lay ahead of him and he felt paralyzed.

"Jorg Gibskopf."

Only then did his stunned nervous system react. Jorg

Gibskopf. It was as though the stranger's voice, producing the syllables of his name, had activated an alarm. His eyes fell on the pinched face and penetrating eyes of the man, and his reaction was a panic from which there was no escape.

"Jorg Gibskopf!"

In that second he leaped backward. He bolted through the door, and slamming it shut behind him, he raced down the steps, his heart beating wildly. The deep-seated fear, which he had tried to suppress for the past few days, welled up, paralyzing his legs. Hell! Something had gone wrong!

He heard the shouts resounding after him as his feet pounded down the stairs. He took them headlong, three at a time. His mouth was open. He gulped at the air, and his lungs seemed ready to burst. At the landing between the second and first floors he heard the rapid footsteps of the men chasing him.

"Don't let him escape!"

The order was shouted sharply by Inspector Cordeille. The young men raced down the stairs, intent on capturing the fleeing quarry. André Cordeille hurried across the room to the window. He opened the shutter wide and called to the men at the lookout post.

"He's coming toward you!" he shouted. "He might be armed!"

Cordeille watched as the lookouts appeared from all sides, revolvers drawn. They crossed the street at a run, trying to reach the entrance of the house before the foreigner hurtled out of it.

"Stop!"

The shout reached the ears of Jorg Gibskopf the very instant he was about to hurl himself through the entrance. He did not heed it. His entire being was concentrated on one goal. To escape. To run for his life. To put a great distance between himself and his pursuers. He did not know who they were. They might be police. They might be from the DST. Worse yet, they might be Israelis.

"Stop! . . . We're going to fire! . . ."

He had already reached the pavement. One yard. Another. The darkness would help him. He accelerated. His legs felt heavy, as though concrete, yet they still moved like lightning.

One of Inspector Cordeille's men fired a shot. The sudden blast shook Gibskopf. He bent over and changed direction. He ran with sharp and sudden turns, zigzagging in and out. As he raced into the street, he did not see the large truck suddenly turning the corner. The driver gave a warning blast on his horn, but he was unable to brake in time. The front wheels of the heavy vehicle smashed into the Dane. The last sound Jorg Gibskopf made in his life was a bloodcurdling scream that echoed in the silence of the dark street. Windows were thrown open here and there and rudely awakened tenants looked down into the street below, trying to see what had happened.

André Cordeille, who had seen it all from above, descended the stairs slowly and joined his men, who had surrounded the panic-stricken truck driver. He was trying to restart the motor to back the truck away. "You saw!" He cursed and pleaded by turns. He was breathing heavily and sweating, almost weeping. "You saw . . . It wasn't my fault . . . He ran right under the wheels . . ."

André Cordeille told one of his men to take the driver aside and calm him down. Another man climbed into the truck, started the engine and backed up, moving the truck off the mangled body of the Dane. The man was dead, his head flattened by a wheel. Cordeille turned away from the sight, breathing heavily.

Phoenix had been destroyed.

Outside the Egyptian Embassy, Motti Klein jumped into the driver's seat of the lead car. Foreign Minister Dayan, flanked by security men, got into the seat next to him. His advisor, the Director General of the Ministry, sat in the back, with Uri beside him. The four other security men piled into the second car, slamming doors shut.

"Drive straight to Brussels," Uri said tensely, resting his hand on Motti's shoulder.

Motti turned around and stared at him. "But . . ."

"Brussels, I said!"

"Right." Motti gunned the engine and the lead car began to pick up speed.

Moshe Dayan gave no indication that he heard the order

that Uri had given, or that it had any significance. He had known Uri Cohen for many years and had requested that he handle his security arrangements when he was appointed Foreign Minister. The links between the two men were strong, and Dayan had absolute faith in Uri's judgment. If there was a change in schedule, obviously it was necessary.

"Well, Uri," the Foreign Minister said quietly after a long pause, "I gather you want to plan the departure for the States from Brussels, not Paris."

"That's right."

There was another long silence. Dayan seemed to be dozing. Then he spoke again. "I'd like to propose yet another change."

"Meaning?"

"I need to get back home for a day. There're some things I have to relay and I'd rather do it in person."

"But . . ."

"I know, I know. But tomorrow is only the seventeenth. The official visit to Washington doesn't begin till the nineteenth. I'll make it. All you have to do is to see to a new flight schedule."

As Uri thought about it, the change in plans was advantageous. It solved a security problem and it would give him a twenty-four-hour interval to reassess the now altered situation. He leaned forward. "You're right. And to tell the truth, I'd welcome a few hours' grace."

Three hundred feet from the place where Jorg Gibskopf had been crushed to death, Phoenix sat in a Renault 16 observing the street. The occupants of the nearby houses had come out into the street, causing further commotion and excitement. A few minutes later, the sirens of the police cars and the ambulance rose above the babble of voices.

For Phoenix, it was a good time to get out of the area. At two fifty his car nosed its way into the narrow rue de l'Amber. He found a place to park not far from his building. After locking the car, he turned and entered the house. His first action was to undress and step into the shower, where, as was his custom, he stood for a long while enjoying the jets of water running over his body. When he finally emerged, he put on clean underwear, set his wristwatch alarm for four thirty, and got into bed. He was asleep within minutes.

At four thirty exactly his watch awoke him. He got up and devoted several minutes to his exercises which dispelled the stiffness that he felt after such a short sleep. After making a cup of coffee, he took out his makeup box and fine brushes. His disguise would take him two hours at least. The Air France plane was due to leave for New York at nine o'clock.

This time, he was creating the character of an electrical engineer: Steve Glenn, age forty-three, a resident of Philadelphia. This was one of the last parts he would have to play. His pack of false documents and passports had dwindled. There were just enough left for a few more characters, if he needed them.

He spent some time softening the sharp features of his face. The Italian had most certainly talked, and it was possible that someone had succeeded in putting a composite picture of his face together. It was also possible that copies of the composite were already in the hands of security personnel at European and American airports. Even though Gibskopf's death should put an end to the manhunt, at least temporarily, Phoenix was taking no chances. Luck had played into his hands when Gibskopf had been silenced before he could talk, but luck was something that Phoenix never banked on.

He turned once again to his disguise. First he tinted his hair light brown. With a fine brush he carefully added gray flecks at the temples. He used a razor blade to cut the excess hair at the back of his neck so that he would look neat and not attract any attention. He darkened his thin eyebrows to soften the piercing look of his eyes and inserted plastic padding to puff out his cheeks and reduce the bold angles of his jaw. He deepened the shadow under his lower lip to make it look somewhat elongated and emphasized the deep cleft in his chin. After he had finished adding wrinkles to his forehead, he examined his face in a mirror. Reflected back was the face of a businessman in the prime of life whose expression gave the impression of relaxation and solidity.

He washed his hands and wiped off the last traces of makeup, then put on a light blue summer suit. He placed his makeup equipment in the false bottom of his small suitcase where he also secreted the packet of documents that he might yet have occasion to use and the eight hunting cartridges with their tubes of lethal gas. He locked the suitcase and, without a backward glance, turned and walked out of the apartment.

At the entrance to the house he stopped by the mailbox and pulled off the paper on which appeared the name of Philippe d'Astine and, in smaller print, Willy Miller. He tore it into pieces and tossed them into the street where a gust of wind caught and scattered them.

He had taken a final leave of the apartment on rue de l'Amber.

Yaki Spillman was asleep at his desk in his office at the Israeli Embassy. It was a warm night, and no breeze came from the open windows. Sweat poured off his face and body. From time to time he opened his eyes, blinked at the strong light, and sank once again into a deep sleep that did nothing to alleviate his exhaustion. He awoke again to feel a hand on his shoulder. Startled, he jerked upright; his eyes fell upon the drawn face of his secretary, Ruth.

"What are you doing here?" he asked in surprise. His throat seemed very dry. He glanced at his watch. It was ten past three. He had told her to go home two hours before. It was bad enough that he had to stay in the office for days at a stretch so that now he could hardly tell day from night.

"Nothing urgent," she said and put a cup of coffee in front of him. "Drink this. It's hot."

"You're crazy," he said. "You should have been in bed hours ago."

"Believe me, I will be when this is all over."

He gave her a long look. She was a small, broad-hipped woman whose face radiated intelligence.

"Anybody phone?" he asked.

"Yes. André Cordeille."

His tiredness fell away from him at once. Reality rushed back in a flood. "Why didn't you wake me?"

"There was no need," she explained. "He's on his way to the embassy. He should be here in a few minutes."

She saw from the way Yaki let out his breath that he felt easier, as if a cold wind had suddenly gusted into the room. He took a sip of coffee and it seemed to revive him.

"That's good," he said. "Thanks. When did André phone?"

"About fifteen minutes ago."

He took another sip of the coffee.

"Ruth, how about boiling up a kettle of water so that there'll be fresh coffee for the visitor." He stretched his arms. "I'll go and wash my face meanwhile."

The cold splash of water on his face and over his neck and shoulders was just what he needed. He put on a clean shirt and gave grateful thanks to his wife who saw to it that he always had fresh underwear and shirts in the office. Who knew when the schedule of successive work days would come to an end. Until it did, he would be unable to check in at home even for an hour to see his wife and children.

When he returned to his office, he found André sitting in the armchair opposite the desk. "Hello, Yaki," he said and smiled wearily.

"You look worn out."

André Cordeille made an effort to keep smiling, but his face sagged. It was true. He was very tired.

"Yes," he muttered. "Aren't we all. Well, Yaki, it's over."

"The message was correct?"

"Quite accurate," the inspector affirmed. He pulled his pipe from his pocket and put it on the table. Then he fixed the Israeli with a stare. "We got him . . . You're finished with the Phoenix affair."

Yaki Spillman felt rooted to the spot. The simple way that André Cordeille had delivered this stunning bit of information took his breath away.

"Where is he?"

"Nowhere now." The inspector picked up his pipe. "He's dead, Yaki."

"When?"

"An hour ago. A little more, maybe." André turned the unlit pipe over and tapped it on the palm of his hand to knock out the lump of tobacco it held. "A milk truck from the country ran over him in the street. Near his house. You see, he was trying to escape . . ."

The office door opened. Ruth pushed it wider with her foot, as she entered carrying two cups of coffee in her hands. She walked slowly across to the desk and put the coffee down.

André Cordeille smiled up at her. "Thanks," he said, and as he stared at the black surface of the coffee, his face grew grim.

Yaki waited for a moment. His instinct told him not to press Cordeille. It was evident that he had been through a long, action-filled night and still had much to do. It was Cordeille who broke the silence and began talking, filling Yaki in on the details of the disclosure, how it had been made, how Phoenix had been killed when he tried to escape.

"The truth is," he said, "that even without the truck, it is almost certain he would have been killed by my men. But this was a different death, Yaki."

"How did he look?"

"It's hard to tell," the inspector said, shrugging his narrow shoulders. "His head was smashed to a pulp. His face was obliterated." He put the pipe in his mouth and struck a match. After the tobacco glowed, he put the spent match into the ashtray. The odor of the tobacco wafted across the room. "In general terms he is identical with the description you sent. His height was about six feet. Broad shoulders. Average build. Not too fat or heavy. As to his face"—Cordeille's upper lip pulled down in a grimace—"that was completely smashed. But from what remained, he was similar to one of the composites of yours. Hard to say exactly. He looked about forty. He had a light beard, graying a little. Apart from the beard and the hair on his head, hardly anything of his face was left."

"It would be interesting to know who the other one was."

"What other one?"

"The anonymous caller," Spillman muttered. "The one who knew so much."

Cordeille pulled the pipe out of his mouth. The question Yaki posed had crossed his mind several times.

"I haven't an answer to that," he replied. "You know, I am

an old investigator. Innumerable cases are behind me. Every wrinkle you see on my face is the result of nights without sleep." He grinned. "I've had dealings many times with anonymous informers that I was never able to identify. Nonetheless their information was exact. I've always asked myself what motivates them." He spread his arms in a gesture of perplexity. "Obviously every one of them has his motives. You have no way of knowing them though. That is why you have no way of checking who the informant was, at least not at this stage; so don't waste your time. Just wait. Either you'll find out——"

"Or you won't." Spillman looked at him wryly.

"Exactly. What's important is that the information was correct."

"The bomb he made: was it a professional job?"

André Cordeille took a pen from his pocket and drew the shape of the tape recorder on a sheet of paper. His hand moved rapidly. At the side of the main diagram, he drew the various parts that the journalist had used to construct the device.

"You see, Yaki?" He put the drawing in front of the Israeli. "The most simple element. Plastic explosive mixed with screws and nailheads. The timing device was mounted under the right-hand reel. It was set for two minutes. The man who dismantled the bomb for us said that Phoenix was a first-class professional. It was a sophisticated and lethal bomb."

"How did you discover that the tape recorder was booby-trapped?"

André Cordeille's face became flushed. "I did a stupid thing," he confessed. "While I was examining the tape recorder I pressed the operating button. Maybe by accident. I shouldn't have done it, but I did anyway."

"What happened then?"

"What happened?" He laughed quietly. "I heard the hum of the machine, but the reels were not turning. I realized there could be only one reason for it. An object was beneath one of the reels that prevented it from rotating. Yaki, it was a simple matter of luck. And that's exactly what happened."

"It was dangerous."

"Yes. If the timer had been hooked to the operating button . . ." He puffed at his pipe. "But it seems that he had decided to make the connection just before he intended to use the recorder."

While André Cordeille had been talking, Yaki had noted down the main points. Soon he would have to transmit the initial findings to Brussels and Tel Aviv.

"That's it," Cordeille rose. He straightened up and turned toward the window. The fringes of the sky had begun to grow pale. The last hour of the night was dying. "This time it's a different story, Yaki. Everything I've done in the last twenty-four hours has the full backing of the politicians." The buildings opposite began to take shape in the first rays of dawn. The leaves of the old trees sparkled with dew. "I hope to complete the detailed report by noon, with all the findings. One copy will be sent to you officially."

He turned back from the window and walked across to the desk. He held out his hand and Yaki grasped it.

"Thanks, André. Thanks for everything."

André Cordeille rubbed the stubble on his sunken cheek. His beard had grown in the course of the night.

"No need for thanks, Yaki."

The door closed behind him. Yaki drank the last of his coffee and waited for Uri's call from Brussels. According to his estimates, the Foreign Minister and his entourage should be there by now.

During the flight from Brussels to Israel, Uri Cohen had remained in his seat, his eyes closed, but sleep would not come. All he wanted was to turn off the voices of the talkers sitting near him in the first-class section of the plane. Time and again he thought of the long telephone conversation he had held with Spillman in the early morning hours. He remembered each detail clearly. On the surface, the death of Phoenix should mark the end of a very complex business. His target, the Foreign Minister, was now sitting no more than a few yards from Uri, absorbed in the sheaves of paper before him, making notes occasionally, summarizing the meetings he had attended during the last two days.

Yet Uri felt a disquiet he could not shake off. He wondered if his strange feeling was akin to the sensation of emptiness that he had experienced many times in the past at the end of a long and arduous mission, when an inexplicable lethargy came over him as though his body were suddenly emptied of air and lead were substituted in its place. This time the feeling was somewhat different. Something was disturbing him. Something he couldn't quite put a finger on. The story he had heard from Yaki was complete: solid, layer upon layer. Impossible to raise any questions about its reliability. Nevertheless, the details of the conversation returned to him over and over again. The facts seemed plain enough. Phoenix, in the guise of a journalist, had planned to plant a booby-trapped tape recorder at one of the Foreign Minister's news conferences, but was foiled, apparently by an anonymous man who had decided to settle an old account with him and had been awaiting the right opportunity. This was one possible explanation. Of course there could be others. But the more he analyzed the possibilities, the more his disquiet grew. If the truck had not smashed Phoenix's face, he would have felt more at ease. Then it would have been possible to photograph the face and show the picture to the Italian for a positive identification. Still, apart from that one point, Uri was unable to find any chinks in an otherwise airtight case.

It was impossible to deny the facts. The man who had been run down and killed was Phoenix. Nevertheless, Uri could not leave it alone. He was convinced that somewhere he would suddenly discover a point left unexamined, and only after studying it would he know for certain that Phoenix had, in fact, been destroyed. Despite his best efforts, he did not succeed in isolating that point during the flight.

It was early evening when the plane touched down at Ben Gurion Airport. Dayan and his group of advisors proceeded immediately by car to Jerusalem, where the Prime Minister was awaiting him at his home to receive a detailed report of the secret meeting with el-Tuhami.

Uri Cohen reached the headquarters of the security service a few minutes before eight. The shadows of night were growing deeper. The lights on the large parking lot had been lit and a few cars were still parked there. Among them was the one belonging to Avital Arnon. Arnon had apparently been called to the office by Spillman who had telephoned from Paris. Uri decided to go to his own office first, where his secretary greeted him with a smile.

"Welcome home," she said.

"I'm sorry to disturb you on Saturday night," he apologized.

"We're used to it," she answered. "Avital is waiting for you."

"Was there anything else?"

"Yes." She held out a sealed envelope to him. "This came from Paris by special messenger an hour ago. I think that's what Avital wants to see you about."

"How is he?"

"In a very good mood."

He opened the envelope and found a copy of the report Spillman had promised to send to headquarters immediately. He read the closely typed page rapidly, but there were no facts other than those he already knew.

He turned to the door. "I'm going to Avital."

He found the door to Avital's office open. The chief of the service rose when he saw Uri and, with his hand outstretched and a broad smile on his face, came to greet him.

"Thank God this business is over," he said, grasping Uri's hand in both of his. "It's amazing how the Frenchman got to Phoenix!"

"Yes."

"Spillman's report is fascinating. I want to send out fresh orders immediately."

"Such as?"

"I've made notes." Avital patted Uri's shoulder affectionately and returned to his chair. He sat down and picked up a sheet of paper. "First, we have to tell Avshalom and Yirmi that they can relax. All special operations can cease and normal surveillance work resume. Secondly, the Italian and his crew can be allowed to leave the country tomorrow. One more thing——"

"Avital!"

Arnon broke off and looked up at his colleague in surprise. Only then did he observe his grim expression.

"What's the problem?" he asked.

"The problem is that I don't know." Uri leaned his elbows on the table. "Something's bothering me in this report.

Maybe I really ought to see it as you described it: 'It's over.' But I can't seem to get the words out."

Avital grinned. "You'll never change," he said lightly. "Whatever happens, your suspicious mind will bring you to an early grave. Good God! You've got plain facts in front of you. You've got the method Phoenix intended to use to hit the target. You've got the bomb. You've got the body. What more do you want?"

"The body," Uri muttered. "The body."

Suddenly it was as if a ray of light had pierced the darkness. The heavy mist that swirled around his head and inside his brain began to disperse.

"How do you know that the body is actually Phoenix?" he asked with a sudden passion.

Avital was nonplussed. "What do you mean?"

"Sure. We have a body; a body with a face smashed to a pulp," Uri replied. "We have an address. A bomb. The description of his behavior the moment before he tried to run. We have a general description that coincides with many of the details we already had." Uri shook his head in negation. "Sounds convincing." He hunched his shoulders as though pierced by a sudden chill. "But convincing only on the surface. And that's the trouble. We have no way of proving that the body is actually the body of Phoenix. For that we'll have to wait a few days until we get the results of the postmortem. Right?"

"Right."

"So first of all, Avital, there's no need to issue any new orders. In my view, we have to leave things exactly as they are until we know for certain the results." He spoke hurriedly as though afraid to again find himself caught in the mist of confusion. "You understand. Maybe they have hit on something here. Something else. Someone about to commit a crime? The man ran? Sure he did. Anyone in his position would have run. Do you see what I'm driving at?"

Avital stared at Uri's agitated face.

"I understand and I don't agree," he said slowly. "Is it the body that's bothering you?"

"Something about it. I feel it. But for Christ's sake, I still can't put my finger on it exactly."

Avital did not answer immediately. He found it difficult

to dismiss the doubts raised by his suspicious colleague, who did not trust even conclusions as clear-cut as these.

"Listen. I have an idea," he said finally. "Let's take Spillman's report and go over it together, point by point. We'll do an exercise in information analysis. Let's see what we come up with!"

It was a practical suggestion. For a long time they pored over each detail of the report, but it was foolproof. Each part joined up with the next. The only element that Uri could point to as a cause of doubt was connected with the anonymous caller who had reported to André Cordeille.

"Maybe it's there that your problem lies," Avital said, smiling. "I don't have an answer either. We still don't have enough background data on Phoenix. Maybe now, with fingerprints and the rest, we will be able to discover something about his past. Perhaps the informer was connected to Phoenix and had some special reason to want to trap him."

"Maybe . . ." Uri bit his lower lip. Avital had eased his doubts. With further investigation there was a possibility that the man's identity might be disclosed, and in the process, the informer and his motives might also be revealed.

"Take the advice of a friend," Avital said gently. "Go home, have a bath and shave, and get a good rest. We'll meet again tomorrow for a summary. Meanwhile, I'm prepared to delay changing the orders until after the postmortem on Phoenix."

Uri pulled himself slowly out of the chair. A bath, he thought. And a shave. His hand rubbed across the sharp bristles. And in that instant, he knew he had the key to the puzzle.

He slammed his hand on the back of the chair.

"Now I know what's been bothering me all this time!" he exclaimed in amazement. "The beard!"

"What beard?"

"Phoenix's!" He snatched up Spillman's report. His eyes searched for the sentence describing the dead man's features. "Look, here!" With a rapid movement he thrust the paper before Avital, his finger pointing to the line. "The man had a beard. We have no details on it."

"Meaning?"

"If it was real or false!" His voice was barely audible. Tiredness had overcome him. "You see, Avital. If the beard was pasted on, then it apparently really is Phoenix. But if it's a real beard, then it can't be Phoenix. Phoenix changes characters constantly—sometimes bearded, sometimes not. So the real Phoenix must be clean-shaven. Don't you see?"

Uri lifted his hand from the page. It was trembling. Avital took a deep breath. Uri was right: he had sensed a false note and had been certain it existed. Now he had found it.

"God almighty!" Avital burst out. "We have to clear up that point at once!" He ordered his secretary to call the embassy in Paris immediately. "Ask for Spillman. If he isn't there, then Goldberg."

Yitshaq Goldberg had returned to Paris from Brussels shortly after Dayan had taken off for Israel. Uri had wanted him to assist Spillman in summarizing the Phoenix affair. Uri and Avital waited for a tense five minutes until the ring of the telephone sounded in the office. Avital snatched up the receiver.

"Yes?"

"Goldberg here."

"Avital speaking. Where's Spillman?"

"I sent him home for a short rest," came the calm response. "Meanwhile I'm continuing the preparation of the reports and instructions we will have to submit to the security services in Belgium and France. That's the end of the matter, isn't it?"

"Not yet. Hold everything."

"What's happened?"

"You and Spillman will have to find that out immediately." The tension in Avital's voice came through to Goldberg. "Tell Spillman to get in touch with André Cordeille immediately. He must ask him one question, and wait for an answer. When you have the answer, call my office. Find out if Phoenix's beard was natural or fake? Clear?"

"I've got it. We'll check at once."

Avital hung up and turned to look at Uri's drawn face. "We'll know where we stand soon," he said.

The reply came in at ten o'clock from Goldberg. Avital

listened in stony silence, then finally said, "Hold on a moment, Yitshaq. Uri is here. I'll tell him first and then you might get additional instructions from him."

He put the receiver down. His face was grim. "The beard's natural. At least six months old . . ."

Uri drew a deep breath. "That's what I was afraid of," he said. "It's not Phoenix. So we are back where we were, and the French have a problem of their own. But ours is ten times worse. Give me the phone. I want to talk to Yitshaq."

Avital handed him the receiver. "Listen, Yitshaq." Uri succeeded in controlling the hoarseness caused by his nervousness. "I am certain now that Phoenix is going to operate in the United States. You must be there. Fly to New York at once and wait for me there. I'll come on Dayan's plane, probably at midnight. Tell Spillman that, in spite of everything, we want to know who the dead man was. I want a complete investigation. It may be connected in some way."

"Right," came the answer. "We'll meet in New York. I'm sorry about the disappointment."

"Me too. We all share in it."

Uri replaced the receiver.

"When are you flying to New York?" Avital asked.

"At noon. Dayan has a few appointments in Jerusalem. He'll go to the airport from there." Uri said. "We'll fly by Swissair. God!" He suddenly struck his clenched fist against the table. "This business is beginning to terrify me, Avital. I'd like to cancel the tour."

"That's impossible."

"I know. I know." He stood up. "But I'm telling you. I'm scared."

"Let's keep a sense of proportion," Avital remarked evenly. "I understand what your fears are, and I share them. At the same time, I know that Kedmi and Spector aren't on their backsides in New York doing nothing. It looks like Phoenix will try to pull something off in New York or Washington."

Avital stood up and came around the desk. "Let's call it a night," he suggested. Uri nodded and the two men left the headquarters together.

The light was on at Uri's home in Ramat Hasharon when he returned. His wife Shula stood in the doorway.

"I was hoping that you'd remember us," she said with a welcoming smile and kissed him on the cheek. "I heard on the news that Dayan came back unexpectedly. Where have you been?"

"I had a meeting with Avital." He took off his shoes. "And I'm dead tired."

"Don't you want to eat anything?"

"I just want to sleep," he said emphatically.

He hugged her affectionately, his lips resting a moment on her forehead before he released her and walked toward the bedroom. He undressed and put his clothes over the chair by the double bed. As he stretched out, he looked at the telephone that was within arm's reach. Please let that bastard instrument not ring this once, he thought, and the instant his eyes closed, sleep overtook him.

For several hours, the small house lay in complete silence. Then the persistent ringing of the telephone wakened Uri. He sat up abruptly, startled out of his sleep.

"Uri." Shula had wakened too. "The telephone . . ."

"Yes. I know." His throat was dry. He picked up the receiver. "Who is it?" he asked.

"Avital," came the reply. "I'm waiting for you at headquarters. I suggest you collect your things. You'll be going straight to the airport from here."

"What time is it?"

"Seven twenty," Avital replied and hung up.

Uri yawned and dragged himself slowly out of bed. Shula watched him in silence as he pulled on his trousers. He went to the bathroom, shaved hurriedly, cutting his chin in the process. He had to splash cold water over his face a few times before the bleeding stopped. He went back to the bedroom and, after putting on his shirt and shoes, took his small suitcase.

Shula sat up. "What about breakfast?"

"I'll grab something at the office," he promised with a smile. "It'll be all right. I'll telephone you from New York."

"Uri . . ."

He stopped and looked around. "Yes, Shula."

"Good luck."

His smile grew wider. "I hope so," he said.

The drive to headquarters was slow at this hour of the

morning. It was a peak travel time and the stream of traffic on the road poked along. It was eight fifteen by the time Uri drove into the headquarters parking lot. He left his suitcase in the car and walked with rapid strides toward the stairs. The elevator was on another floor and, rather than wait, he ran up the steps. This time he went past his own office without entering.

A surprise awaited him in Avital's office. When he opened the door he found Avital deep in conversation with a small dark man of about thirty-five. The two men did not notice his arrival until he said good morning. They stopped talking immediately, and the stranger with his sunken cheeks and burning eyes smiled. His white teeth gleamed under a black moustache. It was only then that Uri recognized him and held his arms out wide as a feeling of deep emotion flooded over him. The small man stood up and came toward him. They embraced for a long time, as though it were difficult for either of them to break out of the arms of the other.

"Hanania," Uri murmured. His voice was choked. "Welcome home."

"This time for good," came the reply.

Uri released his grip and grasped the man's sturdy shoulders with both hands. He looked hard into the smiling face that had aged so much over the past few years.

"When did you arrive?"

"This morning," answered the man who up until two days before had been known as Hamid Mashawi. "I left Tripoli the day before yesterday. Last night I reached Amman, and this morning, at four, I crossed the Allenby Bridge. Home, Uri. Home at last."

Uri gave him a penetrating look that said more than any words could.

"Sit down," Avital motioned to Uri. "Hanania has the complete story which explains many things, among them the episode of the dead man in Paris."

Uri pulled his chair toward Hanania Siani and fixed his eyes on his face.

"I have to get used to Hebrew again." Hanania smiled, somewhat embarrassed. "I was afraid of the language. I was afraid that sometime I might become worn out and fall asleep in the office and let out one word too many in my sleep. Of course, I could always have explained it away." His face grew serious. "I was their Hebrew expert after all."

When he began to talk, he spoke without pause, and his listeners' amazement grew. He described how he had, step by step, succeeded in attaining positions where he had been able to collect information, until he had the entire picture. It all began, he emphasized, with the persistent rumors that came to Qaddafi that Sadat intended to engage in a direct dialogue with Israel. First, the Egyptian President had expressed his secret wish before a closed circle of Arab leaders. But to this group he stressed that such a thing would be possible only if an authoritative government came to power in Israel.

At first, Qaddafi had wanted to send assassins to kill Anwar Sadat. But his advisors warned him that an attack against Sadat would mean a retaliatory invasion of Libya by the Egyptian army. They advised him to embark upon sabotage operations against Sadat's regime. That would clear the way for Sadat's opponents to remove him from power and would increase the likelihood that Egypt would join the rejectionist front that had set a policy of "no peace, no recognition, and no negotiations with Israel."

Meanwhile, Adam Ahmed had already begun to function at the head of a special team to recruit paid assassins, and Qaddafi was adamant that these assassination plans continue uninterrupted. After the political upheaval in Israel when the Likud party headed by Begin took power, Qaddafi had burst into a terrible rage on learning that Moshe Dayan had been appointed Foreign Minister. Qaddafi had claimed for years that the cunning Dayan had managed to drive wedges in the Arab world. He saw in Dayan a real danger to Pan-Arabic unity. As Qaddafi saw it, the clever policies of Dayan had made possible a partnership between the Arabs and the Jews, and in fact had even established open links between Israel and Jordan. Now, with Dayan back in the government as Foreign Minister, Qaddafi was certain that contacts between Israel and Egypt would simply be a matter of time. Therefore, he gave orders to liquidate the Israeli. His destruction, he believed, would uproot any chance of a dialogue between Israel and Egypt.

"Only three days ago I came upon the missing details,"

Hanania stressed. "And when I tell you, you will understand, Uri, why I had to come home immediately. In my estimate, every moment counts. I do not know who advised Adam Ahmed on how to plan the assassination, but whoever it was, he was quick-witted and clever."

"What are you trying to say?" Uri asked.

"I mean the method."

"The activation of Phoenix?"

"Phoenix and the others."

"Meaning it isn't only Phoenix," Uri murmured. "There are others too . . ."

"That's right," Hanania nodded. "The Libyans knew that there was a definite possibility that somehow or other we would get onto the plot. They acted on a correct assumption. But if the Israelis did find something out, it was almost certain that, once they succeeded in catching an assassin, they would then relax. So the Libyans decided to send out three killers, without any one of them knowing about the other two. One of them was bound to succeed."

Hanania smiled. "I now know who they are. That's why I came back. The name of one of them, as I've just heard from Avital, is Phoenix. You don't know his real identity, but neither do the Libyans. The others are a Frenchwoman called Jacqueline Charlotte and a journalist by the name of Jorg Gibskopf. Those are the three. I understand that the Frenchwoman is out of the running because she is facing trial on a murder charge. She killed some American model. Right?"

"I've no idea," Uri admitted. "None of us had been following that affair." He turned to Avital. "Hanania's information explains almost everything."

"It looks that way," Avital agreed. "It seems that Phoenix found out that he had two competitors. He discovered who they were and decided to eliminate them. I shouldn't be surprised if it turns out that he murdered the model to rid himself of the Frenchwoman."

"Then he is apparently the mysterious informer who called André Cordeille," Uri said. "Why? That's my question. Why did he have to take such pains to destroy them?" He turned to Hanania, who had remained calm. "Can you explain that?"

"I know why, Uri. The Libyans made a deal with each one

of the three. Each received a huge advance payment. But the final price was far greater. The condition they laid down was that the killer would get it only after he struck. If the target for any reason died by a hand other than his, he would receive nothing. Phoenix, who is apparently the most dangerous of the lot, decided to remove his competitors from the field to assure the reward for himself."

Uri began to fit the latest pieces of the puzzle together. "Avital, do you remember the negotiator, Pierre de Maline?"

"What about him?"

"I'm now convinced that he was murdered by Phoenix. It was de Maline who provided Adel el-Magrabi with the names of the assassins. Phoenix must have managed to extract the details from him and then killed him."

Avital moistened his lips with his tongue as though they were dry. "You will have to protect Dayan with your very bodies," he said to Uri. "If you can't prevent Phoenix from getting close to Dayan, he will kill him."

"He was in Paris only yesterday." Uri leaped out of his chair. "Now he's on his way to New York, if he's not there already! We have to get Hanania's information to Kedmi right away!"

At that moment the race against time became even more of a reality.

On Saturday, September 17th, a cold wind was blowing across New York City. It blew in from the ocean and brought with it intimations of the end of summer. Masses of gray clouds rolled rapidly over the great city. At the shore, waves thundered in and crashed, tossing their foaming spume onto the white sand with a dull roar and then ebbed, to be swallowed by a new line of breaking waves. The sudden chill lasted through Sunday. In Scarsdale, the shriek of the wind between the branches of the tall trees was even harsher than that between the colossal buildings of Manhattan.

The Air France plane had arrived in New York at midday on Saturday. Phoenix remained in the city, spending several hours in one of the double-feature movie houses on 42nd Street. There was no reason for him to alter his habit of leaving Scarsdale in the early morning and returning after dark. Until he completed his mission, it was necessary to avoid the eyes of the inhabitants of the neighborhood, even though they did not tend to show much interest in their neighbors.

The gray Ford had been parked in one of the large lots at the airport. It was dusty and grimy. Before going into the movie house he had left it at a carpark and paid to have it washed and lubricated. When he emerged from the theater, he found his car ready, clean and shining. He reached home at eight thirty.

First he checked out the entire house, examining the doors and windows. He began his tour on the upper story and ended it in the basement. Nothing had changed during his absence. While he was in the basement, he estimated its area. It was divided into two sections. There was a storeroom and a workroom whose area was about sixty-five square feet. The two parts were separated by a thick wood partition, in the center of which was a gray door of laminated plastic. He was sure that the place would suit his needs.

Among the tools in the workroom was a drill and a set of bits with varying bores. He selected the widest of them and fitted it into the drill. For a quarter of an hour he worked at drilling a hole in the center of the door at eye level. Then he took the Mossberg rifle from its hiding place and measured the precise diameter of the barrel. He drilled a second hole at hip height, ensuring that its diameter would encircle the barrel of the gun perfectly. He tried the fit several times. Finally he took a file and carefully rubbed smooth the rim of the hole that was to engage the barrel. He then examined the fit of the barrel one more time and found it was perfect. The next task was to mount a transparent glass plate over the upper hole. This he did using transparent tape which he stuck around the edge of the plate. He then examined his field of vision and was satisfied: he could observe the entire area of the large workroom.

After finishing this task he replaced the tools and went up to the bedroom where he undressed and went into the bathroom. He spent his usual prolonged time under the streaming jets of the shower. He loved the water. It removed the dirt that had adhered to his skin during the previous hours. A little later he went down to the kitchen and took some cheeses from the refrigerator and ate his fill. He finished the light meal with a full glass of Bacardi mixed with Coca-Cola, then climbed the stairs to the upper floor.

After taking a long drink, he put the glass down on the shelf next to the bed. He took down the photographs of the Israeli and American security men from the top shelf of the closet and examined the faces of the young men for a long time. He had to refresh his memory. He would repeat this examination many times. Each face had to be imprinted on his mind. He had to know who would be near him.

His watch alarm awoke him at four forty-five in the morning. After a quick shower he went down to the kitchen and ate more cheese, then took a salami from the cupboard and cut thick slices, which he wrapped in paper. He left the house and went out toward the majestic trees that spread out over the entire area of the broad hill. In a minute or two, he would certainly hear the lively barking of the beautiful Alsatians whose owners had released them for their early morning run.

He did not have to wait long. He heard their barks from a considerable distance. He pursed his lips and sounded the silent whistle that was picked up by their sharp ears immediately. Suddenly the two of them appeared between the distant trees. They bounded toward him in a zigzag run, their ears up and their bushy tails held high. They came within a short distance of him and stopped, uncertain. They examined him with their heads to one side as though wondering where their friend had been recently. He made friendly noises at them; they replied with low growls, hesitant at first, but finally receptive. Slowly he took two slices of sausage from the packet in his hand and dropped them on the ground. Once again, it was the female that sprang forward first although the male was close behind. They swallowed the slices quickly. He approached them, his hand outstretched, and again they made friendly sounds. The bond of friendship was reborn. At that moment, he straightened up and turned toward the house. The dogs were surprised.

Usually he played with them, breaking into a run among the trees with them bounding after him. This time he seemed to ignore them at first. But then he stopped and took out two more pieces of sausage, this time keeping them in his hand. They leaped after him mischievously and hungrily devoured the slices out of his hand. They seemed to understand. He was playing a new game which had a reward.

When the man reached the kitchen door he stopped and pushed it wide open. This time the dogs stopped, again showing signs of hesitation. He sounded his friendly whistle. They sat down, wagging their tails at the sound, but showed no willingness to go through the door. He smiled and placed a few slices of sausage over the threshold, inside the door, and went inside. He waited for them inside the door, certain of their response. The smell of the meat tempted them. He heard their low growling, as though uncertain. Again it was the female who dared first and entered the kitchen with slow steps. She fell upon the first slice. The male, as usual, followed her.

The man carefully closed the kitchen door. He took more sausage off the table and began to descend the steps to the basement, holding the delicious-smelling food out to them. When he reached the door that divided the storeroom from the workroom, he opened it and tossed the remainder of the sausage into the center of the large area. The Alsatians leaped after it and he quickly closed the door. He looked through the glass plate mounted over the upper hole he had drilled in the door. The pair of dogs were struggling to tear pieces off the sausage. He stepped back. On a table nearby lay the rifle and two of the shells that Freddie McKnight had prepared for him. He loaded the Mossberg and pushed its barrel through the hole that he had cut at hip height.

The first shot surprised the fine-looking animals. The bullet struck the wall opposite and the glass tube filled with nerve gas was smashed. The dogs looked up. A low snarl broke from their throats as though they sensed the danger. Suddenly a shivering came over them. The snarling became a thin, broken wail. Their breathing became heavy; their legs collapsed. A strange foam appeared on their rough tongues. They sank down, panting helplessly. Paralysis spread through their bodies. He fired the other shell. A few seconds passed. Through the glass plate he watched death overtake them. The dogs lay with their legs outstretched; their heads lolled as though severed. A trembling passed along their spines and then the silence of eternity descended upon them.

He was satisfied. Freddie McKnight had done a good job. On the basis of the test he had just done, he concluded that he would have to fire three cartridges into Cottner's shop, pumped out of the barrel one after the other. His glance rested on the wall where the two steel bullets had struck. They had made large pockmarks, shattering the bricks with the force of their impact. There was no doubt that they would penetrate the thick glass of the shop windows like a thread slipping into the eye of a needle.

He returned to the kitchen and heated up some water. When it had boiled, he made himself fresh coffee and drank it calmly. After an hour he descended to the basement again. He withdrew the barrel of the rifle from its hole and carefully cleaned and oiled it. He wiped the inner and outer surfaces with a rag, removing all the excess drops of oil and brushing off any dust. After he had finished, he opened the door and went in. He stood in the corner of the room and pulled up the floorboards. He dug a hole for the bodies of the dogs and, with a shovel, pushed their bodies into the hole and piled the earth over them. Then he replaced the floorboards and took the excess earth out in buckets to the yard and spread it among the trees and bushes. When he returned to the basement, he swept the floor carefully so that not a sign was left to testify to the events that had taken place there that morning.

At seven fifteen on Sunday morning he drove his car to Manhattan. Scarsdale was still asleep. He passed almost no cars on his way to the main highway and reached Manhattan a few minutes before eight. Manhattan on Sundays was quite different from Manhattan on weekdays. The city came alive much later. He found a parking spot along Madison Avenue and walked slowly up the street lined with shops. By the time he reached Charles Cottner's antiquarian shop, the heat had increased. The unusual chill of the day before had disappeared.

He stopped outside the window of Cottner's shop and

studied the size of the area to determine the best angle for his shots in order to hit the center, above the main counter. The spreading of the gas from this point would be rapid and lethal. Satisfied, he turned and strolled on until he found a coffee shop that was open and ordered breakfast. Before paying his check he crossed to the phone booth. It was ten o'clock. He wondered if Jarbil had obeyed his orders to be present in his office even on the weekend. He got his answer quickly. Jarbil took the call.

"Who's speaking?"

"I am," he replied in a low voice.

"It's a long time since . . ." The Libyan made an effort to say something, but the stranger interrupted him.

"No unnecessary talk," he said. "Have you got what I want?"

For three minutes the Libyan related the most general information about Dayan's schedule. He said that the Israeli was due to arrive that night in New York from Israel. There he would board another plane for Washington. He would remain in the American capital until Wednesday when he was to return to New York.

"On Thursday he will not leave his hotel," the Libyan emphasized.

"Why not?"

"It's the Jews' holy day. The Day of Atonement."

"I see you have learned a little about Judaism," the stranger mocked. "Go on."

The rest was useless to him. It was a stream of accurate facts but the Libyan did not know the exact times. It appeared that the Israelis at the embassy in Washington had spread conflicting information on all sides, so that even the Libyan's sources were confused by the flood of contradictory data.

"At which hotel is he staying in New York?"

"The Regency. At 600 Park Avenue——"

"I know, Jarbil," he interrupted the Libyan. "Is that all?"

"I might have something more. When will you call?"

"When necessary."

He hung up and left the phone booth. He turned to the cashier and paid his check. Then he left and walked down Madison Avenue until he reached the spot where his car was parked. He continued from there in his car toward Park Avenue. He had to learn the route between the hotel and the shop. He wanted to determine the length of the journey exactly. He might not need to know it, but his love of precision forced him to learn any detail connected with his target.

After covering the distance, he parked his car near the hotel. He went into the wide lobby and spent two hours there. He wondered if the Israeli security men had already taken residence at the hotel. During those two hours, as he sat comfortably in an armchair holding a copy of *Time* magazine, he watched the faces of passersby, but his eye did not catch the face of a single security man he recognized. It appeared that the Foreign Minister would indeed fly directly from New York to Washington, reaching the hotel only at noon on Wednesday.

In the evening, at dusk, he returned to the house in Scarsdale. Once again he looked over the photographs of the security men. It was much later when he turned on the television and watched a noisy thriller in color. He went to sleep close to midnight. On Monday morning he went for his usual walk among the trees. At nine fifteen he called Jack Stone's law office. He spoke in the rasping voice of old Willy Miller. He started off by telling the lawyer that he had returned home to New York and wanted to know if the lawyer had any more news. Jack Stone was pleased to hear his voice and told him that he was still awaiting news.

"It's almost certain that we'll get the message only a day before Mr. Dayan's scheduled to visit the shop," the lawyer stressed. "That's why I suggest you keep in touch with me every day, so that you can bring the box to Charles Cottner immediately."

The old man promised to do so.

That same morning, at ten thirty, two young men entered the antiquarian shop on Madison Avenue and asked to speak with Mr. Charles Cottner. They were ushered into Mr. Cottner's small office, which was at the end of the narrow corridor connecting the first floor of the shop to the basement where the objects of great worth were to be found.

Charles Cottner was widely respected among the members

of his profession. He was an acknowledged expert in the field of Middle Eastern archaeology and was sought after as a lecturer at universities across the United States. The fifty-seven-year-old man was tall and dignified in appearance. His shoulders were bowed over a hollow chest, but he nonetheless gave the impression of a man in the prime of life. His face was gentle, with a high forehead sweeping back toward a thin line of hair that fringed his crown. He wore narrow gold-rimmed glasses, and his gray eyes looked directly into the eyes of anyone he was talking to. He sat behind a seventeenth-century antique desk in his small office which was crammed with those antique objects that he particularly loved. As was his custom, he rose from his chair when the sales manager opened the door and asked the two men to enter.

"Mr. Cottner," he said, "these two gentlemen would like to speak with you."

A pleasant smile spread across Cottner's face as his glance fell on the faces of the two men. The shorter of the two had dark skin and penetrating black eyes. The other was like a young athlete. His hair was fair and he was some years younger than his friend. Something about the face of the older man was familiar to Charles Cottner.

"Whom do I have the pleasure of meeting?" he inquired, after asking his unexpected guests to sit down opposite his desk.

"My friend's name is Yirmiyahu Spector," the older man said, "and I am Avshalom Kedmi. I think, Mr. Cottner, that we met a few years ago. I came here with Mr. Dayan."

Charles Cottner's eyes twinkled.

"Of course!" He extended his hand and shook Avshalom Kedmi's warmly. "You are one of the security staff of the Foreign Minister."

"He was Minister of Defense then," Kedmi said with a smile.

"I am aware of the change," Cottner said, nodding his head. "I too am among those who follow the career of Mr. Dayan. He is an old acquaintance of mine. I imagine that you have come to coordinate arrangements in connection with his visit, have you not?"

"That's exactly the reason," Avshalom confirmed. "My partner," he rested his hand on Yirmi's shoulder, "wanted to become familiar with these procedures up close. So, Mr. Cottner, here we are on a routine visit."

It was, in fact, the last of their security checks. On Saturday the two men had checked out all the places Dayan was scheduled to visit. Dayan's arrival was scheduled for late the next night, so on Sunday they took time off to visit several museums. In the evening, when they returned to their hotel, Yirmi reminded Avshalom that they had not yet visited Cottner's shop.

"We have to stop by there," he said as they lay stretched on their beds in their room at the Regency Hotel. "It's the only place we haven't been yet."

"No special problem," Avshalom said with a yawn. "I've been there in the past and we'll be able to attend to everything very quickly tomorrow."

After a few hours' rest they drove to Kennedy Airport. Yitshaq Goldberg's plane from Paris had preceded the Foreign Minister's flight by two hours. In this interval, Goldberg filled them in on the details of what he called the "imaginary Phoenix affair." The story astonished them.

"That explains the cable we got this morning." Avshalom showed Goldberg the message. "That's apparently the reason Uri is convinced the Phoenix is here."

After the Foreign Minister's plane landed, there was a short delay before Dayan continued on his way to Washington. While Dayan was hurried to an isolated VIP lounge, Avshalom reported to Uri on the operations that he and Yirmi had carried out since their arrival in the States.

"I want to wind up this business," Uri said. "This time too we are working on hunches, and anyone who thinks that hunches aren't worth anything can go to hell!" He seemed more determined than Avshalom had ever seen him in the past. "I'm certain that he's here. I am convinced that he will try to make his strike in New York because, under the circumstances, his chances of escaping are better here than in Washington. You and Yirmi remain in New York. Yitshaq and I will go on with Dayan to Washington and take charge of security there. If you come upon anything concrete, get in touch directly with the embassy. I'll be there several times during the day."

Now, as Avshalom sat with Yirmi opposite the owner of the antiquarian shop, he wondered if indeed he would have anything to report to Uri. As far as he was concerned, this place was completely in order. But the grim warning of the branch chief gave him no rest. Meanwhile Charles Cottner opened a file full of letters and withdrew the letter and photograph he had received from the lawyer Jack Stone.

"Actually," he said, spreading out the letter and picture, "I had been intending to call Mr. Stone for a few days. Unfortunately, I was out of New York." He smiled apologetically. "I had a few lectures to deliver. So today I decided to attend to the drawing up of the certificate of authenticity for this rare object."

He picked up the photograph of the ancient box and looked at it dubiously.

"Is something disturbing you, Mr. Cottner?" Avshalom asked.

"Yes and no." He handed the picture to Kedmi. "This is an unusually rare object. Personally, I know of the existence of only two other such boxes. But this looks like the best-preserved one."

"In that case," the Israeli persisted, "what bothers you?"

"Frankly, because this is such a rare object," Charles Cottner explained patiently. "I recalled that I once saw one like it in the collection of a friend of mine, a well-known antique and art dealer. Actually, I was certain about it. Before you came, I even telephoned him. But apparently I was mistaken. He denied having it. So I imagine that everything is in order. I envy Mr. Dayan," he said, smiling. "It is very lovely."

Yirmi leaned forward and took the photograph off the desk.

"Mr. Cottner," he said, looking from the picture of the box to the face of the dealer, "has it ever crossed your mind that this box might have been stolen?"

Charles Cottner's face became slightly flushed. "Why?"

"Because you telephoned your friend to make sure it wasn't his."

"The thought did occur to me—yes. It is indeed a very rare object."

Yirmi and Avshalom exchanged glances.

"Mr. Cottner," Yirmi turned to the dealer again. "May I take the photograph and also the address of the office of your friend, the dealer, the one whom you believed once owned the object."

"Certainly," the man replied. He seemed surprised. "But why?"

"We have a strange custom," Yirmi said with a smile. "We like to doublecheck everything. I know that it's a most annoying habit. But every profession has its quirks."

Charles Cottner laughed.

"That's quite all right, Mr. Spector." He jotted down the address. "The gentleman's name is Alex Kraskin. His office is on Fifth Avenue. You can tell him that I sent you, as you are interested in acquiring that piece. Ask him if he knows who its owners were. All right?"

"By the way," Avshalom said, "I would like to ask that you not mention our visit here to anyone."

"You can rely on me, Mr. Kedmi."

As soon as they left the shop, they hailed a taxi and gave the driver the Fifth Avenue address. They were silent during the ride; there was no need to talk.

The moment Avshalom mentioned Charles Cottner's name, Alex Kraskin's secretary treated the two visitors like special customers. "If Mr. Cottner sent you," she said, smiling, "I have no doubt that Mr. Kraskin will see you immediately."

Within minutes, they found themselves standing at the entrance to a richly furnished private office. Alex Kraskin rose to greet them. Although he was smiling, the look he fixed on them was cold and questioning.

"I understand my friend Charles sent you to me, gentlemen." He studied the faces of the young men carefully, as though sizing them up. He wondered what such unprepossessing men could possibly want to buy from him when every item he owned was worth a fortune.

Yirmi produced the picture he had taken from Charles Cottner.

"Mr. Kraskin," he said, "this item has been offered to us for sale. We have been told that it was once in your possession. Could you tell us if this is the case, and if so, to whom the item was sold?"

Alex Kraskin glanced at the photograph.

"No," he said with deliberate coldness, "I have never owned this object; I don't even recognize it." He looked at them with indifference. "Is there anything else I can do for you?"

Yirmi smiled pleasantly. "Our source insists that he knows that this object was in your possession."

Alex Kraskin's temper flared. The painful memory of the visit from the stranger was still fresh in his mind. Nor had he forgotten the blow he received from the silver knob of the black cane.

"I don't wish to talk about it any longer!" His exclamation was sudden and seemingly uncontrolled. "I have already told Charles! And now you two come in here with all these annoying questions!"

Kraskin had no idea who these two men that Charles Cottner had sent were, but he knew how dangerous the stranger had been to him, dangerous to the point of death. Alex Kraskin sensed that the man before him was equally dangerous. Better for him not to have anything to do with that box. He must sever any connection with it. He took a deep breath and his swollen face became flushed. Anger burned in his small, deep-set eyes.

"I am sorry to trouble you, sir," Yirmi said evenly. "We had no intention of disturbing you or causing you anxiety." As he and Avshalom got up to leave, they heard the thick voice of the antique dealer.

"Tell Charles that I have never had any connection with that object!"

"That guy knows something," Yirmi said as they rode down in the elevator.

"Yes. That's clear."

"What do we do next?"

"Go immediately to the lawyer. What's his name?"

"Jack Stone."

"Right. We'll find out exactly what he knows about this business." Avshalom looked at Yirmi. "You were always suspicious about the visit to Cottner's shop. Why?"

"It was too pat," the young man said simply. "Everything looked all right, and I guess that's what was wrong. The whole thing was just too neat. That's all. It was just too neat."

When they emerged onto Fifth Avenue, they found a cab and gave the driver Jack Stone's address. He received them in his inner office.

"What can I do for you, gentlemen?"

"We've come in connection with the will of David Hirshkowitz of Flint, Michigan," Avshalom explained.

"Oh! The antique box—the gift for Mr. Dayan!" He expressed surprise. "But we informed you that the item will be sent to Cottner's shop in accordance with the wishes of the deceased . . ."

"That's not the arrangement we're interested in," Avshalom said. "We're checking out everything in connection with Dayan's visit. What we want to know is if you have checked out all details connected with the bequest."

"What does that mean?" The lawyer was taken aback. "What are you referring to?"

"For example, how did the Hirshkowitz family contact you?"

Jack Stone felt relieved. "Very simple," he explained. "A cousin of the late Mr. Hirshkowitz was here. A rather funny old man he was. The name's Willy Miller. He is the executor of the will, and he asked me to deal with all the arrangements connected with the antique box."

Yirmi studied the lawyer's face for a moment. "That sounds fine, Mr. Stone, but I need to ask you a few more questions. Believe me, we have a reason."

"I'm happy to answer every question I can."

"Did you check the identity of the old man? What was his name again?"

"Willy Miller." The lawyer became serious. "No. As the matter of fact, I didn't. I had no reason to. The old man was pleased and paid for my services promptly. In any case, we were happy to be involved with the matter, particularly since it involved Moshe Dayan."

The lawyer noted the rapid glance the two Israelis exchanged.

"Is there something wrong?" he asked.

"Before we answer," Avshalom said, "I have another question. If you did not check Mr. Miller's identity, and you evidently had no reason to do so, did you check with the lawyer who confirmed that the item had belonged to David Hirshkowitz's collection?"

Jack Stone suddenly felt embarrassed. These penetrating questions made him feel uncomfortable, particularly since they were questions he would have asked under similar circumstances.

"No," he admitted with an effort. "I didn't check."

"Would you mind calling the lawyer in Flint now and clarifying the matter?"

"Certainly."

Stone asked his secretary to bring him the file on Willy Miller. Jack Stone found the phone number of the lawyer in Flint and asked her to put through a call to his office.

Two minutes later, she was back in the doorway. The lawyer was on vacation until the end of the month.

"There's only one thing left to do," Stone muttered. "Get in touch with Mrs. Hirshkowitz."

They waited as the call was put through and listened as Stone spoke to the elderly widow.

"Hello, Mrs. Hirshkowitz. My name is Jack Stone. I'm a lawyer in New York and I need to have some information. I think you can help me. Did your late husband by any chance have a cousin named Willy Miller?"

It seemed that she did not catch the name; Stone was obliged to repeat it. As he listened to her reply, a grim look came over his face.

"Thank you, Mrs. Hirshkowitz," he said. "It's possible that we've made a mistake. Anyway, thanks. By the way, your husband was an antique collector, wasn't he?"

He listened to the reply.

"If you don't mind, I have one more question," he said quietly. "Did you recently sell someone a valuable box from his collection?"

The longer the conversation went on, the tenser Avshalom and Yirmi became. It was clear from the drift of the questions what was happening. They looked at each other quickly, and Yirmi clasped his fingers together so tightly that the knuckles turned white.

When Jack Stone replaced the receiver, his face was damp with perspiration, in spite of the coolness of the office.

"I regret, gentlemen," he said in a low voice, "that I have been made a fool of. Mrs. Hirshkowitz was married forty-three years to her late husband and she never heard of a cousin called Willy Miller."

"If I'm not mistaken," Avshalom remarked quietly, "she did not sell a rare box from the thirteenth century B.C. either. Correct?"

The lawyer lowered his head. "Correct. A few weeks ago she sold several pieces in the collection, but according to her she sold all the valuable items months ago. None of the things she sold recently dated back to the pre-Christian era. She told me that she remembered very clearly each object that was sold from the collection. She recorded everything carefully."

For a moment no one spoke, and then Avshalom said, "Do you remember how this old man looked, this Willy Miller?"

"Yes. But what's all this about?"

Avshalom hesitated. "It's a security matter of the highest order, Mr. Stone," he said, drawing a deep breath. "Please don't press me, and let us have your complete trust."

"I have no reason not to trust you," the lawyer said. He was feeling a dull sense of disquiet. "Particularly not after what I've just found out. What do you want to know?"

"The entire Willy Miller episode. What he was doing here. What he wanted. How he spoke. How he looked. In short, everything you remember about him." Fortunately Jack Stone was blessed with a sharp memory. He recalled many details about the old man. When he began to describe his gait, speech, and behavior, how he had paid in cash for the lawyer's services, the final shadow of doubt was dispelled.

Willy Miller was Phoenix.

"Mr. Stone." Avshalom was straining to control the inner turbulence that was building up in him. "You said that you sent letters to Willy Miller at two addresses."

"Yes."

"One in Paris and the other here, in the New York area. Correct?"

"In Scarsdale."

"The local address interests us."

"By all means."

Jack Stone jotted down the Scarsdale address and handed it to Avshalom.

"It's a high-class neighborhood," he explained. "The residents are mainly people of means. You'll find only a few Jews among them. That's why I was certain Willy Miller belonged to the circle that could afford to live in an area like that. What else can I do for you?"

Avshalom paused before replying and reread his notes.

"You are still supposed to be in contact with the old man. He is waiting to receive a message from you as to when Mr. Dayan will be at Cottner's shop. Is that correct?" he asked.

"Yes," the lawyer replied, "that was our arrangement. He was to bring the box to the shop as soon as he knew the date of Mr. Dayan's visit there."

Avshalom felt his throat constrict from tension. The murderer's plot was perfect and very clever. He clearly excelled at planning and had created a dangerous trap only after he had studied the character of his target. No matter what method Phoenix chose to use, he had succeeded in creating a flawless snare. Although perhaps too flawless, and it was here that his vulnerability lay.

"How were you to let him know about Mr. Dayan's plans?"

"By telephone. I arranged for him to call my secretary every day. If there was anything, she would pass the call through to me. He will certainly call the office tomorrow morning."

"We'll need your help," Avshalom stressed.

"You know that you have it. What do you want me to do?"

"When Willy Miller calls you tomorrow, tell him that our embassy in Washington called you and told you that Mr. Dayan will be at the shop the day after tomorrow."

"Wednesday?"

"Yes. He'll be there at one thirty."

"That's all?"

"You'll have to have a convincing conversation with him," Avshalom emphasized. "He must not sense that something is wrong. Please understand me. Treat him just as you have up to now."

"I can handle that," the lawyer promised. "But let me ask one question. Who is Willy Miller?"

"I wish I knew," said Avshalom. "I wish I knew."

Avshalom Kedmi's attempt to make contact with Uri Cohen in Washington was not successful. The branch chief was not in the Israeli Embassy building and no one knew when he was expected. Therefore, after a brief consultation with Yirmi Spector, Avshalom began to move. The afternoon hours passed quickly as Avshalom tied the loose ends together and worked out a plan.

At nine o'clock that evening he tried again to reach Uri from his room at the Regency Hotel. He was told that the branch chief had said he would be at the embassy from ten o'clock onward and at ten thirty Avshalom reached him.

"Are you certain it's him?"

"Yes."

"Can't you say more about it?"

"Not now," Avshalom explained. "Details only when you get to New York. Or if anything happens before then."

There was a brief silence, during which it seemed that Uri pieced together the hints dropped by Kedmi. It was plain to him that his men in New York were about to act. Yet anyone overhearing their conversation would have had no hint as to what was going on.

"Are you sure you don't need me there now?" Uri asked eventually.

"Best avoid any alteration in plan," Avshalom replied.

"Are you putting the partners in the picture?" he asked finally. Uri was referring to the American security personnel.

"No."

"Why not?"

"For the same reasons that I don't want you to move."

"I see."

Kedmi had decided to use only his own men; if he needed help, it would be available from the security staff of the Israeli Consulate in New York, and even from El Al.

"All right." The matter was settled. "Call me when you

have something to report." He hesitated for a moment, and then added: "Avshalom . . ."

"Yes?"

"I'm relying on you. Best wishes to Yirmi."

Avshalom put the receiver down slowly. Yirmi stood near the table, watching him with interest. This talk had been crucial.

"Did he understand?" Yirmi asked.

"Yes, he understood. We have a free hand," Avshalom replied in a low voice. "The matter is entirely up to us."

He turned to the window. Only at that moment did he truly feel the weight of the responsibility. As a field agent, he had been used to the feeling of sudden isolation that falls on a man sent to accomplish a mission, but this time he had to act decisively and command others in an operation that was of critical importance. His eyes followed the headlight beams of the cars that whizzed by along Park Avenue. He was in another world—an alien world.

"Everything ready?" he asked Yirmi.

"The men are ready. The cars too."

"Have you told them when we're leaving?"

"Yes. Three in the morning. How many of us will there be, Avshalom?"

"Seven. You, me, Shuka Levi from the consulate and four of his boys."

The vacant smile that played at the corners of Avshalom's mouth came from sheer weariness. He was like a mountain climber who approaches the peak, but before reaching the desired goal, suddenly feels a terrible need to rest, to stretch out on the edge of the rock, to spread his arms and legs in passive repose—to refresh himself in preparation for the last stage, the hardest of all, despite the short distance that remained before him.

"Listen, Yirmi." He turned from the window. "Give me a small whiskey." He laughed at the look of surprise that spread across his friend's face. "I know. You're not used to seeing me drink. Just a drop."

Avshalom picked up the glass that Yirmi held out to him. He took a small sip and grimaced. It had its usual bitter taste.

"You know, Yirmi," he said, "Dr. Carmi was right. Phoenix failed because of his drive for perfection. Do you see?"

Yirmi took a drink and looked at Avshalom with comprehension. "It happened because of our visit to Charles Cottner," he said.

"That's it exactly," Avshalom agreed. He took another sip. The liquor slid down his throat with a slight burning sensation. "His quest for perfection frustrated him. If he had chosen a less extraordinary antique item—valuable, yes, but with others like it—we would never have discovered him. But he had to be certain that he was throwing Dayan the best bait he possibly could. That's why he sought something rare, something guaranteed to rouse the interest of an expert."

"We haven't got him yet," Yirmi said in a flat voice. "Not yet . . ."

"We're on the way and we'll get there." Avshalom spoke with calm assurance.

They spent the next few hours stretched on their beds, resting. Each of them was bound up in his own train of thought. Neither one could sleep.

At one thirty Avshalom sat up and got out of bed.

"Yirmi."

"Ready."

A few minutes before two o'clock in Shuka Levi's room at the rear of the first floor of the consulate, the briefing began. Shuka and his four men were already assembled when Avshalom and Yirmi arrived.

"Shuka has explained the mission to you in general terms," Avshalom said quietly. "I suppose you are asking yourselves questions as to what this is all about. Unfortunately, we can't go into details. By three o'clock we will be positioned in lookout spots around the house. We are dealing with a highly skilled professional. One unnecessary move, one false step can ruin the whole mission, with lethal results. Is that clear?"

He studied the faces of the young men before him.

"One more thing. When this business is finished, it will be best if each one of you forgets it ever happened. Not one of you was involved in it. Not one of you has ever met or taken part in this meeting. If anyone asks you questions about this—today, tomorrow, a year from now—you know nothing.

"Are there any questions?" Avshalom paused. "If not, that's all. It's time to move out."

The man who lived in the large house on the hilltop awoke as usual at about five o'clock in the morning, roused by the twittering of the birds as they fluttered and hopped among the branches of the trees outside the bedroom windows. He slipped out of bed and stretched, then exercised for several minutes before entering the shower where he let the water flow over his body for a long time.

At five thirty he went out of the kitchen toward the hill for his morning stroll. The masses of autumn clouds were shot with the first light of day as he walked among the trees, reflecting on what lay ahead of him. He was in an excellent mood. In his judgment, he would accomplish his mission in a few days and then disappear. He smiled when he thought of the uproar that would follow the killing. A world-renowned leader murdered in New York at the hand of an unknown assassin. The event would send shock waves throughout the world. He could just sit back and follow the various developments with interest. He would have unlimited time to do so. In any case, he would have to wait in the large house for days or even weeks until the storm blew over. Meanwhile, his bank account would be richer by two and a half million dollars. It was an immense sum. For him it meant a new chapter in his life, a life of serenity in any corner of the world he chose to settle in: a life from which he could derive all the pleasures his heart desired.

When he returned to the kitchen, he brewed a pot of coffee and fixed breakfast, which he ate in a leisurely fashion. After he had finished, he carefully washed the dishes in the kitchen sink and returned to his bedroom. He sat on the bed and studied the photographs of the Israeli security men spread out before him. He wondered which of them would accompany Dayan on his visit to Cottner's shop.

A few minutes after nine o'clock he telephoned Jack Stone's office. His secretary Mabel Freedman answered the phone.

"Hello, Mrs. Freedman." He cleared his throat. "This is Willy Miller speaking. How is Mr. Stone this morning?"

"He's well, Mr. Miller," she assured him. "I think he has some news for you. If you'd like to hold the line a moment, I'll put you through."

She buzzed Stone and told him that Mr. Miller was waiting on the line. Jack Stone picked up the phone quickly.

"Good morning, Mr. Miller."

"Good morning to you," came the reply. "Do you have anything new today?"

"Indeed, I do, Mr. Miller." From his calm voice it would have been impossible to guess that Jack Stone had passed a sleepless night, tossing and turning. "Mr. Miller, you are to send the box to Mr. Cottner today if possible. Mr. Dayan will reach New York tomorrow from Washington. He will call at Mr. Cottner's at about one thirty on his way from the airport to the hotel."

"Well, that's really news." The old man sounded delighted. "Believe me, Mr. Stone, I'll feel a lot better when I know that I have carried out the final bequest of my cousin David's will. You can tell Mr. Cottner that I'll deliver the box today."

"I'll be glad to."

"And one more thing, Mr. Stone."

"Yes?"

"If you have any more special expenses, I'll be happy to see that you are reimbursed."

"There's no need." The lawyer laughed, and it pleased him to discover that in spite of the strain he was under he could still laugh. "Don't forget I still have two hundred dollars left. According to our agreement, I'll donate them to the Jewish Appeal."

"Of course," came the reply. "Well, let me thank you again for your efficient service."

After he put down the receiver, Phoenix remained seated on his bed for a while, his gaze fixed on some unseen object. Everything was all ready, the plan complete. The jaws of the trap were about to spring shut. The framework was solid. By tomorrow it would be over. Twenty-eight hours lay before him, hours of waiting and expectation.

He left the bedroom and went down to the kitchen. He opened the freezer and removed various packages of food, until he came to the small parcel on the bottom. He took it out and quickly removed the plastic bag and unwrapped the towel. The ancient box was revealed in all its rare beauty. He placed it on the table and busied himself replacing the food in the freezer. Then he returned to the second floor and spent an hour applying makeup. Willy Miller was born again. But these were to be the old man's final hours.

At ten thirty the main door of the house opened. The old Jew appeared on the threshold, supporting himself with a silver-knobbed black cane. Under his left arm he carried a small parcel. He opened the door of the gray car, placed the parcel on the passenger seat next to the driver's, then climbed in and drove off.

Tuesday, September 20th, was drawing to a close. The dome of the sky, paved by masses of gray cloud, was shot with fiery shades of red, as though flames flickered at the edges of the clouds scudding before the shifting wind.

Among the vehicles that streamed from Manhattan to Scarsdale, as dusk swallowed up the last light of the fading day, was a gray Ford. The elderly man who sat at the wheel, driving at a steady speed of fifty miles an hour, had spent a pleasant day. At eleven thirty he had entered the antiquarian shop and had been cordially received by Charles Cottner. The dealer had expressed wonderment at the ancient box, to such a degree that he did not even try to hide his envy of Mr. Dayan, who was about to acquire it.

A few hours later, after enjoying lunch at a restaurant in the center of Manhattan, Miller had called the Libyan Embassy in Washington. He wanted to check the accuracy of the information he had received from Jack Stone. His conversation confirmed what he already knew. Jarbil even gave him the number of the flight on which Moshe Dayan was to leave Washington the next day.

Phoenix had decided to go to bed early that night. He needed to be rested and alert. He also had to leave early the next day in order to get a parking spot for the Ford opposite Cottner's shop. It would be the last time he would travel the route that began in Scarsdale and ended in the upper reaches of Madison Avenue.

It was already dark at seven fifteen when the Ford slipped

into the carport opposite the entrance to the dark house. He got out of the car and, after locking it, took the stairs in easy stride. A stranger watching would have been amazed at the sight of an old man taking the steps with such agility.

He pushed the key into the lock and turned it twice, then entered and closed the door. His hand slid along the wall to find the light switch. The moment the light flashed on, he knew that something had gone terribly wrong. Facing him, a few yards away, stood two men. One was dark-skinned with smoldering eyes and the other, younger than he, was tall and fair. Both held submachine guns in their hands.

He froze on the spot.

Israelis, he thought.

His breathing was heavy as though after a long run, but he did not move a muscle. There was no point in trying to overcome them. One squeeze on the trigger would be enough to pepper him with holes. The building was bound to be surrounded by more of the bastards.

He straightened up. The bent figure of the old man vanished.

"Good evening," he said coldly.

"Good evening to you, Mr. Miller. Or should it be Mr. Phoenix?"

His heart began to pound harder. The pulses in his temples quickened. The stranger opposite, the dark one, was not smiling. His face was cold.

"So that's it," he said.

"Yes," came the reply. "And don't try to make a single unnecessary move . . . take off your clothes carefully . . . first the overcoat . . . then the shoes . . . your trousers too."

He was dealing with professionals. They were not about to be taken by surprise. He thought of the trap that he had set. It had sprung too soon. And not over the target. Its jaws had closed on him. He wondered where he had slipped up. He had to find his error.

The two men watched his slow movements in silence. He tossed his black cane aside, then removed his coat and his shoes, one by one. He unbuckled his belt and, sliding his trousers down, stepped out of them. The two men watched him closely. Now there was less danger. He had no weapon in his hands. He straightened up and glanced toward the corner of the room. The Mossberg rifle was there, leaning against the wall.

They caught his glance. "There's no point," the older of the two said. "We have the shells. All six."

He stood before them, dressed only in his underwear. A tremor ran through him. It was a peculiar trembling that he had never experienced before. They were treating him in a way he had not expected. There were no threats, no attempts to hurt him, yet their silence put fear into him. It was the end. A long and arduous path had finally led nowhere. The feeling of finality grew more profound and with it a sense of the sterility of his life. Somehow, by making him remove his clothes, they had humiliated him. They had stripped him of his skin. He was ridiculous, pitiable. His powdered face was that of an old man, his body that of a powerful young one.

"Where did I make my mistake?" he asked.

"Your quest for perfection undid you," the Israeli replied. His voice was cold. They already knew what they intended to do.

"I do not know what you wish to do with me," he said, trying to suppress the hateful trembling, which infuriated him. "But I have a final request."

"I am listening."

He drew a deep breath.

"I wish to kill myself."

For the first time since he had been caught he noticed a reaction in the Israeli. A spark flashed in his large eyes with their black pupils. He was a man of his own age, a professional like himself.

"You want to join the dogs?"

"You found them."

"We went over the house inch by inch." The Israeli fixed him with a sharp glance, his eyes boring into him. "As to your proposal, I think it's a good idea," he said. "At least you will save us an unpleasant task."

There was nothing more to say. The Israeli pointed toward the stairs leading down into the brightly lit basement. Phoenix walked slowly. The silent young man with the fair hair followed behind him, the submachine gun held firmly in his hands. Although his finger was on the trigger, he had no intention of firing.

Phoenix was to perform the act that would bring about his end. It was his only remaining desire. Like the scorpion that injects paralyzing poison into its body when the flames of fire close in upon it, so as not to feel the agonizing pain that awaits it, he would punish himself for his painful failure.

He passed through the door that separated the two sections of the basement. The two strangers remained behind. The shorter Israeli tossed two of the shells that Freddie McKnight had prepared into the center of the room.

"That quantity should be sufficient," the Israeli said and closed the door. He took out a handkerchief and stuffed it into the hole that had been made for the barrel of the rifle. Then he straightened up and watched what was taking place through the glass that had been mounted over the peephole.

Phoenix bent over. He picked up the two cartridges and stared at them for a few seconds. Then he removed the cardboard casing, uncovering two shells shaped like tiny rockets. He removed the steel caps and drew out the two capsules of nerve gas. He bent over again and, carefully, as though concerned not to damage the glass tubes, he placed them, one beside the other, next to his feet. When he straightened up, he drew a deep breath. Then he raised his foot and brought it down with a rapid movement, shattering the two small tubes. He did not feel the glass splinters piercing the sole of his foot. He only felt a sudden, strange, burning sensation as if a tongue of flame were enveloping him on all sides.

He sank to the floor, writhing like the dogs whose bodies lay under the floorboards a few feet from him.

On Monday, October 10th, Foreign Minister Moshe Dayan's long visit to the United States ended. The following day he arrived in Israel on board an El Al jet; and two hours later he was conferring with Prime Minister Menachem Begin.

In the first week of November, President Anwar Sadat

of Egypt announced that he was ready "to go to the ends of the earth, even to Jerusalem, if this will bring the negotiations for peace nearer."

From that moment on, events moved at breakneck speed.

On Saturday night, November 19th, at eight o'clock in the evening, a Boeing 707 aircraft bearing the insignia of the Republic of Egypt and the figures 01 landed at Ben Gurion Airport. The stairs were rapidly placed against the entrance to the plane and Anwar Sadat descended.

At the foot of the stairs, the President of Israel, Ephraim Katzir, and the Prime Minister of Israel, Menachem Begin, awaited the Egyptian President. The three men stood motionless as the military band played first the Egyptian national anthem and then the Israeli "Hatikvah."

Along the length of the red carpet there stood a long row of Israeli statesmen, members of the new government, members of the previous government, and other notable figures. Among them was Foreign Minister Moshe Dayan. As each man was presented to the President of Egypt, Sadat acknowledged them, but when he reached the Foreign Minister, he smiled broadly as though coming upon an old friend.

"Moshe," he said warmly as they exchanged a firm handshake. It seemed that these two men shared a special connection.

A short distance away, a small group of men stood together—the senior staff of the Israeli secret service. It was a charged moment for them—a moment toward which they had concentrated all their energies during the preceding months. In the midst of the emotion that this meeting engendered, some of them were troubled by whether they were witnessing an isolated event or the beginning of a road that led to peace.

At that moment, tens of thousands of citizens of Jerusalem were moving toward the approaches to the city. The chill of the night did not hinder them. They were awaiting the arrival of the President of Egypt.

The reverberations of the twenty-one gun salute died away. The flags of Israel and Egypt fluttered in the light breeze, their edges meeting each other, as the long convoy of cars ascended the road that wound through the hills of Judaea.